Love and Death

AMONG PIGEONS

Love and Death

AMONG PIGEONS

Lawrence A. Wood MD

ISBN: 978-0-6923-9274-4 (sc)
ISBN: 978-1-4834-4029-3 (e)

Because of the dynamic nature of the Internet, any web addresses or links contained in this book may have changed since publication and may no longer be valid. The views expressed in this work are solely those of the author and do not necessarily reflect the views of the publisher, and the publisher hereby disclaims any responsibility for them.

Any people depicted in stock imagery provided by Thinkstock are models, and such images are being used for illustrative purposes only. Certain stock imagery © Thinkstock.

Lulu Publishing Services rev. date: 11/5/2015

Then the Lord God said, "I see that is not good
for the man to be alone. I will make the companion
he needs, one just right for him."
Genesis 2:18

Dedicated to my wife, Vanessa.
My companion, the one made just right for me.

Foreword

The most significant people in my life are Jesus Christ, my mother and father, our children, and, of course, my wife, Vanessa. In that group is another significant person, but I can't tell you his name, because I don't know it.

This man, is from my past and, at the time, I believed he was very insignificant and useless. In fact, I didn't think much of him, at all. My actions toward him bordered on hatred. No, it didn't border, it was hatred. Yet, decades later John-the-bum turned out to be one of the most influential people in my entire life!

John, which is not his real name, but the name we gave him as children, is the inspiration for my first novel, *Among Pigeons*. Roman Barnes is not John-the-Bum, however. Roman is the character who developed once I tried to understand the life of the homeless man I mistreated in my youth.

However, that is not where the story ends. I wrote *Among Pigeons* to inspire the reader. In reality, it inspired me first. Then he inspired my wife, who never met him, but understood my need to tell a story and support the homeless. Together we founded Fan of the Feather in November 2009, an organization dedicated to supporting homeless veterans. Three years later we bought a home and named it The Promised Land, where we house and offer programs to support a homeless veteran's return journey to the life he wants to achieve. All of this from my "meaningless" encounters with a no-named bum!

My dream is to have a central center to provide support, counseling, and housing to homeless veterans or those at risk. Standing at the entrance will be a bronze statue of John-the-bum, surrounded by pigeons. His arms will be raised in triumph, because in the building behind him will be a homeless man or woman's first steps toward a victorious life.

Is that the end? No, it is not. John-the-bum's story is still not over and neither is my desire to honor him and tell his story through a fictional character.

Love and Death Among Pigeons is the continuation of Roman Barnes' story as a homeless man. It took me a while to develop a theme, and then I noticed how many homeless people have pets, particularly dogs. Regardless of their lack of so many things I take for granted, and in spite of their limited resources, they use what they have to take care of a dog! Why?

I hope *Love and Death* helps answer that question. However, this book is not meant to be a psychological exploration into the mind of the homeless. My thesis could be wrong, but it is expressed in what I hope is a very entertaining and suspenseful manner.

This is a longer book than the first and I thank my editor, Stephanie Jackel, for pushing me to be more descriptive and detailed. I thank my wife Vanessa for believing I could do more. She was right and I thank God for her. She proves there is nothing better than having a suitable companion, handpicked by God.

As much as I want to let Roman go, I recognize he has many stories to tell and I hope I remain up to the task of telling more of them in an engaging fashion, thereby showing the reader that homeless people are very human and deserving of respect. I'm convinced that the same characteristics which make for a successful life are the same ones which keep every homeless person living for another day. The same hope I have for my future, they have for their tomorrow. The same tenacity I have to achieve my dream, they have to achieve theirs. Yes, homeless people have dreams.

Through *Love and Death*, I hope the reader realizes his commonality with a homeless person and will see them as equals, not adversaries. It should be us AND them, not us VERSUS them. I want you, the reader, to recognize you are less than six degrees of separation from any homeless person. In fact, many people are a paycheck, or one natural disaster, from living on the street.

Many are one decision away from living among pigeons.

Chapter 1

"This is bullshit!" shouted Graham. He emphasized each word. He stood up from his chair and stared directly into Reverend Franklin's eyes. He face was red and his breathing was labored. Some spit was noticeable at the corner of his mouth. Not enough to drool, but enough to reflect the overhead lights. Graham noticed the moisture at the corner of his mouth and wiped the wetness from his mouth.

The reverend was not threatened. He had seen this before. During these sessions, he was very adept at asking questions that would get to the core and make someone search his feelings, and the question he asked Graham about his mother was the last straw for him. Graham had enough.

As I looked at him, I saw more than anger. There was pain, and his outburst was more than a response to a question he didn't like. He was making a declaration. He was asserting his independence.

When I first attended these meetings, it was clear the reverend was a matador and the angry one was the bull. Right now, Graham was the bull—snorting and stomping, preparing to charge and gore the man before him. Franklin waited patiently, already knowing the moves coming his way. At times, he seemed sadistic, but I guess he knew what he was doing. He had been facilitating such sessions for years. He sat ready for his opponent. His gaze at Graham was soft, yet steady and confident. There was no anger in his face. He waited, as we all did.

Graham made his declaration again, "You people are shit. This is bullshit!" It was a waiting game. We stayed in our seats, heads down so as not to provoke him any further. Eye contact was not a good strategy. I don't know if it's true, but I told my daughter,

Jenna, on a trip to the zoo, not to stare at the gorillas. It was a sign of aggression and they would get mad. A crazy thought now, since as I recall, they never looked at visitors, anyway. They always had their back to us, showing their ass to us, occasionally taking a shit and walking away. I guess it was their only way of being defiant.

So we followed the protocol and those of us in the circle of chairs treated Graham like a caged gorilla and let him snort and shit, so to speak. It was working. His breathing was less rapid and his ruddy color was less intense. In a way, I was rooting for him. The reverend seemed to manipulate people with his questions and his calm demeanor. Sometimes he appeared arrogant, as if he knew exactly how to control the situation. I wanted Graham to stay angry and do what I wanted to do—charge at Franklin, hit him, roll right over him and teach him a lesson. I wanted to wipe that smug look from his face. I wanted him to represent my anger. I was ready to declare my independence, as well.

I imagined our forefathers used the same language. Surely when the colonists were fed up with King George and his taxation, they must have shouted it. I bet the Declaration of Independence had been changed from some very raw language to the beautiful prose which now reposed in the Smithsonian. I believe it must have started with, "Dear George, this is bullshit!" What other language could express a person's frustration and anger any better than those words.

I never heard my mother cuss. Even when she was mad at me or my father, she let her feelings be known, but there is something very unnatural to express yourself as calmly as she did. She probably cussed out my father plenty of times, but reserved it for times when I was far from her lips. Cuss words were invented for a reason. The very words, though they have no real meaning, must have developed from some guttural response, some deep feeling which had to be released and which no known word could express adequately.

"We, therefore, the representatives of the United States of America, in General Congress, assembled, appealing to the Supreme Judge of the world for the rectitude of our intentions, do, in the name, and by the authority of the good people of these colonies, solemnly publish and declare, that these united colonies are, and of right ought to be free and independent states; that they are absolved from all allegiance to the British Crown, and that all political connection between them and the state of Great Britain, is and ought to be totally dissolved; and that as free and independent states, they have full power to levy war, conclude peace, contract alliances, establish commerce, and to do all other acts and things which independent states may of right do. And for the support of this declaration, with a firm reliance on the protection of Divine Providence, we mutually pledge to each other our lives, our fortunes and our sacred honor. *King George, we are not taking your bullshit anymore! Fuck you!"*

I was entertaining myself, while the situation was slowly defusing in the room. I imagined Benjamin Franklin delivering those words to King George, personally. In his proper wig and colonial dress and heels. It was a funny image and I chuckled inside.

I looked up, to see Seal looking over at me. He saw the humor in my face and smiled. He understood, but it was a bad moment. We were like kids, to be scolded. What we heard was silly, but we were forbidden to smile; nonetheless, just as a kid listening to my father, I couldn't help but smile. I looked at Seal again and his smile was bigger than mine. I could feel a cascade. It was dangerous, but unavoidable. I smiled so big my teeth were showing and that was the catalyst for Seal. He exploded with his signature laugh.

Seal was born hearing-impaired. He could make sounds, but could form very few words. But his laugh was the loudest and most raucous laugh of anyone on the planet. Once he started, it was as if he couldn't control it. He bellowed like a seal, hence his nickname. Of course, this was the wrong time for humor. I was able to contain my behavior to some extent. Seal, on the other hand, could not, and he barked and barked.

Understandably, Graham took offense. He didn't know Seal and his subsiding anger was at full blast, again.

"What the fuck are you laughing at?" He could hardly finish the sentence. He seemed to be talking and hurling himself at Seal. It was too late. By the time he finished his sentence, he was on top of Seal and wrestled him to the floor. Poor Seal could only use some defensive maneuvers with his legs and arms to stop the assault. I raced to his defense, as did others, and pulled Graham from Seal. It wasn't easy. There is no one stronger than an enraged man. There must be some chemical released in the body which

3

makes him superhuman. It took five of us to subdue him, and I think it was because Graham decided to stop. Had he chosen to, I believe he could have thrown all five of us from his shoulders and pummeled Seal to his death.

Franklin was so cool about the situation. He was standing, and he finally spoke.

"Needless to say, that ends our session."

As I escorted Graham to the exit, he bellowed back, "Needless, my ass." I wanted to chuckle again, which would have been another mistake. Finally, Graham and I made it outside and his anger seemed to retreat immediately, as if all he needed was fresh air. Or maybe it was his companion. She never came inside when Graham came to the counseling sessions.

I had my arm around Graham's shoulders as we approached her. The droop of her head and her eyes revealed she either was afraid or humble. I didn't know which, but she stood in her place, as we walked by. I had seen her before and she never spoke. I assumed she spoke to Graham. He didn't speak to her, but she followed close behind, like a puppy.

"Well, that was kinda crazy, man," I said to him.

"Ain't nobody gonna talk about my momma."

It would be hard to reach him, but I thought I would give it a try.

"I don't think he was talkin' about your momma. He was just trying to make a point about you and your relationship with your mother."

"Well, that ain't none of his business."

His response was clear. It was none of my business, as well. It was best to leave the incident alone.

"Well, it is a beautiful night for a cussing out, don't you think?"

Graham's face lifted and he chuckled. "You damn right it is. He got a good cussing, didn't he?"

"I couldn't have done any better, myself. And I'm a sailor," I said.

It was a good laugh at the end of a long day. When I looked around, I had to admit, it was a nice evening. The sun was a rich tangerine and I could feel a mild breeze. Leaves were swaying like clothes on my grandmother's clothes line. It was a lazy slow and hypnotic motion. There was not one cloud in the sky to interrupt anyone's view of the sun and the blue sky. If I hadn't realized where I was going, I would have labeled this a perfect day. This evening I was taking a last walk, with one my friends, back to his camp.

The anxiety of leaving him was mounting—like a last supper or sending a son off to war. Reverend Franklin had no tolerance for violence. Only two others had been expelled from the mission, and it was for fighting. He forgave drunkenness, but fighting was the one and only reason for immediate release. So Graham was gone and he understood that.

"I didn't wanna come no more, anyway," he explained. "What did they have to offer me?"

How could I answer that? I don't know how. He wasn't interested in shelter. He was comfortable where he was. He wasn't interested in giving up his marijuana habit. He was trapped in his own wall of familiarity. It took months of talking to him to convince him to come to HOPE's open house.

It was my idea to have us recruit people to come to a counseling session once a month. They didn't have to be a resident of the mission. The idea was to have people come and possibly reach someone who wanted to change. Graham wasn't one of them. The first two times I came to the park to get him. This time, he was on his way to HOPE without any prompting from me. Tonight could have been his breakthrough. He wouldn't admit it, but he was looking for one.

"So maybe I can come out and visit you and we can talk, every now and then," I suggested to him.

"Sure," he reluctantly replied, "but I ain't up to talking about too much personal stuff."

"I understand."

"I keep that to myself."

"Maybe you'll be up to sharing one day."

"I doubt it, but one day all will be known. Can't keep everything in the dark, forever."

"Yeah," I said. My mom told me that.

Graham looked at me and said, "I bet you got some stories, buddy."

I didn't like the way he looked at me. He said it as if he knew something.

"We all have stories. Everybody got drama."

"I got lotsa stories," Graham replied. "You think you know things. I know things." Graham emphasized.

Graham looked around the sky and finally replied, "I don't need no drama, though—livin' on the street is enough."

I entertained his thought. "Maybe you should write a book."

"Good thought. Maybe I should." He took a moment to think and then continued, "I don't wanna get anyone in trouble, though."

There was more paranoia on the streets than anyone could imagine. Who in the world could he get in trouble, I thought. I had to catch myself again. It was an arrogant thought and I had them more frequently, now that I was a resident at the mission. I was forgetting my three years as a homeless man. I was beginning not to relate to the homeless I left behind. I was thinking I was no longer one of them and we had nothing in common anymore.

It's amazing what a room can do. Three meals a day, and I was thinking as if I were a millionaire. Not just any millionaire, but one who had inherited his money and had no idea the worth of a dollar or the struggle behind it. Arrogance is what separates people from each other. Those with a home are better than those without. White people are superior to everyone. Black pride got it like that over anyone's pride. Straight people are more than gay people. Modern man is more sophisticated than the ancients. Arrogance causes hatred and wars.

Graham's arrogance was apparent, right now. He knew things; things no one else knew. Who was I to argue? It was not my place to diminish a man who was down. To survive, you had to have hope or a delusion. The two were closely related.

He quickly slipped his eyes over to his companion. I understood she must be a handful, but with his temper, he must have been a handful, as well. Maybe they deserved each other.

Graham continued, "You should know this by now."

Yes, I did. I was fifty-one and had seen more than I bargained for. I met Graham in the jungle, an area of heavy foliage in the park at the edge of the city. I met several people there I would call friends. It would be hard to explain to those who have not fallen so far, to understand we had a community and a camaraderie, just like everyone else on earth.

I've seen so-called pre-historic societies on the Travel Channel.

They appeared to be just like us. They had no money, to speak of. They had no medical care, no dental care, for sure. Yet they had celebrations and arguments and they laughed. They laughed heartily. Didn't they know their conditions? If they did, it didn't matter. In their own way, in their own language, they loved each other. We, the homeless, were no different.

From the corner of my eye I glimpsed his woman, Graham's constant companion. She didn't smile. I just rolled my eyes, though she didn't notice, since she was not looking at me.

What in the world did he see in her?

Her nappy hair, hidden under a wool cap, made me believe this white woman had some black in her. She was probably a pretty woman, if she got cleaned up. Of course, I could say that about any of us. Our smell and dirt were enough to allow people not to see us. I questioned my opinion of her. I was seeing her as most people see the homeless. I did not want to see her.

Her tennis shoes were far from the white they were intended to be when they were new. The shoelaces were almost black. Her jeans and T-shirt looked clean, but she smelled like Graham. All homeless people seemed to smell the same. The smell is old and musty, as if they had been locked up in a basement for years.

We reached the park and I declined Graham's invitation to go to their camp and chat some more. He was a good guy — mostly quiet and not so sociable, but he was a Southern gentleman. Manners were his specialty. I believe this white man would have been an abolitionist in another era. Maybe that's why we got along. He was kind.

When I was in the streets, I stumbled upon his camp, during one of my many binges. He never said a word about my being drunk, he just sat me down, talked to me, until I went to sleep. When I woke up, he offered me his food — a biscuit and a piece of chicken. He never spoke of that day again. I never knew if he forgot or he was being a gentleman. Obviously his woman saw his kindness, but she sure could learn a few things from him. A half-hearted hello would have been nice. I guess he got what he needed from her, though.

It must have been about six months since I last went into the jungle. I missed some of the boys, but it also had some bad memories and, from our counseling sessions, I learned it is best not to return to the past. It might keep you. I was finally off the street.

It was always my plan to find a job and a home, but after awhile I didn't think about it on a regular basis. A few months of wandering was enough to get me accustomed to life on the street. I learned where to go for my needs, and my needs were no different than the rest of the population—food, clothing, and shelter.

My plan was reduced to daily survival, and the hope of my return to the level of society from which I dropped was not a priority, anymore. My plan finally became a dream. My father told me dreams were worthless, unless you woke up and started doing the things needed to make the dream come true. Well, a constant survival mode gets in the way of doing the things to accomplish dreams. Of course, he would have disagreed, but he was never homeless. In fact, dreams became nightmares, for me. The last dream I had of my wife and daughter was so real, it was frightening. I awoke feeling as if I had been chased by a monster, and it was running fast and I was running in slow motion. A feeling of doom stayed with me for hours after. Dreams were not only unimportant for me, but were to be avoided.

I said goodbye to my friend and his girlfriend and headed back to the mission. It was where I lived now. The center of HOPE had the right name. It was meant to be inspiring, but after months in the program, I had not reached that level; I did have a bed and I stopped drinking. It was progress, but it didn't feel like it.

It was about thirty minutes to sunset and a little cooler. I thought of Graham and all my friends in the park. It wasn't my plan to leave them, but my life had many twists leading me to a place I had no intention of going. Six months ago, I was a hero. I helped the cops catch a major gang leader. I tried to avoid the spotlight, but Reverend Franklin hunted me down and offered me a room at HOPE. Since winter time was approaching, I took the offer. Though the city offered the homeless shelters for the winter months, there was no guarantee there would be room. There was always more demand than beds.

Then came the rules. I had to go to counseling. The first few days of no alcohol were hell, but I made it. Then I had to take some classes to become a solar technician. I heard the government was giving money to programs which did the training. Whatta joke.

Did they really believe they could make respectable solar technicians from alcoholics, drug addicts, and guys who were nuts? Who would hire us? It was another wasteful government program, but I followed the rules.

The rules—it's why so many don't want to come inside. The rules were so restrictive. We had to wake up on time, sleep on time, eat on time, go to class on time, and on and on. It felt like prison. One needs independence to be a grown-up. One of my father's favorite sayings, "So many adults, too few grown-ups." Once I was grown up, now I had fallen to be a mere adult, which is not a great accomplishment, since it means you only lived long enough to be of age—not much of an achievement. At least, that's what my father would say. I understand him, now.

My stroll back to the mission didn't feel purposeful. I wasn't sure I wanted to return. Part of me wanted to return to the streets. Ironically, I felt grown and free. Of course, that is a ridiculous notion, since society frowns on the homeless. What accomplishment is there in being on the street begging and searching for food like some bird? Ambiguity was another part of my life. It could drive a person crazy. Was this schizophrenia I was toying with or just life? The Navy released me because of my personality disorder, but they didn't say I was psychotic. They said I had animosity toward authority. I knew that when I joined.

Rather than walk the edge of the park before my return to HOPE, I decided to walk down into the city and take in the sights. The large park was set on a hill above the city. It was the site of an army fort from the Civil War. The hill was a great vantage point for watching for approaching rebels, hence the name – The Summit. Today, it was a great spot for viewing the city below. So many visitors came to Summit Park for the view and the peace. Though I couldn't see the mission from here, I could spot the industrial neighborhood to the east. HOPE mission had been established in an older building in the area. On the best of days, I could see the river, farther to the east, but there were not that many good days. Haze was a constant companion, in the air. I rarely had an opportunity to walk around, anymore. I once read the park had been expanded over time to its present size of over 500 acres.

We were all so busy. We HOPE residents constantly had tasks before us. Probably to keep our minds from drugs, alcohol or any other idol. Tonight I was given the opportunity to walk Graham home, since it was his last visit. We would see him again at breakfast, if he decided to come, but no more open house.

Open house was my idea. I convinced the reverend it would be good to have people, other than residents, come and sit with us during our counseling sessions. Of course he was reluctant. My best argument was, he expected us to change, while he wasn't under any such obligation. I reminded him of one of his principles: *If you want to change someone, you must first change yourself.* He had no answer, and the open mike sessions began about three months earlier. They turned out to be pretty successful. There were no incidents until tonight, and I didn't think it was enough to cancel them. It was Franklin's threat to do so. I decided I would ask him when I returned.

I stood at the Lion Gate. The large park had twelve pedestrian entrances, each named after an animal. Each entrance was adorned with an arch, with a replica of the animal it represented. There were six traffic entrances, named after famous Americans, with a bust of Lincoln at one entrance. My father took me to the Frederick Douglass entrance and took a picture of me, but I haven't seen the photo since I was in my teens.

The Lion Gate was a five minute journey, as the crow flies, from the mission. Since I don't fly, I had to walk five blocks west to Gerard Street, then another twelve blocks north. I couldn't have picked a better night to walk.

What a great evening to run away. The evening air was so inviting. Before I got too far from the park, I could smell the spring blooms. Spring is traditionally a time for love and change. Love was not an option, but change was a very entertaining thought. Every blinking city light asked me to visit. Every car horn asked me to follow. I watched people walking to and fro, in freedom. I didn't know if their life was any better than mine, but I imagined it was.

Everyone I passed looked content. They walked as if they were going somewhere. Their walk was eager. Their faces did not express questions, but anticipation. They had a goal. Occasionally, I walked past someone who appeared to be strolling, just like me, and I wondered if they were just like me—just enjoying the night. I wondered if I could stop and speak with them, and we could have a talk about the city's architecture or identify the restaurant from the fragrance which floated past our nostrils. No such luck. They never noticed me or looked my way, maybe too busy in their own thoughts.

There was my favorite liquor store. I had been sober since September14th of last year, but it still called out loudly to me. I might have answered if it had not been for Reverend Franklin, who tooted his car horn at me. I guess he was worried about me. I hopped in the Lexus and he drove away. It was quickly evident to me he was not driving us back to the mission. I was curious, but didn't ask. I instinctively knew we were about to enter a father-son discussion.

I was sure we were about the same age, give or take a couple of years. However, he had the authority, and that made all the difference. A lesson I learned in the Navy. There were officers younger than the senior enlisted, yet the enlisted gave them the respect their position required. The old salty sailors called the young ones, "Sir," and it was the right thing to do. I had my doubts about that, but then again, that was my problem—authority.

"Roe," the reverend started. "How did it go?"

He liked to call me Roe, and I corrected him several times. I finally gave in. I wanted to be called Roman. I liked my name. It was unique. Despite how I felt about myself, my name pointed me back to royalty and power. Unlike the names I was hearing lately, I was grateful to my parents for giving me a name which meant something. When I said my name, I always seemed to stand a little taller. Roman Barnes; that's a name! I guess a person should have at least a name which carries them through the tough times. When you have no money, no family, and no friends, you still have a name, and it should be one which wears well, like a suit. I had very little choice now of my wardrobe, so the only thing left was my name. Thank God for that!

As I expected, the reverend's tone was soft and paternal as he asked, "So how's it going?"

I smiled to myself, because I was able to predict him so well. "It's going okay. I mean, life is better than it was, right?"

"That's for you to answer. Is it?"

I really had to think about my answer. "Yeah. Yeah, it is."

"Was Graham okay?"

"Yeah, he was all right. He's a tough guy."

"You think so, huh?" It was clear Reverend Franklin was implying Graham was not so tough. I took offense out of respect for my friend.

"Yes." I made sure my affirmative answer was without equivocation. "Yes, he is. Think about it. The guy lives on the street, survives every day, takes care of a woman, is despised by the population in general, and still manages to live."

"Does he want to live?"

"What the hell does that mean? If he didn't, he'd be dead." I was surprised my voice was not raised.

"Sounds like I've offended you."

Sometimes he could talk to a person without being sociable. I never knew when he was a friend or a counselor. Something inside him must have told him to be silent. He would say it was the Holy Spirit. I would say he had enough sense to realize I might hurt him, if he kept up this line of questioning.

There was just a moment of silence and he asked, "How's the training going?" The reverend was talking about the job training I started a couple of months ago. At the end of six months I would be certified as a solar power technician.

"It's okay."

"You don't sound very enthusiastic."

"It's not a very enthusiastic subject." How could I be excited? When I thought about it, solar power was not a major concern for the world. People talked a lot about it, and wind energy and nuclear power, but they didn't do a damn thing about it. What job would be waiting for me at the end of my training? None. Who was hiring in this pitiful economy, anyway? It made politicians feel good about creating such a program, but they forgot the most important aspect—the job to go along with the title! Everybody in the chain did their little part to their satisfaction. Of course the person they were trying to help had no satisfaction, but at least it kept us off the streets for six months. Maybe that was the goal all along. It was a stall tactic, until someone could figure out what else to do, and no one ever did.

"You're doing well, though." It occurred to me this was another stall tactic. We made a few turns and none of them put us on a path to return to the mission. I decided to ignore the route and wait to see what was on his mind.

"Yeah, I'm doing okay. I've always been pretty good in school. I just never liked it."

"Is that why you joined the Navy?"

"No." I could be as evasive as the reverend.

"What happened, then?"

I hesitated to answer. Sometimes what I wanted to say I couldn't say to a man of God, but the Holy Spirit gave me permission. "Shit. Isn't that what always happens?" I waited for him to be offended, but he just smiled.

"Yes it does, all the time."

"How do you deal with it?" I asked.

"The same way you do. Hope. Tomorrow will be better, right?"

"I guess so."

"You *hope* so." His clever response was enough to put a smile on my face. We drove on until I recognized where we were going. I didn't know why, but it was obvious we were not randomly driving around to create some time for conversation. The reverend had a purpose and a direction in his head. I rode in silence for two reasons. One, I like riding in a car. It was one of the most relaxing activities I knew. I hated driving, but the experience of riding was like the moments after sex—calm and peaceful. You just wanted to fall asleep.

Second, I wasn't going to give him the satisfaction of being curious. I refused to ask our destination. I would find out soon enough. I felt I was in a chess game. He makes a move. I make a move. Franklin made his move while I contemplated mine.

Another ten minutes of weaving in and out of the night traffic, and he pulled over to a building. Parking was not an option, so he double-parked and got out of the car without a word, but a telling glance. He won this round. My curiosity was satisfied as to the destination, but not as to the reason. The reverend walked to the apartment building and sat on the stoop, waiting for me. I finally followed and sat next to him. We watched the traffic together. We watched residents move in and out of their buildings.

"So you're playing the ghost of Christmas past, tonight, huh?" I said.

"Something like that." He waited a while and asked, "How do you feel?"

Franklin was a smart guy. He studied people for a living. One way or another, he was determined to know me. In a way it was flattering. He could have ignored me, but he was genuinely interested in people and tonight he was interested in me.

He asked again, "How do you feel?"

"All right, I guess," is all I could say.

"What do you remember?"

I had to laugh at the dumb-sounding question. I remembered everything. We were sitting on the stoop where I sat millions of times with my best friend. I grew up in this building. I remembered fighting Joel Johnson, right in front of this building. His dog bit my leg and he laughed. The whole block turned out to watch us fight to the death, but death was far from us. My mother responded to the noise and separated us with a force I never knew she had.

I had lots of memories, but why should I tell the reverend? He interrupted my daydream. "When's the last time you came here?"

"I used to walk around here all the time, but after awhile I stopped."

"Were you avoiding it?"

"No. I don't think so. Just that the place changed, people moved, you know."

"Do you wish it were the same?"

What a stupid question! I'm sure my expression let him know what I thought, but I responded politely, "No, but it's funny...." I didn't really know how to finish the sentence.

"What do you mean?"

"Just weird." I felt stupid I didn't know what to say.

"What is it that you feel?" He emphasized "feel" to help me organize my thoughts.

"I don't know...I don't know."

Franklin remained quiet. I had seen him do this before. He would ask the question and leave a person to himself to figure out the answer. Usually the person would eventually have an answer. I thought and thought but no words would come to me, so my mind returned to a time I sat here with Raymond, and I talked about a crush I had on a girl named Mary. At eleven, she was beautiful, but I wondered if she were as good-looking now. If she wound up like me, I didn't want to see her. It would have been a great disappointment.

"I don't feel so good right now." The words finally came out.

In his most patient voice, the reverend said, "Why?"

Of course the answer required more words on my part, but they were hard to come by. "Life doesn't always turn out like you want it to, does it, Reverend?"

"Many times, no." Another man of few words, at least tonight. He could give some fiery sermons, he could get animated and loud, but this evening he was a different person. It made me wonder if being in the pulpit was a show. He turned it on, like an entertainer, when he felt the need. It made me wonder if the Holy Spirit was real. Sometimes I felt the spirit, but I didn't always know if it was my imagination or my emotions. Maybe it didn't matter.

I directed the reverend's attention to a building across the street. "See that building right there?" I asked. He acknowledged with a grunt.

"There was a girl I was in love with, who lived in that building."

"Really."

"Yep. I loved me some Mary. She was black as charcoal and I loved it. I would sit here and watch for her to come in and out of the building, and every once in a while she would look across to me and I'd wave. She would wave back, but that was it."

"What do you mean that was it? Did you guys talk?"

"No, we never did," I lamented.

"Never!"

I had to think about it a moment, but the answer was the same. "Never."

"Well, that was a safe love, huh? I mean nothing to get involved in."

"Yeah. The best kind," I replied.

"Are we cynical about love?" Franklin asked.

"No. Just cynical."

"So you don't trust anyone, is that it?"

"I trust everyone. That's my problem."

I wanted to talk more about Mary, and he used the opportunity to analyze me. I turned the conversation back to her.

"It's funny, she never played outside. She would just go in and out of her building. Sometimes I wondered if she really lived there."

"Did you see her in school?"

15

"She went to a private school. She wore a uniform on school days. Kinda weird to have a crush on someone you don't know, huh?"

"Not really. That's where all crushes begin. I had a crush on my fifth grade teacher. I didn't know her. I knew her name, but that was it. I didn't have conversations with her. She just taught me and everyone else in the class, but I was shaken by her. I stared at her, fantasized about her—"

"C'mon, Reverend. You can't be talking like that."

"Like what? I can't like girls?"

"Well, you can, but geez, I mean not with me. I'm a regular guy, you know."

"I happen to be a regular guy too, you know."

He may have been right, but I didn't see it. He was always in the king's chair. Who could talk to the king like a common person? Now I was sorry I conjured up Mary. There was only one way to end this discomfort.

"Rev, it's getting late, let's head back."

Chapter 2

Of all the days, this was the loneliest elevator ride Detective Renaldo Jackson had ever taken. Usually there were others coming and going on each floor. The only stop on the third floor was for naught. The door opened to an empty hallway. He waited for someone to enter, but the door finally closed and he was on his way to his final stop, on the fifth floor. Again, no one entered the elevator and he walked out into a busy floor of fellow officers, engaged in conversation.

As he walked through them, they greeted him with cheer, but he had trouble returning the salutations with any enthusiasm,though he looked forward to seeing his friend and former partner.He strolled to the end of the hall. His stride was cool, but his excitement was building. Finally he saw Detective Gregory Innis at his desk, involved in paperwork.

Innis did not notice the shadow over him until he heard a voice. "Stop pretending, School."

"School" was Detective Jackson's nickname for his friend. Innis had to turn his head to see Jackson, but he already knew who it was, and his big grin began before he turned to see the clean cut, well-dressed man leaningover him.

"Well, well, well," Innis said as he stood.

"Don't hurt yourself, now. You're not as young as you used to be," Jackson chuckled.

"No, I'm not, but I'm still smarter than you'll ever be," came the reply. It was a short greeting as they hugged each other.

Innis pulled away from the embrace. "Did I wrinkle your shirt?" He knew how neat Jackson preferred to be.

"No worries. I'll send you the bill."

Innis gesturedfor his friend to sit and Jackson eagerly took the offer to sit across the desk.

"Where's your partner?" the younger man asked.

"Out in the street. He likes that sort of thing."

"Yeah. I remember that. Don't you get to do that stuff?"

"Naw, that ain't my thing. I'm still doing the same thing, different clientele."

"I see." A short pause to think of how to advance the conversation and Jackson asked, "So how's it going? I mean, you like it here?"

"Yeah." He meant it, but he wasn't sure his sincerity showed in the curt answer. Four months ago, Detective Jackson transferred to the Homeless Liaison Squad. It was at his request. His need to change had been building for over a year, and by the time he and his partner busted a sex ring, he was exhausted with his position. He was not one for patience, anyway. During that time, he thought he could be more helpful in helping those who couldn't help themselves and that opportunity came with an opening in the Homeless Division, or HD. He felt he had to explain himself.

"It's different. I like it."

"Don't sound too enthused, okay?" his friend quipped.

"No, really, I do. It's more rewarding," Innis said, trying to convince his former partner.

"No, I don't know. Catching bad guys is catching bad guys, isn't it?"

"No, it isn't. When you do it for someone that no one listens to, you feel really good about it."

"What do you mean?"

"Hard to explain." Innis took a moment to gather words in his head and arrange them to make some sense.

"Do you remember what it was like when you were a kid and someone accused you of something and you didn't do it, and the only one who believed you was your mother?"

"Yeah."

"How did it feel?"

The answer was so obvious, Jackson didn't want to say it, but he said, "Good."

"You know why?"

"Because she believed in me."

18

"It was more than that. She had authority. She was important. If your little brother believed you, it wouldn't be the same. He had no power, no authority, no ability to change anything. Your mother had all of that."

Jackson nodded in agreement. "Man, you get deep sometimes. Who would have thought of stuff like that? You should've been a psychiatrist."

"I'm a cop. That makes me a psychiatrist, by default." The statement made them smile.

"So,Doctor, have you had lunch?" Renaldo Jackson asked.

"Not yet. Lot of crappy paperwork to do."

"Take a break. Buy me some lunch."

"Buy you?"

"Yeah. You get the doctor's salary. I'm just trying to make it on a lowly detective's pay."

As Greg rose from his chair, he said, "You poor pathetic man. I remember those days."

They walked to exit and Jackson returned the fire. "Shut up."

The couple made their way through groups of detectives. They took the short trip down the hallway to the elevator, pressed the button and waited for the elevator to arrive. Neither one said anything to the other, thoughGreg noticed his friend's expression seemed to be in a distant place. He knew heavy a conversation was coming, but he reserved the right to wait until they were in a more private space.

Once outside the building, the atmosphere changed dramatically.It seemed more cheerful. Since the sun was out, the weather was much more pleasant on this spring afternoon. The rain clouds predicted by the weathermanon the previous night's newscast never arrived, but of course on tonight's broadcast they would have pointed attention to the computer models as a scapegoat.

The two men walked across the street to a small park and found a bench which seemed secluded from everyone around. This was the opportunity Greg was looking for, to ask his friend about his countenance.

"So what's up, buddy? You want to talk or do you want to eat?"

The concern on Renny's face became more intense. Greg wasn't sure whether it was the sun or did his friend really want to rub his forehead so hard. Renny gave a loud sigh and slumped

19

against the bench's back. He opened his eyes for just a moment and then quickly shut them and began rubbing his temples.

"Are you all right, man? You look ill. You getting a migraine?"

"No," replied the younger detective, but it was obvious he was under a lot of stress and he was ready to speak about something. Detective Innis just had to find a way to tease the information out of his former partner.

"Let's start with something easy, how about that?"

"I don't think there's anything easy. At least not anymore."

"Man, that sounds serious. What happened to you?"

Innis surveyed his friend, looking for clues as to what could be on his mind. What could be disturbing this seasoned detective? He worked with him for years, enjoyed his company, and they became close friends. Which explained why his friend came to him now about something troubling him.

Detective Innis decided he would ask more probing questions to help bring the conversation to ahead. "Is it the divorce?"

"I guess it's the divorce. I guess it's a lot of things."

"A lot of things," DetectiveInnis repeated.

"A lot of things is a lot of things."

Renny looked at him with disbelief. Greg was trying to be clever, but Renny also understood his friend was trying his best to get into his mind. It wouldn't be that easy, since it wasn't easy for the younger man to understand all the thoughts which kept him awake at night. They kept him on the verge of migraines, on a daily basis. Despite the complex set of issues swirling in his head, Renny understood his best friend was sitting right next to him, and Innis had to make good on the ploy of taking them out to lunch. If there was one person who cared about Renny's life, it was his mentor who sat beside him.

"You always seem to do the right thing," Renny finally responded.

"No, not really. I made lots of mistakes. We all do."

"See what I mean? You know the right thing to say, at the right time, and you seem so understanding. Where do you get that shit from, anyway?"

Greg just smiled. "I'm a genius, man. Don't you know that? I've been telling you that for years."

Detective Jackson finally sat up. He was ready for the discussion ahead, or so he thought. Renny stared into the street watching the traffic and finally he mumbled, "Easy come, easy go."

This was the conversation Detective Innis was determined to never have. Both detectives had been very good at keeping their unspoken promise to never speak of the money they found last year during a big bust of a major human trafficking ring. For weeks after the case was closed, they were heroes. They were interviewed on television and they received medals for their work.

It was a significant news story because they had come upon a major sex ring being operated beneath the city. It was known as the Tunnel of Love. During the conclusion of the case, they found a large stash of cash hidden in an elevator shaft. Greg never knew how much Renny discovered. He took his partner's word for the amount, since he had left it up to his partner to count the money before fellow officers arrived at the scene.

However, there was one thing he did know, his partner's financial problems. It was a great opportunity to stow away some of the cash. No one would ever know. Everyone had to take their word for the amount they found, but maybe fellow officers were becoming suspicious.

During that time, almost a year ago, Renny Jackson was crying on his shoulder about his financial situation. He was desperate about his mounting bills from the mountain of material possessions he was amassing for his wife and his daughter. It would've been the perfect opportunity to take a small amount of money. They turned in close to $1 million. Detective Innis was never sure whether it was more than $1 million, less than $1 million, or exactly the amount they turned in. He never really knew, but he understood his partner's need for money, and he was willing to turn his head and never question and never discuss the amount they reported.

It seemed Detective Renaldo Jackson's conscience was bothering him now. Detective Innis felt as if they were sitting on a confessional bench, and he was the priest about to hear a story he was unwilling to receive. It is a story which would put him in an uncomfortable position. He wanted no part of any knowledge of the money.

Innis decided to interrupt the conversation. "I'm hungry and I need something." He stood and walked toward the vendor cart, selling different kinds of nuts. His favorite was the cashews, covered in a sweet cinnamon coating. He bought a bag and reluctantly returned to the bench, still wanting no part of the conversation to come.

He tilted the open bag of sweet nuts toward his friend, and Renny dipped in his hand, pulling out a handful of the treats. He shook the fist full of nuts and threw five or six nuts into his mouth. Innis took the bag and put one nut at a time from the bag to his mouth, treating each nut as a delicacy.

"I love these things," remarked Renny. He grabbed another handful and shook his fist again, as if preparing to throw some dice. It always amused his partner.

"I'm all about comfort food," Greg said, with a mouthful.

"Yeah, I know."

"So how's Carmen?"

"Her usual self, I guess."

This was not the best of conversations, either. Jackson and his wife were going through a divorce and, as with any divorce he witnessed, it was not pretty. At times, Innis could not distinguish between the marriage and the divorce. The major issue in both was the same. The usual culprit was money.

If Detective Innis could think of a better conversation, he would have come up with a topic, but this moment wasn't about him, so he stopped trying. There was not much good news to even speak of, anyway. If they talked about the world, what good was going on? What could he say about the economy that could improve his friend's posture or demeanor? The economy was in shambles, and politicians' constant fighting about how to improve it filled television and print space, but no one was willing to do anything.

He could talk about his relationship with Lois, but no sooner had this thought come to his mind than his former partner asked about her.

"How's things with you and Lois?" Jackson asked.

"We're doing all right, I guess."

"You still playing the strong, silent type? Even with me?"

Innis chuckled. He was known as the silent type, but he didn't play the coy and silent type with men. He liked playing the game with Lois because she was just as good as he was. It was a challenge trying to get into her brain. He also knew she was using the same strategy to try to get into his brain. It made for a very long courtship.

"You're not pretty enough for me to play the game with you, Renny."

"You know I am. You just don't want to admit it."

Renny's sense of humor was enough to make them relax. Jackson sat up from his stooped position. He squinted at the sun and threw his arms up over the back of the bench.

"Are you guys going to get married?"

"Who knows? The subject really doesn't come up."

"What do you mean, it doesn't? Every woman wants to get married."

"Maybe so, but Lois is way too cautious to bring up the subject."

"Why don't you bring it up?"

"Because I'm too smart."

Renny could only shake his head in disappointment.

"You guys will play that stupid game until you're both in wheelchairs, and then what?"

"We haven't gotten that far, yet."

"Well, I guess I shouldn't really push it, should I? Not that I have a perfect model for you to follow."

"No offense, Youngblood, but no, you're not."

Innis did not intend for the conversation to return to his friend's marriage, but somehow it did. Somehow it always did. He wasn't going to try to avoid it again, this time.

"So tell me, what's going on with you and Carmen?"

"I'm supposed to see her later today. We were supposedly going to counseling, but I don't know why."

"Do you want to go to counseling?"

"At this point, I don't want to do anything."

"I can't say I can blame you."

"I usually get blamed for everything." Jackson said.

"You know what your problem is?" Innis said. "You're trying to be the man."

"I am a man, fool!"

His indignation made Greg take notice. "You may be trying to *be* the man, with the wrong woman. You can't be a man with a woman who wants to be a man, too. My grandmother always told me that you can't have two women or two men in the same house

23

at the same time. Two women can't rule the kitchen, and two men can't rule the same castle."

"So what am I, the woman in the kitchen or the man in the castle?"

"Doesn't matter who you are. Carmen has made it clear you don't count, brother."

"You telling me,"Renny agreed.

"There are only two kings on the chessboard and they both are trying to kill each other. Kings and queens work together. Kings are territorial, queens are possessive."

"And I suppose you think that's profound?" Renny responded, sarcastically.

"My gramma thought so. She was a smart lady."

"Well, let's leave it at that. I ain't arguing with your grandmother."

"Good choice. I didn't, either. At least, not most of the time. When I did, she put me in my place.You know what she used to tell me? 'You smellin' yo'self, boy.' You know what she was trying to tell me?

"What?"

"I was acting too grown. I thought I was a man."

"Was she telling you that she was the man?"

"Yup."

"So you can't win."

"Nope."

"So women are women and women are men and men are… What?" said Renny, exasperated.

"I don't know anymore."

"Well, that's sad. Yeah, you shouldn't get married."

"Exactly. I wanna go to my own house and be the man. I don't need the fight."

Renny smirked. "Lois would kick your butt, anyway."

"The point is, she's not. Life's good."

All Renny could do was look at his former partner and smile. "You always have the answer, don't you? You always do the right thing."

"Not always."

"Okay, let's forget the bullshit. Let me ask you, are you happy?"Renny asked.

The question was unexpected, but Greg struggled to answer. Eventually he said, "Yeah, pretty much."

As he watched Jackson lower his shoulders, he wanted to raise his spirits—at least to the level they were a moment ago.

"Look, man, you will be happy, too." Innis tried to complete his sentence, but Renny's rolling eyes made it difficult. "You will. This will all be over after awhile."

Renny's lips tightened in contemplation of a thought. "Yeah." He thought some more and repeated, "Yeah."

Happiness, contentment, peace, or joy were not a part of Detective Jackson's vocabulary and certainly didn't describe any part of his life.

"School, why did you transfer to the Homeless Liaison Team? I mean, really."

Innis thought of a way to explain his decision. "Remember that homeless guy we helped several months ago?"

"Yeah. It was almost a year ago, right?"

"About."

"What was his name, anyway?"

"Roman."

"Yeah, Roman. Cool name. If I had a son, I might name him that. Roman Gabriel Jackson. What do you think?"

His partner looked at him in disbelief. "Whatever."

"You didn't like him, though. You barely spoke to the guy."

"But we helped him, just the same. There was something very satisfying about helping that guy. He had nothing, he wasn't important." Innis couldn't think of any more descriptions for Roman. "But we helped him."

"We do that all the time. We help people all the time. Rich people, poor people, all races, *etcetera*."

"That's the point. He was an *etcetera*. No identity, an asterisk."

"So you're saying it made you feel good to help a nobody."

"Yeah, I felt good. Not to mention—"

Innis stopped as he noticed his present partner walking toward them. Detective Solomon Turner preferred being a street cop. He didn't like the "suits," as he called most other detectives.

"What's up, Solly?" Greg asked.

Before Turner answered Greg, he addressed Detective Jackson. "How ya doing? Haven't seen you in a long time."

"Not since the child abduction case. We were just talking about that."

"Made you guys heroes. How does it feel, hero?"

"Another day, another dollar, ya know?"

"I know."

Solomon finally turned his attention to Detective Innis.

"We got a call to the jungle."

"What's up?"

"Some guy got stabbed to death."

"They know who it is?"

"No, not yet. Maybe we know him."

So many of the homeless were unknown. It was frustrating to settle on "John Doe." Innis turned to Jackson and said, "Another *etcetera.*"

Greg and Renny stood up and shook hands. That was insufficient, so they hugged each other. Detective Turner interrupted the moment by saying, "You guys can get a room later."

Solomon and Greg walked off together; Renny watched for a moment and then walked in the opposite direction.

Greg turned to his new partner. "Who reported the death?"

"Some woman."

"They holding her?"

"At the scene, so that's where we're headed."

"Is she homeless?"

"Don't know the details."

The couple walked into the police garage and got into their vehicle. As with his other partner, Greg did the driving.

"Do we need the siren?"

"If you do that, I'll have to ride in the back. Don't wanna blow my cover, ya know."

"I think everybody knows you're a cop by now, Solly."

"They keep telling me that, but there's always someone who doesn't know me. I fooled you guys, didn't I?" He was referring to the case they shared nine months ago. Innis and Jackson had no idea Turner was an undercover officer.

"Okay, ride in the back."

"I love being chauffeured. Home, James."

Greg snickered and headed to the jungle with the siren blasting their arrival. The drive took about ten minutes, since traffic was not very congested. Greg pulled the car up to the curb, and he and Solly walked through the park, across an overpass, and noticed police tape and red and blue lights flashing below. They were going the wrong way, but made a short detour, approaching the crime scene. Yellow tape surrounded an area of a hundred square feet. There were two porta-potties lying on their side in the circle, but no body was apparent.

Solly introduced himself and Greg to a uniformed police officer, and they were directed to another officer standing in front of one of the mobile bathrooms.

"You Detective Turner?" the officer asked.

"Yeah." He pointed to Greg. "This is Detective Innis."

The officer continued, "We got called here about an hour ago."

"Where's Homicide?" Greg asked.

"I thought you were Homicide."

"Well, we are and we aren't. We're HD, Homeless Division."

"So you got this or not?" the officer retorted.

Solly was a bit irritated with his tone. He felt it was too arrogant for the officer to be talking to detectives in such a manner.

We got it," Solly informed him.

Greg asked, "Who called you?"

"911 dispatch."

Solly looked at his partner with disappointment. He shrugged it off, but before he could question the officer, he received his answer.

"That female over there called 911."

He directed their attention to a woman standing outside the tape. Her red eyes made it clear she had been crying. She stood shifting side to side.

"So what do you have? And don't say a murder."

The officer walked them to the blood-stained door of one of the overturned johns and peered into the opened the door. A man, his clothes saturated with blood, urine and feces, lay against the back wall of the porta-potty. His eyes were closed and his mouth open as if in shock of what was to come, and whatever he saw had come and gone, without a trace.

"Oh, Jesus!" exclaimed Solly. His partner looked over his shoulder with disgust at what he saw.

"Where's Crime Scene?" Greg spoke to the uniformed policeman.

"They should be here soon. We called everybody at the same time."

"Somebody hated this guy." Greg began to describe the scene. "His shirt is open, several stab wounds." He noted more. "Oh geez, look at the wounds around his heart. They wanted this guy dead and fast."

"And the least amount of sound," Solly added.

"Who said he was homeless?"responded Greg.

"I've seen him around. Don't know his name, though."

"Ah, so that's where she comes in," said Solly, indicating the woman at the perimeter.

"She didn't tell you?"

"No. She's been bawling most of the time. She doesn't talk."

"She doesn't talk or won't talk?" Innis said.

"Comes out the same."

Greg ignored the officer's comment and headed to the woman. "I'm Detective Innis, this is Detective Turner. Is it all right if we talk with you about your call?"

She nodded her approval and wiped her eyes a few times. They walked through the gatheringcrowd.

"How about we walk up on the bridge?" Innis asked her. She didn't say anything, but she heard him. She walked up the hill to the overpass and gazed down at the nasty, stench-filled crime area.

"What's your name?" Solomon queried.

"Kathryn." Her name came in a very strained tone.

"Do you know the man down there?"

"No." She was starting to cry again.

"Did you find him?" Solomon continued.

"No."

The detectives looked at each other. Why were they talking to this woman?

"Did you call 911?"

"Yes." Finally she was composed enough to say more. "I called after I saw him in the stall."

"You said you didn't find him."

"I didn't. I mean, I wasn't the first to see him."

Now their curiosity was piqued.

"Who saw him first, then?" Solly's questioning remained calm.

"I don't know. I heard someone scream and when I looked, she was running away."

"She," was Solomon's only response.

"Yes. She ran down the hill into the bushes." Kathryn didn't know it, but she was pointing to an area known as the jungle, a heavily wooded area of foliage. It was well populated by the homeless.

"Can you describe her?" Greg wanted to know.

"No. She was so far away."

"How do you know the person was a woman?"

"She ran like a woman."

"What was she wearing?" Detective Innis wanted to know.

" A green hoodie is all I could make out."

"Thank you, Kathryn," Solly said. He was good with names. They dismissed Kathryn.

Greg asked Solly if he knew the man in the john. His partner answered, no. If Solly didn't know him, then no one did. He had been on the streets as an undercover cop for five years. He loved it. It was his enthusiasm which made Greg consider transferring to the department. "I love helping somone who has nothing," he would repeat from time to time.

As the detectives looked into the deep brush, Solly said, "Bad *ju-ju* in that place. When is the city gonna clean it up?"

Greg replied, "Probably when somebody gets killed."

Chapter 3

He couldn't bring himself to believe this day would be any different, but Renaldo Jackson was stepping out on faith, again. In his past fifteen years in law enforcement, he had seen the worst and the best in people. He witnessed the meanest of people turn their life around and become of, all things, preachers. He had also witnessed good people turn to murder for the simplest of reasons—greed.

His life seemed to follow the latter. He was convinced money was the root of all evil, regardless of what his therapist said. It was not only the root, it was evil. And if money were a person, he married her eleven years ago and now he was on his way to divorcing her.

Renny's wife, Carmen, had a love affair with money which overshadowed her love for him. Her relationship with all things denoting wealth was suffocating, but he learned he was an enabler. He bought her whatever she wanted, or tried to. He gave up his dreams to support her dream, and her only dream was to be rich—and if not rich, then to have the appearance of being rich.

He already had a strong family history of migraine head-aches, and the stress of his marriage and his job was fertilizer for the blinding headaches.

As he got out of his car and walked into the park's interior, he rubbed his head. He could feel the tension in his shoulder, but failed to relax it. Rubbing his temples felt good, but his self-massaging never delayed the pain, as far as he could remember. Renny thought of taking a pill as a pre-emptive strike, but was too late now. He should have taken his medication thirty minutes ago. Today, his mustard seed faith whispered he could handle a conversation with his future ex-wife.

His major stress proved to be his inability to spar with her. She had a doctorate in illogical thought, and she used it well against his bachelor's degree in criminal justice. "Today will be better," he repeated to himself. "Today, she will listen. Today, she will hear me."

His affirmations immediately dissolved at the sight of her standing against a tree in the distance. She was a painting in waiting. Separated rays of light cut through the tree top and showered her image. Her red blouse was the perfect accessory against the tree bark. From fifty feet away, he knew exactly why he loved her.

Renny was convinced this was a ploy. Carmen was always scheming, but what could she want this time? She got everything she wanted, but always wanted more. His stupidity was, he gave it to her. By every standard, he was an enabler. His therapist made it official.

At twenty feet, it was obvious she was talking on the phone. Somehow it made his approach a little easier. This was their first time alone. Their counselor would not allow it until she trusted they could speak without turning the conversation into their usual verbal brawl. She didn't reach that conclusion until last week, after careful consideration and evaluation of their previous twelve weekly sessions. At times, he felt like a child in those sessions. Why did he need permission from a woman who was younger than he? He was tired and more annoyed at the thought of giving his power to another female—another controlling bitch.

That was his lot in life. He hated women, but he was a man and he loved women. During one of his private sessions, Dr. Fowler tried to figure out his relationship with his mother, but Renny didn't feel it was any of her business. He vaguely answered her questions. She was lucky he discussed Carmen with her, at all. However, he calculated it might be to his advantage. Maybe if he could convince the doctor Carmen was an evil snob, then he could live his life pain-free. Maybe he could live without the constant guilt his former wife placed on him, regularly. He was responsible for every wrong in their failed marriage.

Carmen wouldn't even give him credit for their daughter, Neena. She was his child. Everyone said he "spit her out," but Carmen always gave her attributes to someone, anyone, but Renny. Her eyes looked like Carmen's mother and she had Carmen's body shape—thin and spider-like. In fact, it was her nickname, given to her by her basketball teammates—Spider.

Carmen was as slender as the tree she leaned against. He could hear her sign off from her conversation, and she finally looked at him. Her lips glowed with the flesh-tone shade of lipstick. Carmen's eyes invited him to come ever closer, but it was another trap. She was a black widow spider. She pulsed with sensuality.

Finally, Renny was within speaking distance. "Hey, how ya doin'?"

Carmen looked down at her phone screen one last time and then put it away in her pocketbook. "Good," she replied, softly.

She surveyed him and looked directly in his eyes, looking past his face, into his brain.

"What do you want to know?" It was the best start to a conversation he could find, and even that seemed as if she had planted the thought in his head.

"Are you okay?" Carmen asked.

"Sure. I'm fine."

She never stopped looking into his eyes. "Do you want to walk or sit?"

A choice? It was a rarity. Usually she demanded or instructed or conducted. He felt paranoid. He was waiting for a fight. He was prepared for the worst, yet she was so calm it unnerved him. She chose for him.

"C'mon, let's walk."

It wasn't a bad choice. The sun beckoned everyone to the park. Joggers were in their element andlovers were called to fill in the background. As they walked, an artist was capturing the scenery, dabbing colors quickly on his canvas. Renny stopped to see what would become of the splashes of color. At first it was formless, but with time he could see a tree, then leaves, then the beginning of a building in the background. It was amazing to watch the transformation. Carmen stood close to him and they watched, in silence.

"That's amazing," he remarked to her. "How does he do that?"

"It is pretty cool."

The young man looked up at them. He had a few paintings lying around him. They were fresh paintings, available for sale.

"Spider would like that one, don't you think?"

Carmen agreed. "Yeah. Those are her colors, too."

"She loves her tangerine."

Carmen's smile grew larger, but she pulled on his arm and encouraged him to continue their walk. She wrapped her arm around his.

"She doesn't need any more stuff," Carmen said.

"Yeah. I guess not."

At one point, Renny noticed the level of his migraine pressure was almost gone. Carmen had managed to calm his fears and he was mindful of her arm still wrapped around his. For the moment they were lovers, again.

"What would you like to talk about?" she asked.

"I dunno. What are we supposed to talk about?"

"Whatever we want. We are grown-ups, ya know," she reminded him.

The label of being grown-ups was not always accurate for them. They could fight like cats and dogs.

Renny gave her the controls. "You help me here. What do you want to talk about?"

"How about you?"

"Me." He was taken by surprise.

"Yes, you."

"There's not much to say about me. Nothing's changed."

"Well, tell me about the job. What's going on? Any interesting cases?"

He thought a moment. "Same ol' stuff. Ya know. Saving the world. Keeping it safe for you citizens."

"Us citizens appreciate it."

He looked at her and said, "Us superheroes are humbled by your gratitude."

"Silly."

"Have you eaten, yet?"Renny asked.

"Yes."

"Let me guess. Chicken on a bed of lettuce."

"And."

"I wasn't trying to be smart. I was just noting."

"You note wrong."

"What?"

"You're wrong. I had a hamburger."

"Stop lying. You did not have a hamburger."

"And why not?"

"Because you have a piece of lettuce stuck in your teeth."

Immediately she released herself from him and wiped her gums, feeling for debris with her tongue.

She flashed her teeth at him. "Where? Is it gone?"

Renny looked carefully and said, "Yes."

She looked past his eyes once again. "There was no lettuce, was there?"

"No. And there was no hamburger, was there?"

"No."

"I know."

She mocked his answer, "I know."

Carmen slapped his arm and they continued on their walk, but she checked one more time for some lettuce.

"You can be so mean, sometimes," she remarked.

"It's the nature of the beast."

"You detectives are all alike."

"No, we're not. I'm the good one. My partner is the—" He hesitated, searching for the right adjective. "Hm. My partner is the good one, too."

"That doesn't sound like a good combination. I thought you had to have one good one and one bad one."

"That's TV, girl. You just have to have the right partner. Greg and I used to alternate."

"How's he doing?

"Good, I guess."

"Where did he move to, again?"

"Homeless Liaison Team."

"Hm. Not much glamour in that, I bet."

That was like her, Renny thought. She was all about the glamour. She dressed for the glamour, walked for the glamour. If Hollywood called, she would be ready. She was red carpet-ready.

"Yeah, he never was about that," he said, defending his partner.

"He always looked like he was thinking."

"He always is."

"Do you miss him?"

"He was cool to work with."

"That's a 'yes,' I'm guessing."

"That's a 'he was cool to work with'."

"Does he like what he's doing?"

"He says he does. I mean when I talked to him earlier, he seemed smitten."

"Smitten. Does he have a girlfriend?"

"No, I mean he looks like his new life has captured him. He's involved. He talks about it like a girlfriend. I can see he likes it, but he has trouble explaining why."

"Or maybe you don't get why."

"Whatever."

They walked in silence for a while, taking in the sights around them. Carmen interrupted with, "What do you see?"

"What do you mean?"

"I mean do you see the trees or the people?"

Renny was perplexed by the question. "I see both."

"I always wondered what gets your attention."

"I thought you knew that."

"No. So tell me, what do you see?"

"I see a lot of things."

"I always wondered that about the therapist we see. Does she ever look at people without analyzing them? Does she analyze her friends, you think?"

"So you're wondering if I'm the same way. Do I see criminals at every turn. Is that what you mean?"

"Do you?"

"No. I don't know where the on-off button is, but I do turn it off."

"Do you do it automatically or do you have to think about it?"

"Woo! Aren't we full of questions."

From the look on her face, he realized he needed to reassure her. "But that's a good thing. It's a good thing. Shows you're interested. That's how I knew you wanted me, when we first met."

"Stop lyin'. You didn't know anything."

"Hey, I'm good at what I do. Remember how we met?"

"Of course I do. It was about that stalker."

"Remember you called me 'detective,' all the time?"

"Yes."

"And remember the day you came rushing in the office, looking for me?"

"Yes, yes. What's your point?"

"Do you remember," he prodded her. "What did you ask me that day?"

Carmen had to think a moment. "I don't remember. What?"

"You asked me for my first name."

"You make it sound as if I came to ask for your name."

"Didn't you?"

"Ooo, you can be so arrogant, at times."

"Observant is not arrogant. It's awareness. Besides, there are two things that scream, I'm interested."

"And they are?"

"When someone asks you personal questions."

"And the other?"

"When the status changes from impersonal to personal. And there's only one way to know that."

She just looked at him to finish and Renny continued his thesis.

"You can't be personal when you call someone by their title. You call someone by their first name, it means you want to know them. You want to get close. So when you asked me what my name was, I knew you wanted me."

"Like you didn't want me."

"I didn't say that, now. Shoot, if you didn't already have a stalker, I might have been yours. No room for two stalkers, know what I mean?"

"You want to get something to eat?"

"Aw, shucks," he replied with a sly look.

"What?"

"Now I know you want me." He didn't let her look of disbelief stop him. "Whenever you want to make love, you want to eat, first."

"Shut up!"

"Just sayin'."

After a pause, she asked, "You hungry?"

"Sure. What do you want?"

"No. You tell me what you want."

Her statement was so sincere it took him aback. Now it was his turn to look into her. For a moment they were lost in each other's gaze.

"What?" she asked.

"Just looking for truth."

"Do you see it?"

"The entire time we were married, I looked for that from you."

"What? The truth?"

"No. I always looked for you to ask me what I wanted."

"Please."

"You don't understand."

"You damn right about that."

"I mean I wanted you to care as much for me as much as I cared for you. I wanted to know that I mattered."

"So you're telling me I treated you like you didn't matter? That's bullshit."

"Wait, wait. Don't get defensive."

"How do I not get defensive? You're making some shit up to, to…what? I don't know. You attack me and I'm not supposed to get defensive? You must know me better than that."

"I was talking about me and my feelings, not you. Isn't that why the therapist asked us to get together?"

"And you use the opportunity to get back at me for something I did," Carmen fired back.

"Okay, okay. Forget it. You win."

"Oh, there you go again. You win. It's not about winning, unless you have to win. Is that what your attack was about? You wanted to win?"

"I wanted to explain."

"Explain."

"Never mind," he said, in a disappointed tone.

"There you go, again. Another technique of yours. You say some sly shit and then want to quit as soon as I voice myself."

"How did this get to be about you?"

"You made it about me. Trying to put some guilt trip on me."

"You know what, Carmen? One day it will be about me."

"Whatever the hell that means," she retorted.

"It means, one day you will not have a say. The topic will be me. All about me. Nothing but me, because I deserve it. It's always about you and Neena. Sometimes I want it to be about me."

"Go 'head. Make it about you. Make your accusations. Make up shit. Do whatever you have to do to make it all about you."

"Well, this didn't end well."

"Does it ever?"

"Let's just sit down." Renny escorted his ex-wife to a nearby bench. They sat and stared into the distance. Carmen sat, slightly turned away from him, her right leg crossed over her left. Her free foot bounced up and down. She leaned forward on her extended arms, with both hands clenching the bench seat.

Renny tried to figure out what went wrong. He was always trying to figure out what to say to Carmen and how to say it. It was an exhausting chore, and he was always wrong. Wrong—that was another word which excited her. He would try to end their many arguments with "I was wrong." That didn't work, since she would reprimand him for making the issue a right and wrong issue.

Finally, he settled on the word "inappropriate," and she appeared to approve the term. Carmen manipulated him to the point he was no longer the man he thought he was. Greg told him he was frightened by her, and he denied it, vehemently, but every once in a while, he knew his old partner was right.

He was afraid to speak his mind. He was afraid to upset her. He was afraid she did not love him. He was afraid she would leave him, and she did. She was always so concerned with their daughter, Renny believed they would stay together for her sake.

At times, like this one, it no longer mattered. His sanity was in jeopardy. His manhood was on the line. His only sense of worth came with his position as a detective. He saved lives and that was a good thing, until he came home. He was respected until Carmen looked at him with disdain. He could never figure out why she was always so angry when they argued. Latinos were infamous for their passion, but she could take her emotions from zero to sixty in seconds. Yes, he was afraid of her, but what real man would admit that?

The silence was more than he could handle, so he tried to resume an earlier conversation. "I see the people, mostly," he said.

Carmen was smart enough to understand that he was trying to make up and replied, "I would have thought you were a tree man."

"You serious?"

"No," she smiled. They were back from the brink. It was easy for her. She could move between anger and love in moments. The trick, for Renny, was to figure out how to minimize the hostile events. In the fifteen years he knew her, twelve of which they were married, he hadn't figured it out. But he was not the only one. It appeared to be a man thing.

Once, at a church service, the pastor told the story of Jesus and the woman at the well. Jesus understood her and she went away rejoicing. Renny thought, if only I could do that. If only I could tell a woman her story and tell her of her pain and be so cool about it, she, and any woman, would trust him. Of course, it was Jesus and if he had such power, he knew he would just abuse it. It was the male pattern. Knowledge was power and power was for personal pleasure. It seemed his only power was an apology and humiliation. It felt like slavery.

"So what do you think of that guy?" She pointed out a man sitting under a tree.

"What am I, Sherlock Holmes?" he joked.

"Yes."

Renny stared a moment and began his summation. "He's homeess. He's been on the streets for years. He used to be a computer programmer, until he lost his job to alcohol. Once he was a very good-looking man and his blue eyes used to be the first thing you would notice. He doesn't trust anyone, just like geeks, and this park is his only place for peace. He watches the people he doesn't trust and probably makes up stories about them, too."

"You're good."

"I made it all up. I don't know him, but he probably is homeless, though."

"How do you know that?"

"The backpack. What grown man walks around with a backpack?"

"It's convenient, maybe."

"It sure is. It holds all his belongings." Renny scanned the people walking by.

"There," he said pointing to a woman jogging by. "Tell me about her."

Carmen hestitated. "Okay, she lost fifty pounds over the past twelve months and is thinking about opening her own weight-loss venture. Let's see, she wants a baby, but is afraid it will mess with her new body."

"Come on, now. Where did that come from? At least I started with a real premise."

"And I didn't?"

"Hell, no! That doesn't make any sense."

"You're right. I was describing my friend."

"Who's that?"

"You don't know her."

"You sure?"

Carmen looked to him and said, "You would want to know her now, but not then. It's my friend, Tracey."

"You mean Tracey, the one with those two big dogs?"

"How do you know her?"

"I don't know her. You told me about her dogs. Two mastiffs, right?"

"Yeah. I think she weighs less than one of them, now."

"See? You never know what or who I know. I think I tell a better story, though."

"Everybody has a story, right?" Carmen responded.

"Everybody. Even the trees."

"So what's my story?" Carmen queried.

She did it again. She manipulated him to the subject she wanted. But he couldn't really blame her, since it was the reason they came together today. Their therapist almost demanded it.

"What can I tell you, about you?" Renny wanted to know.

"You can tell me what you know about me."

"What if I'm wrong?" He was easing his way into the conversation.

"How can you be wrong? Perception is what you are telling me, not the truth."

"It's that simple, huh?"

"Sure it is. Do you want me to start? I'll tell you about you. How 'bout that?"

"Yeah, how 'bout it."

"You are so paranoid," she teased.

Renny had good reason to be paranoid. She would tell him unflattering things. She would not try to encourage him. Her life's purpose was to emasculate him. If there were some supernatural being who stripped men of their soul and manly essence, it was Carmen. However, it was less painful to hear her than to tell her of her overbearing nature. He always felt he was in a competition with her. He never felt he was her partner. He was her servant and according to her, not a very good one.

Of course, she would never listen to his side of the story. Her side was the only side, the only truth, and the wall of denial she built was a fortress. There was only one entrance, which he could never find. Whenever Renny thought he finally earned her trust, the breakthrough was fleeting. Each time he vowed to give up, Carmen found a way to draw him into her lair. She had skills. He had nothing. Maybe he should stop thinking like a man, but there was no alternative.

She, on the other hand, had mastered the male role and was increasingly more dominant. The therapist told her so, but denial was a bitch. Her level of denial was so strong, he was sure the therapist would have ended the sessions long ago, were it not for their daughter. Ironically, the sessions were not even for them. They were for a fourteen-year-old girl. Again, he was not the priority.

Renny braced himself for the assault. His face was blank, yet he was in flight-or-fight mode. Though in their twelve years of marriage, he finally was trained to flee or, at least, retreat into silence. Arguing with Carmen required debate skills he never learned. On the street, he had the power to push someone if they didn't cooperate. He punched a suspect a few times without repercussions. Of course, he never did so in the precinct, but it was a common practice to manhandle the disrespectful people he met. Physical power was the only language some of them spoke and he was fluent.

This was a different scenario, altogether. Carmen was the black belt, he was the trainee, and the rules changed regularly. There was no rhyme or reason to her thoughts or responses, but they were always readily available for his destruction. So, he listened.

"I think you think about money too much," she said.

Renny nodded, as if to agree, but his mind was racing for answer to the charge. Yes, he thought about money and he thought about it all the time. If she would curtail her spending maybe he could breathe, maybe he could spend time being a father, rather than think of more ways to get money. The Jackson family was on the brink several times, and at any given moment they could be at the edge of the cliff, again. The past year was their best year in a while, but the reckless spending continued. Renny was in his own apartment since the separation, but, of course, he was still responsible for Carmen's budget, if there was one.

His thoughts turned back to her comments. "I think if you would just have faith that everything would work out, it will," she said.

She sounded so calm, thoughtful and philosophical. What she really meant was, could he keep his mouth shut as she spent his paycheck.

"I have to tell you that it's hard to speak to you about money. You get so wound up," she continued.

Carmen looked at him for any signs she should continue, without a backlash from him. His blank stare into the concrete was not reassuring, but he encouraged her to continue with a nod.

"Go 'head," he said, taking in a deep breath.

"Can you explain to me what makes you so upset about money?"

Renny's tight lip must have told her he wasn't ready to speak.

"Really. I want to know. I'll listen."

Liar! That's what he wanted to say. He told her over and over again what caused his concern. It all boiled down to her and that's what she would never accept, so there was nothing he could say. He could say it softly or he could shout. He could say it sarcastically or he could say it with sincerity. Renny had tried every way he could, with every vocal intonation he knew, but it was a wasted effort. Even if he took responsibility, Carmen would enter into a psychological analysis of his past life—a life she thought she knew only because he told her of a few events. She filled in the blanks and was convinced she was correct.

"No. I think you should just keep talking. Let me do the listening."

It was all he could do. He didn't know why they had conversations. He could never sway her from her beliefs. She called him greedy, because he wanted to save money. Yet, Carmen benefitted from the savings. He was cheap, yet she bought just about anything she wanted. The real issue was her own greed, and if she felt her lifestyle being threatened, she pounced like a momma bear.

Renny finally figured out the cause of her depression. She would say it was her hormones or that she was bored. What she meant was, she felt restricted from spending money. Money saved her many times from anger, depression, and boredom. She would deny it. After all, the reason sounded so shallow, and she was smart enough not to sound shallow.

"Do you think it has anything to do with your poor upbringing?"she asked.

He answered her question a long time ago and was slaughtered for his response. It had nothing to do with his economic status as a child. It had everything to do with a woman who was relentless and unsympathetic to the basic laws of money. Make money, save some, spend some, and prioritize.

Carmen had a different philosophy. I want what I want, not what I have. Spend it all, for tomorrow you may die. Could he say that to her? No. Did he want to say that to her? Yes. Was it worth it? No. Was it a waste of time? Yes. Did he want to slap her, right now? Yes.

Chapter 4

Sundays have become my favorite day. Years ago, when life was so different, when I had a job and a family, it was Friday. Like millions of other people, I looked forward to the weekend. It was family time. Now, while I was here at HOPE, I was burdened by so many rules I had little free time; certainly there was no weekend. There was only Sunday. It was the only day we had to choose our own schedule, our own activity, and only if we followed the rules during the week. That is the life of an alcoholic. Booze was my escape. I seemed so free. Now, I was trapped and for what purpose?

Today, I was using my freedom to study for an exam the next day. I was three months away from being a solar technician. What a waste. I heard so much about green jobs, and I was part of the wave of a new revolution in America, but I knew it was not true. The school was turning out hundreds of us. How many jobs could there be? Not to mention, it was boring. It did have one very important advantage though. I was busy. Regardless of my future in the new economy, I was busy, for now.

The school administrators filled our heads with dreams of an industry waiting to explode with opportunities. In fact, they said, it was exploding, right now, before our dull, lifeless eyes. I was destined to have my own business, they said. I was making the highest grades in my class. I was one of the brightest students they had ever seen—me, an old man of fifty-one years. The best thing about the school was knowing I could do it. It wasn't as hard as I thought it would be. The math was my strongest subject. The science was pretty interesting.

Once I attained the reputation of being the best, I wanted to keep it, so I studied. The mission library was small, but not routinely used, so I had the room to myself. I took advantage and spread my papers across the table. At times, I would put my feet up on the table and take a rest from my reading. I couldn't do that when I was on the street.

Many days I would go to the public library for shelter or some water from the fountain or to use the bathroom. Depending on who was patrolling the building, I could stay for a while. Sometimes I wasn't allowed to enter the library, at all. There were fewer and fewer places to go find some rest. Most restaurants were locking their bathrooms and demanding you buy something before they gave you a key or a token. One place even had a buzzer to get in the restroom. I guess we homeless people were a bigger problem than I thought.

Sundays were even better since I became a house manager. I got my own room. I was a celebrity and I saw it working on my behalf. The year before, I helped the police solve a big crime and I was allowed to stay at HOPE, as long as I went to school. Solar technician was the job they pushed on me, since the government was throwing money at the school and the mission. I didn't really care. It was something to keep me occupied. So, in recent months, I had a room to myself, and today I had the library to myself. Life was good, though very routine. Rules can do that—make life so routine and regular.

Yes, Sundays were the best. That is, until Reverend Franklin entered. I almost tipped over in my chair. I was just on my way into a deep sleep, or so it seemed.

"No wonder you're at the top of your class. You study just like I did," the reverend said, smiling.

I quickly moved my feet from the table and righted the chair on the floor. Still grinning, the pastor grabbed a chair and sat.

"How's it going?"

"Better than it looks," I replied.

"Don't get defensive. It's okay. The smart ones get to relax, you know."

I didn't think so. The lazy ones get to relax, I thought, but his sarcastic smile told me to just relax and not feel like I was caught stealing.

"I don't know how much more of this I can take," I confessed.

"You can't take as much as you can take."

"Hm, another parable. Tell me, do you get a book of them in school?"

He laughed and I believed it was genuine. I had to admit, I was trying to get under his skin a little, but he was not the least bit offended.

"There's a whole book of them. I'm sure you got one, too." He stood up and went to a shelf and extracted a book and thrust it at me. It was the Bible.

"I guess I did get one," I said.

"Yeah, most of us do. We just don't understand the wisdom, unless we've been through it. You have to go through things to be wise. Can't just pick it up, out of a book."

The reverend sat down again.

"Looks like you're on track to ace another test."

"I'll do okay."

"No need to be modest. What, are you suddenly not gonna do well?"

"Shouldn't brag, Pastor. You know that."

"See? That's wisdom. Have you ever noticed that it comes in the shortest sentences?"

What was there to do, but smile? As I looked at him, he stopped smiling, though slowly. There was something on his mind and he was here to talk to me about it. I couldn't imagine what it could be.

"The police called me today," he said.

"For what?" He had my attention and I sat up straight. I couldn't imagine it had anything to do with me. I had been nowhere, done nothing. For once, in a long time, I was living a disciplined and boring life.

"It's about Graham."

Now I was getting irritated because he would not tell the story outright. He seemed to be deliberately keeping me in suspense.

"What about Graham?"

"He's dead."

"How would you know that?"

"They found a dead man in the park and they were making calls, and from the description, it was him."

"What description? You didn't know him." I was surprised at my own anger, though it was muted.

"They described him on the phone, but they brought a picture, the other day."

"When? Why didn't you come to me?"

"You were in class. Besides, they will be back."

The way he looked at me was ominous. He looked at me as if he thought I might be involved in something illegal, or at least, suspicious. I didn't know what to say to such a look. Was he asking me something? Was he afraid for me?

"Really? To see me?"

"Yes."

This moment didn't feel right. I felt accused of something I didn't know about, nor could I have had anything to do with it. It was a powerless feeling. It was the same feeling I had when my parents died. It wasn't as intense, but real nonetheless, and standing over me like death.

"Why are you looking at me like that?" I was really concerned.

"I told them you were one of the last to see Graham."

"What! Me? How do you know that?"

"Well, I don't. I just told them what I knew."

"Well, you don't know shit, do you?"

It was at that moment I looked toward the door and saw the two men walking in.

"Oh, shit." There went my Sunday. I knew them. The two men calmly came in and introduced themselves. At least one of them did.

"Sir, I'm Detective Solomon Turner and this is Detective Innis."

"We've met," I said. "I remember you."

"Yes, we have."

They sat down and Reverend Franklin excused himself.

Detective Solomon continued, "How have you been?" He was pleasant and almost seemed to care. Though Solomon asked me the question, I looked at Detective Innis with my answer.

"I'm good." I was waiting for them to get to the bottom line, but cops are not like that. They like to probe and watch. They were looking for something in my face or body language, I was sure. If they were looking for guilt, they would never find it.

"We were talking to the pastor the other day," Solomon started, "and we understand that you saw Graham recently."

I noticed Detective Innis was the same as my last encounter with him. He was silent and he watched me, intently. He watched as though he was trying to read my mind, as I was trying to read his.

I answered Detective Turner, "I saw him the other night."

"You walked him home."

"Yes."

"What did you guys talk about?"

"He was upset about the open house."

"What happened?"

"I guess he felt embarrassed. The sessions can get pretty intense, and he didn't like the questions the reverend was asking."

"What questions?"

"I thought you talked to the pastor. Didn't he tell you?"

"Of course he did, but different people tell different stories, have different memories. You might remember the very thing we need."

I was skeptical.

"Well, the pastor was asking him about his drinking. You know, about how it started and why and stuff. The usual questions."

"And that offended him," Turner chimed in.

"Not really. Not until he brought up his mother."

"Who brought up his mother? The pastor or Graham?"

"The pastor. He asked him if his mother was a drinker. That's when he went off. Pastor should have known better than to talk about a guy's mother."

"So when he went off, what did he do?"

"Just started cussing and yelling. Then I walked him home."

"Nothing else?"

"That was it."

"Okay, what did you talk about on the walk?"

"He calmed down after that. We didn't talk about much after that, just random stuff."

"What's random stuff?"

"I don't even remember. Just stuff. Oh, he did say something about being smarter than people take him for. I understand that. If you're homeless, people don't believe you have much sense."

"I guess they figure you wouldn't be homeless if you did."

48

I just glared at him. Maybe that was a ploy to get at me for something. Maybe to drop my guard and say something. The other detective, Innis, continued to watch. His glare matched mine and in another world, at another time, we might be at each other, but when I lost my home I lost a few character traits, too. A man with a home and a family has much to defend. Without them, I felt I was at the mercy of the world. Occasionally, there was something to stand for, but not often. In the beginning, I fought to get my family back, but over the years it was clear there was very little to defend. The loss of possessions was not a big deal. Long ago I lost the urge to guard.

Detective Turner broke the stare. "Okay. So what else can you tell us?"

"Nothing. That was it."

"If you remember anything else, will you call us?" Turner extended his hand to shake. I didn't respond immediately, but I finally grabbed his hand. He shook it and then handed me his business card.

"If you lose it, the pastor has another one."

I took the card, but didn't look at it. It was my way of saying, "When pigs fly."

The two detectives left and I placed the card on the table.

"Whatever," I mumbled.

When I sat back down, I realized something. They never brought up Graham's companion. I could figure only two reasons. They deliberately didn't tell me because they were fishing for how much I knew, or they didn't know. There was only one way to find out without asking them, and that was to talk with the pastor. So, I went to his office.

As usual, the reverend's door was wide open. On the rare occasion it was closed, he was in a one-on-one counseling session. Even then, he preferred to counsel outside the building—on a walk or a drive. It was obvious he was not in, but I walked inside, anyway. I wanted to know him and the best way was to see what he kept.

There were many pictures on the wall. The one of his brother had to be his favorite since it was encased in a very nice wooden frame. They looked just alike. I asked him, once, were they twins, but they weren't. The frame was new and there was a feather at the bottom right corner, between the glass and the photo. Franklin had a thing about birds. There was some Bible quote on the entrance door about birds. Something about how God loves them and people, but loves people more. I should have memorized it by now. I saw it almost daily, but looked past it rather than at it.

There were some unopened boxes on the floor by his desk and a black T-shirt on his desk. It had some writing, but it was not readable since it was carelessly folded. Looking out the window behind his desk, there was a good view of the neighborhood. I could see a couple of blocks either way. He could view the people he served from here, but it was a sterile view. From his office, the world was quiet and calm. From here, it looked like a great place to live.

"What do you need, Roman?"

Though his voice was sudden, it wasn't startling. I barely looked away from the street when he asked. For a moment I was lost in some peace I found in the view.

"Nothing. Just wondering what you were up to," I lied.

Franklin came around to his chair, and I moved to accommodate. I went around to the front of his desk and finally sat down.

"What did the police have to say?"

"Probably the same things they had to say to you," I responded.

"Did they show you the picture of Graham?"

"No."

"Good. It was not flattering. In fact, it was horrible."

"What do you mean? Did someone beat him up pretty good?"

"More than that. They stabbed him."

My stomach felt as if I was stabbed. My body felt cold.

"Were you able to help them?" the reverend asked.

"I don't think so. There wasn't much for me to know. I just know he was a good guy. That's about it. I didn't hang with him when I was on the street, but I saw him from time to time. I just started to know him when I went recruiting."

"Yes, for the open mike night."

"Yep. He always asked questions about it, so I knew he was interested. He wanted to come."

"Sorry I made him mad."

"C'mon now. Don't start feeling guilty about that. You didn't have anything to do with his death."

"I know, but I wish he could have left on better terms."

"Trust me,Rev, he was okay when he left. We didn't even talk about you."

"Liar."

"Now didn't you say the Bible says you shouldn't call a person a liar?"

"Fool."

"That's even worse."

"The Bible says you shouldn't call a person a fool. 'But who-ever says, "You fool!" shall be in danger of hell fire,' Matthew five, verse twenty-two."

"I don't know the Bible that well, but I see the word in there a lot."

"If you see it a lot, then you are reading it a lot. Good for you."

"That doesn't answer the question. Why does the Bible use it so much?"

"The Bible describes a fool, what a fool says, what a fool does. It doesn't give you permission to call people a fool."

"So it describes a fool, and if I see someone acting like what is described, then I can't call them the word the Bible says they are," I replied argumentatively.

"I see you like to challenge. That's good. Keep asking the questions."

"Seriously, Pastor, I think I know some fools."

I made him laugh, again.

"I bet you know some, too," I poked.

"I have my suspects, but I don't want to get political."

"Ha! Rev, that was funny. I didn't know pastors could be funny."

"Now that's just silly. I tell jokes all the time in church."

"Yeah, but that's for a purpose. I'm talking about just being a regular guy. Are you a regular guy, Pastor?"

"That's all I am"

"That's humble, that's not regular."

"Sure it is. Aren't you humble?"

"I guess I am, but I'm humble by circumstance. You're humble by nature."

"Whatever brings you there."

"I like your way better. Life has just pressed me so far down, I can't help but be humble."

"I'm not sure we're talking about the same thing. Sounds like you're talking about humiliation. There's a difference between being humble and being humiliated."

"Still sounds like being brought low."

"No. Humiliation is being brought low. Your esteem is trounced, stepped on, beaten. Being humble is an attitude of not thinking more highly of yourself than you should. You can have great self-esteem and be humble."

"There's very little esteem down here, Pastor."

"Where's here?"

"I'm not talking about HOPE. I mean at this level of my life."

"And what level is that? Remember, I said that humility is an attitude, not a location."

"Easy for you to say."

"If it's so easy, why don't you say it?" the pastor volleyed back at me.

"Clever."

He sat back in his chair. It was as if we were playing chess and he just announced checkmate. The more I thought about his response, I guess it was checkmate. I had no moves left.

"Checkmate," I said.

He looked out into the street for a moment, then returned his attention to me.

"What do you want, Roman?"

I had to think a minute. "I guess what everybody wants. Peace and happiness."

"I'm so sick of hearing that."

His answer took me by surprise. That's not something a counselor should say, I thought.

"What? Is that a bad thing?"

"It's a crappy thing to say."

Crappy. I guess that was a Man of God's substitute for a curse word. Whatever he meant, it was rude. What he probably wanted to say was, "That's bullshit." Sometimes the only word which will work is a curse word.

My mother explained expletives to me when I heard her

curse for the first time. I was shocked. My parents were having an argument and when my father stormed out of the kitchen, I heard her shout out to him, "Go fuck yourself, Martin!" Wow! I don't think she knew I was in the house, but when she went after him, she stopped and apologized to me. I told her it was okay, but she kept apologizing. It wasn't as if I never heard the word before. My father cursed all the time. I used it, but, of course, she never knew. She would have killed me.

I remember the night she came to my room and apologized for the last time. I felt funny, consoling my mother as if I were the parent. I was trying my best to relieve her of her guilt, but she came to her peace when she said, "You know what, Roman? Sometimes there is a word that expresses all your feelings that cannot be expressed by any other words. There are words in your head and words in your heart and words in your gut. The words in your gut are closest to your real feelings."

I told her I understood and I never heard her abusive expressions again. Occasionally I heard a damn or two, but that was it. But I always knew when I wasn't around, my mother must have given my father an earful.

"What are you smiling at?" Reverend Franklin asked me.

"Just thinking about my mom and dad."

"You miss them?"

"Yes, but I'm glad they can't see what I've become." My statement was not convincing, so I asked, "They can't see me, right?"

"You ask some good questions. The Bible says the dead know nothing, so I guess the answer is, no, they can't."

"Good. It wouldn't be a pretty sight."

"I'm sure they would still love you."

"But disappointed."

"You're disappointed. Don't put that on them," he corrected me.

"Yeah, I guess you're right."

"What do you think would have made them happy about you?"

"I don't know," I replied. "Be a success."

"There you go again. Mindless drivel."

"What's mindless about being a success? Everyone wants to be successful."

"True, but success is different for different people. What's success for you?

"Being a man."

"What does that mean?"

"It means taking care of your family."

"I see. So in your eyes you're not a successful man."

"I'm not a man, period."

The room went silent. I know he was staring at me, but I couldn't stop the tears I felt forming in my eyes. I tried my best to think of something else. I wanted to wipe my eyes before the tears ran down my face. I just thought of the tears and that seemed to stop it. I stood up and walked toward the door.

"I need to study. I have a rep, you know," I told the reverend.

"When you go through the door, the thought will follow."

"What?"

"The thought you just had, it will be there, still."

"Well, at least it will be my thought. I don't have to share it with anyone."

Franklin stood up and moved to the front of his desk, then sat on the edge. He said,

"My father used to build houses, really good houses. He could do anything—the plumbing, lay concrete, anything. I asked him one time why he hired guys to help him. I told him he could save money by doing it all himself, and the family could have more of the money he made. He told me that's what he did with his first house. He did it all. It took him two years. He said he got smarter when it came to the second house, and then the third. He learned the lesson you can build a better house, a lot quicker, with help.

"Roman, you can do it all by yourself, but maybe you can build a better house, a lot quicker, if you let someone else help you."

"I hear what you're saying. I'm just a little stubborn."

"You're a man. A man wants to do it all. Until they understand, they can't. Even God said it's not good that man should be alone."

I understood. Actually I was glad he stopped me, since I forgot why I came to see him. It was clear he was not aware of Graham's companion. She never came up in the conversation. He didn't know, and the detectives didn't know, either. They would have never let that detail go unanswered. My dilemma was whether or not to broach the subject. I liked knowing what others did not know. I was always told information is power, but I had to give it up. I had to tell him.

"You're right, Pastor, it's not good that someone be alone, particularly a woman."

He had no idea what I was talking about.

"Are you talking about your wife?"

"No. She's not alone. I sure she's doing okay by now. It's been four years."

"Who, then?

"Just talking, Pastor," I said, trying to hide my intentions. My intention was to go out and look for Graham's companion. I didn't know for sure, but I was confident she was alone. I didn't really care for her. I didn't know her, but I liked Graham and it was the least I could do for him.

"I don't know you to talk, Roman. You're one of those efficient kind of guys. You don't talk unless you have something to say."

What was he trying to say to me? Was there a sign on my face which made it clear I was about to jump the fence? I was not confined to the mission, especially since I had proven my reliability, but we called the act of going out to the real world as "jumping the fence."

The mission was growing, building plans would expand the territory of HOPE, and a fence surrounded the compound and protected the growing property. It was not intended to keep residents in. It was a minor deterrent. All the residents were there as a result of their own will. There was a curfew, however, and it was up to managers to make the night count. Of course, if a resident left the premises without notice and missed curfew, they could be terminated from the mission.

"Pastor," I cautiously said. "Can't study here so well. I'm going out to the park."

"Sorry, did the cops disturb you?"

"I guess they got me off my game. I need a new atmosphere."

Franklin looked at me with a hint of suspicion, but he had no way of knowing what I knew or what I was about to do.

"You'll be back by curfew?"

"That's a strange question."

"I don't know you to study in the park."

"Pastor." I said it to make his statement sound like paranoia.

"Just asking."

"You have trust issues, don't you?"

That brought a smile to his face, since he knew I was repeating a question he posed to me several months ago.

"Go on, just be back."

He didn't say be back by curfew. He must have known I was up to something, but he trusted me. I expected him to stop me as I walked through the door, but he didn't. I went back to my small room and picked up my backpack. I knew what was in it, therefore no need to pack or search it. I kicked off my flip-flops and put on thick white socks and sneakers. As I left my room, I threw the backpack over my shoulder and walked out, without fanfare or ceremony.

I walked along the street, not knowing where I should go, but my best guess was to go where I left Graham. I couldn't imagine where she would go without him. They had friends, or at least he did, and she was likely to remain close.

I was on a mission, but I was also enjoying the journey. Most of my days were filled with school, studying, and executing my duties as a manager. The air was not fragrant and clean, but the idea of feeling free made me inhale forcefully. I was energized and I had determination. For the first time in almost a year, I was on my own, free of rules. I was driven by my own desire to find this woman. Yes, I felt like me, again.

It was a city street, but my mind made it a beach. Normally, the air would have been stale, but it was fresh. My nostrils flared to fill me with bus and car exhaust fumes. It was a symbiotic relationship. What was waste to the car, was oxygen to me. I needed this. I would find her.

Chapter 5

Detective Innis sat at his desk, shuffling through photos. He stopped at a photo of the overturned porta-potty. He immediately remembered the smell at the crime scene and instinctively wrinkled his nose. The smell of a dead body was nauseating enough, but to discover one lying in a pile of human waste was beyond imagination.

The photographer who took the pictures had to have been medicated. They took pictures from every angle—far away, up close, from above ground level and eye level. It was disgusting on every level, but there was a story in them. He and his partner, Solomon, would find the clue or piece together the story, once the initial wave of revulsion subsided. It would take a while.

Greg tossed a photograph across the desk to his partner, Detective Turner, and said, "What are you missing?"

Turner snatched it as it slid across the desk and replied, "Oh, yeah, it's gotta be me that's missing something."

"It ain't me."

"Okay Mister-All-That, what do you see?" challenged Solomon.

"Same ol' shit."

"Funny, man. I see the same shit you do."

Greg thought for a while and then returned, "Maybe that's it. Maybe that's all we're supposed to see. Maybe all of that is meant to be a diversion. We're all so disgusted with the smell and the sight of shit that we overlook something."

"And we are overlooking what?"

"I don't know, but it's in there. Why else would somebody stab a guy around his heart and then turn over the toilet on him?"

"That's all rage, man," Solomon informed his partner.

"Why so angry at a homeless guy?"

"There are crazy people out there. You know that."

"Okay, okay. There's theory number one. It's a nut case. That means it will happen again."

"So this could be a serial killer. That's scary. They don't come along often."

"Could happen. Remember the story of the guy in Orange County who killed—what? Four homeless guys?"

"Yeah. He was a former Army guy, wasn't he?"

"I think so."

"Well, they caught him, so it's not him."

"Did he have a partner?"

"Or is it a copycat?"

"Or maybe it was personal."

"If that's the case, somebody hated him."

"What if they didn't?"

"If they didn't hate him, why kill him?"

"Exactly."

"Yeah, exactly."

A revelation came to Greg. "They were looking for something?"

"And this homeless guy had it? What in the world could that be? Sure as hell ain't money."

"What could a homeless man have that anybody would want?"

It was an absurd question to Turner. "Nothing."

"Don't be mean," chastised Innis.

"All a homeless man has is a few clothes and other possessions. Nobody would want that."

"See? That's why I am all that," Detective Innis boasted. "That homeless guy, Roman, had a coat that belonged to guess who?"

"I remember. Dantes, the Costa Rican warlord."

"And we found out from the urine. They urinated all over him, after they beat him up."

"So the common thread, no pun, is waste products. Shit and pee," Solomon said, amusing himself.

"I don't know. I'm just talking. Okay, if it's not clothes, then what would someone want?"

"I don't know."

Detective Innis stared at his partner.

"What?" Turner wanted to know.

"That's it."

"Sure it is. What's it?"

"Knowledge. *You* don't know, but maybe this guy did know, know *something*, that is."

"Oh God, this is gonna get complicated. Now we will have to know all about his life. I don't even remember his name."

"Graham."

"Graham," repeated Turner. "So if Graham had this knowledge that somebody wants, then we have to know how he got it and what it is."

"I think we'll know what it is, when we know who he was."

"Your homeless friend doesn't seem to know much."

Solomon detected a slight twitch on his partner's face. It was as if he were trying to stifle a dislike for the man.

"What's the matter with you?" Turner asked.

"Nothing. He probably knows more than he's telling."

"Do you want to follow him?"

"No." Innis' face was caught up in another thought.

"Then, what?"

"What did that lady we talked to at the scene, say? She saw some guy, or gal, walking away, into the jungle, right?"

"Hell, she wasn't very helpful."

"Well, either she identified the killer or Graham's friend—"

"Or a complete stranger who didn't want to get involved. There's too many variables with this one. Too many ifs."

"Pick one."

"And if we pick the wrong one, we can waste months going the wrong way," Turner said.

"How many wrong turns does it take to make a right?"

"What the hell are you talking about?"

"Nothing. So which one makes the most sense—a madman, an argument gone wrong, or a deliberate killing?"

"They all make sense."

"Then pick one."

"Okay, this is not getting us anywhere," Turner said with frustration. "You pick one."

"All three."

Now Innis' partner was fully frustrated.

"Wait, wait. Don't freak out. Listen," said Greg, trying to calm Solomon. "If it's all three, then there has to be a theory which makes them all true. One, you have to be mad to kill someone like that. Two, you have to be angry to kill someone like that, and three, he must have had something or known something that somebody wanted very bad."

"Okay, they wanted something. So did they kill him because he wouldn't give it up, or did they get it and then killed him so he wouldn't talk?" Turner continued.

"I say they never got it."

"How so?"

"Because he was killed in such a savage manner. If he gave up the info, then they would have killed him politely."

"Oh, yeah, nothing like a polite killing."

"You know what I mean. I mean clean. Why leave such a mess?"

Turner was interested now. He could see the story forming. "They left a mess, because they thought he had what they wanted, with him. They didn't tip over the john to make a mess. They tipped it over looking for something."

"Now you're talking, partner. Bring it home"

Solomon continued his theory. "If they got it, no mess. If they were looking, then they search everything."

"Including the potty."

Both men were excited. The events played out in their heads as if it were a movie.

"So guess what we have to do?"

Solomon knew the next logical step. He didn't want to hear it, but his partner said it.

"We have to search the john."

"That's disgusting. No, I'm not doing that. Besides, it's probably been cleaned up by now."

"It's still a crime scene, buddy boy. We have to search it," Greg came back.

"What could be in there, anyway?"

"I don't know, detective. That's why we're gonna search it."

"I'm not doing it. That's what crime scene investigators are for."

"And you. We are supposed to help. Teamwork, remember?

"Team, my—"

"Don't say it. It would be too easy. Not to mention nasty, just plain nasty."

"And for some reason you don't think sifting through shit isn't nasty?" Solomon said in disbelief.

"It's the professional thing to do. You're a professional," Innis said as he stood. "Come on, let's go."

"Where?"

"To do your duty." He couldn't stop himself from laughing.

Turner followed with, "Duty. That's funny. I thought you were the serious one."

As they walked down the hallway toward the elevator, Turner glanced occasionally at his partner. When he thought about it, this was the first occasion he'd heard a laugh from him. Detective Innis was such a serious man. He always seemed to be thinking hard. For one moment he appeared human, and it was interesting that the thought which made him laugh was the lowest form of humor. Maybe it was a black thing. Black people laughed at the most base jokes. They would laugh at the most inane statements, as long as cursing was involved. Solomon wondered if that was a racist thought; it couldn't be, since he was black. Maybe he was just insightful.

The elevator arrived and another glance at his partner revealed he was back to his old self. The ride to the basement to fetch their car was silent, and Detective Turner felt it was best to remain quiet and let Innis think. After all, he was good at it. The narrative they just created came from his thoughtfulness. Innis would speak again when he was ready, after he had completed his thought or needed some help to complete it. Solomon didn't even ask where they were going as Innis drove, though he had an idea.

Innis broke the silence with a most unusual question. "Why did you get divorced?"

Turner tried to read his partner's mind. Why would he ask such a question? Maybe he was trying to be sociable, finally.

"I guess I was unreasonable," Solomon confessed.

"Impossible to live with?"

"I wouldn't say all that."

"What did she say?"

"I was a control freak," Solly answered.

"You? A control freak?"

"I don't think I am. I'm like everyone else. Don't you like things a certain way?"

"You're too young to be set in your ways."

"I'm not set, just uh, I don't know what to call it."

"You're a cop. You live in a world of chaos, so you need control. Your job is filled with chaos, solving a crime is meant to bring order. Can't do that very well at home, can you?"

"Never thought about it like that."

"We're all control freaks," Greg consoled his partner. "We all start out trying to save the world, then end up trying to control it."

"Is that why you never married?"

"No, I had a crazy life. By the time I grew up, it was too late."

"Ah, that's so sad."

"Shut up, punk," Innis replied, softly. There was no sarcastic smile, so Solomon wasn't sure how to take it.

The rest of the ride was quiet until Innis pulled over to the curb. "Come on, let's do this," he said.

They walked into the park and made their way to the crime scene. The porta-potty was gone, but they circled the area carefully searching the ground. When they came together, Solomon said, "Nothing."

"Yep, nothing."

"Okay, what are you missing?"

"I don't know, but I'll find it." As Innis spoke he kept looking at the ground, slowly surveying every inch of land around him. Just then his phone rang.

"Innis," he spoke softly. He listened. "Okay," he said with a moderate amount of enthusiasm. He was not one to get very excited. His threshold for laughter and being excited were quite high. Innis lowered the phone and turned to his partner. "The lab thinks they found something," he said as he walked toward the car.

Solomon took a moment to follow, but Innis never turned around to see if he was coming along.

Detective Turner finally caught up with his partner. "What did they find?"

"An eye," Innis said in a flat tone.

"An eye?!"

"Yeah, something like that."

"Something like that. What is something like an eye?"

"We'll find out."

They made it to the car and Innis drove them to the crime lab. Once on site, they found Dr. Shriver. The doctor was sitting at his desk typing into his computer.

"What's up, Doc?" Detective Turner greeted him.

Dr. Shriver continued to type, but acknowledged their presence with a nod, which annoyed both Innis and Turner.

"Doc, you called us, remember?" Innis said.

"I remember very well, detective. Look at this." The doctor swiveled the laptop around so the two men could view the screen. They watched an animated film of an eye, but they could not make out what was happening.

"That's lasik," he said.

"Oh, yeah. That's the surgery to get rid of glasses. Is that the way they do that? That looks disgusting," Solomon said.

"Looks freaky," his partner added.

"Man, do people really let someone slice up their eye like that?"

Shriver had to rein them in. "People don't let someone slice their eye, they let an ophthalmologist perform surgery on their eye."

Solomon looked the doctor in the eye momentarily. "You had it done."

"Yes, I had it done. I love it."

"Okay," Detective Turner said in agreement.

Innis wanted to get to the purpose of their visit. "So did you find an eye?"

"A piece of an eye."

"Where? Innis asked.

"In a pile of human waste."

"Oh my God, Doc. You didn't sift through that shit, did you?" Solomon asked.

"It's what we do, son. Would you like to?"

"Glad to have you as a partner, Doctor. Carry on," came back Solomon.

Innis entered the conversation. "What made you look there, Doc?"

"It may be nasty, but it is part of the crime scene. So we sucked it all up, brought it here, and sifted through it."

"And you found something." Innis tried to move the conversation forward.

"Yes, I did. Come." He walked over to a desk with a microscope. He adjusted the instrument's focus and then gestured for the detectives to view the object under the scope. Innis was the first to look, then his partner. Solomon remarked it looked like a contact lens.

"Close," the doctor answered. "It's a cornea," he continued, as he brought his pointed right index finger close to Solomon's left eyeball. Solomon didn't budge, but he did glance over to Greg.

"Got it, Doc," Detective Turner said, pushing the doctor's finger to the side.

"So what do we do with it," asked Greg.

"Every cornea is distinct, like a fingerprint."

"Okay, but there is no fingerprint. You have it. What are we supposed to do? Find someone with half an eye?" Greg said.

"It's not half of the eye. It's just the front part of the eye. And you're right. Look for someone with severe eye pain."

"Where would he go? I mean where does someone go if their cornea is torn off?" Solomon queried.

"First to their surgeon; if not that, then to the ER or to any doctor."

"That's a lot of doctors, Doc," Innis said. "Besides it would be more than pain if someone had their cornea ripped off."

"You guys didn't watch the video, did you? It's not the whole cornea, it's just the front part of the cornea. This guy still has one, but its skin is torn off."

Solomon said, "That's disgusting."

"And it hurts. You ever scratch your eyeball?" the doctor inquired.

"Yeah. I was fifteen and my sister scratched my eye when we were playing around. I thought I was gonna die."

"What did the doctors do?" his partner asked.

"They put a patch over my eye. They said I had an abrasion. I felt like my sister stabbed me in the eye with a knife. Worst pain I ever had."

Detective Innis confessed to having had an abrasion, as well.

"Well, gentlemen, this guy has an abrasion ten times the size of yours, detective. Guess how much pain he's in."

"Doesn't mean it came from the killer," Detective Innis added.

"Oh, yes it does. A piece of it was found under the victim's fingernail."

Innis gave a soft answer. "Bam."

The two men left the laboratory and found the elevator, on their way to their desks, sitting facing each other.

"Okay, Innis, what next?"

Greg leaned back in his chair and expelled air through his mouth.

"I don't know." He thought a moment before speaking. "How in the hell do you find a guy with a ripped cornea? What do we do? Go around looking for somebody with an eye patch? Who says the guy is still in the city? Do we visit every emergency room? Can't do it. How many eye doctors are in this city?

"Maybe you're looking at it the wrong way," said Solomon, but immediately he knew from his partner's stare, he had made an unintended pun. "No, man. Not like that. I mean maybe we need to see it from another perspective."

Greg smiled and Solly tried explain again. "I can't use any word that doesn't have to do with sight. So let's just do it another way."

Innis chuckled and Turner could not resist joining him. Their moment of levity was interrupted when Greg's cell phone rang out with a hip-hop ringtone. Solomon was surprised by his partner's ringtone choice, but Innis didn't acknowledge Solomon's reaction. He checked the phone's screen and looked surprised by the identity of the caller.

"Hey, Carmen," he said in a cheerful tone. His greeting was met with a shrill cry. It was loud and everyone in the office could hear it. Innis rapidly pulled the phone from his ear and then called out to her. "Carmen, Carmen. I can't understand you. What are you saying?"

She tried to speak, but each time she howled over her words. Solomon's face was frozen in a frown. The others in the room tried to ignore the call, but it was not possible. Carmen was screaming.

"Carmen, Carmen. Please stop. I don't know what you're saying." He looked around to see his fellow officers looking at him. He didn't know what to do. He tried again to interrupt her wailing. In a moment of clarity, all he, and everyone else, could hear was the name Renny, then the screaming began again.

"What about Renny?" Greg asked, though it was useless. "Carmen, please. I can't, I can't understand you. Did Renny hurt you? You have to stop, please."

Greg's pleading was not helping. "Carmen, are you home? Just tell me, are you at home."

He waited for a clear answer, then he replied, "I'll be right there. Just stay there. I'm coming there, right now. Do you understand? I'll be right there."

Innis stood up and ended the call. His partner stood with him and asked, "You want me to go with you?"

Innis walked quickly. 'I don't care." He was intent on his mission, and the best Solomon could do was to walk quickly alongside and remain quiet. The drive was silent except for the sighs from Greg. Greg was naturally quiet, but this silence was forced. His stone face revealed suppression of anger, or maybe tears. Solomon couldn't tell.

Finally Greg turned into a neighborhood street and both men spotted the swirling lights from an ambulance and police cars. Solomon looked for a change in expression from Greg, but there was none. Greg pulled the car over, stepped out, and continued his purposeful march, while his partner followed slightly behind, like a puppy.

They reached the steps of the apartment building and were met by a uniformed police officer. The officer tried to intercept him, but Innis shoved the uniform's arm away from him. It was reflex, but the cop moved in front of Innis. This just caused Innis to stare him down. He wouldn't speak, but the puppy, Turner, pulled his ID and flashed his badge at the officer and the face-off ended.

Innis bypassed the elevator and bounded up the steps. Coming out on the third floor, they saw the hallway filled with more officers, a gurney and EMTs. There was no hesitation in Greg's steps as he headed toward the apartment.

The door was open and immediately Greg encountered more law enforcement personnel. This was the first moment it occurred to him he might see something he was not prepared to see. He slowed his progress and looked for someone with an explanation. His attention turned to the man who grasped him by the arm and led him down the apartment's hallway to a bedroom. It obviously belonged to a girl. This had to be Neena's room.

"What's going on, Mac?" Detective Innis asked of his fellow detective.

"Greg, it's not good. I'm sure you won't take my advice and go home. It's too late now, so let me try to prepare you." The detective paused a moment to see if Innis was paying attention and in control.

"I'm cool," Innis assured Mac.

The atmosphere was calm for a short moment only. Carmen rushed into the room and grabbed Greg. She held so tight he could not see her face, and he had to pry her away from his body.

Meanwhile, Mac glared at a uniformed officer who stood at the bedroom door. The officer said in an apologetic tone, "Sorry, sir."

"Yes, I'm sure you are," Mac responded with irritation. He commanded the officer to leave.

Once Carmen was separated from Innis, he could see the blood-stained clothes.

"Jesus Christ. What the hell happened? Did Renny do this?"

He looked her over to find the source of bleeding. Carmen looked so weak. She stared through him and it was obvious he would not get answers from her, so he looked at the other detective.

Mac motioned for him to follow. As Greg tried to move, Carmen clutched at him. He escorted her to the bed and coaxed her to sit. She sniveled, and Greg looked and found a box of tissues. He offered her a few and then left, but reluctantly.

As the detectives walked down the hall, Mac said, "Detective Jackson is dead."

The matter-of-fact statement was enough to make Greg stop and look into Mac's eyes for the truth.

"Did she do that?" Innis inquired.

Mac shook his head, in the negative. "Looks like a suicide."

"What?" It was an incredible situation for him to imagine.

Mac didn't confirm or deny Greg's disbelief. They walked to the kitchen. Solomon was at the door and as they approached, his eyes told a story of sadness. His tightly pursed lips were a warning. He dropped his head as Detective Innis entered the room. Mac handed him a pair of disposable gloves.

"Oh, Jesus!" exclaimed Greg as he looked at the body before him. He felt a little lightheaded and began to sweat. His stomach suddenly felt as if he had swallowed acid. He couldn't focus on the body, so he looked at Solomon. His partner shook his head and his face expressed regret. The short distraction was enough for Greg to regain his control and he looked back to the body.

Detective Jackson's body was positioned as if someone had thrown him across the room to the floor. His legs were spread apart and his arms were spread like wings. It was undignified. Blood droplets were sprayed around the cabinets and counter tops. His skull was fractured and small pieces of brain tissue were scattered on the floor.

Detective Innis looked up at Mac and said, "You were right. It's not good."

"I'm sorry, Greg." Greg wasn't listening. At first sight, he couldn't look at the body; now all he could do was stare at his friend—his dead friend.

"What did Carmen say?" he asked of Mac.

"Nothing much. She's hysterical. I'm just glad his daughter isn't here."

It was another punch in the gut for Greg. "She's going to be messed up for so long, after this."

Mac produced a photograph placed in a plastic sandwich bag and handed it to Greg. "He left a note."

Greg studied the photo then turned it over to see the message. It read, "Yes, there is more. Keep hope alive."

Greg frowned and Mac asked, "Do you know what that could mean?"

"No."

"Mrs. Jackson is way too distraught to answer that question for us."

"Did she find it?"

"Yeah, she was here. A neighbor called 911."

"I can believe that. I've never seen her like this."

"Understandable. Were they having problems?"

Detective Innis glared at him.

"Just doing my job."

"Do it tomorrow."

"Understood."

Detective Turner stood by his partner quietly. It was his best strategy. He had been in this situation before and then he used the standard line, but it would be inadequate now to say, "Sorry for your loss." He didn't know what was adequate, so he stayed close in case his partner asked him for any support.

Greg walked back to the bedroom and watched Carmen from the door. It was hard for him to enter, as if there were an invisible shield at the entrance. Carmen sat slumped at the edge of the bed. She looked exhausted. She wasn't crying, but her face was wet. Finally she looked up at Greg with her red eyes and, though she didn't speak, it was an invitation for him to come to her.

He sat down beside her, close enough they touched, shoulder to shoulder. Carmen bowed her head again. Greg was not sure what he should do. From his perspective, this woman was unfamiliar. He knew the strong Carmen. He knew the woman who could argue with anyone and win, or at least wear someone down until he surrendered to her will. This Carmen was broken and had no defenses left in her. Greg did the only thing available to him. He put his arm around her, and she gave in as she rested her head on his shoulder. Greg knew he would have to go through this once more, when Neena arrived.

Detective Turner watched from the bedroom door. He had no strategy to deal with this, either.

Chapter 6

The jungle was an untouched mass of brush and trees, in the valley of the park. One day it would succumb to the desires of land developers and politicians, but for years it was forbidden territory. It was a refuge for the homeless. The police would come within its borders for official business only. It used to be my home, and the only real change was those who lived here and the height of the bushes. There were walkways to navigate the area. The man-made paths led to areas of flat land, where the occupants cleared away the foliage. It wasn't a place for the fearful. If you had the guts to stay, it offered a natural form of protection, since no one had a reason to enter.

Though it had been months since I lived here, I could remember the routes and where they led. The obvious place to go was to the Mayor's area. He knew a lot about the activities in the jungle. He made it his business to know what was happening; therefore, his name.

I stopped by the public library on my way. There were a few guys on the steps. They sat and chatted as if they were in a bar. A friend of mine used to say being outdoors was the joy of homeless-ness because there was room for all of us, but that didn't stop the human imperative of being territorial.

I recognized Pez, at the top of the stairs. I bounded to the top and sat beside him. "What's up, Pez?"

"Same ol' shit, different toilet," he replied. Though I heard him say the phrase several times before, it made me laugh again.

"No, looks like the same toilet, too," I replied.

"Right," he agreed.

"Hey, you heard about Graham?"

"No, what happened?"

"He got killed." My statement didn't seem to affect him, at all.

"No shit."

"By the bathrooms at the jungle."

"That's messed up. Who did it?"

"Don't know."

He arched his back to stretch and let out an audible yawn. It was then I remembered why we called him Pez. His mouth opened so wide, it looked as if his jaw was unhinged, just like the Pez dispensers from my childhood. It brought a little smile to my face. I don't know if the smile was from looking at him or from my childhood memories. I always looked forward to getting a new dispenser with the funny face. Even without the candy inside, I would play with the head and flip the head back, way back. It was genius. It was candy, though not good candy, and it was a toy. No wonder it was such a hit with us kids.

I would try to entertain my parents with it, but their fun never lasted as long as mine. I could entertain myself for hours, it seemed. My father was quickly bored, and my mother would feign a smile for a little while. Adults were so dull, I thought. It was hard to imagine they were children at one time.

Pez pulled out a cigarette from his backpack and lit it. My father smoked and I always liked to smell that first aroma from the first drag. It was the fresh smell of tobacco. Afterward, it smelled burned. Without letting my father know, I would take a slow and quiet deep breath to enjoy it. Instinctively, I breathed deeply as Pez lit the tip and sucked the end. I wasn't sure, but I think I may have closed my eyes for a split second to savor the smell. I hope he didn't notice.

"Probably won't catch him," Pez declared.

"Why you say that?"

"Why would anyone care?"

His question hit me hard. I felt the same as when I first heard of Graham's death. I understood what he was saying, but his reality check hurt, just the same. Why would anyone care? Half the time we didn't even know anybody's real name. We were all John Doe to the cops. No one got the chance to know us. Who cared if we had a family? Some of us had children and wives. Some of us were children, once.

Some of us had an education which eventually became useless. Most of us had dreams—dreams deferred, dreams forgotten, dreams killed, and dreams trampled, but I have since learned that, long after dreams are abandoned, they smolder deep in men's hearts. That is where the pain lies. Within the wall of arrogance, deep inside a stone heart and an aloof spirit, is an unfulfilled dream—a suffocating dream.

My dreams were strangled by gambling debts and finally drowned in alcohol. I saw my dreams fly away with my daughter, Jenna. She adored me, and I allowed my selfishness to destroy her life. At the time, I always reasoned I was doing it for her. I gambled, knowing I was making money for her. I was confident I was doing the right thing. I was pretty sure about my intentions. I knew every absurd risk was for her benefit. My wife Sharon shared my dreams and I misused her trust. My denial had me walking a dark street, believing I knew my destination, only to find myself in an alley each morning.

It took years to realize I had been on the road to hell, believing I was following God's will. Yes, I even got God involved. He wanted me to gamble. Other people worked hard for their money. I wanted more and God was on my side. He understood because I was a child of the Most High. He would do for me what he wouldn't do for His other children. I listened to His every word, gave Him my time on Sunday. I prayed to hit the lottery, and when it all became obvious I was believing in an inattentive God, I became angry with the God who created me to be great, but left me a beggar.

No God of any greatness or compassion would abandon his child, but he left me. He left me homeless. He left me a drunk. He left me without a family, and I found Him useless. When I came to my senses, I realized that what I accused Him of doing to me, in reality I did to my wife and daughter.

Still I could not bring myself to apologize to Him. There were atheists who ridiculed Him and He ignored them; they lived a fruitful life. If He were a decent God, He would have destroyed them long ago. He allowed them to persist in their insane life, but at least they had families and love and money—everything I didn't have. Yet in my madness, I wanted what everyone wanted—a purpose.

I finally answered Pez, "Somebody cares. I don't know who, but somebody does."

He took another drag on his cigarette and methodically blew the smoke into the air. He watched the smoke rise and fade into the atmosphere.

"Keep hope alive," he said.

I smirked at his comment. He was such a cynical bastard, but who could blame him. His life was on the steps of a public library. If I could give him a purpose I would, but he probably wouldn't take it. I started down the stairs and Pez called out to me and repeated, "Keep hope alive."

When I turned to answer him, he wasn't even looking my way. He just looked at the sky. It wasn't worth saying goodbye. I knew I had to leave quickly. I felt a heaviness which wasn't present earlier. The air was stifling here and I needed a fresh wind, so I continued on my way.

I passed Erma's Hometown Bakery. I never knew a person who could smell fresh pastry and not consider stopping to buy. I was no different and I bought a half dozen pastries, raspberry jelly donuts being my favorite. I intended to buy two, but the final count was seven pastries, since I got a free one based on my purchased six. I didn't find it a problem, since I was certain the woman I was searching for would be hungry, and sweets were a favorite of the homeless, and crack heads, too.

I also passed by my favorite liquor store. It felt good to pass and not have the urge to stop. I recognized I was a changed man, and I walked a little taller as I moved on, with barely a glance in the window.

Downtown was in a stalled renovation period. Storefronts were boarded up, buildings were closed, and unfinished buildings were in various stages of completion. The recession was over, according to the government, but I also knew the official announcement from the government was a hoax. I learned long ago, anyone could use numbers to come to any conclusion needed, for any time and purpose. Numbers do lie, and the homeless didn't count, at all.

I turned into the park and before descending into the jungle, I noticed the porta-potty was gone. I smiled as I thought about who would steal it. Everything in the jungle was subject to theft. It was a common occurrence. Of course, who would want their own personal porta-potty? Someone couldn't pick it up and place in a grocery cart. The more obvious answer was, the police hauled it away.

I passed a few carts, filled with clothes, blankets and trinkets, on my way down into the valley of death. When it rained, the water was funneled to the bottom of the slope, and a stagnant stream was created until it evaporated. Enough moisture was present to make me misstep and slip. I was able to stop my fall by grabbing hold of a branch, but my feet continued into the bottom of a large puddle. "Shit!" What else could I say? Such utterances were great to alleviate a situation, and I was back on my feet without much of a thought.

I came to a clearing and met up with Alderman. He was once a member of the Aryan Nation and served prison time, only to find himself in another prison. Alderman was a big white man and his tattoos were frightening, but his life was changed, as was the case with all of us. His days of bigotry were as far away as his last home-cooked meal. We were friends, now. The jungle had its own social revolution. We were equally broken and equally forgotten.

"What's up, big man?" I greeted Alderman.

"Nothing much. What are you doing down here?

"Looking for the Mayor. You seen him?"

"Not for a while. I think he moved out of here."

"Really?"

"I know he went to the shelter for the winter, don't know if he made it back here."

Looking at him, I was sad for him. This was where I left him when I entered the mission several months back. He had no place to go. I knew how he survived, but I was not happy he was here. I wanted to help him, but such was another objective, for another time.

"Hey, do you know Graham?" I asked him.

He didn't know him, so I needed to move on, but I decided to stay. I pitied Alderman. He was a big man brought to nothing, and there was no better backdrop than to sit in the trampled brush of an abandoned piece of park. I sat with him.

"Have you eaten today?"

"Yeah, I had breakfast at The Federation," he said.

The Federation was another organization determined to do the impossible—end homelessness. It was a large organization, in business for seventy years and its mission to end poverty and take everyone off the streets seemed a harder task than years before. Yet they remained optimistic; at least, it was their public persona. I wondered what they said in the board room.

The federal government got involved and they couldn't do it, either. Billions of dollars couldn't end the dilemma, which caused many people to ask, why spend the money. In these hard times, the organizations tried harder and harder to get others to give, but those with money were feeling their own fall to a place which brought them much closer to me than they wanted to be.

There were many on the street who lived a life so remote from the life of a bum, it was easy for them to give a dollar and walk on. They had done their part, but today was a different day. The long recession made us a mirror. We, the homeless, made it clear to many where they could be spending their next years. Fire could make someone homeless, in an instant. A tornado could carry a home into heaven and leave behind its residents to live in hell.

I didn't know if I should try to start a conversation with Alderman or just sit with him. He seemed content to sit on a crate and stare at the skyline before us. I tipped over an empty grocery cart, to use as a stool. My movement didn't interrupt his deep thoughts.

"What are you thinking about?" I asked.

He just shook his head to indicate *nothing*. I guess my company was enough. The view of the city's building tops was a pretty sight. From our vantage point one could not see the street. Flags waved in the wind and birds flew by with an independence everyone admired. There was freedom in the breeze, and I could see envy in his eyes.

He broke his stare, by starting a conversation. "How's it, living in HOPE?"

Alderman was referring to my exit from the jungle. Once we were jungle-mates, now I was a visitor. It was as if I had moved to another country and I was returning home for a while. He wanted to know what it was like on the other side of the moon. He came from the other side, but had been out here so long, it was a distant memory. He was trying to remember what his life was like when he was five. It was that far away. I could relate. Some memories are so distant and vague, it makes one wonder if they were real.

"It's okay," I replied. "I mean, believe it or not, I miss this place."

Alderman looked at me with disbelief and said, "Really. What do you miss about this place?"

"Fresh air."

Now he looked at me now as if I were stupid, so I felt the need to clarify my statement, saying, "The illusion of fresh air."

Alderman smiled and took in a deep breath through his nose. I responded with my own smile and said, "It's not the best smell, but is better than stifling air. At least the air, out here, moves and it's not recycled. Fresh air surrounds you at every moment. Don't have to look for it, it comes to you."

"That's deep, man," he said. I wasn't trying to be philosophical, but it came out that way.

"The wind is kind of like opportunity. It just keeps on coming."

"I'm waiting for my fresh wind," Alderman said staring into the sky.

"Suck it in," I encouraged. "It's there." I could tell he didn't believe me. I wasn't sure I believed it, either, but it sounded good. I had to find encouragement wherever I could.

The pastor was good at keeping me uplifted, but my best source was myself. Most of what I knew, or pretended to know, came from my parents. My mother was quiet and said little unless it was important. She waited for me to say something she could pounce on. She lived to teach me. My father was always talking. He didn't care whether it made sense or not. He did all his thinking out in the open, for all to hear. Of course, his alcohol consumption ignited his passion for words.

He did have a talent for mumbling wisdom. His talent for drinking was equally paramount. He could savor a bottle of Hennessy, all day. Savoring vodka was another talent, and he passed it on to me. Vodka was my preference, but I settled for the cheapest of wines. However, today I could boast of being sober for 183 days.

"You're a funny man, Hero." He gave me the title after I helped the police solve a crime a year or so ago. For the three years I was on the street, I never acquired a nickname, but I was given one at the time I left the street. As a rule, I wasn't called anything. I had no name. I was anonymous to the most invisible people I knew. The few times they called me, they called me Roman. I guess you had to be out here for quite some time to get a nickname.

"Glad to amuse you," I said. We chuckled together.

"You like it in there?" Alderman asked me. To use the phrase *in there* could only come from a man who served time in prison. *In there* was to be trapped. It was the loss of freedom and he saw the mission as a prison. I couldn't totally disagree.

I must have spent thirty minutes with Alderman. It was time to return to my objective, and I wished him good luck. The good luck phrase would drive my dad crazy. "Good luck?" he would say. "You know what that means? It means 'bye.' It means I'm not going any farther with you. You're on your own." He would always make a big deal of it. I made it a point never to say the words in his presence, but I picked up the phrase again and I felt the pain and disconnect when I used it toward Alderman.

I wanted to help him, but I didn't know how. I didn't have money. I didn't have a place to live. What could I do? I spent some time with him, and then I felt as though I was abandoning him. As I walked away, I wondered if he had the same thoughts as my father. I never looked back to see. I had to go, and I didn't want to get involved with another problem to solve. I wanted to be free to do what I came to do.

After about ten minutes of walking through the brush, I heard the familiar bark of a small dog. Tiger was a small mutt, about six pounds or so. He was a mix of about five breeds. He looked like everything, from a Collie to a Chihuahua. Tiger could be a major contestant in the Ugliest Dog contests. Once I was in his sight, he recognized me and his tail wagged so wildly I thought he was going to toss it into the woods. This crazy dog liked me for some reason I would never know. I didn't care. I seemed to attract dogs, even though I didn't like them. I placed my limp hand close to his face and he got more excited.

"Hey, Tiger," I said.

It didn't take long before I noticed the Mayor curled up in his blanket. Something was wrong. The Mayor would have rolled over to greet me, but all I could detect was some minimal movement beneath the blue blanket. It had a large print of a tiger on it.

The Mayor was into cats. If he could have his way, he would have had a small cat as a companion, but a cat would never be as loyal as Tiger. A cat would be long gone.

"Mayor?" I was cautious as I approached. I wasn't sure what I would find. At least I knew he was alive, because the body beneath the blanket moved. I called to him again, but my call was timid. I didn't want to startle him. This was not like him. Why was he sleeping at this time of the day and all by himself?

Like a cat, I crawled up to his body and place my hand on his shoulder. "Mayor," I said in my gentlest voice. "You okay?"

I could feel he was fragile, before I saw his face. He finally responded to me with a grunt, followed by several coughs. His cough was wet and almost made me gag at the sound of it. Since he was on his side, I turned him face up. He looked awful. This man had been homeless for more than ten years, so I couldn't have expected him to look healthy, but his look was different. The Mayor was sick.

Tiger was still excited to see me and wherever I moved my hand, there he was. I swatted him away. I had to divide my attention between the stupid dog and my friend. Finally, Tiger got the message. He sat quietly while I looked over his master.

"Mayor, what's wrong?" I shook him a little to get him to respond, and he opened his eyes. He looked through me, but I knew he recognized me from his smile.

"I knew it would be you." I had no idea what he meant. "Of all the people, it would be you."

"Stop talking nonsense, Mayor. What's going on?"

"I'm sick, fool." I tried not to smile, but he was one fool talking to another.

"What happened?"

"I don't know. Just sick. I think they gave me something."

"Who gave you something?"

The Mayor was full of conspiracy theories. Whatever was going on with him was probably the result of some government agency action. If he weren't so nuts, I would have thought he was a former spy. I don't know what he had against the government, but he had it bad. These days everyone had something against the government. Everyone knew it was full of useless people. I was glad I didn't vote anymore. Democrats and Republicans vied for power in a government which did nothing for people. It was like any business. It was more interested in surviving than being helpful, and the people of this country donated millions to elect people who were no smarter than a small dog.

When I grasped his face to bring him to his senses, I was startled. "God, you are hot," I exclaimed.

"No kidding. You should feel it from in here."

He was right. I snatched the blanket from him. I jostled him more than I meant to, but the dirty blanket was wrapped tightly around him. He needed air. He groaned as I pulled it away. That's all Tiger needed. He was anxious again. Jesus, I thought, will this stupid dog just stay put. I pushed the dog aside. "Sit," I shouted, and I was amazed to learn the dog understood. Maybe he knew other orders. "Stay," I commanded. Then I turned back to the Mayor. A quick glance: Tiger was still sitting, patiently.

I took the blanket and rolled it to make a pillow for my friend. "How you been?" he asked me. I didn't know why he was concerned with my well-being.

"I'm good, I'm good." As I spoke to him, I was loosening his clothes. He was so sweaty and his constant coughing was irritating me. I never could stand noises. When I was a kid, I would cry at the sound of the doorbell.

"Do you have some water?" I asked.

I found his backpack and looked through it, finding it full of papers. I spotted his grocery cart and searched it to find a bottle of water. I offered it to him, but he drank it as if I were forcing liquor into the mouth of a child. "Come on, Mayor. Drink it." He followed my instructions, but with reluctance.

Maybe it took me too long, but I realized I was wasting my time. I needed to get him help beyond what I could offer. I looked around as if I expected to see someone walk by. What a silly notion.

"Mayor, I'm going to get you some help." He didn't respond, so I didn't know if he ignored me or didn't hear me, so I repeated myself and he acknowledged my intentions with a nod.

When I stood, Tiger was at me again. I think the dog was asking me to not leave, but I had to go. "Stay," I said. The dumb dog obeyed. I trekked up the hill and walked out of the jungle. I didn't really have a plan. I hoped I would see a police car drive by and

I could flag it down. My plan was evolving as I walked. Maybe I would see a cop walking his beat, but of course I saw neither.

I passed by a coffee shop and saw many people inside, talking on their phones and typing on their computers. I stopped and made myself enter, but I still had no idea as to how to approach someone and ask for help. However, the problem was solved for me. A young lady asked from behind the counter, "May I help you, sir?"

I hesitated, but I put my misgivings aside and said I needed her help. "What can I get for you?"

"I have a friend who's very sick." Her body took a step back and her smile dropped. She didn't know what I wanted.

"He needs an ambulance."

"Oh," she said, but her face expressed confusion. Her name tag introduced her as Amy.

"Amy, please. He's very sick."

I think she recognized my sincerity, but still didn't know what to do, so she asked me to wait a moment as she walked over to another employee. I watched their short conversation and she returned. She pulled out the phone under the counter and called 911.

"Thank you," I said. "Thank you."

Her eyes darted back and forth from me to the phone as she answered the questions of the dispatcher on the phone. Then she handed the phone to me and I explained what was going on with the Mayor. The woman on the phone assured me help was on the way. I gave the phone to Amy and thanked her again. I had to get back to the park entrance to direct the 911 personnel where to find my friend.

It had to be just five minutes, and I heard the sirens. The emergency vehicle slowed and I waved my arms as if I were hailing a cab. They came to me and together we hurried to the site. I called out to the Mayor and found him rolled to his side again. As I tried to put him on his back again, the emergency people pushed me aside. "We'll take this, sir."

This was the second time I was addressed as "sir." A year ago, I was rarely addressed, at all. No one knew my name, no one cared, and no one treated me politely. I was the same person, the only difference was, now I was cleaner. I was shaven and my clothes didn't smell. They thought I was somebody. If they only knew. They were here and were offering to do what was necessary for the Mayor. I watched as they lifted him onto a gurney and called for aid. Two other men arrived and the four men carried him up the hill to the back of the ambulance.

I couldn't go since I was not a family member, but I knew where they were going, so I headed for St Mary's. Sometimes I ran, sometimes I trotted, most of the time I walked quickly, but I made it to the emergency room. I was sweaty, but I didn't stink, which was another change. I had deodorant and it was working. I still thought I should have lied and said I was a family member. My dilemma now was to decide if I should go to the registration desk and inquire, or find a way in the back door. Then it occurred to me, I didn't know the Mayor's name. I heard it a few times, but not enough to remember it. He was the Mayor and all of us referred to him as such.

If I went in the back door, I could just look for him and there would be no need to ask any questions. I went to the vehicle entrance. After the commotion of bringing him here, there was little activity at the ER sliding door. I remember passing by a fire department when I was a kid. I would look inside the open garage door and there was no one inside, every day. I wondered where the firemen were and were they really ready if a fire call came to them? I guess they were. I was always wishing to be at the fire station the moment the call came. It never happened. I just saw the drama in movies. There was no drama here, either. I guess the EMTs were inside with their feet on their desks, eating donuts.

I spotted the large square button on the wall. If I pushed it, the doors would magically slide apart to allow me inside, to search for the Mayor. Of course, it would make a lot of noise and every-one would look to see who was entering. I was sure there was a side door and I looked for it, but as I passed the sliding doors, there stood a security officer. Plan A was dead. There was no plan B.

This was a moment when I could see my mother wagging her finger at me. "If you don't have a plan for you, someone else will have one." It was hard to take her seriously, since I was so much taller than she. I was her height when I was thirteen. By my sopho-more year in high school, I towered over her. "Who do you want making plans for you—you or life?" she scolded.

It seemed life was making the plans at this point, until I came back to my current objective. I was really out to find Graham's girlfriend. So much time had passed, and sundown was well underway. It was time to return to the original plan. The people of St. Mary's would take good care of the Mayor. I had to believe it to move on. The original Plan A was back in effect, but I still didn't know where to go. If I wanted to start again, in the jungle, I had moved a long way from there. I was tired and the sun would be gone when I made my way back. Distractions—another lecture topic I could hear from my parents.

Oh my God, I thought. The stupid dog, Tiger was still back at the park. Dammit, there was another distraction. The medical people asked me who the dog belonged to, and I said it was mine to avoid having them call Animal Control. Now I was stuck. I had to go back and get him. Shit, shit, shit!

I wasn't in shape enough to run or walk fast, so I decided to use my bus pass. Standing at the bus station was a different experience. No one thought of me as unusual. They acknowledged me, but were not disgusted by me. I was one of them. I was a citizen. They assumed I was a useful member of my community. I spent three years on the streets and had to learn the look of disgust and how to avoid it. Now, I was trying to get used to the idea of being a regular guy again. It wasn't so easy. I didn't spend much time out here, anymore. I was with other misfits, at the mission, and we learned to be irregular, together.

As an alcoholic, I had to remind myself I was not drinking anymore, but I was still an alcoholic. It was a notion which was hard for me to accept. When could I stop being called an alcoholic? I heard speeches from men and women who were sober for more than twenty years and they introduced themselves as alcoholics. Such a thought was frightening to me. When does the label go away? Was there a time in life when you can stop calling yourself something you're not? Is being an alcoholic the same as being black? My aunt Minnie used to tell me she only had to be black and die. So I guess, I will always be black, an alcoholic, and then die.

Why can't someone be a *former* alcoholic? Can I change my mind, change my lifestyle and then my title? Those are the rebellious questions I was always asking. Rebellious—another label I was given. I guess I will always be a rebel, as well. Aunt Minnie, there are a lot of things I will always be, some of which I don't want to accept. Dog hater; I don't mind that label, and yet here I was on my way to get Tiger. Of course, it served the dual purpose of looking for Graham's woman. All of my random thoughts served to keep me entertained during the bus ride. It worked. I got off the bus and headed for the jungle.

I don't know why I was surprised, but there Tiger was—lying under the grocery cart. Not for long though, he was after me with an urgency I hadn't seen before. I wondered if someone had tried to catch him or frightened him. Some folks could be pretty mean.

"Okay, okay," I said trying to reassure the dog. He stood on his hind legs and pushed against my leg with his front paws. Then he would stand on all fours, wait a moment, and do it again. All the time his tail was wagging. I didn't know what to make of this other than to recognize he was glad to see me. With his repetition, I finally picked him up and he seemed to appear calmer. Is that what he wanted—to be carried? Did this dog have enough sense to ask to be carried?

I kept Tiger in my arm as I searched the Mayor's possessions. It didn't appear anyone had rummaged through them. I found some dog food in a plastic bag, so I took a handful and put it in the bowl also in the cart. Now I understood. Tiger was telling me he was hungry. He ate the handful without looking up for a moment. All I could do was watch.

I didn't like it out here, so I had to find a place which seemed more secure for me. I couldn't go back to HOPE with Tiger. I gathered the remaining dog food and put it in my backpack. I put Tiger on a leash I found, and we headed up to the street. He was definitely quieter, now. He just walked along my side, occasionally looking up at me. I thought he was asking where we were going and I was stupid enough to answer, at one point. "I don't know, but we have to find a better place than this dump." He wagged his tail as if to say he understood.

I was sure the pastor was anxious about my whereabouts, but he found me on the streets, so he should be confident I was okay. In three years, I learned to survive. But I never learned how to do it with a dog.

Chapter 7

Pastor Franklin sat at his desk looking through a box of black T-shirts. He was sorting them on the floor according to size. At one point, he unfolded one and held it up for inspection. He heard a voice from beyond the shirt, which obstructed his vision. "Is it the end?" he heard. The pastor lowered the shirt to see the two detectives at the door.

As they approached, the pastor answered, "We're close." He stood up to greet them and extended his hand for a handshake. "Is this *deja vu* all over again?"

Solomon smiled and grasped the extended hand. Franklin offered them a seat. Turner took the chair in front of the desk, and Innis lifted a box from another chair to the floor and sat.

"You must have unanswered questions."

"Perceptive, you are," Solomon said in his best Yoda impression. It made the pastor smile.

"So, what can I answer for you?"

"We would like to speak with Mr. Barnes, again," Detective Turner responded.

"He's not here."

"Oh, when will he return?"

It was a struggle for the pastor to answer, but finally he said, "I don't know." The response was hard for the detectives to accept. The reverend could tell from their expressions they were not sure he was telling the truth.

"I'm a minister, for God's sake."

Turner was quick to respond, "I'm sure it was for God's sake, Pastor." Franklin got the pun.

"He left yesterday."

"Did you kick him out?"

"No, Roman is a very good resident. He follows the rules, is doing well in school."

"Then why did he leave?"

"That I can't tell you."

From the second chair, Innis said, "Can't?" The pastor insisted he used the correct word.

"So do you just let your residents leave, at will? I thought this was a program."

"It is a program, not a prison."

"Do you know where the rest of your people are today?"

"Detectives, I know how to run this facility, so if I can help you, please ask the appropriate questions."

"We have, Reverend. You don't seem to have the appropriate answers," jabbed Solly.

"Well, how about restricting the questions to what you really want to know. What are you interested in?"

Detective Turner answered without hesitation. "We're interested in a lot of things. You never know what you'll find. You find the truth, if you keep asking. Seek and you shall find, isn't that what the Bible says, Pastor?"

"Everyone knows a little bit, don't they?" He realized he had to explain his statement. "I mean about the Bible. Everyone knows a little bit."

"I would think that's a good thing, Pastor."

"Milk is for babies." The pastor's statement made Solomon turn to his partner.

"Do you think I'm a baby?" he asked Innis.

"You are kinda young," Innis said

Solomon turned back to Reverend Franklin. "What shall we do?"

"Ask and it shall be given you."

"You know what I've noticed, Pastor? A lot of people seem to have a distrust of the cops. Are you one of those people?"

"I can only say I've seen the police treat people unfairly, at times. I've seen them push homeless people off the street to the parks, from the parks to the sidewalk, from the sidewalk to some filthy shelter. Then back to the streets, to find you, again."

"This is not a shelter?" Solomon appeared confused.

"We already established this is a program, detective."

"Oh yes we did. And not a filthy program, I'm sure."

"Detective, you are why people distrust the police. Why do you have such an antagonizing persona?"

"Not a good question, Pastor. Why don't you ask why do I put my life on the line, daily? Why don't you ask why I try to find murderers or why people are killed by people other than the cops, because cops don't kill people, Pastor. Thugs do. And I seek, ask, knock, search and turn over rocks and speak to slimy people to find out things you have a hard time trying to help with. And the worst part is finding people who resent the way I do things. Don't lose the forest for the trees, Pastor. I'm trying to find a murderer, while you're trying to make some sociological point. Make your point, Pastor, and see if you catch a killer."

It took Franklin a moment, but he understood. "*Touché*, detective."

"I'm not interested in *touchés*, Pastor. I'm not on the debate team. The people you care for, I care for. So let's find this mutha." He stopped.

Detective Turner recognized he was about to step over the line. After gathering his thoughts, he said in a much calmer voice, "Can we do this together? We'll debate another day, okay?"

"All right."

"Thank you. Thank you. So when do you expect Mr. Barnes to return?"

"He should have returned already. We do have a curfew and he missed his class this morning."

"What class is that?" asked Turner.

"He's in training to be a solar technician."

"Solar technician," repeated Innis.

"Yes, we received federal money to train technicians."

"So you do the training?" Solly asked, continuing the investigation.

"Well, no. We just have an agreement with a local school, which does the training. They are part of our program."

"There's that word program, again. So you said he's a good student."

"Oh, he's really better than that. He's stellar. We expect many good things from him."

"So where does he train?"

"The community college has a training program. We transport the students each day and bring them home."

"How many students in the program?"

"We have three from this facility."

"Who else is there?"

"There's Derrick Martin and Trevor Grossmont."

"Are they available?"

"Yes."

"May we speak with them?"

"Sure." He began to stand, but was stopped by Detective Turner. "We would like to speak with you first, though."

"Oh, okay." The reverend sounded meek as he return to his seat.

"So, please tell us about the last time you saw Graham."

"All I can tell you is what I said before."

"That's what we look for, consistency and inconsistency."

"Well, we were having our open mike night—"

"Which is?"

"Well, most of our sessions are private sessions with the residents only, but recently we have invited anyone, once a month. It's called open mike night."

"Sounds appealing."

"It is. The numbers have been growing. I think most come for the camaraderie, though."

"That's good, too, right?"

"Well, yes."

"So what made Graham mad at you, that night?"

"I asked him about his mother." From behind Solomon, the pastor heard "Whoa," from Innis.

Solomon continued the conversation. "It's a dangerous thing, talking about someone's mamma."

"I wasn't talking about his mother. I was asking about her."

"Must have been some question."

"We were talking about his drinking and he was offering he was an abusive drinker."

"An alcoholic."

"I didn't use that term with him. He just mentioned his life had gone bad because of a rough life and alcohol. I asked him who he blamed for his life. I listed several things—his job, wife, and so on."

"You asked if he blamed his mother."

"Yes."

"Was that wise?"

"Yes, it was. Alcohol and anger tend to remove inhibitions. You begin to say lots of things you wouldn't normally say."

"So you were trying to make him mad?" Solomon asked in the same monotone voice he used on a regular basis. During interrogation, he rarely showed emotion.

"Sounds kind of mean, but if they say something they have been trying to hide, it can be a breakthrough for them," the pastor explained. "Most of us hide our feelings from others and especially ourselves. Anger can sometimes make someone say what they have been hiding. Even if they don't know they are trying to hide it."

Detective Turner turned around to his partner, then back to the pastor. "That's good, Reverend. That's good. You could be a detective."

"So is that what you do?"

Solly smiled. "So what did he do when he got angry?"

"He just stood up and started ranting and cussing."

"Did he reveal any secrets?"

"He was mostly cussing. He did mention no one could keep him from talking or telling the truth."

"What truth was he talking about?"

"I couldn't tell you that. He was just very angry."

"Could it have been because he *did* blame his mother?"

"Maybe. I didn't know him, really."

"Do you know Roman?" Solly was on a mission with his questions.

Franklin began to squirm in his chair. "You don't think Roman killed him."

"No way, Pastor. Do you?"

"No," the pastor replied. He was insulted. "Roman is a good man. There would be no reason for him to hurt Graham. He worked long and hard to bring him to the open mike sessions."

"So where is he?"

"I don't know. Really, I don't."

"Why would you think he was a suspect?" Innis asked, entering the conversation.

"You were asking so many questions about him, I thought he might be a person of interest."

"He is, but that just means we want to talk with him."

"Yeah, right. 'Person of interest' is the new word for suspect."

"Pastor, you are a cynical man for a minister. I thought pastors were full of hope."

"Are you trying to make me angry, Detective Turner?"

"Are you? Angry, that is?"

"No."

"Good.

"Besides," the pastor continued, "he helped you guys last year bust that human trafficking gang."

Again from behind Solomon, "Good people can go bad."

"And bad people can go good. Roman is a good person."

Solomon didn't miss a beat. "What did you say to Graham when he was angry?"

"Nothing. I just listened."

"And that's all he said?"

"That's all he said. He left and Roman went after him."

"See? That's why we need to speak with him. Seems he was the last to see him alive."

"How do you know? Many people could have seen him afterward. There are a lot of people out there on the street. Some, not so friendly."

"We don't know. All the more reason to speak with Mr. Barnes."

"I wish I knew where he was."

"I believe you, Pastor. Thank you. We'll find him."

Pastor Franklin stood up and escorted the men to the exit. "Oh, don't you want to speak with the other men?"

Solomon, the usual spokesman, responded, "Another day, Pastor. Thanks."

The two detectives talked as Detective Innis drove. "What do you think?" asked Detective Turner.

Innis answered with a sigh. His brow furled and he sighed again. "I don't know."

"I guess the real question is, why would anyone kill a homeless man? I mean, is a homeless man that important?"

"Most people wouldn't think so, but I guess this guy was important to someone, anyway," Innis answered.

"So to find out who he was important to, we need to find out who he was."

"Then, again, maybe he was just so unimportant, taking his life meant nothing."

"Well, that's a horrible thought," Turner said.

"Yes, it is."

"Okay, let's assume he was important. Why was he important? Was he important because of who he was or what he knew?" Before Innis could respond, he added, "Or both." His conclusion brought a smile to Greg's lips, but he prevented it from spreading to the rest of his face.

"First we have to know where he was from, who he knew, who he spent time with, where he worked," Innis said.

"That's where Mr. Barnes comes in." He looked to his partner to return a thought. "You don't like him, do you?"

"Who, Barnes?"

"Why don't you like him?"

"Did I say I didn't like him?"

"Yes."

"And when did I say that?"

"Did you know ninety percent of communication is non-verbal?"

"You learn that in the academy?"

"Yeah, didn't you?"

"Your point?"

"Your face says you don't like him. I saw it the day we met in the tunnel. Remember that?"

Solomon was referring to the case which led to the discovery of a labyrinth of tunnels beneath the city, used by sex traffickers. Roman Barnes was part of the discovery. "Remember when we were in the elevator shaft? The look on your face said it all. And he saved your life."

"Maybe he did."

"See, you won't give him the credit. Did you know him before?"

"We brought him in for questioning."

"Was he helpful?"

"Not really."

"So you guys are old friends."

"Old maybe, friends is another story."

"What story would that be?" Solomon was intrigued.

"Another day, son. We have work to do." Solomon decided to drop it, not to conjure up any unpleasant memories he was sure his partner was trying to keep buried.

"Okay, where do we look for the mysterious Mr. Barnes? You know what I don't get? He has been at that mission for six months, at least. Suddenly he disappears, just when one of his buddies gets killed. Do you think he's afraid of being killed?"

"Or he's the killer?"

"You know that doesn't make sense, Greg."

"When we know who they are, we'll understand."

Solomon laughed out loud. "That is so Zen-like. You are the Zen master, baby. If you build it, they will come. That's what that's like. Got anymore?"

"The truth shall set you free."

"You amaze me."

"Three words, all truth."

Solomon could only roll his eyes. "So do you want to look for him now?"

"No," Greg answered. "I'm tired."

Detective Turner understood his partner's fatigue. "When is the funeral?"

"Saturday."

"How long were you guys partners?" The questions were more to ease his own discomfort than to get Greg to talk.

"Six years."

"Pretty long time."

"Yeah, pretty long."

"He seemed like a pretty good guy. I wonder what happened?"

"None of your business."

Turner excused the rude reply. It obviously came from a man who was grieving, though few would know that. Innis continued to work without interruption. He never discussed Detective Jackson's death; this was the first time Solomon felt comfortable to ask, but it was too soon. Greg was not ready to speak about it, but the answer Solomon received was enough to let him know Innis was aware of the reasons for his former partner's suicide.

Innis broke the silence to let it be known he was going to see Jackson's wife and see how she and her daughter were doing.

There was little emotion in his announcement. Greg pulled the car over to an empty parking space and relinquished the driving to Solomon. "I'll walk from here. See you tomorrow."

Turner nodded his acknowledgement and drove away. He could see his partner standing on the corner, like a wounded dog. He was tempted to stop and ask if he could come along, but it would have been futile. In the rear view mirror, he noted people crossing the street, but Greg stood still. His partner was more than wounded, he was lost. It was painful to watch him, and Solomon was relieved to turn the corner and change his view.

Greg stood at the corner and watched everyone around him. He was looking for someone as miserable as he was, but everyone was so busy going to places he didn't know nor care about. He knew the streets very well, but without warning, a feeling of disconnection came over him. Everyone belonged, but him. He knew where he was going, but felt he was a stranger. He knew Carmen from the beginning of the men's partnership. Renny became a close friend because Renny was very open about his life and his marriage.

When Renny loved Carmen, Greg loved Carmen. When Renny was angry with her, Greg was angry, as well. Today, he wasn't sure how to feel about her. He didn't know what Renny would think of her. Today he had to make up his own mind about her. This was his chance to really get to know her and ask her questions. Their daughter, Neena, was easy to love, like any child.

Finally he made the effort to walk across the street. He was walking in the right direction, but it still felt aimless. Once he reached the building entrance, Greg stood at the door and watched traffic for a moment as he tried to regain his equilibrium. Recovered, he entered the door and took the elevator to the fourteenth floor.

He rang the doorbell and Carmen answered. The pause was only a few seconds, but when one is searching for words to say, it can seem much longer.

"You okay?" he asked her. Carmen didn't answer. She opened the door wider, to invite him in, and then she turned and walked away. Greg followed her to the living room and watched her as she politely sat on the couch. He didn't know if he should sit or stand, and she gave him no indication of what he should do.

Greg self-consciously sat in a chair across from Carmen, but she didn't notice.

"Carmen," he quietly called to her and waited for an answer. When she didn't respond, he called her again.

"I'm okay."

"You don't have to be." When Carmen looked puzzled, he tried to clarify. "You don't have to be okay."

"Yes, I do, for Neena's sake."

"How's she doing?"

"Probably doing okay, for my sake."

"Is she here?"

"No, she's with my mother. This is not the best place for her to be, right now. She can't even go into the kitchen. I barely can. It's funny, though. He didn't even die here."

Carmen was stating the obvious. Detective Renaldo Jackson killed himself in his own apartment, but the association was still very strong. They were married for twelve years, until a year ago. Though she and Neena moved into this present apartment four months ago, her ex-husband's presence was always with her. Neena reminded her daily. She loved her father and spoke of him daily, but the most eerie were her eyes. Neena's eyes were her father's eyes. The cadence of her speech and the words she used, were his words. Renny lived and Carmen saw him every day.

"I know this is really hard, Carmen, but can you tell me what the note meant?"

She quoted the note, as if she had recited it over and over. "Yes, there's more. Keep hope alive."

"Yes, what does that mean?"

Greg already had an idea of what the note meant; he was more concerned if Carmen knew. It was important to him to make sure the message was received. From many conversations, he knew Renny felt unimportant in his home. Did she know that and was this the best time to place any guilt on her? It was an automatic response for him. He was protecting his partner.

"He told me many times he felt insignificant at home," she struggled to say.

"He wasn't, was he?"

"Of course not. Life just changed for us."

"What changed?"

"I can't really tell you. He just spent more time with you than with us. Did he talk to you?"

Now was Greg's chance to tell the truth, but it was not the right time. It would be mean and inappropriate.

"We talked mostly about cop stuff. Besides, I wouldn't know what he was talking about, anyway. I'm single."

She smiled a little. "He told me you've never been married."

"It's not for everybody."

"Yes, it is. It's not good that man should be alone."

"You like the Bible?"

"I'm not sure. It says some comforting things, but God seems so far away."

"My grandmother would tell me, He's as close as air. I can take Him in at any time. When I was feeling bad, she would tell me to take a deep breath and let God in."

"Let Him in, huh? I could use a whiff."

"Well, according to Grandma, it's that easy. Breathe Him in."

"I can barely breathe. I don't have the energy to bring Him in, let alone some air. I'm curious. Did it work for you?"

Greg shrugged. "It's just something she would tell me."

"Yeah, I thought so." After a moment of silence, she spoke again. "Do you believe in God?"

"Yeah, sure."

"That didn't sound very sure."

"No, I do."

"Do you know Him?"

"I'm not sure what you mean."

"I was talking to my priest and he asked me if I believed in God. When I told him yes, he asked me that same question."

"Do you know Him, you mean?"

"I was like you. I didn't know what he meant, and he explained a lot of people believe in God, but don't know who He is. They don't understand His personality. I think he was trying to help me understand God was still a good God, even though He let Renny kill himself. Father said Renny killed himself for reasons we will never know, but God loves him."

"Did it help? Do you feel better knowing that?"

"I'm not sure I know that."

"I'm sure God loves Renny. That's the kind of God He is."

"Maybe so. He may love Renny, but does He love me?"

"Oh, honey, of course He does. Why wouldn't He?"

"Maybe He blames me for his death."

"Oh, no, don't say that. Why would God blame you?"

"Maybe the note is about God and not about Renny. Maybe God let this happen, so it would be about Him."

"I don't know how to answer that. It sounds—I don't know, but it doesn't sound like something God would do."

"How do you know?"

Greg fumbled his response. "I don't know."

"You don't know Him," she said.

Greg was stumped. He had no answer. He couldn't bring any comforting words to mind. He wanted to sound sure and bring Bible wisdom to her, like his grandmother could. Grandma had a verse for every occasion. She was a deaconess, and at this moment he concluded his grandmother knew God, but he didn't. At this moment, he wanted to know Him, and he answered Carmen, "I guess I don't."

"Yeah, you're like the rest of us. You believe in Him, but don't know Him."

"Carmen, I don't think this is helpful. What can I do to help you?"

"I don't know. Nothing, I guess. Don't worry, Greg. We'll be all right."

Carmen's shoulders slumped and she looked into the space ahead. Her eyes focused on an invisible image before her. Greg watched her gaze and he was able to see himself. He must have looked like her on many occasions after finding out about Renny's death. He could look at her and understand that, though she could have a conversation, she was not really present. She sat on the couch, but she was in some other dimension, an alternate universe. Her body sat across from Greg, while her mind was wandering. She sat in a living room, but her soul was homeless.

"Carmen?" he called, trying to bring her back. Greg wasn't sure she could hear him, but he called again and she brought her gaze toward him. Greg stared back at her to keep her with him. He watched her eyes fill. He was mesmerized by the flow of her tears. He studied their path all the way to her lap. Carmen was too weak to wipe her face, so Greg did it for her. Her gentle smile told him she was appreciative.

This was not the Carmen he knew. She was always loud and primed to argue. Of course, he expected her to be sad, but he never anticipated her complete decline to depression. Maybe Carmen did love her husband. The woman he heard about and the woman before him were vastly different. Her reputation as a strong woman was demolished, and Greg was not prepared to aid the Carmen he saw. He came to say some nice words, give her a friendly hug of encouragement and leave her, which would have satisfied his basic human requirement to help, but Carmen's state was one of hopelessness. Greg did not know how to restore hope.

Many times he expressed his condolences to victims, but his statements to a stranger were followed by his exit. Right now, he wanted to run, but it would have been cowardice. Greg forced himself to do the best he could offer, and it was an arm around her. It was enough. He felt her melt and she wept in the only way she was able—softly. She didn't have enough energy to cry any other way.

As he comforted her in the only way he was able, Detective Innis' cell phone sounded a short tone, alerting him to a message received. This was not the moment to answer, but it sounded again, so he thought it best to quickly check the text. Carmen didn't notice, as he pulled his phone from his side. The message was from Detective Turner and it read, "We found Mr. Barnes."

Chapter 8

Detective Turner sat across from Roman Barnes in an interrogation room. Atop the bland, unattractive table between the men sat a plastic cup and a pitcher of water. The window behind Roman was draped with blinds, partially closed. If fully open, one could view the city, seven stories below. The view of the city streets from the room offered a sense of security. Any danger seemed as small as the people and cars which traveled below.

Roman was looking out of the window earlier, until the detective entered the room. He had been out on the streets for two days looking for Graham's woman friend and, though he knew how to survive, his level of insecurity was rising daily. For now, he was safe. For now, he was a part of a game he played before. Same ol' shit, different toilet.

Detective Turner asked him expected questions. He asked Roman to repeat his last day with Graham. He recalled the day. Graham was angry because of a question the pastor asked about his mother. He was more than angry, he was furious, and Roman felt guilty for the escalation of the atmosphere. He was Graham's friend and he started to laugh, not because the situation was funny, but he looked at one of the residents and his reaction set off a firestorm of laughter. Seal's laugh was never stifled. He was severely hearing-impaired from birth, so he was not aware of the booming sound of his laugh, which resembled the bark of a seal.

Graham blamed Roman. He probably felt betrayed by his friend, and he pushed Roman. Roman would have fallen to the floor, but the huge body of Tuba, another resident, limited the damage to Roman's only being tipped over onto the large man. At the sight, Seal's roar grew louder, while the pastor tried his best to quiet him. When Tuba stood, his large frame was enough to restrain Graham's ire, and he left.

Roman recounted his walk to the jungle. He omitted telling the detective about the woman. He didn't know why, but it felt right to do so. She may have been involved with his murder, but he wanted to know for himself, and it felt good knowing he knew something the police did not. He had the upper hand and they didn't even know. He had the power. Their badges, weapons and interrogation room were no match for the strength he derived from his knowledge.

His father always told him knowledge was power. He heard, regularly, the only thing someone could take from him was his mind. However, Roman had seen so many mentally ill men on the street, he could argue with his father on the topic. Today he was of sound mind and he had the power. His mind was intact and ready for battle.

Apparently, the detective was not satisfied and he continued to ask questions. "Did you guys argue on your way back to the park?" he asked.

Roman thought he answered the question fifteen minutes ago, but he responded again. "No. We were cool. I wasn't the problem."

"Who was the problem?"

"It wasn't the pastor, if that's what you're leading to."

"I don't lead, I follow," Detective Turner answered.

"Meaning?"

"Meaning, I'm a detective. I don't set people up, plant evidence, lie, or cheat my way to an arrest. I follow the clues, wherever they lead. I'm not in the business of judging. I'm on the side of justice. I find bad people and I let the lawyers do the rest."

"Not what I'm used to."

"Not my fault. Do you remember the first time we met?" Roman nodded he did. "I'm sorry about your friend."

Turner was referring to the murder of Roman's friend who was killed in the jungle the night they discovered the tunnels. We called him Rooster, but *Pequod*, tattooed on his back, boasted of his Native-American tribe. He was close to killing the detective until Turner identified himself, but the incident left his friend dead from a gunshot to his abdomen, from the smugglers they were chasing.

"I remember. Why are you so interested in a nobody?"

"Is that what you thought of him? Maybe he was more than that. Maybe he was human. I would think you could relate to that."

"Most people don't care about us." Roman was surprised he was identifying himself as homeless. He hadn't felt like that for a while.

"That's a pretty cynical thought to carry around with you. Isn't it heavy?"

"I've seen lots of heavy stuff, and very few lifters. We're nobodies, to others, I mean."

"There's no such thing as a nobody. I can look Graham up on the Internet and probably find something about him." Turner raised his phone from his side, tapped a few buttons and asked, "Want me to find you?"

"Don't waste your time."

The detective put his phone back in its clip and continued the interrogation."Do you remember how my partner and I treated you last year?"

Detective Turner's response was not convincing, since Roman made no effort to acknowledge the remark. The silence didn't affect either man and Detective Turner continued the conversation.

"Why did you leave HOPE?"

"Because I can."

"Mr. Barnes, can you see how you make yourself look suspicious? I mean, I ask a simple question and you give me a stupid answer. Your good friend is killed, you're the last man to see him alive, and you hit the streets. Why?"

"It's the life of a black man. We're always suspicious."

"And you think that's funny?"

"You're black, what do you think?"

"I think you're obnoxious. I think you don't give a damn about people and you don't think much at all. But I can't believe you have always been this way. I think you were human once, how long ago I don't know, but once you must have been human. How long has it been, Mr. Barnes? When was the last time you cared?"

"How did he die?" asked Roman, after a moment of thought.

"He was stabbed, Mr. Barnes."

Roman's eyes dropped to the floor as if he were trying to imagine his friend being murdered. He might have responded, but it was too late. A knock at the door ended this session. The two men looked at the two-way mirror and Detective Innis entered the room. He walked over to his partner and asked for some time alone with the suspect. At one point, he lowered his voice as he spoke to Turner. He patiently waited for Turner to leave, and then he sat across from Roman.

"I've seen this routine before," Roman said.

"I bet you have," Detective Innis said, staring into Roman's eyes. "How many times have you been arrested?"

"You didn't look it up?"

"No, but I bet it's more than once."

"Your point?"

"Do you like being a person of interest in a murder case?"

"I don't like being harassed and I don't like your insinuations, but I do like my chances that you have no reason to believe I killed anyone."

"I don't like you," the detective admitted.

"I'll live."

"I wish I could say that about others," Innis snapped back.

Roman detected a different tone of anger in the detective before him. His anger was personal, though he didn't know why.

"What is this about?" Roman asked. Innis' answer was not what he was expecting. The detective reached into his sport jacket pocket and pulled out an object, then tossed it onto the table. Roman began to understand his anger.

"You know what that is?" the detective asked.

"It's obvious, isn't it?"

The detective was not interested in his sarcasm. He asked again, "Do you know what that is?"

"What are you trying to get to? What is it you really want?"

"Forget the mirror," Innis assured Roman. "This is between me and you. No one is listening."

He watched Roman's face and he could see him thinking about his situation. He tried once more to comfort the man across the table. "Really. No one is behind there."

Roman thought, and thought some more. Finally he confessed, "A feather."

"I'm not interested in the description. What's the meaning, Featherman?"

Roman had not heard the title since the last time they met. Decades earlier, he was a member of a gang, the Feathermen. The name came from the gang's original intent—to raise and fly pigeons. The title was presented in a more menacing tone, this time.

"What are you after?" Roman responded.

Innis began to explain his question. "I was nineteen when I got this. It was outside my sister's house on Cresswell. You know Cresswell, don't you?"

It was a rhetorical question. Innis didn't wait for an answer and continued, "It was April seventeenth, about nine o'clock. There was a shooting which resulted in the death of my niece. She was only three years old, and a slimy group of Feathermen killed her. They shot her and her father and raced off down the street. I didn't know about it until my sister called and blamed me. Do you know why?"

"You're a Hammer-Head," Roman stated.

Roman knew this from the hammer tattoo on the detective's left wrist. He spied it the first time they met, and there was no doubt Detective Innis recognized the tattoo of a bird on his neck. They were enemies from long ago.

"She said if I had not been in a gang, it would never have happened. I was a Hammer-Head, and I hate you and every other Featherman out there."

"I didn't do it," Roman responded, coolly.

"Oh you did, all right. You may not have pulled the trigger, but you and your fellow gang boys killed her. Every Featherman killed her."

"I'm sorry about your niece."

"Is that what you think I'm after, an apology? Do you believe your sorry self will do anything for me after almost thirty years?"

"Is it revenge you want, then?"

"Don't get fuckin' philosophical with me, Featherman. You know what I really want. I want my niece back. I want my sister to forgive me and until she does, I won't forgive you."

"Sounds like you and your sister are not doing well."

Roman's casual manner was more than Innis could bear. He stood and lunged at Roman, but the person of interest was nimble enough to avoid his full force. Roman stood quickly and backed away enough to be out of reach of the detective's hands. Roman grabbed the detective's arms, but Innis' hands were able to grab his shirt and back him to the wall.

"What the hell is wrong with you?" Roman shouted.

"I let you go a year ago," the detective said in a forced and restrained voice. "Not this time. You were a piece of shit thirty years ago, last year, and today. Don't look for someone to come to the rescue. I meant it when I said no one was listening. It's me and you, baby."

"Did they find out who killed your niece?" Roman did not resist the detective's pushing. The wall stopped Innis' intention to push him into eternity.

"You're not listening. You're responsible, *all* of you are responsible."

"And you're not?" The question was enough to stop Innis' assault on Roman. The detective backed away but never took his eyes from the Featherman. He still wanted to harm Roman.

"I wasn't there," Roman said in a conciliatory tone.

"Feathermen were there, you were there."

"I can't help you then, if that's how you think. You Heads were as violent as they come. We never bothered you, until you tried to expand your territory. You thought killing our birds would make us quiver? You just gave us a reason to live. Revenge is powerful."

"Yeah, tell me about it," Innis agreed.

"We found the bloodied pigeon feathers when you guys slaughtered our birds. It became a symbol. We found hundreds."

"And you placed them as a warning to your next victim."

"Sometimes, and sometimes we placed it after the deed to send a message, but as you said, that was thirty years ago."

"Thirty years for you, yesterday for me."

"I can't treat your guilt."

"Don't fuck with me, Featherman." Innis' anger was about to rise again.

"You need to listen. I wasn't there," Roman insisted. "I was in boot camp. I hated every day of it, so I know I wasn't there. I didn't do it. I didn't sanction it."

"Did you know it was going to happen?"

Roman didn't want to answer, but a direct question deserved a direct answer. "Yes."

"You son of a bitch!" the detective said as he drove his suspect against the wall.

"You need to look at yourself. Your sister obviously blames you, but more important, you blame you. Admit it, being part of a gang was stupid. You and I both know that now. It was cool, then. You got caught up, like me. I didn't make you join the Heads and I didn't make you violent. You chose violence, and violence is the 'son of a bitch,' not me. You chose it, and now you want to make me pay for your fucked-up choices. I made mine and I'm paying the price. Be a man and pay your debt."

"What the hell do you know about debt?" There was disdain for Roman as Innis asked the question.

"I'm not your therapist, either."

"You're nothing."

"Yeah, keep thinking that, if it helps." Roman sat down and watched the detective stare at the ground until he finally sat, as well.

"Nothing helps." Innis handled the feather in his fingers. "That poor little girl. Makes no sense."

They each took a moment to calm themselves. Roman began the conversation anew. "What happened to your other partner?"

The question snapped Innis back to the reality of the interrogation room. "What do you mean?" he asked Roman.

"I remember that guy," indicating Turner with a pointed finger at the mirror. "But that's not who you were working with before. What happened to the other guy?"

Innis stared for a moment and then answered. "The other guy, as you call him, was Detective Renaldo Jackson." Innis went silent again.

Roman studied him to try to understand the irritation, interrupted by silence, and then a blank stare from the officer.

"Did he die?" Roman asked.

It was troubling for the detective to admit, but he said, "Yes. How did you know?"

"I've seen the look before. You never know when someone on the street is going to be killed or just drop dead from some disease. But you can always tell someone is gone, when you ask the question. It's always the same look. Like they're looking at someone who is right in front of them. They can see them, but no one else can. It's a dead stare."

Roman stopped because he saw the detective's eyes wander as if he were looking for something, or maybe someone.

"I'm sorry. How's your sister?" Roman continued.

Detective Innis glared at his adversary and thought he had great gall to ask him any personal questions, but he answered anyway. "She's doing okay. She's married. Has three kids, but Monique was her first. I thought she was going to kill me. It was as if she was more angry with me than you." He corrected himself, "Than the Feathermen."

Despite his guilt or his hatred of Roman, he could not deny his connection to Roman. They were enemies, yet who else could understand the gang life but another who lived the same life? His partners knew about gangs and their behavior, but didn't really understand them and their choices. He was one of the few cops who understood the life and the language. At times, he wanted to talk about his old life to someone who knew. The man sitting before him knew. He had to shake his head and smile because he recognized the irony.

"What's so funny?"

"How life turns," Innis said.

"It turns quickly, very quickly." Roman was thinking of his own life.

"My grandmother would correct my mother all the time about that. She, my mother, would say how quickly time flies. My grandmother would answer, 'only if you don't pay attention.' My grandmother was the only person I ever heard talk like that. She had peace. In all this mess, she had peace. Yeah, she was something."

"How do you think she got her peace?"

"She'll tell you, God. There was a song she sang all the time. *This Joy I Have.*"

Roman completed the sentence of the song, "'The world didn't give to me. This peace I have, the world didn't give it to me.'"

"You a church man?" Innis asked.

"Aren't we all? I was dragged to church every Sunday and sometimes on Wednesdays."

"Yeah, how about those Wednesdays? I never did get the point. Once a week is enough, at least, for a kid."

"But it stayed in your head, didn't it?"

Detective Innis recognized he was engaged in a conversation, not an interrogation. For a brief moment he saw Roman as a person, a good person. The dynamic changed, so he asked, "Why did you leave the mission?"

"I was bored."

"So you just left your stuff and got out?"

"Yeah."

"And you didn't tell anyone."

"There was no need to. It was a freedom walk, a power walk, a declaration."

"You don't think it was rude? I mean, to just leave, don't talk to anyone, don't thank anyone? Seems like a cheap way to say fuck you."

Roman didn't have an answer, so he just shrugged.

"Do you know something?" the detective asked him.

"What do you mean?"

"Do you know something about Graham's death?"

"No." He scowled back at his interrogator.

"But you knew Graham."

"You know that already. Listen, there is nothing I can tell you," Roman tried to convince Innis.

"You know something. Maybe you don't know you know it, but you know something."

"Well, that means I still can't help you."

"Do you want to help me?"

The question made Roman feel uncomfortable. He used to play poker, and the inexperienced players had a look or gesture which expressed how confident they were with the cards they held. This particular question made him feel he might be showing he was withholding information. Then, again, bluffing was a big part of the game. Was the detective bluffing or not? Roman called his bluff.

"I'll give you all the help you need," Roman answered.

Detective Innis leaned back in his chair and smiled. Roman was sure this was another ploy. Of course, he wanted to ask if the smile was an indication of his distrust. They were in the game, and Roman's response was to remain calm and unresponsive. His face remained frozen. He was being read and he was determined to present a blank page.

"Featherman, it's over," Innis said. When Roman didn't

respond, he repeated himself. "It's over between you and me. We're not gang bangers, anymore. It may seem strange, but we are on the same side, now. We have to let it go. My mother used to tell me that all the time. 'Let it go, baby.' I used to be full of anger and revenge."

"Used to be." Roman wasn't sure the detective was being sincere. "What made you change?"

"A lot of things. The death of my niece started the change. Nothing I was doing was worth that. My mother and grandmother would tell you it was prayer."

"Can't argue with that."

"Oh, I used to, though. I would come home to find mother praying for me. I would pass by her room and see her dancing and praying in tongues. It would scare me, at first. I remember the first time I went to a church where they prayed like that. I went because I was trying to get in some girl's pants, so when she invited me, I went. I didn't know what I was in for. It was the longest church service of my life. People would get up and dance. They started speaking a crazy language, and the music had them in a fever. And every time I thought they would stop, the music started up again. I swear one song must have lasted thirty minutes."

"Did you get in her pants?"

"You kidding me? I was through with her, when she started speaking in tongues. She scared me. I couldn't wait to get out of the place. Then wouldn't you know, my mother joins a church just like it, and she starts speaking in tongues."

"My grandmother told me I was marked. She told me God was not gonna leave me alone. 'He gone hound you, 'til you surrender,' she would say. I guess she was right," Roman related.

"What are you saying? Are you a believer, now?"Innis wanted to know.

"I'm not sure," Roman replied. "But God keeps showing up. Sometimes I feel hounded. Are you a believer?"

The detective had to think a moment. He told people he believed in God, but he was not sure he manifested his belief. He didn't really talk about his faith. He didn't attend church regularly, so what could he answer? "Yeah, I guess I am."

"You don't sound convinced," Roman challenged.

"Neither do you. You ready to get out of here?"

"Yes."

"I will find your friend's killer."

"I hope you do."

The two men stood up and headed for the door. Innis opened the door and they entered an empty dimly-lit room. It was the observation room for those who wanted to listen in on the interrogation.

"You were right. It was just me and you," Roman said.

"I've changed," Innis said.

As they went into the hallway, Roman left with a parting remark, "Must be that hound dog."

Detective Innis responded with a shrug. He watched Roman walk down the hallway to the elevator. He felt a fondness for him. The man before him was trying his best to walk tall, but life was a heavy burden on his slumped shoulders. He was a survivor and Detective Innis admired his ability to continue day to day. This man never gave up, which caused the detective more pain. His partner gave up, and this man continued. It didn't make sense.

He watched the man disappear into the elevator and when the door closed, he walked into another room. Inside, Detective Turner stood over another man who sat in front of a monitor. The monitor displayed a live picture of the interrogation room his partner had just exited. Turner looked at Innis and said, "You've changed?"

"I have, but I'm still a cop," Innis said, and he closed the door.

Chapter 9

It was day three of my search for Graham's girl. Being interrogated by cops was not my favorite thing. They always seem arrogant. Was it because I was homeless or because they had a badge? It didn't really matter, I don't like cops. Even though they were kind enough to house Tiger while they harassed me, they always seemed to play mindless games. I picked up the dog from the police kennel. He seemed so happy to see me. I could not return the same emotion. If anything, I was loyal, though. Maybe that's what the dog sensed in me. I guess dogs can sense intangibles like love and loyalty.

As I walked, I tried to think of all the places she would go. She wasn't in the jungle and she wasn't at the usual sidewalk "cafes," as we called them. The cafes were the places where many homeless people congregated. They were usually in front of buildings, such as the library or office buildings, after they closed for the night. My best thought was, she found shelter in a home. My worst thought, she was dead.

My walk was not the usual wandering, but had purpose. Purpose was the key to life, I thought. Purpose made me feel important. Purpose was clothed in hope and hope gave me life. I remember my father telling me something about purpose and hope. Something about their being twins or something like that.

Though I was strolling leisurely, I studied every alley, every hallway, and every apartment building entrance. Where else could this woman go? Another hour and the sun would be completely settled in for the night.

The pedestrian traffic thinned to a few people walking the streets, along with me. The work day officially ended. I crossed the street with a young woman who made a quick detour halfway into our crossing, into a coffee shop catty-corner from me. When I reached the other side of the street, three young men were approaching the same corner and would have passed me had they continued, but they turned the corner and were now behind me, by about twenty feet.

My street paranoia was returning. A moment ago, these young men were chatting it up. Now they seemed to be whispering. I sensed trouble and I hoped I was wrong. My fears increased and, as they closed the distance between us, their actions confirmed my suspicion. Tiger was growling. The sound was so low, it was almost as if he were talking under his breath, as if he were cussing them out. At least I learned that much from him over the years. He barked when he was happy; his little tail would wag so fast it shook his whole rear.

Tiger was cautious now. He was sending a warning and, as the boys came up to me, his growls grew louder.

"What kind of dog is that?" one of them asked.

I didn't want to answer. I knew they didn't care, but I said, "I don't know."

The same boy continued to tease. "You don't know? Is that your dog?"

I wasn't in the mood. "Look, son, don't worry about me. I'm not looking for any trouble."

"You think we're looking for trouble? I just asked the name of your dog, that's all. Now I'm thinking it's not your dog. You steal it?"

Tiger's growls grew more intense, so I picked him up and it seemed to be what he needed. The growling stopped.

"Yes, it's my dog," I insisted.

Another of the boys asked, "How come you don't know its name."

"Did I say I didn't know its name?" It was not a good idea to man up against three guys, but sometimes instinct will overtake a person. I heard of the fight or flight phenomenon, but it seemed this situation was headed for a fight. I could not imagine a flight scenario.

My question raised the stakes, and the leader, the one who started the conversation, pushed me into the alley. I could have resisted, but I didn't. I was trying to keep the dog from doing anything more to antagonize these three.

"Come on, you guys. This can't be that much fun. Little dog, and old man. Where's the challenge in that?"

The leader backed me up against the alley wall. I thought of him as a boy, but we were the same height and he glared at me. Maybe he was trying to prove his manhood. Maybe they were looking all along for someone to intimidate, and I was a good candidate. I put Tiger on the ground and he snapped at the young man. The young man snapped back, kicking Tiger hard enough to slide him a few feet.

The young people used a term about flashing. At this moment I understood the concept. In an instant, in a flash, I saw nothing, but I responded with a punch to the young man's jaw. I never planned it. I just wanted to leave, but the damage was done, the boy was on the ground for a brief moment. I'm sure he was in as much disbelief as I was, at how the situation had escalated to this point. The challenge was real and these three were armed to end it. One of them pulled a knife, but the leader wouldn't let him use it.

Tiger was up for a fight, but when he snapped again at the pant leg of the leader, he was kicked so hard, he yelped. The sound was heartbreaking. I could tell he was hurt this time, since he was motionless, on the ground.

The leader's gaze on me was uninterrupted. "Does your dog bite?" he said, recalling an old vaudeville joke.

The three laughed, and I wanted to hit him again. I was caught in a cat and mouse game. They were intent on hurting me and if I struck him once more, it would not have made a difference. When I was younger, I would not have given a thought to three boys. Decades later, the odds had grown from three to one, to ten to one. I was about to be walloped, yet I had no fear. I guess this was the moment my grandmother told me about. She spoke of death regularly, and I didn't like it. It scared me, but my grandmother said there was nothing to fear. When she died, she seemed to be smiling.

Here I was, facing death, but I wasn't smiling. I wasn't afraid, either. I wondered if this was the moment my Nana Fay told me would come. The battering began, but I was not one to be beaten without a vigorous retaliation. My intentions and emotions were not enough. The three boys were eager to hurt me. I fell to the ground and the pounding continued, until a shout ended the assault.

I had heard the voice before. The person tried again, "Hey!" but the sound was not clear, though understood. When I looked to see who came to my rescue, I understood the muffled words. It was Seal. Though he was deaf, he could speak a little. Most of his speech was very difficult to understand, so he chose to sign or write.

Seal dismounted from his bicycle and approached us in the alley. It was the break for me to see what happened to Tiger. He had recovered, but watched from a distance. I didn't blame him. I had enough, too.

The three boys were swollen with testosterone. They were willing to take on anyone, and another damaged man was just another opportunity to mark their manhood and their territory. Seal approached, and the boy with the knife lunged toward him, knife raised. It seemed to happen in an instant—Seal grabbed his wrist and twisted it so it seemed the boy stabbed himself in his own torso. I was in as much shock as everyone else. The boy slowly slumped to the ground with his own hand on his own knife, embedded in his side. Finally his hand fell away as he hit the ground.

The only person not surprised was Seal. He stood in anticipation of the remaining two boys' onslaught. Suddenly, the odds were reduced to an even match. I stood up and attacked the leader. As with most bullies, he had very little defense. He was not used to defending himself. His purpose in life was to wreak havoc on the weak. He was an arrogant predator, never suspecting there was always a bigger and smarter predator to come. One day he would be the prey, and apparently it was today.

We tussled, but experience will always trump youth. I wanted him to run away, so I never really hit him. I just threw him from side to side, but he would not quit, which was his mistake. He came at me again and I could see his defeat in the making.

When I played basketball, I always saw the play developing before in happened. I could still see it, but I was certainly too slow to take advantage of the opportunity to drive into the hole which wasn't there, but would soon be open. He came and I side-stepped and pushed his extended arm. It twisted him around and there his face was there for the taking. I hit him, and he was unconscious before he hit the ground. Even then I wanted to catch him, before he struck the cement, but I wasn't fast enough. I really didn't want him to break his neck in the fall.

I wondered how Seal was doing with the last boy. Just as I turned, I saw Seal spin and kick the boy in the back of the head. It was brutal and full of vengeance and final. The last young man lay on the ground.

Seal and I walked through the bodies. I went to the boy with the knife in his side. I was relieved to see he was breathing, but in obvious pain. He looked at me like a tranquilized animal. His eyes followed me, while his body remained still. I felt sorry for him, yet angry. I'm sure he thought I would harm him further, but I had seen more death than his, and I wanted to see no more. Certainly I was not about to cause it.

I felt a hand on my shoulder and turned to see Seal beckon me away from the mayhem. He seemed so calm and unaffected by the altercation. When I asked him what he was up to, he responded in sign. I understood the pastor sent him to look for me.

"Where did you learn to fight like that?" I asked. Seal signed something, but he could tell that I had no idea what he was trying to say. He pointed to his belt and then did some martial arts moves with his hands.

"You know karate?" He vigorously shook his head and hands to indicate "no."

"What?" I responded.

He signed again, but I didn't know what he meant. He shook his hands as if to say never mind. He was right, it wasn't important right now.

He indicated he wanted me to follow him. I couldn't, I told him, and he frowned. I gave him a limited explanation. "I have some business to take of," I said.

My answer didn't sit well with him. Now he wanted answers. "What?" he signed.

"Seal, don't tell the pastor you found me. Okay?"

He looked so puzzled. I knew I was confusing him, but I was not about to let anyone know my plans. If I wouldn't tell the cops, I sure was not going to tell anyone else.

"Trust me, Seal. Trust me. I'll be back, I promise."

I could tell he wasn't convinced, and I just placed my hand on his shoulder. "I promise," I reassured him.

Seal was stuck in thought, then walked over to his bike. He motioned for me to follow him. He offered his bike to me. "You sure?" I asked him.

He was sure. He signed for me to take care of myself. I told him I would; he took one look at the three boys and quickly walked away. His quick steps became a trot and he disappeared.

I lifted the bike away from the wall and looked at the boys. I called to Tiger, who was smart enough to stay away from the fray. He little legs jogged toward me, but when he approached the three bodies, he hesitated. I encouraged him and he braved his way through the mess. They were moving, though slowly.

As I lifted the dog up, for a short moment I wondered whether or not I should help them. The quick answer was no, and I left.

It wasn't easy peddling and carrying the dog and my backpack, so I put him on his leash and let him run alongside. Every once in a while I would look down to see Tiger looking at me, seemingly asking for help. I made a pit stop and sat against a building. I took some dog food from my pack and put it in a paper bowl for him. He ate as if he were starving. Maybe he was.

I knew he would want some water, eventually. After Tiger's snack we walked to the corner store and I bought a bottle of water. I took some money with me when I left the mission and used it to buy my one meal for the day. I was resentful of using some of my money to buy this dog some water, but we shared. I put some in his bowl, the rest for me to guzzle.

If I could just find someone to watch the dog, I was sure I had a better chance of finding Graham's woman in a quicker time. I felt like Clark Kent, when Lois asks if she should go with him to some disaster. "No, Lois, I can do it faster by myself." She, too, looked like a lost puppy when he rejected her.

A couple of days with Tiger, and I was learning his habits. After every meal he wanted to poop. We walked along the curb, he sniffed every inch until he was satisfied the location was appropriate. He did his business and those passing by looked at me to pick up his mess. I wasn't prepared for that, so I had to tolerate their looks of disgust. I was used to it, anyway. Being homeless for three years was excellent training ground for Humiliation 101.

Tiger seemed to be content. I took a protein bar from my backpack and we started again on my quest. I felt I had looked everywhere for the woman. As we walked, daylight gave way to dusk. There was little reason to continue looking for her at night. When I first became homeless, I was afraid to sleep at night. I didn't know the secure places, so to sleep in the park during the day was best for security. Was she doing the same? Was she holed up somewhere passing away the night, without sleep? I had to stop thinking about her and find a place for us. Us—that was a strange way to think of me and the dog, but I guess it is what we were—a couple. Better than nothing, I guess.

We passed by a construction site. Several trucks and construction materials were enclosed in a chain-link fence. It was easy enough for a fifty-one year-old man to scale. I made the decision to sacrifice the bike. I never did like them, anyway. They slowed me down. Of course, I had to figure out how to get the dog across. I walked along the fence and found a small opening. It was apparent someone had pried it open. Someone might be in there, but it was no concern for me. It was a large site and there was room for many. There was also the possibility of a guard dog inside, as well.

I coaxed Tiger through the opening, but he wanted to come back through. I decided to climb the fence first, and then he easily followed. I felt like a ninja. I remained still, hugging the dog, listening for a dog or another person or anything to give me warning. There was no sound, no warning. All I had to do was pick a spot and bed down for the night. I chose a dump truck. I crawled beneath the truck and rested my head on my backpack. It wasn't warm, but so quiet. The dog seemed to get comfortable more quickly than I did. He waited for me to stop shuffling and once I did, he nestled against me without any trouble or thought.

I wasn't sleepy. What was there for me to do? I really wanted to start my search again. The pastor was doing me a favor when he sent Seal to look for me. He could have reported me to the cops. Surely he would send them after me when Seal returned without me. Which would mean, at most, I had another day. I couldn't avoid them and search for her at the same time.

Sleepy or not, I stared at the bottom of the dump trunk and marveled at the workmanship. I had no idea what I was looking at, but the tubing, wires and enclosed boxes all seemed to be in their proper places. The dried dirt on the under-shell could not hide the genius of the design. I tried to follow the paths of metal channels and wires, but I could not come to a conclusion as to the purpose of anything thing I saw.

I thought of my father and me, and how he tried his best to teach me about cars. He could fix just about anything on his car. If he couldn't fix it, he had friends who could. Looking at the aggregation above me, I had some regrets I was not interested in what my father tried to teach me. I didn't really need it now, but I felt so inadequate, since I could not name any part.

Studying the under-parts of the truck was enough to relax me and put me to sleep. It was like counting sheep. I counted and followed the pipes until they led me to my quiet place. All was right with the world.

When one is tired, it's easy to fall asleep. It doesn't matter whether it's on a bed or on the ground. Sleep is king. It can overpower anything and certainly my present situation was no match for my body's desire to rest and recuperate. However, there is another force at work and that is the desire to survive. From the deepest sleep, there is a mental watchdog which surveys what cannot be seen, just senses, and that is what keeps me and my homeless friends on the alert. We are like birds. We may walk confidently, but we do so skittishly. We are always on the lookout for the predator. Yes, we are the prey.

I had two watchdogs and I could feel movement on my chest. At first, I thought I was dreaming, but as I became more conscious, I was aware Tiger had placed his two front paws on my chest. He was expressing himself, again, with his low growl. It meant danger. Once I grabbed him and brought him closer to me, he stopped. I turned my head from side to side to see if I could spot what captured his interest. I couldn't see anything. I listened more intently and I could not hear anything. Maybe Tiger was just as paranoid as the homeless. After all, he was a homeless dog.

It was a beautiful and peaceful view from beneath the truck. It was so still I could imagine I saw the rays of light move through the air. It was a clean yellow light from the street lampposts. I was surrounded by dirt, but the light was unaffected. It was pure and quiet.

At one point, though, I thought I noticed a shadow in the distance. Tiger must have seen it, as well, because his eyes fixed on it. I looked again and it was there, then it was gone and it re-appeared. I moved the dog to my side and his low growl started again. I had to investigate, so I put my finger to my pursed lips and quietly shushed him. To my surprise he listened. He must have heard the command many times from the Mayor.

I slowly rolled from under the truck, trying to maintain my eyes on the spot I last saw the shadow. I reasoned the person was not a security guard. A guard would have had a flashlight. So who was this person? Was this a person, at all? I looked back to the dump truck and saw Tiger lying on his belly, watching me. What a coward!

I returned my attention to the shadow. It wasn't there, so I listened for anything to give a clue. I squatted and looked around under the vehicles, but there was no movement. I wasn't convinced I was imagining some motion, so I stayed in position and watched. Tiger and I were one.

I heard a crunch in the dirt. Whatever was out there was stalking me, as much as I was stalking it. I was caught in another cat and mouse game. I just didn't know if I was the cat or the mouse. There was another crunch, and I was able to tell from which direction. It was my move, and I decided to crawl beneath a water truck to try to come from behind the noise. I knew I was creating a crunch of my own and the shadow was triangulating on me. It was a question of who was going to have the better strategy.

I stepped and crunched, stopped and listened. I repeated the pattern over and over. My stalker must have been doing the same, until I heard nothing for a while. Time passed long enough for me to question my reality. Did I hear someone or not? I waited long enough, so I stood up and waited again. I didn't want to psych myself into giving up to an imaginary friend, and I didn't want the shadow to become real. I was stuck in indecision. I couldn't move.

My stalker, on the other hand, declared himself. I knew what to do. I stayed still and listened as the slow pace of foot crunches came my way. My father told me once I was too impulsive. He told me I should learn to slow down. "Sometimes you need to sit still and let things come to you," he told me. As with so many things he said, it didn't make sense then, but on this night his wisdom played out right before me.

Fortunately, I was standing against a truck, so there was no need for me to move my feet. I leaned against the large truck and waited. It was in an awkward stance, but I made up my mind to remain still. Yes, patience is a virtue. The figure slowly emerged from the front of the truck and was slightly illuminated by the street lights. I was right. This person was not a security guard, which was a relief. We were just sharing the same real estate, but I didn't want to startle him. I was in another moment of indecision. Should I speak out or just wait for him to notice me?

It was becoming more obvious he didn't notice me. The body of the truck was so large, I was hidden in its shadow. I felt like a ghost, as he came closer. I decided it was time to step out and let him know I was here. As I did so, I whispered, "Hey."

We were finally aware of each other, but all my intentions were for naught. He elbowed my head into the side of the truck and I could feel myself falling, but I was not going to go down by myself. I grabbed his jacket and we fell together. It was all we did together. On the way down, we wrestled for the position best suited to conquer the other. As we fell, we rolled beneath the truck and continued to wrestle.

"Calm down," I struggled to get out of my mouth, but he wouldn't listen. Didn't this fool understand we were the same? We were two vulnerable homeless guys trying to get a decent night's sleep. There was no need to fight each other, but he wouldn't stop. I had enough power to throw him away from me. I quickly rolled from under the vehicle to tackle him, before he recovered. As I threw myself on him, I heard a quick hiss and my eyes began to burn immediately.

"Oh, my God." The pain was mounting, especially in my left eye, but I was not going to let him get the best of me. I kept lunging and grabbing until we rolled under the truck, again. I was fighting him and fighting to keep my eyes open. I was in the most vulnerable position. My assailant used our rolling momentum, and he was on top of me.

With my eyes open, they were so full of tears, I could barely make out anything, but I did notice the glint of metal coming toward me. I wasn't quick enough to swat it away, so my only option was to turn my head, to avoid the weapon. I wasn't quick enough. I felt a sharp pain on my left cheek. I was losing this battle and I was prepared to do anything, anything at all.

The action was so fast I couldn't think. Every move was by instinct only, and in one motion I opened my eyes and punched the face of my assailant. His head hit the bottom of the truck, making a loud thud and he stopped. The wrestling match was over. He fell on my chest and didn't move. I was too concerned with my eyesight to notice much more. My tears were flooding my face and I had to choose pushing the body away from me or wiping my eyes. I chose the first option, and the unconscious limp body rolled away from me.

"Sweet Jesus," was my mantra. I didn't know any other words to mutter. I don't know how long it took for the Mace to wear off, but I was able to keep my eyes open longer and longer. I looked up to see Tiger looking inquisitively under the truck.

"Stupid dog," I chuckled.

I turned to my unconscious adversary and felt sorry for him. We were not really enemies, we just found ourselves in the same cage, and each of us gave in to the paranoia of the streets. If I lost to him, would I be alive? I think it was best, for both of us, I was the victor. I was the merciful gladiator. I was so gracious, I pulled the body under the truck with me and I was able to view the face.

Tiger began to growl again and I shushed him. He minded me by lying down. His little nose was so inquisitive. I rested against one of the huge tires and watched the dog sniff the unresponsive frame.

"Come here, ya dumb dog," I commanded. "She'll be okay," I told him, as the body began to stir. Tiger obeyed and came to me, resting against me, and we watched her together.

It took her a few minutes to clear the cobwebs from her head and when she did, she was well aware of what happened and where she was. Her recollection startled her and she partially sat and looked around for me.

"Relax. I'm not going to hurt you." The statement didn't make sense, as I looked into her dazed face, so I modified it to say, "I won't hurt you, again."

I guess I must have sounded convincing because after she rubbed her head, she stared at me and then laid her head on the dirt. I heard a muffled sigh and she looked out into the city. I bet she was going through the same moment of indecision as I. Did she want to leave or stay?

I tried to calm her fears, even more. "Do you remember me?"

I was sure she should. I walked Graham and her to their camp the night he died, but she didn't answer. The few times I saw her, I noticed she never talked. Maybe she couldn't talk. I decided not to press the point. I guess it is what she needed. Actions speak louder than words, they say, and my actions said she could rest her head and close her eyes until her cloudy head was fully cleared. Besides, I fulfilled my goal. I found Graham's woman. We could both rest.

Of course, now that I found her, or more accurately, she found me, I didn't know what I was going to do. She made it clear she was able to take care of herself. Maybe it was all I needed to know. She was okay. Maybe all she needed was to understand I was not there to abuse her.

The stories of women being abused on the street always turned my stomach. Probably those stories were my incentive to find her. Of course, I didn't really know her, but I was doing it for the man I knew—Graham. And I didn't really know him, but at least we had conversations. He was kind to me and I liked him. There were a lot of people out here I cared very little about. Some were so nutty, it was no wonder they were homeless. Some were only looking for their next hit of their preferred drug. Marijuana was at the top of the list, but oxycontin and crack cocaine were not too far behind.

Regardless of their reason for being on the streets, the women were in double jeopardy. All of us lived at the edge of civilization. We had our own culture and cliques and rules, but the women were not a part of it. It was definitely a man's world, on the street. As civilized women voiced their rights, the homeless woman had no voice. She was the least powerful woman on the planet.

The war on women was a cute political phrase, until one witnessed the assault and battery of homeless women. Birth control was not an issue. Rape was the issue. Abortion rights were not the issue. Discussions regarding the rights of a fetus were muted against the right of a battered woman of the street.

Pregnancy was not an issue. Few could become pregnant

when their period was erratic or not at all. The stress of the street altered their bodies, as if nature understood this was not an environment to conceive anything, other than hope. Giving birth to hope was the great accomplishment, and many women were barren.

I understood her attraction to Graham. He was her protection and for now, she accepted me as her savior. If I wasn't against her, I was for her. I couldn't say I was for her, but I could say I would protect her, for the night. She was safe and whatever debt I felt toward Graham was paid.

Tomorrow I could return to HOPE, if I was still on their roster after four days of absence. I wondered if Seal told them anything. I doubted it. During my time at the mission, he was a trustworthy guy. He didn't say much, not only because he couldn't, but because he believed in action. Maybe it's what his disability taught him. Being a man of his word meant living an exemplary life. I used to ask how he survived on the street. He demonstrated his survival skills very well. His disability was probably his best defense. No one expected much from him. His primitive speech was disarming, and I'm sure he liked it that way. His motto: Speak ugly and carry a big foot.

I watched Graham's girl, noticing she would not look my way. She showed no gratitude. I was looking for her, but she really didn't know who I was or that I had just accomplished my duty. I could have molested her, so she could have, at the very least, thanked me for respecting her. My anger toward her response to me was minimized as I thought I heard her sniffle. I didn't mean it, but I probably hit her in the nose. I hoped I didn't break it.

I moved closer to her with caution and she looked me in the eye, as if to say I was not welcomed. "Are you okay?" I asked.

She did not answer, so I asked her again. She lay back on the ground and turned away from me. This didn't turn out as I intended. In fact, the situation escalated as her sniffling became louder. She stifled her crying to the best of her ability.

"Look, I'm sorry," I said. "I really didn't mean to hurt you." She allowed me to touch her shoulder, and I tried my best to explain myself.

"Believe it or not, I was looking for you. I'm really not going to hurt you. I've been out here for three days looking for you."

My confession didn't seem to affect her. She was able to control her crying, until all I could detect was a moment when she gulped some air.

"Hey, tomorrow you can come with me and I'll get you a room at the mission, where I stay." Again, she stayed curled up, not caring about anything I said to comfort her.

I gave up. I slid back and sat against the tire. The dog looked at me for answers. I just shrugged at him. I swear the dog was human. My answer appeared to satisfy him. He looked ather one time and then curled against me for a long-awaited rest. He glanced at me as if to say, "Let's get some sleep."

I was in full agreement and in response, I said, "I hear ya. Go to sleep. I gotcha, dog."

He seemed to understand and he rolled over on his back, exposing his belly for me to rub. The idea of massaging his bare belly was an obnoxious thought. It felt pornographic, as if I were about to engage in what seemed to me like some sort of aberration. I turned my head away and said, "Ain't gonna happen, dog."

I looked over at Graham's woman and she was still. I hoped she was all right, but I wasn't about to disturb her again. I felt bad when I thought of punching her lights out. I never meant it, it was instinctive. Luckily she decided to stay with me, for now. My plan was to get her to HOPE and then I would be done with this self-assignment. I wanted, very much, to be done with it. Looking for this woman was a pain. It wasn't her fault, but I would otherwise never have been a part the fight earlier. It was fortunate Seal showed up.

As I licked my wounds, I was getting angry with her. I was sympathetic when I thought of Graham. Right now, I could feel some stiffness coming over me. I was fifty-one and I was in two fights today. My thoughts were racing through every kick, punch, and grab. I was exhausted in mind and body. Tiger was asleep and the woman seemed to be resting. It was my turn. The two of them were a thorn in my side. Tomorrow would be a better day. She would be safe. The dog would find a home, and it didn't matter to me if it was the pound. My obligations would be over and it was enough to put me to sleep.

My sleep was interrupted, again, with the idea of being caught by the construction workers returning to their work site in the morning. Being homeless sucks. I was stuck in a revolving and irritable cycle of sleep and consciousness. My sleep periods were deep. So deep, I was afraid I might miss the opportunity to save myself from any intruder. My awake states were so groggy, I felt drunk. Enough was enough.

I noticed the first hint of daylight. It was time to move on. Tiger was already awake. He understood the routine. The woman was in the same position as last night. I started to think she was injured more than I originally thought. I crawled over to her and touched her shoulder. She didn't move. Oh hell, I thought, she was in real trouble. I came to rescue her and ended up killing her. My father once told me the very thing you fear, is the thing you cause.

I was afraid to get the answer, but I slowly turned her over. Her eyes were closed. Why didn't I just mind my business. First, I was questioned about Graham. I was sure to be suspected of killing this woman, too.

A man's imagination can take him where no man has gone before. My thoughts were taking me into another universe, but I was brought back to reality when she opened her eyes. She looked at me, but her stare was lifeless, no emotion, at all. I don't think I showed it in my face, but I was so relieved.

"We have to go," I instructed her. I moved away from her and she sat up. She followed me to get my backpack and we climbed the fence. I was right. The bicycle was gone. I asked if she was hungry and she said yes, which was the first word I ever heard her say. We walked to the nearest fast food restaurant and I ordered some breakfast for us.

As I sat across from her, she quietly ate her breakfast sandwich. She would glance at me occasionally. I didn't know if she was angry with me, grateful, or numb from our eventful evening together. I guess wisdom does come with age. When I was married and my wife wouldn't talk to me, I was angry. Today, I was smart enough to leave Graham's girl alone.

My identity for her was Graham's girl. I had to change that, at least. "What's your name?"

"Talitha."

"Talitha?" I repeated. She looked at me and then continued to eat. Yeah, regardless of what she looked like, her name screamed her ethnicity. She was black. Jesus!

Chapter 10

The heavy rain was subsiding and it was easier to see the scenery through the car's windshield. As Greg watched the rain flow down the glass, the scene before him became clearer.

"These times have sometimes been the best times of my life," he said.

Lois was in the passenger side of the car and she watched her man without comment. She watched him stare in the distance. They had been sitting in the car for the past twenty minutes with minimal conversation, and she was unsure whether or not she should interfere with his silence. It was a hard day for him. They came to this location directly from the funeral of Detective Renaldo Jackson. He didn't want to stay for the repast.

"That was some service," Greg tried to say in a cheerful voice.

Lois recognized he was trying to come out of his funk. It was small talk, but it was more than he had been willing to do all day.

"Yes, it was beautiful."

"How many funerals have you been to?" he asked.

She didn't expect the question, but she managed to answer. "I guess about three or four. I was supporting friends. I haven't had to go to a funeral for a family member, yet."

"How did you feel?"

She had to think again. How could she answer such a question? The only answer she could give was so obvious, so why did he ask? Maybe she was just thinking too much about it. The simplest answer should be the best.

"I was sad, of course." Lois tried her best to make her tone as calm and non-threatening, as possible. "I mean, everybody was sad, but I guess the family members were taking it harder than I was."

Continuing to look out the windshield, Greg responded. "I remember when my niece died. She was only three."

"I remember you telling me a little. It's hard to get over that."

"It's even harder when you know who did it. Well, I don't know, but I know."

"You talking about that homeless guy?" Greg answered by nodding his head.

"I don't really know if he did it, but his gang did. Besides, he has an alibi."

"What's that?"

"He was in the Navy. Isn't that ironic? He's defending this country, while his friends are killing people in this country. Funny. I don't get that."

"Didn't you say you were in a gang?" Her question made him finally look at her.

"No, I didn't mean it like that," she desperately tried to clarify.

"Yes, you did."

"You okay?"

It was a minimal smile, but he flashed it at her to reassure her he was okay, with her. Today was not a good day for smiling or anything, as far as he was concerned.

"No worries," he said. "It was a stupid question, anyway."

Lois wanted to agree, but it would have been rude. She was known to be heartless. As a member of the audio-visual team at the police station, she was characterized as arrogant and cold. She heard many co-workers whisper "bitch" in describing her. Of course they always said so as they walked away from her or thought she was out of earshot.

Despite her defenses, this man slipped through. He never seemed to be interested in her, and for the two years since she had been transferred to her present position, she was not interested in him. They interacted, regularly, on many cases. It was always business with him, unlike his partner, who was always trying to get to know her. She never told him about Renny's advances, though it was well known Detective Jackson was a flirt, a major flirt. Detective Innis was different. He always seemed to be on a mission and had no interest in anyone. There were no rumors about him. The women in the department had no gossip to offer about him. He was clean. His bland behavior must have been the key to their relationship. They didn't need each other, they wanted each other.

"You never told me much about it."

"You mean about my niece? I thought I did."

"You told me she was shot—"

"Murdered."

"Yes, murdered, but you never told me the details. I didn't think you wanted to talk about it."

"You were right."

"Do you want to talk about it now?"

"Every time I go to a funeral, or even hear about one, I want to talk about it. Renny knows the story—*knew* the story."

"Is that who you used to talk to?"

"Yes. He was younger, but he was cool. I guess when you're with someone every day, you can't help but get close to him. He would talk to me, too. I know his life like it was mine. Sometimes I felt like his father and sometimes like his brother. Today, I know I was his friend."

"I could tell you guys were more than partners. You never talked about personal stuff, at least in front of me, but it was the look in your eyes."

"Now that's funny. What are you trying to say?"

"Nothing bad. I forgot the name of the poem, but there's a line that reads, 'A look that's meant for one, but everyone can see,' or something like that."

"You make it sound like we were lovers."

"No! But when you think about it, friends and lovers are the same, but with different boundaries."

"You can be creepy, sometimes," he said to Lois.

"Yeah, I heard that one before, too. I can't explain it, it's just the way people act around each other. Friends act different around each other than co-workers."

"Renny said the same thing about us."

"What!" she remarked with amusement. "What did he say?"

"He told me I wanted you."

"Really? What did he see?"

"Probably the same thing you saw. You wouldn't have let me into your world unless you already knew I wanted to come in."

"Yeah, you were knocking."

"And you let me in because you wanted me there."

Lois smiled because she knew he was telling the truth. She could only answer with, "Whatever."

She returned to the forgotten subject. "Do you want to talk about your niece?"

"Kye. Short for Kia. She was so cute, and she just loved her Uncle Greg. She put me out of work for three days, once."

"No, she didn't."

"Oh, yes, she did. I had never been out. No injury, no illness, nothing."

"What did she do?"

"Scratched my eye. We were just playing, and out of nowhere she swiped her hand across my face. Man, that thing hurt for days. I had an eye patch for three days. I was miserable. I couldn't do anything. All I wanted to do was take pain medication."

Greg was silent for a moment as he recreated the incident in his mind, then he continued. "She was so cute. She was going to be the one who changed the family. She was going to go to college. She was going to be the one who left the neighborhood. She was the one who would end the poverty in our family. I guess it was unrealistic to put all of that on a baby, but we did."

"We all do that with our kids, don't you think? They're the future."

"Yeah. She never made it to the future."

"It's ironic. You became what you wanted from her."

"I would rather she did it, though."

"I know, baby. I just want you to know, I'm proud of you."

"I wasn't even there, the night she died. I was off with some woman. I don't even remember her name. For some unknown woman, I lost my life. My mother used to play this song about some man who lost everything because of a woman. What was the name of that song?"

Lois watched him think. Greg was with her, now he was gone again. Without warning, he returned singing a tune. "Reverend Lee, he went to the water. He was hotly pursued by ol' Satan's daughter."

He stopped. "You remember that?" Lois indicated no, shaking her head.

Greg started to recite the song. "This is a song about a man that thought he had it all together, but he soon finds out that he doesn't have it all together."

Lois' stare indicated she had no idea of the song and, more important, had no idea of how to respond. Greg thought it was unfair of him to speak so cryptically to her.

"I'm talking kind of crazy, huh?"

"Not crazy. I just don't understand."

"I thought I had it all together. Then, someone dies and I know I don't have it all together. I want someone to blame, someone to hurt. I want revenge. That's crazy, I know. After all these years, all I want is revenge."

"Will you ever get it?"

"I don't know. Maybe. I don't know. Most of the time, I don't even consciously think about it, then someone dies. Someone close dies, and what is so hard for me, I couldn't help. I wanted to help Renny. I couldn't."

"You can't help everybody."

"I help people every day. I protect people. I catch murderers, and I think it helps. I even joined HD, because I wanted to help those who couldn't help themselves, like Kye. She couldn't help herself. I was supposed to help her."

"Why are you blaming yourself?"

"Funny, I didn't at the time, but you should have seen my sister's face. Kye was her life. My sister had no husband. Kye's father did what so many men do, he bailed. I took his place. I was the daddy."

Lois watched Greg's eyes fill. She had never seen him this emotional. He looked broken. She watched his shoulders drop, then his head. His lips quivered and she could tell he was trying to keep from melting into a full-blown cry.

"It's okay, babe," she said, trying her best to comfort him. It must have accomplished the opposite because his silent cry became audible, and she heard him repeat, "I'm sorry, Kye."

She decided to leave him to himself. There was no support she could offer, but to let him be, with his thoughts. What could she say to relieve him? It seemed to her a simple hug or rubbing his shoulders would be woefully inadequate, but she offered what she had. You can't give what you don't have, and at this moment she had her hand to massage his neck. She silently wept with him.

Right now he needed to wail, if he chose, and she would be there when he made it through to the other side.

She learned from her mother, there's nothing like a good long cry. Her mother advised her, after she broke up with her first boyfriend. "Honey," she said, "after a while, after all the talk, after all the anger, after everything, only one thing remains—crying. There's nothing like a long, good cry." She was right. It took her about two weeks after the breakup, but without warning she broke out in a cry which would have scared her mother had she been home.

Lois patiently waited, what seemed a long wait, but she could tell he was making his way through. First, he wiped his tears. He lifted his head and breathed deep and looked outside and scanned the scenery.

"I love the beach when it rains," Greg proclaimed. "The sky is so clear after a good rain. It smells good, and best of all, there is no one around. It's quiet."

"It's very peaceful," Lois added.

"Yes, very peaceful. I think that's my favorite word, peace."

"It's a good word. I like it, too," she replied.

They watched the sky and the beach together. They seemed to find each other in the silence. Greg felt closer to Lois. It was probably due to her accepting his vulnerability, but it had to be a better reason. With more thought, he recognized it was in the silence, following his emotional moment. Lois' silence said she accepted him. She never tried to console him or asked him to look at the brighter side of life. She let him be. She allowed him to figure out his situation and allowed him to find the answer. At a time such as this there were no answers, and Lois accepted the situation as it presented itself. She was perfect. Her personal side and her professional demeanor were so different.

In the office, she never appeared compassionate or caring. Life can throw curves when one is expecting a fastball. Lois was a curve. She was a slow curve which came so slowly, it was predictable, but like all curve balls, she suddenly did what was not expected. Greg swung his bat a long time ago and she dodged him, again and again. And just when he thought he struck out and the game was over, she allowed him to get a hit. He was never a good ball player, anyway.

He took his phone from his side and pointed it toward the beach and snapped a photo. They looked at it together and decided it was a poor representation of what they really were experiencing.

"Let's get out," Greg said. They walked the beach, and strangers, if there were any around, might have thought they were just married. He was in his suit and she was in a black and gray dress. It would never have occurred to anyone, seeing them now, they were coming from a funeral.

Greg took some pictures of Lois and she posed in any manner she pleased. She could be very playful, at times. Too bad it was only a camera phone, because some of her poses were on the level of a top model.

"You ever want to be a model?" he asked her. Her answer was an emphatic no, but she continued to play the role and he continued to play the photographer.

"Let's see them." Lois was referring to seeing the pictures. Greg scrolled through the photos and they critiqued each one. Then he scrolled to a picture of Renny.

"Awww, that's cute," Lois said. "When did you take that?"

"I didn't. He sent it to me."

"See, I knew you guys were lovers."

"Stop it!"

"Well, guys don't send pictures of themselves to other guys. Do they?"

"No.

"Well, then, what's up?"

"I don't know."

"Come to think of it, isn't that the photo found at his apartment. The one with the message on the back?"

Greg ignored her and studied the picture. "You're right, buddy. There is more." He wasn't speaking to Lois. He was addressing his friend.

"What do you mean?" she interrupted.

"He wrote it on the back of the photo. I guess he found out too late. There is more to life than money and all the other stresses out there. I wish he knew earlier."

Lois could only agree with a muffled grunt.

"Would it be crazy if I understood why he killed himself?" Greg posed.

"What do you mean?"

"Renny was so stressed out—financially, emotionally, mentally. He just couldn't seem to find any peace. Yeah, that word again. It's enough we dealt with thieves and murderers all day; then he had to go home and deal with a bad marriage. He never had enough money for anything. Carmen was high maintenance, still is. His daughter is like any kid, always needing more."

"I think he was kind of high maintenance, himself. He dressed pretty nice," Lois added.

"Yeah, he loved his clothes. Nothing but the best for him."

"Don't take this wrong, I'm just asking, okay? How did he do it? I mean, afford all of it?"

"He couldn't. He played with his credit cards, maxed them out. He did some moonlighting, he borrowed money, anything to keep his lifestyle going."

"You wouldn't have known it. He always seemed happy."

"The key word, *seemed*," Greg corrected. "More days than not, he was not happy. He couldn't keep up and yet he wouldn't give up. He kept trying to maintain rather than stop spending."

"What is it about money? What a powerful thing, don't you think?"

"Sometimes I can't figure out if it's good or bad. Everybody wants it and no one seems to be satisfied with what they have. Why do we always need to have more?"

"I think it has to do with self-esteem. People need to feel worthy, and things make them feel worthy. You need money to get things. That's what commercials are all about. They're meant to make you feel insecure. Do you have the right toothpaste or the right car, or whatever."

"Envy. That's what they create," he stated.

"Yes, they do." Lois wanted the change the subject. It seemed to be too gloomy. "What's he doing in the picture?"

As Greg looked at the picture again, it brought a smile to his face. "Yeah, he could be nuts, too." He studied it more and squinted as he put his face a little closer.

"What?" Lois asked. She figured he had seen something interesting in the picture.

"Just curious. It is kind of a crazy picture."

Lois turned the phone toward her and smiled as she studied it, as well. "What's he pointing to?"

She was referring to Renny's stance in the picture. He stood in front of a store window and had a smug look on his face. His right arm was out of view as he was using it to hold the camera at arm's length. His left arm was curled and he seemed to be using his thumb as a hitch-hiker would.

"Nothing. He's just being crazy."

"When did he take it?"

"I don't know, but he sent it to me about a day or so before he, uh, you know. I guess this is how he wanted me to remember him. He was a fun guy. He tried so hard to stay afloat, but he just couldn't. I wish I could have helped him. He was so far in debt, I couldn't help or didn't want to."

"Baby, don't feel guilty."

"Yeah I know. It was his life, but I was so much a part of it. I feel I could have helped to turn it around. I catch criminals, I protect good people from bad people, but I couldn't help my friend. If I had enough time, I could have helped him."

"I think you did. That's what the picture is about. He wanted you to remember him as the crazy guy, the fun guy. I don't think he wanted to you to remember the stress which brought him to his end. Maybe he didn't want you to remember the end, but he wanted you to remember him. You know what I mean?"

"I do." Greg looked at the photo again and smiled. "I guess he wanted me to remember our greatest case, too."

"How so?"

"I think that's the building where we found the human traffickers."

"Really? Let me see." She looked. "Oh, you mean the building in the reflection of the store window?"

"Yeah."

"Oh wait. This is not the same picture he left at his apartment."

"Not quite, but the same stupid pose. He was just standing in front of another building."

"What building?"

"I don't know, just some building. Why are you acting like a cop?"

"I don't know. It just seems weird."

"Lord, woman, can you stop for a little while?"

"Okay, okay." She grabbed his free hand and they walked back to the car. "You okay?"

Greg pulled her close to him. "I'm fine. Don't worry about me. I'm a simple guy. I don't want much, except you."

"Well, that's a lot," Lois jested.

"Ain't you conceited."

"What are you trying to say? I'm not a lot? Do you think I'm cheap?"

"Whoa, whoa, whoa. Don't go that far."

"Too late, and I took you with me."

"You shouldn't play with my emotions. I'm vulnerable right now."

"I'm sorry." Her attitude quickly changed at the thought of hurting Greg.

"Suckuh. I can play that game, too." He was playful again.

"Ooh, I hate you."

"Liar."

They finally reached the car, holding their shoes in hand. Inside, as Greg started the car, he noticed Lois was staring at him.

"What?"

"Nothing." She turned away, in an attempt to turn the conversation.

"Nothing," she repeated.

Chapter 11

A transit center is a homeless person's version of a spa. It has all the amenities one would want. Everything was available, as long as the cops would leave me alone. Right now it offered shelter from the rain.

Talitha, Tiger, and I sat in the station and waited for the rain to end. If the dog were any bigger, he would have called attention to us, but a small cute dog can be an asset sometimes. People don't mind. They walk by and smile at it, which translates to a smile toward us. It's like having a baby. A person can't be mad at a man with a baby.

Of course, I would rather the dog be somewhere else. A kennel or the pound would be just fine, but it was too late for that. Talitha and the dog were bonding already. He treated her like she was his best friend. Wherever she went, he followed. He lay in her lap every chance he got, and she encouraged him to do so at every opportunity.

The rain was slowing down and it wouldn't be long before we would be on our way to nowhere in particular, but we would have to move. The security guards or cops would eventually make us move. Some were compassionate, others were mean. I never did understand the mean ones. They would treat me as if they woke up to a roach crawling over their face. I was the roach, and they wanted to crush me for invading their personal space. For now, we were treated as if we were passengers waiting to board a train.

In the past two days I collected a dog and a woman. When I thought of it, my plan was the same for both. I needed to find someplace for them to stay. If the Mayor knew I left Tiger at the pound, he would be hurt. Talitha, on the other hand, did not have my allegiance, so I needed to get her off the street, soon. Sitting in silence and watching people was not advancing my cause, or hers.

"Looks like the rain has stopped." I didn't know what else to say. It was a stupid segue into a conversation with her, but it was better than anything. In the two days I had spent with her, I only knew her name and I wished I didn't know that. What the hell were her parents thinking? Maybe her father's name was … why bother? There was no possible combination of names to bring a family to Talitha. Maybe her momma took a syllable from every important family member she brought to mind during labor.

She looked up to confirm my statement about the rain and then turned her attention back to the paperback book she was reading. Now I understood my mother. She couldn't understand an ungrateful person. It was the only time I heard anger in her voice. She would go on and on with my father about how ungrateful someone at church seemed to be.

One name came into the conversation more than most. My mother did not like Sister Bowman. I thought she was a nice lady, but I learned to dislike her as a result of my mother's regular barrage of insults toward her. Once I asked my dad why she was so mad at Sister Bowman, but he didn't have a satisfactory answer for me. However, the smile on his face just before he answered told me he knew, but it was not my business. I learned to read faces in my childhood, since my parents would say little to me about a lot of things.

"Come on, let's go." It was a command to Tiger. He jumped from her lap without a thought. This dog was born to travel. The woman, on the other hand, slowly placed her precious book in her bag.

"I'll be right back." I think she looked at me, but her glance was so quick, she may have been talking to the dog. Of course he wanted to follow, but I had his leash in hand and he could only go so far. Like two lost puppies, we watched her enter the restroom.

The availability of bathrooms was another reason transit centers were a mecca for the homeless. I looked around to see if any cops were around. Since I didn't spot anyone, I took Tiger with me into the men's restroom. It was spacious inside with several stalls and one urinal meant to be used by several men at one time. It seemed unsanitary, but who was I to complain. I had not completely lost my standards for cleanliness, though I had lost the ability to maintain my standards, a long time ago. I lost my power, but not my dignity.

I brushed my teeth and washed my face. I was tempted to shave, but I put my razor back in my backpack. I wasn't sure I had the time. I might not have the opportunity to take a dump, so I stepped into a stall and was reluctant to sit on the seat. The metal toilet seat was meant to maintain cleanliness, but it screamed of filth. I had to take advantage of the facility, though I didn't like it.

As I sat, I spotted Tiger staring at me. That was all I needed — a stupid dog watching me take a crap. He was a dog, but I felt he understood what I was doing. I felt judged by a dumb dog, but I had no choice. I wondered if he was offended by the smell, but Tiger never showed a look of disgust. I didn't even see him sniff the air. I couldn't believe I was looking to an animal for acceptance. I finished my business and cleaned myself and exited the restroom to look for Lee. That's what I decided to call her. Talitha was just too ghetto for me.

She wasn't immediately in my line of sight. I looked around like a man searching for his lover arriving on the train. Where could she be? The logical place was the ladies' restroom and I went over to the door. I didn't know if I should call out to her or wait. I placed my hand on the door to crack the door and call to her. My plan was foiled when someone pulled at the door and she came out. She looked at me as if I were a pervert. I looked at her as if she were crazy. She walked away and Tiger followed her with the loyalty only a dumb animal could express.

"Lee," I called. She didn't respond and I called again. The third time was the charm, and she turned. Tiger turned with her and they both looked annoyed. I was ready to abandon both of them, right then.

I walked up to her and asked where she was going. She just shrugged, and Tiger looked at each of us asking if he could be in control and take us where he wanted to go. The three of us went out into the street and just walked. I glanced at her and noticed her hair, though still mostly covered with a cap, was still nappy. I guess by covering her unruly hair, she was trying to be more presentable. However, her hair wasn't the problem. Her attitude made her unattractive.

"What happened to Graham?" I asked her.

"He knew it was coming sooner or later."

"He knew what? That he was going to get killed?" I was amazed at her answer.

"He said so many times."

"Why would he think that?"

"Busybodies always end up busy or bodies."

"What does that mean?"

"He ended up a body."

It sounded so cold to hear Graham reduced to an impersonal body. This was his woman, and she spoke of him in such lifeless terms. I thought she liked the man, but maybe it was her coping mechanism of choice—detachment. Not that I could blame her. Life was a fragile enterprise, and it was more so on the street. Men and women died all the time—of disease, murders, and unknown causes, and they were referred to as bodies. The police referred to them as bodies. It was rare to have a homeless person referred to by name, especially when he or she was dead. Everyone seemed detached. It was protocol.

"Do you know how he was killed?"

"I heard he was knifed," Lee responded.

"The police wouldn't tell me."

"Why should they? You talked to them?"

"They rounded me up."

"And now you're asking me questions. You work for them?" she replied in an angry tone.

"No, no. I'm just looking out for you." I was insulted she would think of me as a pawn for the police.

"Me? Am I in trouble?" she asked.

"I don't know. I don't know why anyone would kill him. Do you?"

"Because they could, because he was in the way, or he smelled bad, or he looked lifeless, anyway." She itemized the reasons in a poetic and matter of fact manner.

"What do you mean about being a busybody?"

I waited for her answer as we walked, but she didn't respond. She just gestured she didn't know. I decided not to ask any more questions for now. I was beginning to feel like a cop and it felt dirty.

"I don't mean to be rude," I started, "but I think I should get you someplace safe."

"Safe. I've been on the street for four years. I'll be okay."

"I guess we're all okay, but don't you want to be better than okay?"

"I want to be better than a lot of things, but I'm not better than most."

Her statement hit me like a brick. It might have been honest, but it was so revealing of her self-worth. There was a freedom being out here again, but the drawback was the constant reminder of what I believed of myself. You can never go home again. It was a treacherous journey back to your past. It was never as remembered, smaller than you remembered, and never as satisfying as you remembered. At this moment, I was presented with my past, which had become my present. It made my head spin. I looked at Lee and feared for *my* life more than hers. I wasn't sure how to respond, but I knew I had to answer.

"That doesn't sound healthy." It was the only response which came to mind. It was ineffective and she knew it, as well as I did. She just looked at me from the corner of her eye and smirked. Sometimes I wished I could be as wise as the pastor or my parents. They always seemed to have the right answer to every situation. Right now, I didn't feel grown up. I felt as if we were two teenagers trying to figure out life on our own.

"How long have you been out here?" It was a good sign. She asked me a question. My father told me it was a good sign when a girl asked you questions. "If she doesn't ask you questions, she's not interested," he told me.

"This time, a few days."

"How many times have you tried?"

Tried was an interesting word to use. She made it sound as if I were an addict and was trying to remain sober, once again.

"You mean how many times have I been homeless?"

"How many times have you tried to live in the world? How many times have you tried to figure out where you went wrong? How many times have you tried to fit in and be normal?"

"You sure can be poetic. Do you write?"

"I do, but not because I try. It just comes out. I've written some poems, though."

"Well, you must find a lot to write about, out here."

"Not any more than anyplace else. People are people. We just live in a different reality."

"If you can call this reality," I said.

"What do you call it?"

I had to think a moment. A flood of words came to me. They came so fast I couldn't form a sentence to express myself.

"I call it sewage. I call it lonely. I don't know what to call it."

"Can I quote you on that?" Her sarcasm was evident.

She made me smile. "Yeah, you can quote me."

We walked a while in silence—me, her and the dog. The dog walked at her side.

"Do you want to get off the street?" I had to return to the subject. I found her and now I had to get her to safety.

"Yes, I do."

"Well, what are you going to do, then?"

"I don't know. I been down so long, gettin' up jus' don't seem right."

"There's that poetry again."

"Not mine this time, but the sentiment is appropriate. It's a song I heard a long time ago. It makes sense now."

"Does that mean you don't care about getting off the streets?"

"No, it just means I don't think about it as much as I used to."

"Liar."

"What!" She was astonished at my challenge to her answer.

"I don't believe you. You think about it every day."

"Really?"

"Really," I replied boldly. "I can tell by the way you dress. You don't have much, but you try your best to look good with what you have. When I was out there, I didn't care about anything. I didn't care if I lived or died. On most days I felt dead, anyway. And I certainly didn't care about how I looked."

"I'm a woman. I will always care. Men on the other hand—"

"Okay, let me stop you. Don't go bashing men, especially since you have one, I mean *had* one."

"Graham wasn't my man. We were, I don't know, what. We found each other and it worked out."

"Okay."

"Don't say okay like you know something other than what I said. We were companions. We helped each other."

"Okay," I insisted, to make it clear I was accepting her explanation.

"You don't believe in platonic relationships?" I didn't answer and she added, "I have a feeling you don't believe in much, anymore."

I still didn't answer. It was best to continue walking. It looked as if we were roaming aimlessly, but somehow we kept walking until we entered the park. We arrived with such ease, I felt we both had been heading to the same place. If we were walking separately, we would have ended here together. We wanted to be here, not necessarily with each other, but the stroll was so effortless, I never felt I was being guided to the park, it was just a casual walk. If she could keep her mouth shut, our time together would be okay. A man could only dream.

Lee must have felt the same. She walked alongside me without protest. Tiger must have liked the journey, as well. He walked at her heel with his head up. As I saw it, she was his new best friend. Maybe this was a moment I needed to get rid of her and the dog at the same time.

We finally sat on a bench and watched the passing people. Normally, people would watch us homeless as if we were some zoo attraction. I guess they wondered how we lived or how we ate or how we survived in the wild of their very own neighborhoods. We were the rats among them—mostly hidden, always to be avoided, and best not to be challenged. Staring at a homeless person was like staring at a gorilla in the zoo. It was a challenge, which resulted in warfare. In a zoo, there was a separation of man and beast, by a fence or moat. In this world, the only defense was an attitude. The wrong attitude could result in a nasty fight. A good attitude could result in a good deed. Attitude was the line in the sand.

Lee reached into her backpack and pulled out a plastic baggie with pieces of bread. She flung a few of the pieces into the air and watched them fall to the ground. I looked around, knowing what was about to happen; I just wanted to know when it was going to happen. It took about ten seconds, and a pigeon came and picked at a piece of bread. A second pigeon flew in and wanted the very piece which was in the beak of the first bird, but gave up when other pigeons arrived. The few pieces were gone within seconds, and

Lee tossed more morsels, which attracted more birds. I was tempted to count them, but it was obvious there were at least twenty. They bobbed and weaved and waddled back and forth, gathering the available bread.

"Did you know pigeons prefer seeds? They don't really care for bread," Lee said.

"Beggars can't be choosers." I didn't mean in the cold manner in which I expressed it. There was no way to take it back and say it again. She looked at me as if I was as annoying as I found the pigeons.

Lee ignored me and continued to educate me. "You know what's cool? They mate for life. I guess we could learn a thing or two from them, huh?"

I wasn't sure she really wanted me to answer the question. What the hell do I know about them and why do I want to learn anything from them? She kept looking at me and apparently it was my clue to answer her dopey question.

"If you can learn anything from a pigeon, I guess it would be that." I just could not think of anything else, and she looked at me as if to say I had a birdbrain, but it didn't deter her.

"Do you know how they mate?"

Shit! She asked another stupid question, but I was ready and answered, "I would guess they go out to dinner and then fly off to a hotel?" I was afraid she would look at me with another look of disdain, but my answered tickled her.

She continued her tutorial. "The male bird brings the female to a nesting site and presents her with a stick. She accepts or rejects it. If she accepts it, he brings another one and another and so on and so on, until they have a nest."

"So they don't have dinner first?"

"You are so silly," she replied in a dry voice.

At times I could be silly. My reward was her smile. She threw more pieces out into the crowd, causing more chaos. There was not enough for all of them, but each bird hoped she would throw a piece of food directly at him. I noticed there were a couple of birds which seemed to bully the group. I wanted to shoo them away, but it would only result in all of them flying away and the bully would return, alone. I learned another pigeon lesson. Bullies are found everywhere.

"They share nesting duties, too," she continued.

"As it should be," I responded. "Where did you learn all this stuff about pigeons? Did you raise them or just read about them?"

"I love to read. I read about them."

"Do you know how to tell the difference between a male and a female?"

"The male is the bigger bird, right?"

"Generally," I said. You can tell also by the way they strut. See that one there?" I directed her attention of one of the birds. "What do you think about that one, male or female?"

"Well it's kind of small, but walks proud." She kept thinking. "I think it's a he."

"You just guessed that. You don't know."

"I did not guess."

"Please," I said with disbelief.

"Is it a male?"

"Well, yes, but you didn't know that."

"Oh, but you did?"

"Oh, yes, I do"

"Okay, so how do you tell?"

"I look for the stick."

"Oh you are so nasty. And you learned this how, books or experience?"

"I used to raise pigeons."

"Really!" She was so excited. "Do they really have a penis?"

"No. They have a cloaca."

"A what?"

"A kloe-ay-kah. It's like a sac filled with sperm and the male rubs his cloaca against the female's cloaca and that's how they mate."

"Two cloacas rubbing? Sounds kind of freaky to me."

"Hey they're birds. It's called a cloacal kiss."

"And you've seen this, this kiss."

"Well, when you raise them, you see it a lot."

I could tell she was trying to visualize the mating ritual. "I used to like pigeons," she said. "Now, not so much. They're like people say—nasty, just plain nasty."

I didn't expect to, but I laughed, and it was contagious enough that her smile grew to a big grin. She dumped the rest of the crumbs from her bag, and the birds rushed around her feet. She lifted her legs to avoid the rush.

"Nasty. This could be a post-cloacal feeding frenzy."

"Are you on medication? I mean, I not trying to be mean or get in your business, I'm just asking." I was trying my best not to sound mean.

"No," she said shooing the birds away. "Nasty things."

"Women. That was a short lived-love affair with pigeons. I thought you admired that they mated for life."

"Admirable, yes. Mating, not so much"

"Are you married?" It seemed an appropriate question for me to ask.

"Yes."

Her answer was so short, I didn't know if I was prying into a subject I should leave alone, or she was just answering the question.

"Do you care to talk about it?" Her response was a shrug of her shoulders."What does that mean? Talk or no talk?"

"Look, I just met you and it wasn't the best circumstances, so don't try and be my best friend all of a sudden."

"That means no talk. That's all you have to say."

"I didn't say that."

"Okay. Forget it. Is it too much to ask if you have kids? You would tell a complete stranger that much, wouldn't you?."

"*You* are a complete stranger."

"So, talk." A minimal smile and a quick glance at me told me her attitude toward me had softened. Humor and sarcasm can mend, as well as cut.

"I have two kids." Lee provided the information I needed. I had to get rid of her and I saw my opportunity. Again, my father was right. Wait and many things will come to you.

"How long have you been out here?" I asked her.

I could tell she didn't like the question. I was prying, and she didn't know me, yet she walked with me the entire day and I never saw her take any occasion to leave. I was her first aid kit, her survival guide, and maybe her only hope.

"What're your kids' names?"

"David and Naomi." Thank God, I thought. Maybe they had a chance in life with *real* names. She continued, "I miss them so much. My baby, David, is getting so big. He's five."

A quick calculation was enough to make me understand she didn't raise her children, at least her son.

"How old is your daughter?"

"She's seven."

"What happened? No, that's a stupid question, I know. Not what happened, but where are they?"

"They live with their father," she said, but needed to add, "for now."

I didn't know of too many mothers who didn't have custody of their children. Her story must be serious. I met many mothers on the street, and some had their children with them. It was sad enough to see homeless women, but to see children living day to day trying their best to be children was worse. I didn't know if it was possible, but maybe all they needed was the security of their mother. It was sad, none the less.

The children were innocent nomads in this fierce world. Some people would watch pigeons; I watched kids. They played in the park like I did when I was a child. Some of them went to school. They slept in cars in the evening or some abandoned building. They followed their parents to and fro, never knowing how the day would end.

As an adult, I understood the world and survival of the fittest. How did the children process this senseless world? It must be even harder for them as they walked and interacted with the ordered world. Maybe they had friends with houses and food. I wondered if homelessness was all they knew. Were some born into it? I saw homeless mothers pushing their babies in strollers, randomly traveling to the next chance for food or money.

The older children hurt me the most. They reminded me of my wife and my daughter. My decisions brought them close to living in the street. Living on the streets is not living—it is much closer to death than life. My wife chose life and left, with my daughter, to anywhere not near me. I hated her for it, but in my lucid moments, I knew she did the right thing. I wanted my family with me, but now I had the assurance they were safe. Of course, it was my hope. I didn't know what they were doing or where they were living, but they had to be doing better than I was.

"Are you doing anything to get them back?"

"Everything."

"You don't want to get them and bring them to the street, do you?"

"I don't want them now. I want to get back on my feet and then get them."

I tried to calculate her chances. She was away from her children for years. She was not going to get on her feet for even more years. They would have spent have their lives without her. Why would they want to be with her? What would make them choose her? I couldn't answer the question, but I did witness homeless children choose their mother over everything. There was a bond between mother and child which I never understood.

As much as I did for my daughter, I could never reach the level of relationship my wife had with my daughter. They fought so many times. They would fight more times in a week than I did with her in a year, yet their relationship remained strong. I stopped trying to figure out their connection and tried my best to develop my own. At times, I felt I was in competition with my wife for the best relationship.

"Do you think they want to be with you?"

I could see Lee was struggling with the answer, but she finally said, "You can't separate blood. Blood wants blood. Blood seeks blood. I haven't seen them in so long, but I feel—no, I know they want me. They can't help but want me. Have you ever heard those stories of adopted people wanting to find their biological parents? No matter how much they are loved by their adoptive parents, they must find their blood. It calls to them."

"It seems they are calling you, don't you think?"

"And I will find them and get them back with me."

"How will you do that out here?"

"I won't always be out here."

"Listen, if you could find a place to stay, wouldn't that be a good start?"

She stared at me. She looked into me, looking for the truth. Lee understood this was no longer a casual conversation.

"What do you have in mind? Do you have someplace for me to go?"

"I was just thinking—"

"Are you a social worker or something? Another sociologist? Are you doing a research project?"

"No, I want to help."

"What can you do?"

"I think I can find you a place to stay."

"Where?"

"Where I came from."

She repeated my statement and asked, "If you have a place to stay, why are you out here?"

"It's kind of convoluted."

"That's a big word. Maybe you are a professor, doing great work for your great ego and great project. Sounds like you want to answer the great question you have posed for your thesis. Maybe you're looking to get a great grade."

I didn't understand her response. She was sounding paranoid, not that I could blame her. I tried my best to reassure her. "I just want you to be safe. You know as well as I, it's not safe out here. Do you want to be killed before you get the chance to get your kids back? If you want them back, you have to be off the street. I know it. You know it."

"What, do you have an apartment?"

"No, a room, and I know they're looking for me. Maybe they have stopped by now, but it's worth a try to get you in there. You never know, it could be the start of your way home."

"What about you? Are you on your way home?"

"I don't know. I have no idea if I'm closer or not, I just keep moving."

"You just keep roamin'." Her smile told me she was teasing me as she made a pun on my name.

"Aren't you clever."

"Yes, aren't I?" she answered.

"So what do you think? Wouldn't you rather have a room than a park bench? One day closer to your children, if you choose life. Life is not here, it's with your children, in a home."

I watched her face turn to stone as she thought about my proposition. She could go either way, and this was my one time to convince her to come with me to HOPE. She was thinking, and it was a good thing. She was weighing her options, which she probably had not done in a while.

"Tell me about Naomi," I said.

Her stare into deep space faded quickly. She had to be thinking of her little girl. Finally she said, "She is a pistol. That's what my father always said of her. He was right. Takes one to know one, I guess. She hit her terrible two's six months early."

"Precocious, huh?"

"That's the truth. She rocketed past two, straight to twenty-five."

"I think girls do that naturally," I added.

"Do you have a daughter?"

The question caught me off guard. I had no intention of talking about my life, so I quickly dodged the question by answering, "That's girls in general. They talk sooner and they talk a lot, thereafter."

"Tell me about it," she said accepting my dodge."Naomi was starting to read when I, uh, left."

"Do you want to talk about it?"

"No, not really."

"I understand," I told her.

It's hard talking about a past which should still be your present. It's harder still to know it's your fault. Day after day, you relive the moment you destroyed a family. The only way out was a numbing drug or alcohol. I chose the latter, the cheapest I could find. However, it just created another prison for me. Either I had to think of my lost family or lose myself in a bottle. I liked it there. The bottle had boundaries. Once inside, there was little room for anything else, or anybody. Even my thoughts were crowded out. The bottle was the best real estate.

Being free of my alcohol addiction for the past few months was not always a good thing. I felt like a genie out of the bottle—free, but bound by others' wishes. I was bound by the mission and plans of others. Reality was not always the best solution to my drunkenness. I always seemed to be walking the shoreline of a lake full of wine. On any given day, I was sure I would jump in and try my best to drown.

"Come on," I instructed as I stood up.

"Where are we going?"

"We're headed for HOPE." I walked without looking back, hoping she would follow. I knew she was with me when I saw the dog's shadow at my side. Her shadow soon followed.

"Don't worry," I said. "They will take good care of you."

"Do they have a place for women? I mean, separate from the men?"

"Of course. Why?"

"Have you ever heard of MST?" I didn't know the term, so Lee explained. "It's military sexual trauma. Women have a rougher time in the military than anyone knows."

I didn't really want to know, but I asked, "Were you raped?"

"Yes." The answer was enough for me. I did not want to know any more, but apparently she was ready to talk.

"They don't do anything about it in the military, just like they don't do anything about it in the world. You would think the Army would be more disciplined, have more honor, but it's just a big ol' boys' club."

"Is that why you got out?"

"It was the last straw of several reasons. I was in Afghanistan for three tours. I always heard how badly the Taliban treat their women. I was fighting to defend *their* women, I was told. I was fighting to defend the country from barbarians, but the barbarians were on my side of the fence."

I was not generally a squeamish person, but I never liked hearing about women and the abuse they suffered. I hoped she would stop, but she didn't.

"The men in my unit made me feel as if I was there for their service. They made it clear I was a female with their snarky remarks."

She just wouldn't stop, so I had to ask, "What did they do with the other women?"

"We were ostracized, except for those who played the game. Some of those females were more man than any male I ever knew."

"Were they lesbians?"

"No, they just played the game. They were never intimidated. They played at being a man, so the men would leave them alone. They lost as much as I did. We all lost our femininity."

"That is sad." I had nothing to offer, but my curiosity was piqued. "But you stayed in and did three tours. Why?"

"I didn't want to be beaten. I was determined to be—"

"A man, it sounds like," I interrupted

"No, I didn't want to be a man. It's hard to explain. I just wanted to be competitive. I wanted to do my job and be a part of a team, and they wanted to remind me I was not part of the club."

"Man, I don't remember my time like that."

"Were you around many women?"

"No, not really."

"Bam, there you go."

"What does that mean?"

"It means you don't know shit."

"Now wait, what you are you mad at me for?"

"Sorry, you just don't know. Probably don't want to know." She was right, but I wasn't going to let her know that; yet she refused to stop talking.

"But I found out the barbarians are everywhere. Someone tried to rape me last night."

"Oh, no, I wasn't. You can stop right there." She had gone too far.

"I wasn't talking about you, though I thought you might consider it, too. Earlier last night. That's why I was looking for better shelter inside the fence. Then you showed up, and I was sure you were going to try something, but you didn't."

"You damn right I didn't."

"I said that."

"Well, say it, again."

"You didn't do anything, but you did punch me."

"You tried to gouge my eyes out."

Lee looked at the area below my left eye. "Sorry. You should get that looked at."

"Yeah, soon as my health insurance kicks in," I replied sarcastically. "So, who, um, you know, uh—"

"Tried to rape me?" I didn't know whether she said the word to irritate me or to help me.

"I wouldn't know. They all look and smell alike." She must have experienced many sexual assaults. I decided I was not going to ask her anymore questions. I wouldn't understand the answers, anyway.

We walked a little while longer with a mutual understanding to keep quiet. We turned a corner and there was HOPE.

"Is that where we're headed?" Lee asked.

"Yes, you'll be safe here."

Chapter 12

I walked through the hall to the pastor's office. I left Lee in the cafeteria, since they were serving one of her favorite meals, enchiladas. I didn't want to eat. It was more important to explain my absence to Reverend Franklin. I wasn't sure how he would take it, but I was soon to find out.

I stood at the office entrance and waited for him to look up from his work. Without seeming to stop reading his documents, he said, "Well, well, the dead has arisen."

I smiled. I heard him use the phrase before. I heard it from my own father when I ran away when I was fifteen. It was for only a night, but my father was calm for a change and he used the same sentence when he opened to door to see me standing, anticipating my punishment.

The reverend didn't sound menacing. It was almost welcoming, so I came into the room and stood at the desk. He continued to read and gestured for me to sit. I did as instructed and waited for more commands. Finally he placed his papers on the desk and looked at me.

"Are you back?" he inquired.

"I'm back."

"Where did you go?"

Now came the tricky part. I wasn't about to tell him of my mission to find Graham's girlfriend. It deprived me of bragging rights, though. The police and he never knew of her existence and I could be the hero, but I felt sorry for her. She had been harassed enough. I wasn't about to put her in a position to be questioned and manipulated by the cops. All she needed was a bed and some food. It was my self-appointed job to convince the pastor she was a good candidate for both. The food was the easy part. The bed, on the other hand, would take some negotiating skills.

I started to explain. "You know me, I had to clear my head."

"Is it clear?"

"I guess so. I mean, I don't think it will get any better than this."

"Did you learn anything?"

I could feel the pastor maneuvering. He was positioning for a strike. I could imagine a lioness stalking her prey. He was waiting for the right time to strike, but I wasn't totally without defenses. He might be more cunning, but I was fast. He knew where he was going, and it was up to me to stay one step ahead. It was nothing new. It was my life on the street.

"Well, I guess I should make a decision to do what I set out to do. Finish the program and—"

I couldn't finish. What was I supposed to do after I finished the program? I could recite the party line, but I didn't really feel it. The words were stuck in my head. I heard them, but I couldn't repeat them.

The pastor could see my struggle and he helped me escape my mental trap. "You'll figure it out."

"I'm trying."

"I know."

I took his response to mean he was ready to allow me to return and continue my school and lay my head in peace. Of course my anxiety wasn't fully resolved, since I needed a way to introduce Lee and her needs.

"Pastor," I began. He looked directly in my eyes, and I could see small darting movements of his eyes as if he were searching me. He was scanning me, but the look was penetrating. He was beyond my eyes and deep into my body. He was looking for something.

I continued, "While I was out there, I found a woman. I mean I didn't find a woman, I came across a woman."

The pastor's look became steady. Maybe he found what he was looking for, whatever that was.

"I think she could use your help. I mean, I know she could."

"A lot of people could use my help."

"Pastor, sometimes you surprise me. You can be so cynical at times."

"Did that sound cynical?"

"Yes, yes, it did. Are you tired of doing this kind of work?"

"No, but I will admit I want to get away at times."

"Well, pastor, this would be a bad time to decide that. I need your help. This woman I found out there needs your help. She's a good person."

I could tell I was speaking to a wall. He had checked out. He did not need to hear another sob story.

"Can you do it for me?" He had no idea how much of my guts I had to spill on the floor to ask; but he looked at me so quickly, maybe he did understand my anguish.

"What's going on, Roman?"

I wanted to tell him how I searched for her for two days. I'm sure he would agree if he knew she was Graham's girlfriend, but I couldn't bring myself to tell him. I wasn't able to trust many people, and he had not reached such a level for me. He was a good man and he expressed a lot of wisdom, but my list of criteria to establish trust is much longer. It also made me feel significant. I had information, he wanted and I was in control. Knowledge is power and I had power, if just a little.

"She's a good person, Pastor."

"You said that. How do you know that?"

"I don't know that."

"You feel that."

"Pastor, you know how hard it is for women out there. Most of the time we don't come across them. They have family who will take them in, organizations have more compassion for them. They get snatched up quickly, especially if they have children."

"Does she have children?"

"No, but she has a dog."

"You know we have no place for animals. If I take her in, the dog has to go elsewhere."

"I know that. I'll find someone to take the dog. It's easy to find someone who wants to adopt a dog. You've seen the commercials. Someone will take in a dog quicker than they will take in a person."

"A dog brings love. A person on the other hand brings lots of baggage."

"So is that what it's about, love?"

"Everything is about love, Roman. Everyone is looking for it. Most people look for it, in the wrong places, though."

"Sounds like a song." He understood my sarcasm and smiled.

"And if they don't find love, companionship will do."

"Are we back to the dog?"

"We're back to everything people do to find love. People have children in search of it. That's why people lament when their children grow up. They feel they are losing their love. How many homeless people do you know have dogs? They have no money, yet they find the money to feed their dogs. Are they dog lovers? Maybe. Have they seen the commercials and are filled with compassion and find a dog to take care of? "

"Maybe they had a dog when they became homeless."

"I'm sure that's part of it, but trust me when I say it is about a relationship. Having a relationship with someone who loves you is the basic, most powerful drive in humans."

I couldn't give him an amen on that. Tiger was a pain in my ass since I started taking care of him.

Franklin continued, "Every single thing a person does is to find love. Dieting, overeating, drinking, drugs, everything."

I wondered if his reference to drinking was a dig at me. I thought about his theory. I didn't drink because I was looking for love. I was trying to avoid it. I wanted to forget my family and the pain I caused them. I drank because it felt good. Forgetting my pain was a good thing. What did that have to do with love?

He seemed to be reading my mind. "Do you know why people drink?"

"It feels good."

"Why?

I couldn't figure out why he would ask a stupid question. "People drink every day. They don't drink to always get drunk, it just feels good, it relaxes them."

"Ah, relaxation. Do you know what that means?"

"Of course I know what it means." He watched me, and I realized my answer was insufficient. "It means rest," I continued, but I could see in his eyes he wanted more from me. "It means peace. People come home after a long day, and they just want some rest. It's rough out there. People want peace, somewhere they can find some solace. You think people are looking for love in a bottle?"

"People are looking for love in a bottle, a TV, a dog, a baby, furniture, shoes, cars and anybody."

"I've never heard you talk like this, Pastor. Are you okay?"

"I'm fine. I'm just learning more and more."

"Well, you don't sound like your knowledge is helping you. You sound—" I didn't want to say the word, but I did. "You sound depressed. I didn't know pastors could be depressed."

"Then you think more highly of us than you should."

"Well, you're always teaching us how to live, like you have all the answers."

"I don't have all the answers, God does."

"Well, don't you know what God does?"

"Oh, heavens, no. I couldn't possibly know all He knows. He created everything that exists. I have created nothing."

"Of course you have. You created HOPE," I protested.

"And He created the idea of HOPE in me."

"You have very little going for you, then."

"That was blunt."

"Don't mean to be harsh, Pastor, but you sound in a bad way. Sounds like you need Jesus. Or maybe you need love. I don't mean to be in your business, but have you ever loved somebody or something?"

"Both. Some*one* and some*thing.*"

I looked up at the pictures on the wall and spotted a couple of photos of his brother. He told me the story a while ago, of his brother's death from alcohol.

"No, I mean someone other than a family member. Have you ever loved a woman?"

"Yes, I have."

"What happened?"

"It's interesting, to hear you ask me questions," he said. "You really want to know, don't you?"

"Yes, I do. I guess people don't see you as human like the rest of us, especially us lowlifes."

"Don't say that. No one is a lowlife. You are as valuable as anyone."

"I know that. Just pass it along to the rest of the world."

153

"I'll do my best. Some will listen, some won't. I don't spend much time on those who won't. I don't cast my pearls before the swine."

"My grandfather used to say that."

"Wise man. Was he a happy man?"

"I guess he was. I mean, I was just a kid when he died."

"Sorry."

"No need. I think I was seven or eight when he died. I never did know what he died from, though. I remember him telling me stuff all the time about life, and when he tired of me asking 'why,' he would end the conversation with that casting pearls statement."

"Do you know what that means?"

"Don't waste your time with idiots."

My interpretation amused the pastor. "Yes, I guess that's the best way to put it."

"So, Pastor, what about your love life? You're a man, but you're not married. Aren't you looking for love?"

Before he could answer, I stopped him. "Wait, I know. Everyone is looking for love. So who is she?"

"There is no she."

My face dropped. I wasn't sure what he meant by his answer, but it could have meant more than one thing. I proceeded with caution.

"So, are you…um—"

"No, I'm not gay."

"I'm not making any judgments. It's not my business."

"You already made the judgment, and you correctly state it is none of your business."

"Have you ever been asked that before?"

"Many, many times. Sometimes as directly as you, other times it's the look, but judgment is always close at hand. By asking the question, it must matter to the questioner. If it matters, then there's an accompanying judgment."

"Man, Pastor, I didn't know you were so deep. You read the Bible every day and teach us stuff from it, but that's not your wisdom, like you always tell us. You have your own wisdom, don't you? I mean, you think and stumble over your thoughts just like the rest of us. It's funny. You're just like me. You're not as grown-up as your appear."

"Am I to be flattered or insulted?" He was smiling.

"I'm just talking, Pastor. You're like talking with a celebrity. Who talks to a celebrity and gets to really know them? All we know about them is what the magazines tell us, but if I were able to talk to one, really talk to one, I could find out who they really are, you know what I mean?"

"I thought I made myself accessible."

"You're only accessible to hearing about others and their problems. You're not accessible to telling your problems."

"I'm talking to you, aren't I?"

"Come on, Pastor, you're not hearing me. You're a celebrity. You're the man. You're on a pedestal. You're like God, the Wizard of Oz. You don't ask the wizard or God questions. You just listen."

"That's ridiculous. I question God all the time."

"Really?" I was amazed he would make such a sacrilegious statement. "What do you ask?"

"All kinds of things. It depends on what's going at the time."

"So you question the almighty God, your ruler?"

"All the time."

"Hm. Does He answer?"

"Sometimes."

"Not all the time?"

"What are you getting at?"

"Why doesn't He answer all the time? Why does He create you, then leave you? Why does He say He loves you and then disappears when you need Him the most? Why does He make promises and take a lifetime to fulfill them?"

"That's not God."

"Who is it then?"

"I mean, it is God, but you characterize God incorrectly. The premise of your questions is not right."

"And the premise of your questions to Him, is?"

"Roman, what is going on? You thought you were questioning me, but you are really questioning God. What do you want Him to answer for you?"

"I don't know."

"When you figure out the question, ask. Whatever the question, He will answer."

"Me, He will answer me."

"Even you."

I wasn't offended. I understood his sarcasm. I thought a moment, then said, "Okay, what about this? I've heard you quote something in the Bible about man being alone."

"In Genesis. Genesis 2:18 says that God looked on Adam and said that it was not good that man should be alone. So He created Eve."

"So why are people alone? Why are people lonely?"

"Not everyone is alone or lonely. Many times it's the choices we make, not the choices God made for us."

"You're alone. Is it by choice or by God?" I was really probing.

"I'm not really alone. I have HOPE. This center surrounds me with many people. I couldn't possibly be alone with all the people in my life."

"So we are your companions?"

"Yes, you are my companions."

"We are your Eve."

"Yes, you are my Eve," he replied, with a smile on his face. "Everyone is searching for love. Companionship is a manifestation of love. Even the wrong companion is better for people rather than none. But in the end, it is the relationship we seek, we crave, we will do anything for it. Gang members search for it. Terrorists search for it. Each looks for a sense of belonging, and each finds it in a relationship. It raises our self-esteem to be in a relationship. It is the institution we were meant to be in and establish. Love is found in the relationship, and many confuse companionship with a relationship, and any companionship will do."

"I thought they were the same."

"Now you know the difference. A companion may keep you company, may keep you from being bored, but that's not love. A relationship has love."

"Are we, the people you help every day, are we the relationship you seek?"

"Yes. So I am not alone, even if I want a woman from time to time."

"You want a woman?" Now we were getting somewhere.

"Not like that. I mean a relationship with one."

"So where does God fit in with all of this?"

The pastor opened his Bible on the desk and flipped through

some pages with a deliberate expression on his face. He knew what he was looking for and when he found it, he passed the book to me, pointed his finger at a verse and said, "Read it."

I read the verse slowly so as to get what the pastor was after, but he wasn't satisfied. "Out loud," he said.

"He who does not love does not know God, for God is love."

"First John 4:8," he said, in response. "What is God?" he asked.

"God is love."

"And what is everyone searching for?"

"According to you, love."

"There, young grasshopper, you have it. Everyone, and I mean everyone, is searching for love–or, in other words, they are looking for God. They just don't always know it."

He was a clever man. I had to backtrack over the steps he just led me through. I wondered if this was his or God's wisdom. It was clear. I had no more questions. There was nothing else for me to contribute. My only reply, "Oh." But I kept listening to his logic revolve in my head. I understood.

"Oh, so you're saying the search for love is really the search for God."

"By George, I think he's got it!" the pastor said.

"But wait. Atheists don't believe in God, so what does that mean?"

"There are some who don't believe we landed on the moon, does that make it true? Some believed the Earth was flat. Did that make it true?"

"Guess not, but it doesn't mean they're wrong this time."

"You choose, Roman. I choose God. Who do you choose?"

"Do I have to make a choice?"

"Eventually. Look at it another way. Have you ever lost a person you love?"

I was almost offended he asked me the question. He knew enough about me to know I lost my family. He was trying to provoke me.

"Yes."

"What did you do?"

"I didn't do anything. I was just sad."

"I don't believe you. You were more than sad. Didn't you want to make things right?"

"Of course. I wanted to be together again."

"That's right." He seemed so excited. I must have given the right response. "Everyone who loses love wants to replace it."

"Okay." I couldn't figure out where he was going with this.

"People replace a love with another love—the love of things, another person, food."

"I get it. Lots of things."

"But it's never satisfying, so people keep trying, over and over to replace that love, that first love, so to speak."

"Pastor, I don't mean to be rude, but is this going anywhere?"

"Yes. The road leads to your first love." He pointed to the Bible again and said, "Revelations 2:4."

The pastor was exhausting me. I wasn't interested in Bible study, but I reluctantly searched for the verse he announced. It took me a while. I didn't know where Revelations was located.

"It's the last book."

I wanted to throw it at him, but I thought it would be considered sacrilegious, so I went to the back of the book and searched again. Finally, I found the chapter and the verse. I read it silently, daring him to demand I read it out loud. If he had, there was no doubt I would punch him for frustrating me. I was prepared and he must have read my mind. Yet without a request or prodding, I read the verse aloud.

"'Nevertheless I have this against you, that you have left your first love.'" I looked at the pastor and waited for him to respond.

"The first love is God. Your first love is God. My first love is God. All you and everyone else wants is to return to that loving relationship, that perfect relationship, which comes from God, alone."

It was checkmate. There was no move or response to make. I was exhausted, anyway. He was good at what he did. He had the title of pastor for a reason. He could make a sermon from tissue paper and peanut butter, but it didn't matter because we were interrupted.

"Reverend Franklin, you gotta come quick. There's a fight in the cafeteria."

Chapter 13

The evening sun produced blocks of light as it passed through the windows. It seemed to produce spotlights to illuminate the objects on Detective Innis' desk. There was a set of photographs, his cell phone, and a plate of chicken and rice, partially eaten.

Greg sat on the edge of the desk watching a group of officers discuss a case. He was partially attentive, only hearing some words and some sentences. He couldn't piece the story together, if he was asked. Neither did he care about their case or their progress. At one point, he thought he heard them invite him into the discussion, but he ignored the call.

Greg's mind was amused by the most insignificant things. He watched a fluorescent light flicker, then he looked at the shoes of a woman sitting at a desk about fifteen feet from him. He liked the red spike heels. The strap across her toes matched her red toenails, which were well polished. She could be a prostitute, but it was unlikely. It didn't look as though she was being interrogated, just questioned. She noticed him, and his attention turned elsewhere.

A young man stood at a window. His ears were pierced and gauged to about an inch. Greg could look through the openings in his earlobes to view the city skyline. It was eerie to be able to look through a person's body and see scenery. It was like looking through a camera lens, but it was creepy. As the young man moved his head, a ray of light streamed through, but for only a split second. Greg watched to see if it was his imagination or did he really see light come through. As weird as it seemed, he wanted to see it again. He wondered if he could get a picture of the phenomenon. He waited.

"What are you doing?" a woman's voice asked.

It was Lois. While he was in his trance, she pounced on him without any warning. It was then he realized he was watching and thinking the wrong things. He didn't feel as if he belonged here, at least not lately.

Now he was back to so-called reality, Greg was able to respond. "Just thinking."

"What are you thinking?"

"Nothing much, too much, I don't know."

Lois could hear the struggle in his voice. His brain must have been going a mile a minute and he was not able to absorb it all. He must be trying to describe a dream, but the images were so ridiculous and unfamiliar, he couldn't keep up with them. His thoughts traveled at light speed and he could speak only one word—a word which could describe a scene. It couldn't be done and it was obvious he needed time. However, he was at work and he needed to focus. She knew how to bring him back from the brink.

Lois put a photograph of Detective Jackson in front of him. It worked and Greg stood and turned to her.

"What's this?"

She didn't mean to be rude, but her response came without thinking. "You know what it is." He seemed to be okay with her answer.

"How did you get this?" he asked her.

"It's the picture he had at his side."

"I know. How did you get it?"

"Remember, when you showed it to me at the beach?"

"And?"

"Well, it just struck me as curious, he would have it at his side and also send you one, as well."

"We went through this, didn't we?"

"I know, but can we go through it again? Just one more time."

Greg showed his frustration as he flopped into his chair and invited her to sit in the chair on the opposite side.

She repeated, "Just one more time."

As she sat down, she realized his partner was not in the room. "Where's Detective Turner?"

"Out and about. He likes it out there."

"What do you think of him?"

"A bit scruffy, but okay. He's a good guy, smart. He likes to

get in the mix. He likes pretending. When I met him, he was pretending to be a gang member. He's the one who convinced me to
try the HD. He doesn't like to sit still. I'm sure he'll move on from
this squad to another. He's like a kid who changes his mind over
and over again about what he wants to be when he grows up."

"Sounds like a fun guy."

"Yeah, he's that, too, but like a kid, he isn't settled. Me, I'm
ready to settle."

"Settle down, you mean?"

He detected her double entendre, but was unsure as how to
answer. Damned if he did, damned if he didn't. He felt trapped, so
he turned the question around for her to answer. "How about you?"

"Oh, I don't know. Some days yes, some days no," she
answered.

"How about today," Greg asked.

"Today? Today is all about you."

"Which means?"

"Which means, today I follow, you lead. You're a man. You're
meant to lead, right? Lead, man."

Oh, she was good, he thought. She was so damn sensual.
Women this sensual must take a class in how to deliver the simplest sentence. She could speak about police evidence with a
cadence in her speech at just the right tone and pitch to make anyone ask for her hand in marriage. She must have had plenty of
offers, yet most of the guys in the department thought of her as
a bitch. There was no stopping her oozing her sexiness. She was
born to be the height of femininity, and she was prepared to level
any man who tried to take advantage of it. Yet despite the wall she
created, she chose him, and he was grateful.

Greg watched her. She had an awesome power, but he was
her equal, which is probably the reason they were good together.
Though most in the department knew of their relationship, they
were professional toward each other as much as they could be.

"Your turn, today, ma'am," he said and pointed to the picture.
"What's up with the photo?"

"There's a message in it, and I don't think it's what you think
it is. I don't think he's talking about life after death."

"What did he mean?"

Lois repeated the phrase, "Yes, there is more."

"And that doesn't refer to Heaven, you're saying."

"No, it doesn't," she said. Her voice didn't sound as confident as she felt a moment ago, but she continued her theory.

"First, I don't understand why you and Carmen get the same picture. Second, why *this* picture? Doesn't that make you start wondering? It's a little creepy for a man about to commit suicide to send this upbeat picture."

"It was a bad day for him, but maybe he wanted to leave an upbeat memory."

"No, that doesn't make sense. Maybe to you, but you told me his relationship with her wasn't good."

"He didn't hate her. He wouldn't try to make her suffer after his death."

"Exactly. That's why there is a message."

"Wait, you're confusing me. He dislikes her; likes her enough, though, to keep her from being depressed about his death. Maybe the note was for his daughter. He definitely cared about her."

"Okay, so the message is for her."

Greg looked around the room, to see if anyone was interested in their conversation. Once he convinced himself no one cared, he said to Lois, "I like you a lot, but let's let this one go. I'm tired of re-visiting Renny's death on a daily basis."

"I know, I know. If you really want to put it to rest, you have to get rid of the nagging suspicions."

"Or the nag." She didn't respond, so he continued. "Okay, what are the nagging suspicions, your nagging suspicions?"

"That's it."

"That's it? You have a suspicious picture and a suspicious note. That's it."

"Yes."

"Of course you realize that none of what you see as suspicious is suspicious to me?"

"Yes."

"Yet you are trying to make me suspicious."

"Yes."

"That's called paranoia. There are pills for that."

"Okay, I shut up."

"Thank you. I really need your help on the porta-potty murder. What do you see in those pictures?"

Greg lifted the photographs from his desk and invited her to take them. Lois studied the photos, but was unable to come to any conclusions.

"They're just gruesome. Other than that, I don't know, yet."

"Come on, you're good at seeing patterns. What do you see?"

"Patterns in different crime scenes. This is the same one. What pattern could I, or anyone, see?"

"I don't know. Don't they pay you top dollar to figure these things out?"

"Don't they pay you top dollar to think for yourself?"

"That's mean," he said.

Lois didn't answer. She walked away, across the room through the staff and through the door, out of sight. He re-evaluated his last statement. "Nope, *that* was mean," he said, referring to her sudden departure.

Greg sat at the desk, hoping no one noticed the altercation he and Lois tried to keep to themselves. They had no audience, so he turned his attention to his desk. He picked up the photos Lois threw into the box and looked through them once again. A new look did not reveal any secrets. He looked again for the picture of Renny, but it was not there. He reasoned, Lois took the photo with her. He shook his head as he thought of her stubborn nature.

He watched Solomon stroll toward him. As his partner approached the desk, the man muttered, "What did you do now?"

"What did she say I did?"

"She didn't say anything, which, as a rule, is the norm. However, there was a definite unfriendly tone to her silence. 'Other quiet,' as my wife used to say."

"Where is she now?" Greg asked.

"My wife or yours?"

"Funny. Your wife, fool."

"My wife is back in Europe, Paris to be exact. She never did like police work."

"You told me. Who does, except those who perform police work? Did she go back for good or just visiting family?"

"I don't think she knows for sure, yet. She may be staging, preparing for her eventual return. To tell you the truth, I don't know how I convinced her to marry me."

"You didn't do a damn thing, it was love."

"Yeah, it was love. I guess I had nothing to do with it."

"Very little. Didn't you tell me you loved her? How much did she have to do with that?"

"Geez, Greg. People just don't walk down the street and fall in love. You make it sound like we're animals in heat or something."

"Aren't we?"

"Man, she really messed you up this time, huh?"

"What are you talking about?"

"Love. Isn't that what we are talking about?"

"Whatever."

"Yeah, whatever. Besides, I didn't come here to be your priest. You can give me your confession another time." Solomon raised his hand from his pocket to expose a card. "We have a winner."

"What did you find?"

"I know who Graham is."

"Really. Who is he? How did you find out?"

"Everything is on the Internet, everything."

"So you found him on the Internet," Greg said in disbelief.

"Well, partly."

"God, man, you are making my head hurt. Tell me the whole part."

"I told you the face recognition thing would work. The lab found a match."

"You mean to tell me the photo of his dead face matched? You're right, I didn't think it would work."

"Well, it didn't exactly."

"You are wearing me out. Are you deliberately keeping me in suspense?"

"Did I grab you?" Solomon asked, with little-boy bright eyes.

"I'm gonna grab your neck if you don't tell the story, and quickly."

"They sort of found a match."

"Sort of," Greg mimicked.

"The system captured twenty-five matches, three of them were woman."

"So out of twenty-five, how did you decide which was Graham?"

"The three women were out, obviously. Out of the twenty-two

remaining men, six are dead, two are living overseas, which leaves fourteen."

"Your math is impeccable. Were you an honor student?"

"Six are in college."

"And five are midgets, right?" Greg said with sarcasm. "But wait, the twenty-five must have had criminal records to be in the system, right?"

"Now, you're getting it."

"Graham has a record."

"Yes."

"What did he do?"

"Nothing big. He was arrested for a campus protest that got out of hand."

"Crazy kids. What was it, their tuition went up?"

"They were protesting a speaker the university brought to the school."

"So much for free speech, huh?"

"And he wasn't one of the kids. He was a professor," Solomon continued with the story.

Finally, Greg's interest rose. "I'll be damned, but wait a minute, there's no Graham on this list."

"Yeah, that's the other thing," Solly admitted. "I jumped the gun. Once we narrowed it down, I searched the Internet and found more pictures, and that sealed the deal."

"If you found him, then why isn't his name on the list?"

"Well, it gets kind of murky, here. The professor's name is not Graham."

"Oh, my God, Turner. Get on with this story, wrap it up, come to the end of the road. Who is Graham, then? Is he the professor or someone else? I believe in hunches, and I'm assuming this is a hunch, but I need something from you, so I can get as excited as you. Do you have that or shall I just roll over and die, right now, my life unfulfilled?

Solomon had a smile on his face reminiscent of a poker player with a winning hand. He placed a photo directly in Greg's face. His partner didn't take long to reply, "Oh."

Chapter 14

I followed the pastor closely as he quickly walked to the cafeteria. He entered without hesitation. I stopped at the door and watched, to get a better idea of the situation.

"What happened?" he asked Tuba.

I couldn't hear what the big man was saying because there were at least twenty conversations going on. I entered the room and looked for Lee. I found her behind a group of men, and she looked as if she was going to explode. When I pushed my way through the group and grabbed her arm, she retracted from me as if I were a rattlesnake. But more curious was the fact she never looked at me. Rather than grab at her again, I called her, and she didn't respond; I raised my voice and rested my hand on her shoulder. That did the trick. She was looking at me, and it gave me the opportunity to ask, "What's going on?"

Her heavy breathing slowed and she relaxed. "That's him," she said and her eyes darted across the room. I'm sure I was meant to identify who she meant, but I had no idea.

"Who?"

This time she tilted her head toward the "him," and this time was just as insufficient as the first gesture.

"He's the one who tried to rape me. That one there. Check his neck."

"What about his neck?"

"He has the same mark as your eye."

Immediately I had a flashback to the moment she stabbed me a fork. It missed my eye and hit my cheek. The thought made me touch my face and it still felt a little sore. I followed her clue and walked across the room and looked for the mark of a rapist.

166

I looked for the pastor and he was at the edge of the room, still speaking and getting the history from Tuba. I felt stupid looking at the necks of each man I passed. Then it occurred to me to walk up to Tuba. My father used to tell me the guilty speak first, and he was the first to grab the pastor, probably trying to explain his innocence. I would check his neck for sure, so I went toward him and Reverend Franklin.

I came to Seal and signed, "What happened?"

Of course what he signed in return was much too fast for me to understand. There's a problem with knowing too little, but just enough to make people think you know something. That was the level of my sign language and I owed it all to Seal. "Slow down," I said to him, but he was signing and flipping his arms about like wings. His movements exposed his neck and I saw the mark. I couldn't believe it. This man could not be who she was talking about. I turned to find Lee and she was glaring and pointed to her neck, to confirm Seal was the rapist. Impossible, I thought, but when I turn to him, he looked at me with eyes as wide as a guilty child.

There is nothing more maddening than betrayal. I wanted to choke my first wife when she revealed she was pregnant. She was my girlfriend at the time, and I reacted with a rage I didn't even know it was in me. I restrained my anger then, but this was a man. This situation smelled the same, and without thinking, I grabbed his collar. Had I remembered he was an expert in martial arts, I'm sure I would have tempered my response. It was too late.

We fell to the floor and wrestled. I frantically used my arms to block every blow, but his expertise finally got the best of me. My nose had to be broken, but there was no pain. There was nothing. There was no sound. My field of vision was so narrow, I could see only Seal, which was enough to keep me going. I lunged like a bull, and his kicks were not enough to overcome my momentum. We were on the floor again, rolling and kicking.

The brawl came to an end when Tuba lifted me and tossed me aside. I didn't get the message the first time, but it was clear when he wrapped his arms around me. I felt as if I was enclosed in a casket. I could barely breathe. Then I noticed the pastor escorting Seal through the door.

"You slimy son-of-a-bitch!" I yelled at him. He tried to turn toward me, as if he heard me. It gave me the opportunity to shout

"Fuck you!" in sign language, of course. He allowed himself to be handled by Franklin. However, he was able to gesture the universal sign for disdain.

As he and the pastor went out, I shouted, "Fuck you, Seal! Fuck you, too, you mad, sick bastard."

I was in big trouble and I knew it, but for the moment, I felt free. I didn't care about any consequences. I was sure I did the right thing. I was so involved in replaying the incident, I barely heard Lee ask me if I was all right.

"What?"

"Are you okay?" she asked again.

I was sure I answered her, but maybe not. Lee grabbed my arm and escorted me to the front and then outside.

"Thank you," she said.

"Yeah, sure," I responded, but I was still agitated. Seal had a lot of friends, and I didn't feel safe being outside. She took me from a safe haven to the wilds of the street. As I twisted and turned to see anyone coming for revenge, I must have looked out of control.

"Stop!" she yelled. She got my attention and I stopped, but my eyes were slow to respond to her. I was still looking for attackers. It took me a moment, but I finally convinced myself all was well.

"I'm sorry," I said to her.

"For what?"

"I just blew your chances of staying here."

"So what. Why would I want to stay, now, anyway?"

It was a good point, but I didn't go through three days on the street to have her so close to safety and then lose her security. I was about to explain, when I saw the pastor at the door. He said nothing, but his eyes were shouting commands at me. He turned away from the entrance and walked away. I knew what he wanted and I went inside to his office.

Pastor Franklin was as irritated as I felt. He paced the floor and didn't notice when I arrived. He was not an angry man, so the only way for him to release his anger was to pace the floor. He looked at me briefly and walked back and forth. He must have been trying his best to compose himself. He stopped, then sat on the edge of his desk. He stared at me and thrust his hand toward a chair. I followed his instruction and sat down.

"Don't worry, Pastor, I'm gone. No worries."

"What were you thinking, Roman?"

"I wasn't thinking. I was just–" I couldn't tell him what I was doing or thinking.

"Reacting," the pastor said, completing my sentence. It sounded like the right word. The analysis was not new to me. I heard it all my life, from my parents and then again from my superiors in the Navy. I had been in more fights then I could count. Most of them were stopped well before any damage was done. Occasionally, it was a fight to the death, though death never came. There were times I tried to kill someone. My mother told me my rage would either kill someone or myself, and many times I wished it was me.

When the pastor handed me a tissue, I realized my nose was bleeding. I felt no pain until that moment. I wiped my nose and gently ran my fingers around it to assess if it was swollen, broken, or still in place.

"Is it broken?" I asked him.

"I don't know. I can't tell, but you seem to be talking okay. Can you taste blood?"

"No."

He leaned over me and looked over my face, carefully.

"What happened, there?" he asked pointing under my right eye. "How did Seal do that?"

"He didn't." I wasn't about to tell him how Lee stabbed me, just as she stabbed Seal. One woman and two men with the same mark. He would think I was part of the rape.

"Where's Seal?"

"In his room."

"Yeah, sure he is."

"He's there," the pastor insisted. "Tuba will make sure of that."

"Did you call the cops?" I asked.

"They should be here any minute."

Any minute was not soon enough. "Do you know what happened?"

"I only know the accusation. Do you know more than I do?"

"Not really," I said.

"You brought her here."

"I just wanted her to be safe. I knew you would help."

"Is that arrogance, presumption, or should I be flattered?"

"Which one will work?" I responded.

"Which story would you like to tell me?"

"What do you mean?"

He was insistent when he asked, "Do you know her?"

"No, Pastor. I just found out her name yesterday." Of course, I never included I knew her as Graham's woman, but I wasn't about to dig myself into a hole. I was nervous to ask, but I did anyway. "Do you think I hurt her?"

It sure took him a long time to answer, but he finally said, "No." The pastor was finally showing some sympathy. "Well, I'll get her to our emergency room."

The emergency room was only for those he thought worthy of a chance, but really offered little. When anyone was admitted to the emergency room, a team went to work to find services, housing and medical care. They were an incredible group of people, who could assist those in the deepest trouble and get them into an environment that put them on the road to recovery in days. I saw them get a guy off the street, a dental and medical appointment, and a housing application completed in forty-eight hours.

The Team of HOPE would swoop in like an eagle grabbing a rabbit and take them away, not to kill, destroy and eat, but to revive. They were miracle workers or at the very least miracle finders. They knew everyone in the city. I once heard the pastor say of them, "I don't know nobody, but I know somebody who knows someone."

Lee would be in good hands with them as long as she submitted to their will. I wasn't sure she would. I already figured out she was strong-willed and stubborn. My job was done, though. I delivered her to the right place, and it was my turn to leave. I could see sadness in the pastor's eyes.

"I'm sorry," he said.

"No worries, Pastor. I'll be okay."

"The rules are the rules," he explained.

He was reminding me of the zero tolerance for fighting. I broke the rule and I had to go, but I was okay with it. I was more right with the rule than the reverend seemed to be at the moment.

If I could produce puppy-dog eyes, I believe he would have ignored the rule for me, but I wanted no favors.

I stood up and told him I would pack a few things and be out within thirty minutes. I really didn't need much time. There was little to pack and there was no reason to say good-bye to the other residents. It was clear, they weren't my friends. The most docile and friendly guy in the place turned out to be a rapist. He fooled all of us. I liked Seal. He saved my life. I hated being manipulated. It was a manifestation of the disregard for my intelligence. I wasn't an ignorant man, despite what anyone thought.

There wasn't anything left to say, but the pastor looked so pained. I guess I was his pet project gone wrong. Before I left, I tried to reassure him again I would be fine. The pastor tried to smile and I left for my room. Goodbyes are never any good. I've said it, and it has been said to me, and every one was painful. Even when my wife decided to leave me, she seemed to hurt. I wasn't sure if she was really sorry to leave me or was sorry to leave me alone. I deserved to be alone.

At times, I wished I could tell her she made the right decision. I was of no good to her or my daughter. I deserved to be on the street and on some days, I felt I didn't belong anywhere, except in a bottle of alcohol, of any kind, of any age. Flavor was not important, I just needed enough to drown my brain cells so I was numb to anything. When I looked back on those days, I didn't want to be numb, I wanted to be dead.

In my absence, no one seemed to have been in my room. Everything was still in place, even the toothpaste was still on the bed. It was evidence the pastor was hoping for my return. He wanted me here. I felt bad for him. I didn't know what to pack. I didn't want all of it. I remember when I moved from my parents' house and joined the Navy. I took my music and some clothes. It was all that mattered then, and I was of the same opinion, now. I stuffed my backpack with a pair of pants, two T-shirts, a couple of pairs of underwear, toothbrush, toothpaste, three pairs of socks and my iPod. What else could I need?

A shadow covered the door and I turned to see Tuba. Each time I saw him, I was amazed by his size. I wondered if he was sad I was leaving.

"Cops came and got Seal," he informed me.

I acknowledged his statement with a nod and then pushed past him to be on my way.

"Take care of yourself," he said, and I barely responded with a "yeah" and walked through the empty hallway to the street. It was the hardest part, the moment of separation. Once I was outside, I felt much better. The moment passed and I was free. As tempted as I was to turn and look at the mission building one more time, I resisted the urge. I knew I would feel so much better once I turned the corner and the building was no longer in sight. I used to come to the mission for food, but I knew this was the end. The pastor would feed me, but I wasn't about to relive this moment on a regular basis.

My plan was almost complete, when I heard Lee shout out my name. When I turned, I saw her running toward me. I hoped she was far enough away so she didn't see my look of disgust. I tried to smother it.

"Where are you going?" She seemed so concerned.

"I'll be okay."

"I didn't ask you that. Where are you going?" This woman was annoying. I didn't mean to be so sarcastic, but I pointed down the block and said, "That way."

She just stared at me, then responded, "Jackass."

I shrugged, and she turned and walked away. I guess saying goodbye was hard for her, as well. I watched her for a moment and she must have felt compelled to prolong the separation for one more statement.

"You're a jackass, Roman."

"I'm just trying to move on, the best way I know how."

"Well, the best way you know how is pretty shitty."

"Listen, they'll take good care of you. I'll be fine." How many times did I need to repeat that phrase? She kept looking at me, as if I slapped her. Jesus! Everyone was so sensitive.

Finally she walked away, and I was free to do the same. Though I sarcastically pointed out my direction to Lee, I had no idea where I was going. After walking for two blocks, I began to plan my future. Once, I planned years in advance. Now I lived day to day. The twelve-step programs preach daily living as the way to live. One day at a time, but that strategy seemed so defeatist to me. To be unable to see into the future meant I had no future. I came to accept the philosophy from necessity, not by choice. So with a new game plan, I headed to the park. Just like a homing pigeon, I returned to what was familiar.

The sun was a beautiful tangerine color. Of course, it's better to appreciate God's work from afar. Nature was not my thing. My parents suggested I join the Boy Scouts when I was ten. I resisted, but I never told them the reason. The thought of sleeping with bugs and being vulnerable to the beasts of the wild was frightening. I saw too many movies to be comfortable with such an arrangement. Besides, I never heard of them wanting to go camping.

I told them I would rather go to basketball camp, which wasn't true, but they signed me up and I didn't like it. The coach wouldn't let us play. He interrupted every piece of fun with instructions. He instructed us how to turn, how to guard a player, how to shoot. I grew up watching guys playing basketball at the playground, and they seemed to have fun. I never saw any rules in place, other than some heated arguments over a foul.

Ironically, I passed by a playground and there was a game going on. I watched, and for a moment I was in the game. I felt myself making the right moves and the right shot. The game hadn't changed much from my childhood. It was all about looking pretty. I was never pretty, but today my memory failed me and I re-imagined myself as graceful and all-seeing.

I watched my youthful self make unbelievable passes. I saw every opportunity to score. I was a team player. After about fifteen minutes, my youth faded quickly, as reality returned. My mother asked time and time again, where the time had gone. Yes, where did it go? I was on the ball courts just yesterday, it seemed. There's nothing like reality to come and ruin my day. I was no longer young. I could no longer play basketball with these kids. I no longer had parents. My youth was taken from me as quickly as my recollection conjured them. It was time to move on.

Entering the park was like a homecoming. In the past several months, I visited. Now I was a resident again. I found a tree to nestle against and watched the remainder of the sunset. I wanted to put my headphones on and listen to music, but this was not the best time. Being distracted was not a good strategy. There was a time I needed every distraction possible and alcohol was the best tour guide. I hadn't had a drink in months, since joining HOPE. I wondered if I had kicked the habit.

The pastor said habits can be broken in thirty days, so I was hoping I was free. My memories of freedom in a bottle were returning, but they were minimal. I guess I was free. Small victories were better than big ones. I remembered a poem about a battle and a nail. For want of a nail, the horse was lost. For want of a horse, the rider was lost. For want of a rider, the battle was lost. I couldn't remember the rest, but I know the war was lost because of some damn nail. Small things are the big things.

Being alone and watching the sun descend was not good. I decided to go back to the street and find some other people. I walked to the library and found a row of homeless men setting up camp at the entrance. There was a light which offered some security. The block was full, but I found a spot at the end. I walked by and nodded to some. They watched to see if I was going to harass them. It was a common occurrence for the police to move them away.

"Hey, Roman," someone called. I looked up and saw Alderman. I surprised myself by the joy I felt when I spotted him. I felt I was being welcomed by a friend. My homecoming was complete.

I dropped my backpack from my shoulders to the ground next to him. "What are you doing, buddy?" he asked.

"Nothing much." What else could I say?

"You out again?"

It was a question asked of those in prison. I didn't know if I was out or in. I confirmed my new address as we sat up against the building wall. He offered me some food and I took some from his plate.

"I see the Chicken Lady was here," I said.

The Chicken Lady came on a regular basis with plates of food. The main course was always fried chicken, hence her name. The bird was almost cold, but the good thing about chicken is that it is good, no matter the temperature, especially if you were hungry. Hunger changes the taste buds. Sometimes a person will accept anything to satisfy it. Hunger is like lust.

"She can still make some good chicken," I said as I licked the grease from my fingers.

"Yeah, ol' girl still got it. I don't think she makes it, though. I think she buys it somewhere."

I put the last piece between my teeth and peeled the meat from the bone. "No matter. She buys it at the right place."

"That's right," Alderman agreed.

I had few friends, maybe none, really. Food, however, was on my list of friends. It made me feel good. It supported me when I was down. When I was happy, I knew of no better friend to celebrate with.

When I looked up, Alderman was lighting a joint. He took a long drag on it and held it in his mouth and closed his eyes. I stared and waited for him to return to earth, but he stayed where he was for a while. I wasn't clocking his time, but he made me feel like a peeping Tom. Just as I decided to turn away, he opened his eyes and offered the bud to me. I doubted if I could achieve the same results as he, but I took it and dragged on it. I held on to the smoke and let it settle in my lungs. When I opened my eyes, Alderman was sitting against the wall and barely acknowledged me when I returned the cigarette to him. He grabbed it and took another hit. We were like two old men sipping on an after-dinner Cognac.

"Alderman, why are you up here? You don't stay in the jungle any more?"

"No, man, it's way too dangerous in there now. Did you hear about the guy that got killed over there? I heard they cut his heart out."

The picture it created in my head was so obnoxious, I wanted another drag on the joint. I grabbed it and sucked down another puff of smoke. I wasn't a marijuana type of guy. It used to make me sick, but it was all I had at the moment to calm my nerves.

"Did they really? I mean, did they really cut out his heart?"

"It's what I heard. It's not like it's in the paper or nothing. Maybe they're holding back that sort of information for a reason."

"Maybe."

The cops were always trying to trap someone. Their enthusiasm resulted in wrong convictions or, at the least, harassment of people with no power to fight a well-organized system. I was part of the powerless. Homeless people barely had an identity, let alone power.

I gave the joint back to Alderman and he took the last drag. He slid from the wall to a supine position and I watched him as if I were watching a dance routine, from West Side Story. I liked that play. He exhaled and closed his eyes, and I knew our conversation was over.

I looked down the block and everyone seemed to be settled, as well. I watched some pedestrians walk by, though on the other side of the street. I wondered what they thought of us. We covered the sidewalk. It would be a good night if the police didn't come along and move us. A good night's rest is all I wanted.

I watched cabs drive by. I watched a limousine cruise slowly by and thought there was a couple peering through the darkened glass. A few feet and a car door separated me from prosperity. But, of course, maybe they were worried they were close to poverty. Who knew how close? Maybe they were a paycheck away. One investment gone wrong and they could be on the sidewalk, as well. It would be a story to tell — the journey from a limo to the streets. It never happens suddenly. It's like a slow-motion crash. You always think you're in control of the car, until the final turn and you realize there is nothing left to do but give in to the inevitable.

The limousine moved out of sight. We were two ships in the night. I almost had the urge to wave, to catch their attention. I wanted to be rescued, but they were not the ones, I was sure. Besides, maybe no one was in the back seat.

I pulled my knees close to my body and rested my head on the table I created with my folded arms. I looked for more sights to entertain me, but there were none. Alderman looked so comfortable. It's amazing what a layer of cardboard can do to transform concrete to a bed.

My mother tried to tell me the difference between being alone and being lonely. Tonight I could tell her. I was surrounded by homeless men and women, but I felt little connection to them. I was a part of them, but they were not a part of me. I was not among friends. Alderman was my only connection, but he wasn't my friend. We would not die for each other. We were company and that was enough, I guess.

As hard as the pavement was, I was at the point where my fatigue overpowered the pain in my butt. I drifted asleep, occasionally, but for only seconds at a time. Soon, sleep would win and I slowly lay down on the ground and rested my head on my backpack. It was my last act, and without any sense of time I was in a dream. I could have stayed poolside forever, but some dog started to bark. The barking became louder, until I couldn't ignore it any longer.

There is the moment between a dream and consciousness. It's the moment when you want to return to the dream, and you talk to yourself hoping to pull yourself back into your fantasy. I was there, but as always, the attempts always failed. I was almost awake. It was a real dog and real barking. I could even smell the thing. When I opened my eyes, I could see the thing. It was Tiger.

He was happy to see me, as usual. I quieted him and it finally occurred to me he had escaped from HOPE.

"Geesh, dog. What the hell is wrong with you?"

I also became aware of the dawn. I had slept through the night. It was time to break camp. The police would soon be on the way to break it for us. I looked up to see others beginning to rise. Then I spotted Lee.

"Jesus Christ! What are you doing?"

"I came looking for you. What else?"

"I don't know what else. Why are you looking for me, anyway? You have a bed, food. What else do you need?"

"I don't know. I just wanted to know you were okay."

How pathetic, I thought. "I'm okay. I told you that. I'm okay. Go back. HOPE is what you need."

"A friend is what you need," she softly argued her point.

I wanted to hurl cuss words at her, in rapid succession, but what would be the result? I stood up and stretched the kinks in my back and neck. As I stirred Alderman, I watched Lee with my peripheral vision. She stood motionless and Tiger stood beside her.

I leaned over to gather my backpack and under my breath I whispered, "Shit."

Chapter 15

Detectives Turner and Innis drove the unmarked police car into the mission's parking lot and turned into a spot marked *Reserved*. The partners got out and walked to the entrance of the building, passing by a few men, some with small suitcases.

"Let me ask you something. Why is it, you don't wear a tie?"

Solomon found the question amusing. "On this squad it's not required."

"Did you ever wear one?"

"I used to. I'm not that kind of guy. Maybe it's one of the reasons I transferred. Apparently you like 'em."

"I don't know if I like them, I just wear them, out of habit, I guess."

"You're a traditionalist."

"I am. I've been so contrary for so long, I just want to live smooth, ya know?"

"Shoes don't match," Solomon teased.

"Yeah, I hate that. I can never find shoes that look good enough to wear with good-looking clothes, at least not for this job."

"Therefore, it is best to wear more casual clothes."

Greg looked over his partner's attire. His navy blue knit collar shirt was well coordinated with his dark grey pants. His black leather shoes were clean and cushioned for his daily life of walking and occasional running. Greg had similar brown shoes, but not stylish enough to match his suit jacket and pants.

Inside the building they headed for the pastor's office. As they went, they surveyed every corner of the hall and open doors. Pastor Franklin came out of his office and greeted the detectives.

"Gentlemen, I was just coming to ask you to move your car. It's in a reserved parking spot."

Solomon was the first to respond. "For who, or is that, for whom? I never could get that right."

"Our doctor. He will be here today."

"No worries. We don't plan on being here long. We just wanted to follow up on a few things."

"What things?"

"May we go into your office?"

The pastor escorted the men into the office and each took a seat. Franklin repeated his question. "What things?"

Solomon was quick to reply, "I thought we ended our hostility at our last meeting, Reverend."

"Apparently not."

"Your choice, sir. We all have choices."

The pastor remained nonchalant. "What can I do for you, detectives?"

"Cooperate, sir. Is that too hard for you, Pastor?"

"What can I do for you, officer?"

Detective Innis decided to intervene. "Pastor Franklin, we need your help finding a murderer, a pretty vicious murderer. Pastor, they tried to rip a man's heart out."

"Oh, my Lord."

"I doubt you will keep that detail to yourself, but I had to let you know. It's important you know there is someone very sick out there, maybe a serial killer."

Innis could see the pastor's face soften. It was the detective's intention to place an ugly image in his mind. Maybe the image would be so repulsive, he would tell all he knew. It seemed to be working.

"I'm sorry," the pastor said, finally.

"Thank you, Pastor," Detective Innis responded. "Do you know who Graham was? Do you know anything about him? We really need your help. Help us."

"I really don't know him. As I told you, he came to our open mike sessions, twice, I think. Maybe three. He didn't really have much to say until the last time. Funny though, he did ask some questions a few times."

"What kind of questions?"

"He asked one of our residents about VA benefits. He seemed very interested in that, but I had to stop the conversation since it was not part of what we do. He could get that information on any day. I don't know why he was so interested, unless he was a veteran."

"Did he say anything that made you believe he was?"

"No, nothing other than his interest."

"You said he asked some other questions."

"Yes, he also was interested in where people lived when they were on the streets."

"Do you think he was looking for a place to live?"

"Could be, I don't know."

"Did he ever try HOPE?"

"No. We're full, anyway."

"Is that good or bad? I mean to be full means there are a lot of people out there who are in trouble. Of course, it could be good for business."

"We're not a business," the pastor made clear to Detective Turner. "We're a service."

"Yes, sir."

Detective Turner felt the need to re-enter the conversation. "May we speak to Mr. Barnes?"

"He's not here. I don't know where he is. His residency here was terminated."

"Why did he want to leave" Turner asked.

"He was terminated involuntarily."

"Interesting. What happened?"

"We have zero tolerance for fighting or any violence or threats."

"Which one did he violate, Pastor?"

"He was fighting."

"May I ask, with whom?"

"One of the residents was accused of raping a woman, and Mr. Barnes was defending her."

"May we speak with her?"

"She's not here. She wasn't a resident."

"Wait, I'm a little confused. He was defending a woman who doesn't live here. What was his connection to her?"

"He brought her here. As quiet as he is, Roman thinks a lot and always feels the necessity to help people. I think he's trying to make up for his past."

"What's his past?"

Turner could see the reluctance to answer his question. "Is that confidential?"

"We tell everyone who tells his story, it will remain confidential."

"What happens at the mission, stays at the mission, sort of thing?"

"Yes, that sort of thing. We're involved in counseling, which is private and secure."

"Even if you're in a group session? Isn't that public information?"

"No. The group session is held in a private setting."

"I respect that," Turner said.

"Thank you, Detective."

"May we speak to the young lady?"

"She's gone, as well."

"Wow. So Mr. Barnes brings a woman here and gets in a fight defending her, and now she's gone. These are some slippery folk."

"Not slippery, detective. More like survivalists. It's rough out there."

"Yes, I've heard. Is it rough in here?" Detective Innis chimed in.

"It can be."

"Oh, yes, the fight," Detective Turner reminded the pastor. "So did you kick her out, too?"

"No, I offered to let her stay while we found her some help. Unfortunately, Roman had to go."

"So what happened to the rapist?"

"Alleged rapist. The police came and took him. I don't know what will be become of him."

"Especially since the victim is gone. Why do you think she left?"

"Maybe out of loyalty to Roman, or maybe she thought she might get hurt if she stayed."

"Hurt how?"

"Seal had a lot of friends here. He was very well liked. Maybe she thought they might retaliate."

"But, of course she wouldn't know he had friends here."

"I guess."

"I pick your first guess, Pastor," Turner stated. "I believe she's with Mr. Barnes. Did he ever bring her here before?"

"I've never seen her here before. He told me he found her on the street when he left the first time. Remember, I told you he likes to help people."

"It would make sense if he knew her. Did she leave with him?"

"No, she must have left last night or very early this morning."

"May we see her room? What is her name, Pastor?"

"Talitha. Fountain is her last name."

Turner repeated the name, "Talitha Fountain."

The men left the office and found the room set aside for Talitha. The detectives entered the room, but asked Franklin to remain outside. The small room had a bed with ruffled bedding. The dresser drawers were empty, as was the closet. Detective Innis flipped the bedding to reveal the sheets. He looked at every corner of the bed. He lifted the mattress and found nothing and continued his search behind a chair.

"I guess she took everything with her. Did she bring anything with her?" Innis asked the pastor.

"Just a backpack, is all I saw."

"Where's the bathroom? She probably used that, at least once."

They walked to a bathroom in the middle of the hall. Franklin knocked on the door and no one answered, so they entered. Again, they stopped the pastor from following. There were three shower stalls, and Turner noted a towel hanging on a hook.

"Could this be hers?"

Before his partner could answer, he began looking in the trash cans, which were lined with trash bags. He lifted the bag from the trash can to find some spare bags. Opening one, he placed the towel in the bag, and they left the room after a brief search for any additional objects.

"Pastor, who called the police during the fight? Before you answer, is he here?"

"It was Tuba, and yes, he is here."

"You wouldn't mind if we speak with him?" Solomon pressed.

"No. He's in the Captain's chair today."

"Captain's chair."

"Yes. Every week, one of the residents will take charge of operating the facility. They started calling it the Captain's chair."

"Navy thing?"

"Or a Star Trek thing."

Solomon continued, "I like the Navy thing. I'm a veteran, ya know."

The pastor ignored his statement as he and the detectives walked down the hallway to another room. Tuba was sitting at a desk laboring over some papers. He stood as the pastor entered.

"Sir," he said, as if in the military.

"Wow," replied Solomon. "That's impressive. They love you, huh, Pastor?"

"I love them. They return their love in various ways. I'll leave you with Mr. Tuberville."

Detective Turner walked over to the huge gentleman and shook his hand. "I get it now. Tuba, Tuberville."

Tuba smiled and sat again. Solomon sat and Detective Innis looked around the room.

"Do you like being called Tuba, Mr. Tuberville? I had a nickname when I was growing up, and I hated it."

"What did they call you?"

"I said I hated it." The seriousness with which Solomon answered took Tuba and Detective Innis by surprise. "Just kidding," he followed. "They called me Soul Man."

"That's not bad. Why didn't you like it?" Tuba asked.

"It kind of reminded me of death. We saw a movie when we were kids. It was called *The Soul Man*. It was about this guy who would steal souls. The guy would come in your house and while you were asleep, he would take your soul and torment it. You remember that movie?"

"No."

"No? Remember, the guy was like a vampire. He would rarely come out in the daytime. He would come in the house through any crack in the house, under the door. Then he would find the one he wanted and stand over the bed and call out to your soul and it would rise up out of your body and follow him."

"Follow him where?" Tuba was interested.

"Oh, man, that's the best part. At the end of the movie, you see all the souls he was collecting and—wait, I don't want to spoil the end. You got to see it, though. It will freak you out."

"Sounds good."

"Believe me, it is." Solomon waited a moment as Tuba wrote

in a booklet. He took the pause as an opportunity to change the subject. "What are you doing, there?"

"I have to make out the schedule for the month." Though he was answering Detective Turner, he watched as Detective Innis roamed the room.

"A month! That's pretty far in advance."

"Not so bad, now. When I first started, it was difficult, but it really is pretty simple. It mostly stays the same. I just have to move some names around."

"How about Mr. Barnes?"

"What about him?"

"Do you have a schedule for him? What's he supposed to be doing next week?"

"He's the reason I have to make some changes. He's not here anymore."

"Really. Where did he go?"

"Don't know. After the fight, he had to leave. The pastor doesn't allow fighting, not even the threat of one. He's very strict about that."

"You were there, right?"

"Yes, sir."

"You don't have to call me 'sir.' I'm not anybody."

"That's not what I've seen. You guys are always throwing your weight around, especially on the street."

"Yeah, we can be heavy-handed at times. I'm pretty sure, though, we never bothered you. You're a big guy."

"Big guys are no match for a gun, even a small one."

"True. Where do you think Mr. Barnes went? Did you know him well?"

"Didn't really know him at all. He kept to himself, didn't say much. I was shocked when he went off on Seal. That was crazy."

"It's always the quiet ones, it seems, huh?"

"That's what they say."

"So you don't know where he might have gone?"

"There's a hundred places, sir. How many blocks in this city? That's how many places."

"I see your point. Well, I guess we'll be on our way. Thanks for the conversation." Solomon stood and his partner joined him.

He turned to Tuba again before leaving and asked, "By the way, how's life for you here at the mission?"

"Good. I don't know what I would do without HOPE. I have peace here. I can focus on what I need to do, to get back to the life I want."

"What life is that?"

"I want to get my business back. I lost it about five years ago."

"Sorry. What happened?"

"I had a computer business. I lost it when the economy went sour. I felt bad I had to let my employees go. I tried to hold on, but one by one I had to let them go or they left. They saw the writing on the wall. Kind of ironic. I employed four guys. They may be doing fine now, and here I am, homeless."

"How did you wind up homeless?"

"Slowly. To keep up, I sold things—computers, computer parts, then my car. They foreclosed on my house. That was the last straw. I wish I didn't sell the car so fast. I could have used it to sleep in. I slept on the street for almost two years, then I found this place or maybe HOPE found me. Who knows?"

"Well, I'm glad you're doing okay."

As the detectives went out to the hallway, Tuba thanked them.

"Nice guy," Detective Turner said to his partner, but Innis didn't answer.

Greg finally broke the silence, by asking, "What movie was that, again?"

"*The Soul Man.*"

"Must have gone straight to video. So where did Soul Man take the souls?

Solomon shrugged an "I don't know."

"Don't worry, you won't spoil the end for me. I don't watch movies that often, but I never heard of it."

"Maybe that's why you never heard of it. You need to get out more," Solomon said.

"Tell me the end, fool," Innis cracked.

"I never heard of it, either."

"What?"

"I never heard of it. I made it up."

"You made that up, right then and there?"

"Yeah. I was just making conversation."

"Couldn't you talk about a real movie?"

"I couldn't think of a real movie. I was just trying to be nice. You're the mean guy. You know, I'm the good cop, you're the bad one. You have a mean mug, man."

"It complements your affable, yet agitating style. The pastor doesn't think you're the good cop. He doesn't like you."

"Whatever. I had to be different with him. His defenses are always up. I was just trying to rattle him, so I could get in his head."

"Did you?"

Solomon answered with a shrug of his shoulders. As they continued to stroll, a well-dressed man approached and was greeted by Pastor Franklin, coming into the hallway from his office.

"Speak of the devil," Solomon said.

The pastor and the man greeted each other, and the detectives overheard the man ask about who was parked in his space. The pastor's eyes indicated the detectives. He introduced them. "Detectives, this is Dr. Maloney."

"Sorry, Doctor, we're on our way out. I hope we didn't inconvenience you."

"No problem, detectives. I found a spot."

"But you're used to special treatment, though."

"Not special. The mission just gave me the spot. I didn't ask for it."

"That's what I mean. You didn't even have to ask for it. That's special. It's like the rich guys who don't have to pay for their food at a restaurant. They just give it to them. Don't you think that's special?"

"I think that's kindness."

"Could be that, too. Say, Doctor, did you ever treat a guy by the name of Barnes, Roman Barnes?"

Detective Turner could see he was reluctant to answer. "It's not privileged information, Doctor, is it?"

"No, I guess not. No, I don't believe I have."

"Oh, okay. What do you do here?

"I have a clinic here, once a week."

"Every week? That's amazing. Do you get paid or is it *pro bono*?"

"I donate my time."

"I'm impressed. You must make a lot of money. Well, doctors do, anyway, right? I mean, you give up your own practice once a week to come here. That's admirable."

"It's what doctors do. We give. That's our profession, to give our help to those in need."

"Yes, you're right, Doctor. I apologize."

"No apology needed. If you'll excuse me." Dr. Maloney turned as he said goodbye to the pastor. He stopped when Detective Turner asked him a question.

"Have you ever treated a guy by the name of Graham?"

"I don't think so."

Solomon produced a picture from his pocket and showed it to the doctor. "How about him?"

The doctor scanned the photo, but could not keep his shock to himself. "My God! They really had it in for him."

"Yes, they did," returned Detective Turner. "So you don't recognize him?"

"It would be hard to tell, even if I did. This is horrible. No wonder you kept this out of the paper."

"I'm glad you understand. I only show it to you because you're a doctor. We didn't even show it to the pastor."

"Oh, I'm sure he's seen things just as bad. Unfortunately, ministers deal with death, as well as life."

"True, but this is a bit gruesome. What kind of doctor are you?"

"An internist." His answer was met by no response. "An internist deals with many patient conditions."

"So you're like a Family Practice doctor."

"Not quite. I deal only with adults."

"So, you're a specialty of Family Medicine?" Solomon asked.

"No."

"Sorry, did I insult you?"

"No problem. You are not in the business, so I wouldn't expect you to know the difference." The doctor's arrogance was apparent. "Do you mind if I go to the clinic now?"

"Sorry, Doctor. Please don't let us hold you any longer." Solomon shook the doctor's hand and they left the building. As they walked to the car, Detective Turner looked at his partner and exclaimed, "I love being a detective. Do you love being a detective?"

His far more reserved partner responded, "Yes, I do."

"Do you like this kind of work? I mean, working for the homeless?"

"I never really thought of it as working for the homeless. I thought of it more like working on their behalf. Maybe there's no difference."

"Attitude, I think. It's like motivation. Some people do the same things, but for different reasons."

"What's your reason, Solomon?"

"I love them."

"You love the homeless."

"If I didn't, I wouldn't love my mother."

"What?" Detective Innis was shocked. "Your mother is homeless?"

"Was."

"Where is she now?"

"Living a pretty comfortable life with my father, I mean my stepfather. She was homeless when she was pregnant with me. I was born on the street. I lived out here for about two years."

"No wonder you're so comfortable being out here."

"Not comfortable, just familiar, I guess."

"Do you remember living on the street?"

"A little. Mostly I remember a lot of men. I don't know if my mother wanted them around or they were just attracted to her."

"Maybe both. A woman needs security. She was doing what she needed to stay safe and mainly take care of you."

"You know what? I don't even remember being hungry. I must have been hungry, but I don't remember."

"That's a good thing. You wouldn't want to remember your mother like that, anyway."

"I remember more when she had a job at a pre-school. I was able to attend the school. I asked her how she got the job, and she told me she just made up stuff. She almost made up a new person, but she couldn't make a whole new woman, since that would mean I would be a different me. She didn't want me to be confused, so she only went so far. She met my stepfather at the school. She told me she knew he was the one when he found out we were homeless, but didn't tell anyone. That was over twenty-five years ago. They've been together since then."

"Are you making this up?" Innis was suspicious.

"I could be, but I'm not."

"Because that would be pretty sick, if you were."

They arrived at the car, but stood outside to continue the conversation.

"Did you like what you heard? I mean in there?" Detective Turner probed.

"Very interesting."

"That's what I thought. Now you understand my methods. It's disarming, don't you think?"

"Irritating, too, but it works."

"As long as you heard what I heard, we're good. How did the doc know we kept something out of the paper?"

"That's not all I heard," Greg added.

Chapter 16

My mother used to tell me, if I were to get in trouble, "you get in trouble by yourself." It was good advice. She went on to explain, if I were stupid enough to get in trouble, I should account only for myself. There would be one alibi, one truth, or one lie. Hanging around in a gang complicated matters. Of course, I didn't listen. As a Featherman, I had my buddies. We thought we spoke with one voice, but when trouble hit, there were too many stories to keep straight and coordinate.

My mother was right. The beginning of this day started with my being in a situation I tried to avoid. I found myself with a dog I didn't like and a woman I didn't want.

I didn't have much of a choice. I needed the Mayor to get better and I needed Lee to return to HOPE, or somewhere. In the meantime, we walked the street and eventually returned to familiarity—the park. The park always offered a sense of freedom and comfort. That is, if the weather permitted. On a good day, I could pretend I was on a picnic. On the best of days, the park offered equality. So many people were walking and talking and involved with their lives, they rarely had time to think of anyone else. I was a part of the crowd. I was a regular guy. With a dog and a woman at my side, I imagined the rest of the world saw us as a family.

My mother also told me everyone was hurting. She told me, regardless of the smiles and the appearances of people, they were hurting. It didn't occur to me she was hinting about her life. Today, the crowd never knew I was hurting. The sun was too warm and comforting and the sky was too blue to focus on anyone else. Today was the spring day for poets. Today was a day which would inspire anyone to speak eloquently. This was a lovely day.

While I rested against a tree, Lee slept. It was the first time I saw her relaxed. Today was made for relaxation, as well. Watching her was like watching a baby in a crib. I recalled the days I would get up early in the morning and prepare for work. My wife and daughter were sound asleep, trusting me to be their guardian. Before I left the house, I would watch each of them and it brought peace. My wife was so pretty in her sleep. During the day, she was always so worried about many things, but in her sleep, her mind was at ease. I felt she was placing her trust in me. On my way out, I would kiss her lightly on the cheek, not to disturb her, and she would smile and raise her arm, beckoning me to come closer. I would bend over and, without opening her eyes, she could sense I was close enough to hug. A light hug and I was gone. Her smile persisted as I left.

My daughter, on the other hand, was always oblivious to my being in the room. I could kiss her over and over, and she wouldn't budge. I used to wonder if a stranger could come in the room and do the same. I realized it was my kiss she knew. It was my scent and my presence which kept her in her dreams. She always had great dreams and I was always anxious to hear them. It was the highlight of my day to hear her excitement. "Daddy, Daddy, I had a dream about you." She would grab my attention the moment I walked in the door. I'm sure she calculated the right moment, before my attention was stolen by my wife.

Every morning memory was wrapped up in Lee's face. Her face was the face I wanted to see again, every day. These were the moments I longed to see again. These moments meant I fulfilled my responsibility as a man.

I felt some nudging at my right thigh. Tiger was making himself comfortable against me. His eyes were closed and he was searching for the right spot to rest. I watched him and he looked at me one time and then went to sleep. The dog was at peace, as well. I guess all was right with the world.

It was the perfect time to people-watch and I watched everyone. A group of skate boarders walked by, with boards in hand. I was surprised they followed the rule of no skateboarding allowed in the park. Young people were always testing the limits of justice. I don't think I would have paid as much attention to them, except for the young boy with the long red hair. I had seen him before. I was pretty sure he was homeless. He asked me for some change about a month or so before. He tried to impress me with a story about needing the money to get to church. His baptism was in jeopardy and he didn't have a way to get to the sanctuary.

I recognized the bullshit from the outset, but I gave him two bucks, anyway. At the time, I didn't let him know the only reason I didn't call him on his lie was the fact I was homeless and I understood his struggle. There was no reason to strip him of his remaining dignity. I saw him later in the day, sharing a meal with his girlfriend, or maybe his wife.

I looked for his woman among the pack, but she wasn't there. I wondered if she was safe. I don't know why I cared. Maybe it had to do with the two critters I had with me. If I had to take care of them, he should be responsible, as well. The redhead and his group walked by deep in a conversation I couldn't understand. They laughed and mocked each other and enjoyed the weather with the rest of us.

Two women jogged past and spoke to each other. I imagined they were talking about each other's husband or boyfriend. The spoke so effortlessly as they ran. They were in great shape. I noticed they were wearing the kind of pants which had to be the style these days. Many women were wearing them. They were very tight and it made many women look as if they had an impressive butt. They didn't, I was sure. Take them out of those pants and their ass would fall faster than lead in water.

I saw a man walking a little girl. It had to be his daughter. She looked like him, even at her age, which I guessed was two. Her little hand was locked in his and he accommodated her little steps with smaller steps of his own. At one point, he released her to explore the park for herself. He guarded her like a man watching over the president, and she felt free to roam. She turned where she wanted, waved to whom she wanted, and laughed at God knows what.

I was jealous the man was able to provide his little girl the security she needed to examine the world. Isn't that manhood? At least that's what my father told me. I didn't listen, or maybe the lesson struck me so deeply I made stupid decisions to prove I was a man.

Lee slept for another hour and Tiger didn't stir, to the point I was afraid he was not breathing. Eventually she moved, then turned and sat up. The world must have looked much different after a good sleep, because she stared ahead as if see had never seen it before. She looked like the two-year-old I spotted earlier. Everything seemed new to her. She finally looked at me and said, "Are we going now?"

I took her question to be a hint, so I answered, "Sure." Where were we going to go? I couldn't answer, but we broke camp and headed for the street. It would be entertaining, if nothing else. Lee asked to go to the library and there was no objection from me. Once we reached the steps, she sat and made herself comfortable, reached into her backpack and pulled out a book.

It was common for us homeless to use the library, for the bathroom and to get out of the elements. Of course to do that, you had to be presentable. If you had the obvious look and smell of being a street person, you would never be allowed to stay, but if you could play the part, it meant a few hours of comfort and security.

"Why aren't we going inside?" I asked her.

"Don't need to. I got my book."

This woman was confusing, but what woman wasn't? "Well, wouldn't you rather read it inside?" I coaxed her.

"No. I like it out here. Do you have a book?"

Was she trying to be funny? There was no other answer but no.

"Come on, sit down," Lee said.

It wasn't that I had any other place to be or any other event to attend. I just felt manipulated. She could have read the book in the park. She always had a book in her hand. With a little more questioning of her sanity, I sat down. She looked pleased.

"Have you ever read this book?" she asked. Since I was never a reader, I answered in the negative.

"It must be pretty interesting," I followed. "What's the name?"

"*The Last Good Man.*"

Apparently she was mocking me, but when she flashed the cover at me, I realized she was telling me the truth.

"Weird title."

"But a good story. Have you read any of Cheryl Lofton?"

"No. what's it about?"

Her eyes lit up. She couldn't wait to tell me the story. I really wasn't ready to hear it, but I listened.

"Have you ever heard of her? She's world-famous now, but guess what? She was homeless, once. Her first book was called *The Last Good Day*. It was about her days as a homeless woman. She used a simple technique to keep her going."

What could be so simple, I thought, so I asked, "What did she do?"

"She remembers her last good day and she uses it to try and recreate it."

"What was her last good day?"

"She tells the day she helped her best friend move into her house. She and her friend moved all her stuff. When the day ended, they sat among a hundred boxes and furniture all over the place and they drank wine. They talked about what they had accomplished and they slept on a mattress and talked until daylight and then went to sleep."

"I don't get it. That was her last good day? What was so good about it?"

"Yes," Lee responded as if I had two heads.

"I mean, she must have had better days than that, right?"

"Her friend died two days later in a car accident. She was pregnant."

"What happened to the husband?"

"She didn't have one."

"Wow, that's messed up. So why did she concentrate on that day?"

"She explains it was the only day where she did all she could to help a friend. No man, no movers, no one else but her and her friend. She was there for her. And it wasn't really about the moving. It was about her being with her friend through a stressful time. It was the best time of her life, and she kept that memory with her the whole time she was homeless."

"How long was she homeless?"

"Seven years."

"Jesus!"

The thought of someone living in the street for seven years was unimaginable to me, though I met others who were homeless for more. The Mayor was homeless for fifteen. The street was his home, and I don't think he would be comfortable anywhere else.

"How long have you been out here?" I asked Lee.

"Two." The answer was muffled and I was smart enough to know she wasn't ready to talk about her life. Maybe she was talking about Cheryl Lofton's life as a way of talking about her own.

"So what else did she write?"

The question appeared to take her out of her solemn thoughts. She was excited to talk to me. "She has a whole series. *The Last Good Day*, *The Last Good Woman*, *The Last Good Man*, and *The Last Good Dog*."

"Dog?" What in hell was good about a dog? I looked at Tiger and couldn't find an answer.

"I know, right? Everyone has a favorite pet. It's usually the first one and when they die, people just keep on replacing their pet, be it a gold fish or a dog."

"She sounds like a psychologist."

"That's what she is. She became a psychologist. Isn't that cool? To be homeless and then become a doctor is amazing."

"Yeah, I guess it is."

"So anything is possible." Lee saw a smile come to my face and asked about my thoughts.

"Reminds me of what my daughter used to say."

"You have a daughter?"

"Is that possible?" I asked. Did she think I was on the street my whole life? What a stupid question. But I couldn't blame her. I didn't look the part. I continued, though I was miffed.

"She used to say anything was possible. I remember when I was reading her a story about a ballerina, she told me she was going to be the first ballerina president."

"Was it called *Bettina, the Ballerina*? I love that book. I read the same book to my daughter."

I recalled reading Jenna a story about the presidents. She was about six. She was observant enough to notice they were all men. "When was a girl president?" she asked me. When I told her there hasn't been a girl president, she said she was going to change that and be the first. I reminded her of her dream to be a ballerina. She fell silent for a moment and then her face lit up with an idea. She was so excited. I wondered if she was still so enthusiastic about dance.

I finally answered, Lee. "I think so. I don't remember. She told me she would have concerts and dance for the people. I told her being president was a very hard job and taking care of the country would take a lot of her time. It didn't matter to her a bit. She told me anything is possible."

"Out of the mouth of babes."

My daughter was so positive. I never saw a child who was so good at turning a situation around to her benefit. I used to think there was something wrong with her. Why couldn't she feel sad? She always saw the good in everything, and I couldn't figure out where she got her philosophy at such a young age. I wasn't like that, and neither was her mother. Once I asked her how she became to be so smart and she said she asked God. Then she told me about her Sunday school lesson. She told me to be smart, all you had to do was ask God, so she asked Him. She even showed me the verse, though I couldn't remember it. I could use some of that wisdom. I must admit, though, I never asked for it.

I looked at Lee and her face was back in her book. I looked at Tiger and he looked at me as if to say, "Don't ask me anything." He rested his head on my backpack. As I looked down on him, I was reminded of his owner, the Mayor. I needed to visit him, but I needed a plan. I escaped from a hospital. I could sneak in, as well.

An hour was all I could tolerate of people-watching. Lee read and was oblivious to the passing time. Once I stood, she looked away from her book and her eyes had the same look as the dog. Though I told her it was time to go, I had no plan. I was just bored.

We walked as if we were tourists, watching everything. We watched people not because they were interesting, but to see if they were watching us. Did they know we were homeless? I guessed they didn't, but the question came to mind because I knew I was homeless. I wondered if there were telltale signs.

Our walk was uneventful. Occasionally, someone smiled at us because of Tiger. He was like a baby. He was cute, so people had to make a comment. I could only feign a smile. Lee, on the other hand, wanted to start a conversation. She was too friendly for me. Couldn't we just walk, wherever we were walking? I think Lee was trying her best to be a regular person.

As we continued, I heard some music in the distance. As it grew louder, we walked toward it as if drawn by some force. Lee hummed as we approached the music, and the cadence of her steps synchronized with the rhythm of the music. In time, we came to a clearing and a DJ was playing in a small park. Many people were gathered and dancing to the Latin music. It was obviously infectious because Lee was dancing. She eased into it, but soon the music caught her body and moved her. She was pretty good. She tried to entice me, but I refused. It didn't stop her, though. She was the most animated I had seen since I met her. She seemed to be lost in the music. Even Tiger looked at her like she was crazy, but his wagging tail indicated he liked it. They were both nuts!

The music eventually stopped and Lee spotted some tables and a group of people giving out food. She grabbed my arm and tried to force me to the other side of the street. I refused to follow.

"Come on," she coaxed.

"You go. I'm okay. I got money, anyway."

"You can save your money."

"I'm okay," I insisted. I guess she understood my resistance and she let go of her grip on my arm.

"You're a jackass."

"Jackass maybe, a pigeon, no."

"What!" she asked in disbelief.

"I'm no pigeon." It was obvious she didn't know what I meant, so I explained. "Look how they flock around the food. They're like pigeons. It's like feeding birds in the park."

Lee walked across the street after giving me a look of disgust. Tiger tried to follow, but I picked him up and leaned against the wall and waited, not patiently, but I waited.

Finally, Lee returned with two plates of food. She shoved one in my face. "Here, jackass."

I didn't want to take it, but she would not budge until I took the plate. We walked farther down the street, until we had some semblance of privacy. We sat just off the sidewalk, in an alley. It didn't take her long to interrupt the silence.

"What's wrong with you?"

"Nothing's wrong with me."

"What's all this talk about birds and shit?"

"Nothing."

Lee mocked, "Nothing. Look at you. You're eating like a hungry bird. You're just too proud." It wasn't something I hadn't heard before.

"At least your money will last a day longer." She was right, of course, but I wasn't going to tell her that.

"Is that a man thing?" she asked.

"Is what a man thing?"

"Pride. Cheryl Lofton says it is."

"Who?" She had to remind me of the author.

"No, it's not a man thing. I just don't like depending on others. Don't you like being independent?"

"Yes, but I'm smart enough to know when I'm not. I know how to ask for help."

"Good for you."

"Yeah, good for me," Lee responded.

"Is it a woman thing?"

"What?"

"To nag. Isn't it enough that you got the food? You just have to keep it going. Let it rest. Okay, I give you the credit. You got us some food. Is that okay? You win."

"I'm not in competition with you. I'm on your side, Roman."

I didn't know if I liked her using my name. She didn't know me. There was no need for her to be so familiar. Of course, what else was she to call me? To address me as Mr. Barnes would have been silly. The best course would be for her to be gone. She could stay on the street and beg all on her own, and I could be at peace. Of course, she would have to take the dog with her. That wouldn't happen. It wasn't her dog. I had to keep Tiger until the Mayor was released from the hospital.

With that thought came my *raison d'etre*. My next plan of action was to get to the hospital and check on the Mayor. Surely he was close to being released. Hospitals didn't like to keep us uninsured around for long. I don't know who paid our hospital bills. Maybe the hospitals went to the government for payment. I thought maybe there was some general homeless fund they could use.

"Let's go," I instructed. Lee didn't ask any questions, she followed me. I guess she believed I knew where I was going and she gave into my instruction. My belly was full. Tiger shared some of my chicken mixed with his crunchy dog food. I wanted him to be reunited with his master soon. As we walked to the hospital, I was hopeful the Mayor could be discharged. I also tried to figure out a scheme to get to see him. Of course, I could lie and say I was a family member, though I wasn't sure it would work.

My best bet was to go through the emergency room and have them tend to the cut under my eye. It was getting more tender and red. I was sure it was infected. As I thought about it, I became somewhat resentful toward Lee, since she was the one who stabbed me in the first place. I was trying to help her and she did this to me.

I parted with Lee and Tiger at the emergency room entrance. They would never allow a dog into the facility. When I checked in, the nurse asked for my insurance.

"I don't have insurance," I told her.

Her facial response told me she expected the answer, so she went on to get whatever information she could get from me. There wasn't any to get.

"I thought everyone was insured," I said.

"What do you mean?"

"Don't we have national medical insurance?"

"You still have to buy a policy, Mr. Barnes."

My name had a nice ring to it. The fact she bothered to use it was a sign she cared about me. My father told me to always use a person's name when speaking to them. It made a person feel good. The little things are the big things, and I did feel good.

I thought I would return the favor. The receptionist's badge stated her name as Kathleen. "Kathleen, how do I get it, the insurance, I mean?"

"You go online and apply for a policy that works for you."

"What happens if you don't?" It was a reasonable question, since I never had a policy since I became homeless.

"If you don't get insurance, you have to pay a fine. I don't know what that is, though."

"And if you don't have the money to pay the fine, what happens? Do you go to jail or something?"

"Mr. Barnes," she answered in frustration. "I can't help you with that. I don't know. Please have a seat." Her tone was a bit abrasive, but I forgave her because she used my name again.

Emergency rooms, airports, and malls are a great place to watch people. I guess everyone watches everyone else. A little boy lay across his mother's lap, fast asleep. I tried to figure out which of them was sick. He seemed too comfortable and content.

His mother, on the other hand, kept looking around, impatiently. She cradled his arm and he stirred for a moment. A closer look at his arm and I saw it was bruised. Poor little guy. I don't know how he could sleep with what I diagnosed as a broken arm. Why weren't they taking care of him, right now? I hoped he had insurance, maybe he would be seen sooner.

A pregnant woman sat across from me, and I remembered when I had to bring my wife to the ER. It was a scary time. She was six months pregnant and spotting blood. She had a miscarriage during her first pregnancy and lost the baby, and we thought we were about to experience the same loss. Her doctor was really good about it, though. He instructed us to go immediately to the emergency room and he met us there within minutes. I was scared, but I tried not to let her know. All I could think about was what would I do if we lost another baby? She would fall apart and I would have no idea how to comfort her.

I looked at the pregnant woman again, and I noticed she must be alone. I had been waiting for at least a half an hour, and no one came to give her attention or care. How hard life must have been for her. Of course, maybe she was waiting for someone who was sick. Maybe she wasn't the one in distress. Maybe I had it all wrong. She looked calm enough.

Another three hours passed and I was finally called to a room. It was like an amusement park experience. A young man took my temperature and blood pressure, asked me if I was taking any medications and what was the reason for my visit. I know he was doing his job, but wasn't the appearance of my eye the reason for my visit? I took offense at the word "visit." I visit my friends or my Aunt Helen. People don't *visit* the emergency room, do they? I followed protocol, answered the questions, returned to the waiting room, and waited for another thirty minutes or so before I was called to a room.

The doctor asked me the same questions as the person before. I wondered if anybody talked to anybody in this place. I gritted my teeth and answered the questions. I kept my mission before me. The doctor poked and prodded at the lump under my eye. At one point I wanted to punch him. I didn't realize it was so tender. He squeezed it, and I let out a "Damn!"

"Sorry, Mr. Barnes. It looks infected. I will have to cut it open and let the pus drain out. Okay?"

What did he want me to say? I wasn't a doctor. Why was he consulting with me?

"Sure, Doc. Do what you have to do."

He called a nurse and asked her for some equipment and some drugs. I knew one of them because of my visits to the dentist.

"Mr. Barnes, I can numb the area before I cut it open, but I must tell you that it will be painful to do that. It's very hard to numb an abscess. By the time I numb it, I can cut it, but I'll leave the decision to you."

What kind of doctor was this guy? He keeps asking for my input. He should just be a doctor and take care of it. What the hell did I know about numbing things? How was I supposed to know the difference between the pain of numbing and the pain of cutting? I saw some gray hairs so I assumed he wasn't as young as he looked, but I had to ask anyway.

"How long have you been doing this?"

He smiled and then answered, "About ten years."

The answer was not what I expected. I was thinking he would say one or two, or maybe three years, at the most. Suddenly I trusted him.

"Do what you think best, Doc."

He left the room. During his absence, a nurse set up a table with instruments and some brown liquid. I focused on the blade. I tried my best to slow my breathing and prepare for the worst, though I didn't know what the worst could be. My only reference was the initial injury. It couldn't be worse than having a fork thrust in my cheek.

The nurse left and I waited for another twenty minutes, though it seemed like an hour. Oh shit! The doctor returned. I remember feeling like this when I was a kid sitting in the dentist chair. I would look at the tray and I knew pain was coming when I saw the syringe sitting on the tray. There was no needle this time, but a blade innocently lay on the table, surrounded by gloves and iodine. That was it. I knew he decided to just cut me open. Barbaric son of a bitch!

I told myself to breathe deep, but the more I thought, the more quickly I breathed. I closed my eyes, but it didn't work, either. I wondered if he would give me something to bite on, but it was a ridiculous notion. This was not the Wild West. God, get it over with, doctor!

The doctor ignored me and slowly prepared his hands, put his gloves on, and then rubbed the cold liquid on my cheek. Cut it open, doctor! Get it over with. The remarks were in my mind. I didn't want to make him angry.

"Are you ready?" he politely asked. I watched the blade in his hand and nodded my head to indicate yes.

"This won't hurt much. Just a little cut." He stopped talking for a moment and then said, "There."

Was that it? It was that quick? I watched him put gauze against my cheek and squeeze. It was too painful. Then he warned me the next maneuver might hurt a little. I knew he was lying. It was going to hurt a lot. Why do doctors lie so much? His voice was calm to the point I was inclined to trust him. He took a clamp and used it to stuff a ribbon of cloth in the hole he created in my cheek. He was right. It hurt, but not a little.

Then he placed a band-aid over his creation and leaned back. "There. You okay?"

"You done?"

"Done," the arrogant bastard replied.

Of course he could be so relaxed. I believed he had been doing this for years. He had no compassion. He just did his thing and he was on his way. The nurse did the rest of the work. She gave me instructions and allowed me to lie alone, for a while. Given some time to myself, I realized the doctor must have known his craft. The pain wasn't as bad as I thought it would be. It was just a mild throb. I felt the bandage and looked for a mirror to view to myself. I used a cabinet with glass doors. It didn't even look as bad as I thought. Good job, doctor.

I was tired of waiting, so when I decided to leave, I noticed the doctor had left his lab coat. Thank you, doctor. You really did help me.

Chapter 17

It was not unusual to find Detective Innis with his feet on the desk as he thought about the cases he and his partner were following. Detective Turner approached the desk, placed a folder on the desk, and flopped into his seat.

"We just caught another case," he informed his partner.

Greg didn't seem interested, but he responded anyway. "What else is new? Another murder?"

Turner confirmed his suspicion, then opened the file and studied the information inside. He asked Innis if he was interested in the file.

"How many homeless people are in this city, do you think?" Greg asked.

"The last official count was something like twelve thousand."

Greg pondered the number then continued, "Twelve thousand, out of millions. Out of twelve thousand homeless, twenty or so are murdered. The number is so small, they must all be related. Find one murderer and you'll solve ten homicides."

"So you think we have a serial killer?"

"No, but in such a small population, they must be related. Just imagine a small town of twelve thousand people, and twenty people were murdered."

"You would have a serial killer." Solly stated his response as if there could be no other answer.

"No, that wasn't the best analogy, but you see my point. To have a serial killer means the murderer is common to all. They're all related."

"I don't buy that. Besides, this is a city of millions, not twelve thousand."

"The common thread is, they're homeless."

"Greg, that is all we deal with—the homeless. That's what we do. No conspiracy theories please."

"No conspiracy, just a theory. Find one and we solve seven."

"Now it's seven. A few minutes ago it was ten."

"Don't take me literally. Take the concept."

"Okay. Let's talk about the Graham murder. Do you think it's related to any other murder we have?"

"I don't rule it out. Everything is possible, until only a few things are possible, then only one thing is possible."

"Are we down to a few things yet?"

"No."

"Okay. How about we start with one murder, one murderer? Why would anyone want to kill Graham?

"Not the best question. You're still calling him Graham. We know better, right?"

"Right. So why would they—" Their conversation was interrupted by a man who approached their desk.

Detective Innis removed his legs from the desk and sat upright.

"Hey, Li'l John," he greeted the man.

"How are you guys doing?" Li'l John responded. He pulled a chair over to the desk and sat with them.

"Just wanted to let you guys know I'm leaving town."

"Really? Where are you headed?"

"I'm going to live with my brother."

"I thought you liked the streets," Innis chimed in.

"I do, but he needs my help. We're both getting old. His wife is gone. I'm the only family he's got. It's not as much fun as it used to be. It's dangerous out there."

"We know."

"Yeah, I guess you would. I just wanted to say, I appreciate you guys. You're doing a good thing."

Turner returned the compliment. "We'll miss you, man. Who's going keep us informed about what's going on out there?"

"Somebody. Somebody is always hungry."

Li'l John was not an official police informant, but he was helpful many times in helping them evaluate any leads they received. Most homeless people had a distrust of the police. Li'l John, on the other hand, was a joyful soul. He could be happy anywhere, with anyone.

"How are you going to adjust to life in a real home?"

"If I can make it here, I can make it anywhere. It will be weird, though."

"How long have you been homeless, John?"

He answered so quickly and precisely, one would have thought he was keeping a daily count. "Eleven years."

"Li'l John," Turner said. "I don't mean any harm, but what the hell do you do out there for eleven years?"

"I know, huh? I guess I should write a book. I guess I could write a survival guide."

"Really, you could."

"Yeah, somebody already asked me to do that. I'm not a writer. I wouldn't know a thing about it. I wouldn't know where to start, where to end. Too much stuff in my head, ya know? You guys could write a book. I mean, you write reports and stuff. Just put it all together and you have a book. Have you thought about that?"

"No," replied Turner.

"You should. It would be a best seller. You guys could get a movie deal or something and be famous. Did you know those crime shows on TV have cops as advisors? You could be an advisor. You could be living the life."

"Funny, coming from you about living the life. Why is it you don't want to live the life?" Solly asked.

"I'm a different kind of guy, man. I don't need that stuff. I'm content."

"Li'l John, you mean to tell me you've been content to live on the street for eleven years?"

"It's fun, once you figure it out. It's a game. Like a corporate game. You figure out who the players are, the organizational chart, and you have it made."

"How long did it take you to learn all of that?"

"About three years, but I was a slow learner. Find a benefactor and you could do this stuff in a month."

"You're kidding, right?

"Yeah. I had you for a minute, though. Hell, it just happens after a while. You really do know what to do, where to go. But it's true someone wanted me to write a book, though."

"A publisher?"

"No, Graham."

The detectives became very attentive and Li'l John noticed.

"Yes, Graham. All he wanted to do was help people. He was a good guy. Too bad about him. He was a good cracker."

He noticed the surprise at his last statement. "What? That's why they called him Graham. He was a good white boy."

Innis looked at his partner, then back to Li'l John and asked, "What was his real name?"

"Don't know that. We just accept what you tell us."

"What did he say?" Innis tried to bring the conversation back to the topic.

"What did he say about what?"

"About writing a book, the survival guide?"

"Not much. I didn't think he was serious. I would see him every once in awhile and he would bring it up. No big thing. He would just say that we could do it."

"Did he know a publisher?"

"Hell, I don't know. I wasn't that serious. Just a thought, but I think he could have done it. He was a real smart guy. Always asking questions and stuff."

"What do you mean?"

"Mean about what?"

"About asking questions?"

"He would just ask a lot of stuff. He would ask where to go for food or drugs."

"Drugs?"

"Yep, drugs."

"Was he a druggie?"

"I don't think so. He was just interested in places and people and stuff. He liked knowing stuff."

Turner looked at his partner. "Not such a big surprise."

"Did he tell you why he liked learning so much?"

"So much what?

"Anything, Li'l John, anything."

"Oh. No, not really. You know, there are people that have a thirst for knowledge, you know?"

"Know what?" mocked Detective Turner.

"What?"

"Okay, I think we've said our goodbyes," interjected Innis.

"It's been a pleasure, Li'l John. I hope you and your brother live well."

"Oh, we will. Or maybe I should say he will. He's got money, lives on a big farm. Maybe I can sleep out under the stars every once in a while, so I can feel at home."

"Your brother probably wouldn't mind, at all."

"Oh, he just might. He has a lot of rules. He drove his wife, Lisa, crazy. It probably killed her. Sometimes death sets you free, you know?"

"True," Turner replied.

"Well, I gotta go, guys. You stay safe and help everyone to do the same." Li'l John leapt to his feet and waved to everyone he passed. Turner and Innis watched in amusement.

"I don't know how he does it," said Turner. "Some people have a knack for things."

"Is there a talent for being homeless?"

"I bet there is. Everybody can't do it. Some people die out there. Some people get killed."

After a moment, Greg responded, "Unless you have help. Maybe you can be taught. Maybe someone can mentor you. Maybe someone can show you the ropes."

"What a degree to have–Ph.D. in homelessness," replied Turner.

"Or sociology."

"Say it. Say what's on your mind. What's your hunch? I feel a hunch coming on."

"Maybe Graham was writing a book. All the questions, the notes he was compiling, was for a book, maybe even a survival guide."

"Sounds right to me," replied Turner.

"No, that's not right."

"What? It makes a lot of sense."

"It makes sense to a point, though. You saw the body. Somebody mutilated him, on purpose. It was a message," Innis said.

"Okay, so what's missing? The message is for who?"

"I don't know. Maybe for no one."

In frustration, Turner responded, "Okay, you're talking in circles."

"Yeah, I am. The level of violence doesn't match a planned book."

"Well, it wasn't just planned, he was taking notes, right?"

Innis considered, then replied, "Yeah, he was. Nope. That's not it."

Innis' eyes came to the point for which he was searching. "Got it! He wrote it. He wrote the book already, and there's something in it that will hurt someone."

"Or a lot of some ones."

Detective Innis rose from his chair with enthusiasm. Turner was excited enough just to know there might finally be a path to a solution. There was nothing more frustrating for him than to have a fist full of facts, none of which fit together.

Turner saw some light at the end of the tunnel. It may have been dim, but it was a light, enough to direct their steps; he hoped his partner's excitement was evidence enough to hope. Yes, the light at the end of the tunnel was the gleam in his partner's eyes.

"You got it, partner. We have to find the book," Innis stated.

Chapter 18

Today was made for a celebration. My cheek was almost healed. I had no pain, and the ribbon the doctor packed into the hole was gone. In fact, it was gone by the next day, because I pulled it out.

The birds sang for no apparent reason. I guess they were just glad to be alive. The noonday sun made the blooming flowers so vivid. This would have been a day to celebrate my fifteenth wedding anniversary. Sharon loved the park, especially, during the spring. However, today was not my day to celebrate but to remember my marriage, which ended years ago.

If my life had gone the way I planned, today I would be walking through the park, picking the flowers, to the objections of my wife. Sharon always followed the rules. I was the rebellious one.

Today I had an *ad hoc* family. Sitting on this bench gave me a great view of all the park's activities, but the inactivity at my side was the most pressing. I looked to my side and watched Lee as she slept. Her head rested in my lap, as if I were the perfect pillow. She barely moved and I didn't want to move for fear of waking her. She looked so peaceful and I felt waking her would be interrupting the best part of her day. Tiger lay against my backpack, on the ground. He was content, as well. I guess I was responsible for both, for now.

While they rested, I took the time to create my own peace. The slight breeze produced a mesmerizing to and fro of the leaves and flowers. It was easy to get caught up in the rhythm. Sometimes I didn't need to think about anything. Sometimes *nothing* was the tranquility I wanted. Nothing was the absence of responsibility, no bills, and a stillness I couldn't describe, just feel. As a gambler,

I wanted excitement and stimulation at all times. Being homeless changed my priorities. The daily uncertainty of a sound sleep or food was taxing. Routines were overrated, but my life begged for the mundane, the regular, and the silence.

Lee began to stir, which interfered with my fantasies, but her head was getting mighty heavy. Eventually she sat up and Tiger sat up, as well, and jumped into her lap. What a cute couple.

"Good morning," she said.

"Not quite. It's afternoon, but who's keeping track."

"Oh." She fussed with her hair, as if it would help. It was nappy any way you looked at it, but I guess it made her feel better. Maybe it was a look from me, but she decided to pull her ball cap on her head. It was the best she could hope for, I guess.

She put the dog aside and walked to the park bathroom. I watched and was struck by the way she walked. I felt like a stalker, but she walked like a woman. Of course I knew that, but I never saw much evidence, other than her soft face and breasts. She switched her hips and it caught me by surprise. I had to admit her butt was shapely for someone in her state. It seemed she was in shape. I lost the energy to keep fit years ago. They built a gym at the HOPE mission, but I was never motivated to use it. Lee, on the other hand, either had good black genes or she found the time to exercise. She was at the age to fall apart, anyway. I convinced myself she was the result of hereditary favoritism.

Lee emerged from the bathroom with her backpack. She looked refreshed. Her face was cleaner and brighter. She had brushed more of her hair under her cap. I hoped she brushed her teeth, and it was clear she had when she sat beside me and spoke.

"How are you?"

I thought it was a dumb question, but there was no need to tell her that, so I answered, "As well as can be expected." It was a cliché, but they work most of the time.

"What did you expect?"

I should have known she was one to push the issue. She just wouldn't accept the answer and move on. I think it was a feminine characteristic. My wife wouldn't let sleeping dogs lie, either. Sharon always wanted to talk. It was plain to me, Lee needed other women to talk with and I was desperately trying to decide where to take her.

"I didn't expect much of anything," I finally answered.

"Maybe that's the problem."

"There's no problem. What should I expect? It's a nice day, but that's all it is. Nothing else to hope for, nothing to do."

"Man, how long have you been out here?"

"I told you already." I was annoyed, now. Life was good for the time she was asleep.

"You really need to read *The Last Good Man*. You will love it. It may sound corny, but it really is good. Do you know the author is now a millionaire? Pretty impressive. Going from the streets to a penthouse, don't you think?"

"If you want a penthouse, I guess." I regretted making the statement the moment it came from my mouth. I already predicted her comeback, but I was too late.

"What do you want?"

I predicted her question and I could only respond with a smile.

"What's so funny?"

"Nothing funny, but I amuse myself, at times."

"Really. At my expense?"

"Are you nosy, paranoid, or just inquisitive?"

"I don't know. They sound all the same coming from you," she replied.

"That's paranoia."

Lee lifted the dog to her lap and petted him vigorously. "I'm not talking to you, anymore. Tiger is a much better companion, aren't you, boy?"

I understood she was in a playful mood and I obliged. "That mutt apparently doesn't know who to suck up to."

"Or maybe he does."

I wasn't going to lose this battle, so I reached into my backpack and pulled out a handful of dog food and put it in a paper bowl. As expected, Tiger leaped into my lap and began to devour the food.

I looked at Lee and mocked her previous statement. "Maybe he does."

"Food will last for a minute. Love lasts forever," she said.

My eyes rolled up into my head, gloating with satisfaction. I took a quick look at her to make sure whether her last statement was meant to be flippant or serious. She was still looking and petting the dog, so she probably never noticed my one moment of triumph.

"So may I ask what made you come look for me the other night?" I asked her.

"It wasn't the other night. It was the morning and I came to see that you were okay."

"Why?"

"Because you took care of me and I wanted to return the favor. It's not nice out here and I didn't want you to be alone."

"That's nice, but—"

"I know, I know, you're a man and you can take care of yourself. But I'm a woman and taking care of people is what I do, okay?"

"Not grown men, children."

"Wrong. I take care of everything. It's woman, uh—" she fumbled for the proper word, but could only come up with "womanish."

"Feminine," I corrected her.

"Whatever. It's what we women do. We talk a lot, we mother everybody, even men. It's in our DNA to cuddle, snuggle, kiss on the third eye, and rub things and people."

"Kiss what?"

"The third eye. You need to read more." She pointed to a spot on her forehead just above her nose. "The third eye. Have you ever been kissed there? It's more affectionate than the lips. It's connected to the pineal gland and when you get kissed right there, you stimulate it, and it improves a person's mood. Didn't know that, huh?"

"No, but you're wrong. It's all about the hug. Nothing is better than a hug."

"I can't argue that, I was just telling you about kissing."

"Maybe a hug is connected to the pineapple gland."

"Pineal," she insisted.

"I bet pineapple is tastier."

"You can be so silly, man. You should be more relaxed, like this."

True, it was a light moment. Everybody has them, but I knew it was limited. It would be short-lived because life was just too harsh to let me enjoy anything for too long. It seemed that was the lesson from my whole life. The problem was, the good times were too few and far between.

"Hey, come back," I heard Lee say. "Where did you go? You

were on your way out of the universe. There's no oxygen out there.
I just saved your life."

"Did you, now?"

"Oh, yeah. You don't know it, but I did. Are you going to see
your buddy, in the hospital?

"I will."

"When?"

"I don't know. I will."

"You should have some clean clothes, don't you think? Dirty
clothes and that lab coat you stole don't mix very well."

"I didn't steal it. I have every intention of leaving it there
when I go back."

"Is that a form of borrowing?"

"It's a form of—"

"Stealing. Yes, say it. Stealing."

"Like you never stole anything."

"I didn't say that, but at least I will admit it."

"What did you steal?"

"Well, it's kind of embarrassing, but it was for my friend."

"Your friend. What did you steal for your friend?"

"You know, my friend, my monthly."

"Ooooh. You stole tampons?"

"Yes, when I could. Sometimes I would just get some toilet
paper and use that." She must have seen the look on my face
because she added, "It's rough for a woman out here."

I knew that. I saw many women mistreated, sexually,
mentally and otherwise. There was little protection for them. They
were the most vulnerable of the vulnerable. Well, maybe kids, but
the kids had advocates. Women did as well, but everybody loves
children. When it came to housing, women and children had the
priority.

Men, on the other hand, though most of the homeless
consisted of us, were at the bottom of the list. Maybe because we
lost our place in society. Maybe a homeless man lost his leadership
position and that was a taboo. Men were designed to be the leaders
of the planet, or so my father said. "You lose your place, you lose
everything," he told me. He was drunk when he said it, so I didn't
know if it was wisdom or just a string of words he put together to
make a sentence.

213

"You had your opportunity at the mission," I told Lee.

"The mission's design is to take care of me. I want to take care of others. Remember, it's in my genes."

"Stubbornness, too, I see."

"Yeah, that, too. And add hardheaded and controlling."

"Yikes, I'm scared. Did you learn that in the military?"

"I don't think so. My mother always said I was hardheaded. I guess it was just cultivated in the military. Once I realized I could succeed, all my traits just grew. I liked myself and didn't see myself as a failure. All the things people didn't like about me, helped me succeed. "

"Good traits for being out here, I guess."

"Survival skills."

She was right. Being homeless required skills the average person couldn't handle. I wasn't average when I went to the streets, and I met others who had the grit to survive. Those who died were the ones who gave up. They no longer wanted to do what it takes to live another day. Once, the mission brought a speaker to one of the church services. He was formerly homeless, and he said the very skills he needed to survive were the same skills he needed to come out of homelessness and get a job and eventually own a successful business. I think he owned an investment firm.

He said the first and best investment should be in us. It sounded good, but advice always sounds good from successful people. It made you feel like you could do it to, but that's not true. Everyone can't do everything. I decided there were just special people who control the planet and I was not one of them. I was smart. I knew that much, but I was not destined to control anything. I couldn't control much of anything, so it was amusing to hear Lee speak of being a controlling person.

"You know how to make beef jerky?" I finally asked.

"What? Where did that come from?"

"Survival training. Didn't they teach you how to make beef jerky in the Army?"

"I don't remember that. Is that a requirement or something?"

"I just thought it was a good survival skill."

"Just buy the stuff. They have it everywhere. Besides where would you make it out here? No beef roaming these plains," she said waving her arm to indicate the city. "All you can make out here is rat jerky. Doesn't sound too appetizing to me. The professor should have put that in his book—rat jerky, maybe cat jerky. What do you think?"

I had no idea what she was talking about. "What book?"

"He was working on a book. He wanted to help people, people like us."

"And him," I needed to add.

"No, I don't think he thought of himself as homeless."

"But he was homeless."

"Yeah, he was, but he was different. I think he thought he could end it at anytime. He never seemed depressed by it. He was fascinated. He wanted to help other people survive the streets."

"That's where the book comes in. Was it a survival manual, his story, what?"

"I don't know. He never talked to me about it, but he was always gathering information. He liked learning the simplest stuff. He even asked me about my friend and how I dealt with it."

"Your friend. Oh, I remember." I was embarrassed again, and I repeated the phrase with the delicacy it deserved. "Your friend."

"He even wanted to know if it changed since I was homeless. I told him it was lighter. You know what I mean?"

"Yes, I know. I was married."

"Oh, yeah, I forgot."

"So what did he do with all that information?"

"Kept it in the bin. Which by the way would be a good place for you to get a change of clothes. You and Graham were about the same size. Wanna go?"

I don't remember when my interest had been so roused. "Let's go," I said.

It was a good, quiet walk. Maybe it was good because it was quiet. Tiger walked ahead of us exploring, as if he had no care in the world. He stopped and sniffed and then looked back to tell us the coast was clear. Silly dog.

I was quiet because the day was so quiet. There was little traffic and everyone was looking for their peace. It seemed everyone had gotten the memo, no talking today, enjoy the day. It was Sunday and, as my grandmother used to say, "This is the day which the Lord has made."

"Let us rejoice and be glad in it," Lee finished. I was startled. I didn't realize I was audible. I smiled, knowing we had the simplest of things in common. It was all we said during the remainder of the walk, another twenty minutes or so. We took the Lord's advice.

We approached the door to BIN THERE, DONE THAT. It was a brilliant idea. The man who started the enterprise wanted a place for homeless people to store their goods. The building was donated to him by the city, and Roger "Hero Man" Clapton renovated the interior to hold more than five hundred bins.

The bins were assigned to a person, or a couple, and there were a few showers and bathrooms, which were for use only by their clients. I remembered reading about Hero Man. He got his start by making sandwiches for the homeless. Eventually, local sandwich shops donated hero-style sandwiches to him, to distribute to the homeless. The city council put a stop to his distribution because they said he, or the shops, could be responsible if one of the homeless got sick from the food. So much for good government.

He got the idea about the bin storage facility about five years ago. He pitched his idea to the city as a safety issue, as well as having a place for some homeless people to make themselves presentable for a job interview or job. He was very knowledgeable. He made it clear many homeless went to school and had jobs. They needed to be clean. The city understood his argument. It took them five years, though. Or maybe the council felt guilty about shutting down his other operation, so they gave him the building, at least until they found a need for it. It didn't take long for the bins to be occupied.

Lee and I entered the building. It was bare to the walls except for rows of bins, which looked like trash cans, but were painted orange. Lee registered at the desk, and a young man walked the rows of bins and pulled bin number 57 and brought it to an open space called the holding area.

"Did you guys share one bin?" I asked.

"No, but he had more than I did, so he had some of his stuff in mine," Lee said.

"Can you get into his bin?"

"Yes, but I don't really need to. I never asked, but Graham gave me permission to get his bin. They may not even have his any more."

"Why not?"

"You have to come in at least once a week or they will bring your stuff to the holding area for another week. If you don't show up, they will assume you abandoned it."

"Or died."

"Yes, or died."

"I'm sorry. That wasn't nice," I apologized.

Lee didn't take much notice of my remark. We were interrupted by an elderly gentleman who set another bin beside us.

"We heard," the man said. "This is yours now, but I have to tell you we will need the bin by the end of the week. Sorry, Talitha."

He placed his hand on her shoulder and looked into her eyes for a response. My mother used the same technique. After she asked me a question, she would stare into my eyes. It was annoying and when I asked what she was looking for, she answered, "The truth."

I don't know if he received his answer, for Lee never said a word. I thought I heard a grunt of some sort, but maybe it came from the old man. Her lips were tight. She wasn't about to say anything. The gentleman left and she opened Graham's bin and gently moved the contents to and fro. She found a shirt and pants to match and a pair of running shoes.

"What size shoe do you wear?"

"Twelve," I said.

These are thirteen, but they'll do." She handed me the clothing and shoes, but never looked up at me.

"Thanks. Where do I go to change?"

I felt I was disturbing her. Lee kept digging into Graham's bin. She reminded me of a robot. She had no emotion, she was just digging, in slow motion.

I had to interrupt. "Lee."

Finally she stopped and looked at me, but her eyes were empty.

"Where do I change?"

Her stare reminded me of my mother, but she turned to the bin and pulled out a gray toiletry bag and handed it to me.

"Here. You should shave." Then she pointed to the back. "You can change there. The showers are there. They will let you, this one time."

"Thanks," I said again and walked away in the direction she indicated.

"Wait," Lee commanded. "Do you like what I picked out? Is it okay?"

She looked so weak. For just a moment I wanted to hug her, but I thought it would have been inappropriate. I didn't really know her, but it was an instinctive thought. It would be something I would do for my daughter. My only method of consolation was to praise her selection.

"Oh, yeah. It's great. I feel like Johnny Cash, with all this black."

I thought my joke deserved at least a smile and that's what she gave me—the smallest smile. Almost undetectable, but I saw it.

"I'll be right back," I told her.

"Take your time."

A sign advised to take no more than five minutes in the shower. I knew immediately I was going to challenge the rule. The water was warm, soothing and loving as it fell over me. I stood motionless, almost forgetting to use soap. However, I came to my senses and cleaned and cleaned again.

This was better than a meal. It was better than sex, though it was so long ago I had sex, I had to rely on memory of what it was like. I'm pretty sure most people would be shocked I thought about such things. Apparently dirty clothes dull the sexual senses, as well. If I did talk about it to anyone, they would think of me as some kind of pervert. I couldn't be homeless and be human at the same time. Sex is only for normal people. As if normal people had normal urges, anyway. I had been to many a club during my gambling days and saw and heard about acts which made me blush.

I shaved with caution, as if using a blade on a child. The cleaner I became, the taller I stood. My father told me to buy only clothes which would make me walk tall. There was so much he told me, I had to grow old to get to the same place of wisdom. Maybe there is wisdom in a bottle.

When I returned to the holding area, I found Lee sitting on a bench. She was impressed with my appearance, as well. She didn't say, but her eyes screamed it and I stood even taller.

"I have something for you," she said.

I took the metal container from her hand. It was one of those tins one would use for Christmas cookies. I sat beside her and lifted the top carefully, and found it stacked full of handwritten papers.

"Did Graham write this stuff?" I asked Lee.

She just nodded her head, so I leafed through the stack, briefly reading some of the writings. Most of it made no sense to me, but finally a pattern emerged. Graham was describing the street. Each description was assigned a number, a letter and a color. This was impressive.

I asked, "What was he doing?"

Lee responded by handing me another folded paper. I unfolded it and I was mesmerized by the detail I saw. Graham had drawn details on a city map. The map was further divided into sections with different colored borders, numbers were scattered over the map. I understood the colors and numbers must be connected to the voluminous narrative he wrote. What an undertaking.

"How long did it take him to do this?"

"I don't know. He had it before I met him. I would just see him add to it from time to time."

"This is crazy!" I was still astonished. "Why? I mean, what was he trying to do?"

"Help people. He wanted to help other homeless people. I don't know what he wanted to do, exactly. He didn't talk about it."

"But he left it to you."

"He didn't leave to me, at least, not on purpose."

"Well, it's yours, now. There's a lot of information in here. Have you seen it?"

"No. I don't snoop."

"I think it's okay, now." She didn't like that, so I had to apologize, again.

"Do you see what's in here? This is amazing."

Lee finally took an interest and looked over the map. "Could be dangerous too, I guess," she said.

"What do you mean? You said it was meant to help people."

"I mean, there are things on here that people may not want you to know."

"Like what? Show me."

Chapter 19

Detectives Innis and Turner were on the last interview of the day. Or they wanted it to be. Everyone they spoke with knew Graham but didn't know much about him. Innis' hunch didn't seem to pan out into the reality his hunches had in the past. It was time to stop and go home.

Turner broached the subject first. "Shall we stop?"

"Yeah, this is getting us nowhere."

"Maybe if we think about it a while longer, we'll come up with the answer."

"I have the answer," Detective Innis made clear.

Turner challenged his partner. "Really. You have the answer. You've had the answer all this time, and you let us go through all of this? For what, may I ask?"

"Well, not all the answers, not *the* answer, but some of the answers."

"Well, enlighten me, because all I have is a lot of questions."

"Answer one, Graham was killed. No, make that butchered," Innis started.

"And that's an answer."

"Yes, that's an answer. The question is, why?"

"Well, then, that puts you in the same place as me. Nothing but questions."

"Answer two. He had a companion," Innis continued.

"Question. Who?"

"Answer. A woman, who no one's seen since the murder."

"Did she kill him?" Turner asked.

"No. To kill him would be to kill her protection."

"Graham was her pimp, then," Turner surmised.

"No. None of the people say that. If she was prostituting, someone would have known by now. She was his companion, his lover, his co-writer."

"So back to the book, the alleged book."

"The real book," Innis insisted. "Graham found a reason to be on the street. He found a way to be useful. He was giving back. He was important."

"So who butchered him? What did he know?"

"Everything," Innis said. "We're cops. We know a lot about these streets and the people, right?"

"Right."

"We know what we know because we ask questions and get to know a few people and we've been at it for a long time, right?"

"Right."

"But what if the people we know are giving us answers to protect someone. What if they intentionally cause distractions?"

"And they do this for what reason?"

"Because they are family. They need security. They all need security, and they all depend on each other for that. The code is to keep the world out. We see them as the outsiders, and they see us as intruders. They have their own rules, their own homes they protect. We see them as dirty and unintelligent, and they see us as oppressors."

"Well, damn, you're talking about every grocery store clerk, or almost everybody, for that matter, in the city, and they're not homeless," Turner replied.

"But they could be. How far are you from being homeless?"

"What?"

"How much money do you need to keep you from being on the street? Do you have a financial plan?"

"What's your point, Greg?"

Pinching his thumb and index fingers together, Innis replied, "Most of us are *this far* from there. How far are you?"

"What makes you think I am?"

"The odds, the economy."

"I'm doing okay. I make good money, I save, I buy things, I'm not married. I'm good," Turner said confidently.

"How much do you pay for your apartment? I mean, do you spend more than fifty percent of your pay on your rent?"

"I never thought about it. I don't think so. But so what if I do? I have only myself to look after. So what?"

Innis drew a check mark in the air with his index finger. It annoyed his partner. "What is that supposed to mean," Turner said, eyeing the air.

"It means you're not aware of every dollar, every day."

"Are you?" Solly pushed back.

"Every single dime," Innis told his partner, emphasizing each word.

"I think we got off track. What does any of this have to do with people who are homeless right now, and what does it have to do with who killed who?"

"I'm just giving you answers, that's all."

"Okay, so I'm a cop who is close to being homeless. Whatever. I'm not going to be. I save. I put money away for my future. I make money, I give some, save some, and live on the rest. Even if I find money, I do the same."

"What do you mean, if you find some?"

"I mean if I find some. What's hard about that? I find some money, I save it, that's all there is to it. It's like icing on the cake. I put it away, that's all."

"You put it away?"

"Right. I put it away. It's not that I find a lot of money, it's just a habit I developed. Once I found—"

Innis interrupted him. "Yes, you put it away."

"Yes, I put it away," Turner said to his partner, who seemed to be in another world. Turner wondered whether they were in the same conversation.

"You give some," Innis repeated.

"Yes, I give some and—"

Innis completed the sentence, "... and you save some. Yep, that's it. He put some away. That's what he meant."

"We're not talking about Graham anymore, are we? Who are we talking about now? We're certainly not talking about me, and we're not talking about you, so fill me in, partner. Who the hell are we talking about?"

"Never mind. Did I say all of that out loud?"

"Yeah, very loud."

"Partner," Innis said, "after we finish with this mission, I need to do some things on my own. Is that cool?"

"I guess." Turner thought about it a moment and realized it was not in his power to stop his partner. "Sure. It's cool."

"You're a good man, Charlie Brown. You're a good man."

The two men got in their police car and drove toward the HOPE mission. It was a silent drive until Turner said, "You used to make sense, you know."

"I still make sense."

"From whose perspective?"

"From the only perspective that matters. No offense. Trust me, I know what I'm doing. I understand now. I have the answer."

"Why am I still in the dark watching a tidal wave of questions about to hit me?"

"Solomon," Innis said, "stay in the dark on this one. The less you know, the better you are. Trust me. This is not business. It's personal."

"Are you almost homeless, Greg? Is that what this is all about? Do you need some help?"

"Shut up. I'm not homeless, I'm not going to be homeless."

"I would help, you know."

"Shut up!" This time the command was louder and with enough agitation in his voice to quiet his partner.

The remainder of the drive was silent, but the atmosphere was not so heavy. Innis examined every building they passed. Turner, on the other hand, watched every person. The city was covered. Everything and everyone was under suspicion.

HOPE was their last stop. Talking to people and asking the same question every day, looking for a clue which never comes, was exhausting. Too many days had passed and too many memories became unreliable. Memories could be manipulated. Ask the same question to different people and to one it was a threat, to another, intimidating, and to another, annoying. A question coming from a cop was not just a question, it was an interrogation. Everyone would be defensive. Sometimes it was best to let a civilian do the talking. Thank God for informants.

As they turned into HOPE's parking lot, Innis couldn't resist confessing, "I'm tired of coming to this place."

"Indeed," agreed Turner, "but it must be for a reason we don't get right now. We just keep coming back here. Why?"

"Because we have no other place to go."

"Don't be negative, partner. We're closer than you think. Those who give up would never do so, if they just knew how close they were to the finish."

"Your mother tell you that?"

"No, but my father did. I used to run track. It was his way of encouraging me. He is a preacher, ya know."

"Your father is a preacher? What is his name?"

"Oh, you wouldn't know him. He's not famous. He doesn't have a church."

"So he's not a pastor."

"No, but he's ordained, back home. Helluva preacher, he is, too."

"Are you supposed to say that about a preacher? I can see him being introduced." Innis mimicked a master of ceremonies. "Ladies and gentlemen, it is my honor and my pleasure to present to some, and introduce to others, an honorable man and one helluva preacher."

Turner finished the intro, "Reverend Doctor Sylus Tyberius Turner, the second."

"The second? Why aren't you a third?"

"My mother put an end to that. She would have none of it, thank God."

Innis continued the tease. "I like it. I could call you Sy or Ty or SyTy or—"

"I got it, I got it. That's exactly why my mother put an end to it. The foolishness ends with me."

"Wise woman," admitted Innis. "Though I wish your people would get the memo."

"For real. How about LaShawn? What's up with Shawn and black folks?" responded Turner with a giggle.

"Don't ask me. Where the hell did *La* come from, anyway? It's French for what? I wouldn't know."

"It's the search for meaning. Don't forget Marshawn, Kayshawn, DeShawn, Vashawn, Beeshawn, Knowshawn."

"How about NoMoShawn," interjected Greg.

"Yeah, please, no mo, no mo, please."

The detectives shared a good laugh as they parked the car. Turner noticed Dr. Maloney's car was in its reserved spot.

"What's in a name, right?" Solomon asked.

"We're about to find out."

"Shall we talk to him again?"

"Should be interesting," Innis said lightly.

Rather than stop at Reverend Franklin's office, the detectives asked for directions to the clinic and made their way for another set of interviews. Walking down the hallway, they almost collided with Tuba.

"Whoa, big guy," said a startled Turner.

"Excuse me, sir. Reverend Franklin is not in right now."

"When will he be back?"

"We have a meeting this evening at six, so he will be back by then."

"Where did he go?"

"I didn't ask, he didn't tell."

"That's okay, we'll talk to him another time, okay, uh Mister, uh—"

"Tuba. That's what they call me."

"Everyone's gotta have a nickname," Innis said.

"A lot of people do. It's just something we do."

"A sign of affection, huh? I guess there is something in a name," said Turner, but Tuba answered with a shrug of his shoulders.

"We're on our way to the clinic. We saw the doctor's car. You think he has time to speak with us?"

"You're the cops. You can do what you want," Tuba replied.

Turner looked at his partner and smiled as he agreed. "Yeah, I guess we can."

The two men walked on into the clinic, unaware Tuba watched them until they disappeared behind the clinic door.

Dr. Maloney barely acknowledged their presence. He continued to write his notes in a chart. Once he finished, he looked up and said, "Hello, detectives," then closed the chart and sat upright.

Again, Turner took the lead. "How are you, Doctor?"

"Well, and you?"

"Well, sir. Thank you."

"Are you looking for me or the pastor?"

"We're looking for a lot of people. That's the thing about being a detective. We're always looking and looking, and we look for so many things and so many people."

"Must be exhausting."

"Oh, I don't know. Sometimes I find it exciting." Turning to his partner, he continued, "How about you, detective? Does it excite you?"

Innis played along. "The search? Sometimes I hate it, sometimes I love it. It depends on the day, or the people."

The doctor continued the rhythm of the conversation. "Is this a good day or a bad day?"

"A good day, I would think," said Detective Turner. "Doctor, did you say you had a practice, elsewhere?"

"I did, but not any longer. I'm retired from that practice."

"Is there a reason you didn't mention that when we talked to you before?"

"I didn't think retirement would have anything to do with a murder. Is that irrational?"

"Not irrational, but we get suspicious of everything. We're cops, what can I say."

"Suspicious? Am I under suspicion for murder?"

"No, no, no, Doctor. It's just that until we get a decent lead, we handle everyone as a person of interest."

"So I'm a person of interest?" Dr Maloney didn't appear moved about his status.

"I guess I'm not explaining this well. Greg, do you want to take a crack at this?"

Detective Innis was walking around the room surveying every item, but took his partner's cue to join the conversation. While he picked up an ophthalmoscope, he questioned the doctor.

"Dr. Maloney, every person we talk to is a person of interest, but we prioritize the list. You, for example, would be on the bottom of the list. You have no motive, though I must say you have the means."

The detectives noted the doctor's frown. He did not like having the means. Innis continued, "But having the means and no motive, makes the killer crazy. Having the motive, but no means, makes for a sloppy murder."

"It looks like you're looking for a sloppy murderer," Dr. Maloney added.

"You would think. But Peter Lattimore's mutilation was not random, it was focused. It was like surgery."

"I sound like a suspect again or person of interest or whatever you want to call it."

"Sorry, Doctor," apologized Detective Innis. "It seems I'm not doing such a good job, either. We didn't come here to speak with you, anyway. You just happened to be here."

"Well, if I can help, I will, but I don't know much about his murder."

"You don't know much, or you don't know anything?" asked Detective Turner, returning to the conversation.

"I really don't know anything. I see what you mean, about you guys being suspicious of everything and every word. Not unlike being a physician."

"How so?"

"Sometimes you have to take the smallest clue and run it to the ground to find what you are looking for. Sometimes it's just a hunch."

"Yeah, my partner likes hunches. Me? I just follow facts," said Detective Turner.

"I think most people believe hunches have no basis. They can be quite rational, but they appear irrational because most people in my profession are rational people. They only want the facts; but for some people, the facts can trigger something in a person to explore what others don't," Detective Innis said.

"Sounds like you're trying to make a rational argument for an irrational act," Dr. Maloney replied. "Psychiatrists do it all the time."

Turner looked at his partner. "See, I told you. You need a psychiatrist."

Innis refused to respond, so Turner continued. "Do you have any hunches about Mr. Lattimore's death, Doctor?"

"I wish I could help you, Detective, but I have no clue. Once I wanted to be a pathologist, and be cool like Quincy."

"Interesting," Turner replied. "Did Quincy inspire you to be a doctor?"

"No, my father did. My father was a doctor. To this day, I think of him as one of the best surgeons who ever lived."

"That's nice. Everybody needs a hero. It makes it all the sweeter when it's a parent, don't you think?"

Dr. Maloney was pensive when he answered, "Yes, it is."

Turner stood up and began to leave the room. "Doctor, it was a pleasure. I don't mean to be rude, but we're wasting our time with you. We have some others we would like to speak with."

"Here at the mission?"

"A couple, but I'm done for the day. Unlike TV, we go home. TV detectives have an hour to solve crimes, we get a little more time than that. We're a bit more patient."

"I heard you had only forty-eight hours to solve a crime."

"That's forty-eight to gather evidence. The wheels of justice grind slowly, Doctor. We'll find our man or men. Which reminds me, why did you say 'they' killed Peter? Do you think it was more than one person involved? "

"No, not really. Just a figure of speech."

"Did you know Peter and Graham were the same person?"

"No, not really," the doctor answered.

"I was just curious. You never asked who Peter is, or was."

"I guess I just assumed it was the same case."

"I see," said Turner.

"Does that make me a person of interest, again?" the doctor asked.

"It makes you an interesting person, Doctor. Thank you," Turner responded and the detectives left the office.

Once they were a distance away from the clinic, Turner asked his partner, "What do you think?"

"Suspicious."

"Yeah, suspicious. He just moved from the bottom of the list to the top ten, but we have others to consider."

The walked to their car and drove out of the parking lot just as the pastor was entering. Each car stopped in order for the men to talk to each other. Reverend Franklin lowered his window and shouted, "Did you need to speak with me, detectives?"

Innis and Turner looked at each other and Turner replied, "No, Pastor. We can do it another time. If you hear anything about Graham having a companion, please give us a call."

"Will do," Franklin said and continued into the parking lot to his assigned space. When he walked toward his office, he saw the detectives across the street, looking back at him, as if they were in a stake-out. He nodded and Turner returned the nod.

Chapter 20

I had put off visiting the Mayor long enough. Lee and I walked to a courtyard just outside the hospital and we agreed I would take no more than thirty minutes.

"Do they take dogs?" Lee was not sure she could stay in the courtyard with Tiger.

"No, but try it anyway. If not—"

"I can take care of myself, you know," Lee insisted.

"I'm sure you can. I'm worried about the dog."

My reply brought a smile to her face. How the heck did she have such pretty teeth, I thought. For a homeless person, she took care of herself. She noticed my stare, or my thought.

"Hello. Are you there? Get going before it gets dark, but don't worry. We'll be fine," she encouraged.

Lee saw my hesitancy and gently nudged me along. I surrendered to her urging, not so much because of her insistence, but I really needed to see the Mayor. As I turned to go in, Lee grabbed at the lab coat in my hand. "You look nice. They won't turn you away. You don't need to fake it. Just give it back."

I looked into Lee's eyes trying to decide if she was being in earnest. She just smiled and I walked away toward the hospital door. My mission was on my mind. There was no thought of looking back.

With the lab coat over my arm, I entered the hospital lobby. I walked as if I were about to be discovered as fraudulent. I passed by a shop window and saw my image. For a moment, it wasn't me, but the image of my clothes. I realized it was me when I saw the reflection of the white lab coat. It was me, and I stayed a moment to look at myself. I didn't look at myself often. I didn't want to see the man I had become. Of course, I saw myself in the mirror daily as I shaved or brushed my teeth, but I was not looking at me. I was concerned more with not cutting myself or cleaning my teeth, which were not the white seen on every billboard sign. I still didn't understand how teeth could be so white without some sort of photography trick. Even when I saw real people smile, I examined their teeth to see if was real. People's teeth were changing and I was left behind, again.

However, for this moment I was presentable. I even looked as if I could be the doctor I was going to impersonate. I looked at the name tag and realized I didn't look like a Patel, however.

I asked a very nice woman at the information booth for the location of the Mayor, but I couldn't remember his full name. I did remember "Gus." She was kind enough to look up every Gus in the hospital. There was only one and he was located on the fourth floor, in isolation. I didn't ask why the isolation, I just nodded in appreciation and made my way, to the fourth floor. I don't know why, but I felt more comfortable taking the stairs.

I entered the ward and looked for someone to help me to the isolation room. A nurse sat at a desk and when I asked for her help, she smiled and walked me to room 405. There was a sign which instructed me to wear a mask. I was still baffled about the isolation, but I did as told and entered the room. The nurse donned a mask and entered behind me.

I felt out of place, as she walked around with such comfort. What was I supposed to do? I didn't even know if I was supposed to touch anything. I took my clues from her. She walked to the bedside and aroused the frail-looking man in the bed.

"Mr. Sotheby." When he did not respond, she called to him, again, and he opened his eyes.

Wow. Mr. Sotheby. His name was so formal. He sounded important. His name gave him stature. The only Sotheby I knew was the auction house which sold items for millions. Suddenly, the Mayor was worth millions. Maybe we gave each other a nickname to send a message we were not worth the name we were given.

Thankfully, I never earned a nickname. His name was worth every syllable. Suh-thuh-bee. How sweet the sound. He was transformed immediately, in my eyes. However, he was not the man whose rants on race and injustice I spent so many of my homeless days listening to. He had deteriorated from the day I found him in the park.

I whispered to the nurse, "What happened?"

My question, coming through a mask, made it unintelligible, so I lifted it away from my face and asked again, but the nurse immediately made it clear I was to keep the mask in place. My God, I thought. What did he have? I saw a sign on the door about tuberculosis, but it wasn't serious to me, until the nurse made it clear, again.

"How did it happen?"

"I'll speak with you, outside," she said and she turned to walk away. She couldn't have taken more than two steps before she turned and took the lab coat. "You won't need this, Mr. Barnes."

She left and my mouth was open beneath the mask. I closed it immediately because I thought I might catch some germ which might be roaming the room. How did she know my name? I couldn't think long about it because the Mayor called to me. I went to his bedside and leaned over, watching his eyes. They seemed to wander, as if he had no control, and then he found me and looked into me, but I wouldn't look back.

"Hey, Mayor. How's it going?" I sounded so insincere. I didn't even know if he knew who I was.

"How's Tiger?"

I couldn't blame him for asking about his dog. It was all he had. It was his constant companion and maybe his best friend. At least, I knew he was aware of me and who I was.

"He's fine, Mayor. I think he eats more than I do." My little joke brought a little smile to his face.

"Where is he?"

"He's in good hands. Don't worry," I assured him.

"Where is he?" He was more insistent this time.

"He's with a friend. She's downstairs waiting for me."

"Who is she?"

"A woman I met. I've been taking care of her, trying to get her a place. She doesn't need to be on the street. Women don't belong on the street."

The Mayor nodded in agreement. "Is she nice?"

I had to think a moment, but I told him Lee was a nice person.

"Does Tiger like her?"

"Oh yeah, he loves her. That dog is always with her. He barely lets her out of his sight. He would make a great guard dog if he was bigger."

"He has a big heart. If he likes her, she's okay. He knows people. That makes him the best guard dog."

I hoped I didn't offend him. I wasn't trying to belittle the dog. I was just trying to bring some levity to this gloomy room. The Mayor tried to do the same when he replied, "He likes you."

"He used to. Now he's in love with her."

"What is her name?"

"Lee... well, Talitha." I couldn't help but chuckle a little. "I have to call her Lee. 'Talitha' is a little too ghetto for me, you know what I mean?"

"Now, that's funny. One homeless man judging another one. We all live in the ghetto."

His eyes drifted away and I saw his eyes fill with tears. I looked for some tissues to wipe his face, but there were none in the room. It wasn't worth walking away to search the room. For a moment, I was afraid to touch him for fear of breaking some hospital rule. He looked so sad, I forgot myself and the hospital. I wiped his tears with my thumb, and he looked at me. I could see the gratitude in his eyes.

"They can't help me, you know."

"Of course they can, Mayor. They know what they're doing. They have the best doctors here. I was here a couple of times. See," I said, pointing to my eye wound. "They fixed my face."

He wasn't convinced. The Mayor just stared at me, but I couldn't help but encourage him more. His eyes said it all.

"Don't give up, Mayor. You need to give it time."

"God only gives you so much time. You have to do the best you can with it."

"That's what I'm saying, Mayor. Give the doctors a chance to do their best. Let them help you."

"I'm tired, Roman. Have you ever been tired? I've been tired many times. Tired of work, tired of people, tired of begging, and tired of people looking at me like I don't mean much. But you know what? I've never known what it was like to be tired of living."

I knew where his thoughts were going. I had to interrupt him. "No. You're not tired of living."

A wry little curl of a smile came to his lips. "Yes, I am. I'm tired, son. I'm tired of living."

"It must be the drugs they're giving you. I've heard medications can make you hallucinate and make you suicidal. It's the drugs, Mayor. It's the drugs. Tell them what you feel and they can change the drugs."

"You're afraid," he said. "It's okay. I'm not afraid. Just take care of Tiger. No, let Talitha take care of him. He loves her and she loves him."

"And how would you know that?"

"I don't, but you do. You trust her and I trust you."

"Okay, if you trust me, then listen when I tell you need to let the doctors heal you. They can do it."

"You don't understand. I don't want them to help me. I'm tired of living on the street. You know what it's like. This hospital bed is the most comfortable I've been for years. I don't want to leave. This is heaven. I want to leave in comfort."

All I could do was repeat, "Leave?" I understood. My friend was hurting and no one could understand but me. The nurses and doctors would not understand his life. Should I be honored? Was I chosen to be here?

"Thank you, Roman. I could have died in the jungle. You came along just in time. I don't know if anyone else would have. You saved my life. You brought me to my comfort. I could have died out there."

I watched the Mayor's eyes as they moved about the room. He was looking at something, but I said nothing. At one point, he looked at the ceiling and stared, then he smiled. Of course, I had to look, but I didn't see anything and when I looked back at him, he was still smiling. I was smart enough to recognize this was his moment not mine, so I said my goodbyes.

"Mayor, I'll be back, okay?" He nodded okay and closed his eyes.

As I walked away I heard him say, "Is this all for me?" When I turned to ask him what he meant, his eyes were still closed. The drugs were really messing with his mind. I left and returned to the nurse's station where I found the nurse.

"Is he going to be all right?"

"I don't know. The doctors are doing what they can, Mr. Barnes."

"How do you know me?"

"Oh, it hasn't been that long. You were a patient here about a year ago. I was one of the nurses who took care of you. I'm Nurse Callie. I don't expect you to remember, though. I don't remember everyone, but I sure remember you left without permission."

"Yes, I do remember that. I was doing okay."

"It looks as though life is treating you well."

"Looks. Yes, the looks. They sure can fool you, can't they? Can't judge a book."

"By its cover," Nurse Callie completed my sentence. "So you are not doing well? Is that what you are saying?"

"Well, it's not about me really. What about the Mayor?" I had to repeat the question, using his proper name, Mr. Sotheby, since it was obvious she did not know him as the Mayor.

"I'm the nurse. I follow orders. I don't make diagnoses, nor do I make a prognosis. I'm just a nurse."

"I understand." I didn't believe a word she said. She was avoiding telling me something unsettling, but I asked another question. "How did he get tuberculosis?"

"Who knows, but there are a lot of homeless people who have diseases, and if you come in contact with someone who has TB, then you could get it."

"So there's someone out there with TB who is spreading it to other people? That's scary."

"Well, it's not that easy. He or she is not just going around infecting everyone they meet. It helps if you are in close proximity to them for a period of time, share a room or apartment."

"He was homeless," I corrected her.

"Always? Was he homeless always?"

"I don't know about always, but for at least fifteen years, I know. Probably more than that. Even when I was homeless with him, we didn't spend so much time together we could get that sick from each other."

"He got it somewhere," she reminded me.

"Can you give it to somebody on purpose?"

"You mean like someone going around giving AIDS to people?"

"Yeah, sure, like that."

"It doesn't seem likely, but I don't know. He must have been with someone for a while. This past winter was pretty harsh. Where did he go?"

"I don't know. I was living at the mission." After some more thought, I had the answer. "He was at the winter shelter. He hated going to those places, but maybe he went this past winter. Could he have gotten it there?"

"Possibly."

"Then that's where he got it. Who knows where all those people come from and what they bring with them? Hell, they burn our clothes and shower us down like we were in a prison. Yep, that's where he got it. Damn filthy people." I said.

I wasn't really addressing her. I felt I was talking to some imaginary person before me. I watched her face and she looked frightened. Maybe I was showing too much anger or maybe she thought I had a lot of nerve calling other homeless people dirty. I excused myself and walked down the stairs to find Lee.

I went to the courtyard and I didn't see her, but I wasn't alarmed. I traversed the property again. Where could she be? I trotted to the curb and looked around. Jesus! There had to be a logical reason for her not waiting for me. Logic is the only fallback when confronted with chaos. The chaos came from within.

I watched the traffic and the few pedestrians, and all appeared calm and in order, but what happened fifteen minutes before? Was there a fight or a struggle? I just reassured the Mayor his dog was in good hands. Now, I didn't know the truth. Lee would never hurt the dog, so the only logical reason for their disappearance was something sinister. My mind ran through various scenarios as I rushed from one corner to the next.

It wasn't long ago I was accused of kidnapping a little girl, who, it turned out, was abducted by a sex trafficking ring of thugs. Could this be the same situation? Of course, I would be suspected again. I was the last one with Lee. It would all fall on me to prove my innocence, again. What else could go wrong?

Then, I heard barking. I looked down the street and there was Tiger, barking at me, as he usually did when he saw me. It was his hello. I quickly walked toward him and Lee, who nonchalantly walked along with him, with his leash coiled in her hand. Tiger walked peacefully at her side without the leash. He kept barking.

Once I was close enough, he stood on his hind legs and tapped my legs with his front paws, his tail wagging with excitement.

"Where were you?" I didn't give Lee time to respond. I unloaded another question. "Where did you go?"

She wasn't impressed with my animation. "We went for a walk. Is that allowed?" she calmly replied.

"I thought we agreed you would wait at that, uh–" I couldn't remember.

"Courtyard," she smugly informed me.

"Whatever. You know we agreed."

"We agreed you would be back in thirty minutes."

I had to correct her. "I said about thirty minutes. I could be less."

"It could be more. I guess it could be anything. Fifteen minutes?"

"Why are you so contrary?"

"I'm not contrary. I just went for a walk. I don't care what we agreed to. I went for a walk. Simple. Breathe and listen carefully." Then she emphasized every word of her next sentence. "I went for a walk."

"Geez, Lee. You just don't understand."

"I guess I don't, but you need to relax. All is well."

"All is well, my ass! My friend is dying and no one can help him. I got kicked out of the mission. I'm homeless, living among bums. No offense."

"I'm not offended. I'm not a bum. I'm homeless, yes, but not a bum. Maybe you want to be out here, I don't."

I couldn't believe she would make such a senseless accusation. "I'm out here because of you," I reminded her.

"Because of me. You're homeless because of me? You're delusional."

"If I wasn't concerned about you, I would have never been out here looking for you in the first place."

"You don't even know me, how could you be concerned for me?"

"Well, maybe not you. I was doing it for Graham. I was doing what I thought he would want me to do."

"You thought. Did he ask you to look after me? Who are you, the savior of the homeless? I don't need a savior of your kind. I have a savior. He'll take care of me."

"Well, a fine job He's doing. I hear that shit from the pastor all the time. What kind of God would let this happen to good people?"

"Maybe you're not as good as you think. Maybe you're the asshole I see standing here, right in front of me."

"Well, this asshole saved your ass."

"*My* ass saved my ass."

I looked down at Tiger and he sat like a twelve-man jury trying to make sense of our argument.

"Please spare me the strong black woman speech."

"What?"she responded in a very calm, but confused tone.

"I've heard it before. You are a strong black woman. No man can match you. You are the mother of all mankind. You don't need a man to be complete. Blah, blah, blah."

"Sounds like a good speech, but I'm not black."

"What!" Could this woman be any more delusional?

"So you're not only stupid, you're hard of hearing and can't see very well, either," she snapped back at me.

"So you deny your black side. Typical."

"Now I have a black side," she mocked. "Maybe so, but it's not from my parents. I'm white. I'm not mixed. I'm white. I was born white and still am white to this day. Is that okay with you, Mister All Black Man?"

She was infuriating and I grabbed her arm to impress my point with her. "Don't start with any racist remarks."

"Now, suddenly I've become a racist. First I was a strong black woman. Now that I'm white, I'm a racist. That's always the last thing a black man can do, resort to racism when he has nothing else to argue. It's always racism, isn't it? You can't get ahead because of racism. You can't get a damn job because of racism. You can't do a damn thing because of racism." She snatched her arm from my grip and continued. "Everything is about race with you."

"Not with me," I interrupted.

"Well, it's not with me. I don't give a shit what happens to you. I'm not the cause of your homelessness. I'm not the cause of any of your problems. Get a fucking grip on reality, black man." Her enunciation of "black man" was filled with disdain. I grabbed for her arm again, but she was quick enough to avoid my grip.

"Watch it, black man, or I will cry rape." Her remark made me look around in suspicion. "Yeah, you call on racism, I call on the white woman's final cry—rape. You call on the god of racism and I'll call on the god of rape. They'll believe me. I'm white. You're nothing but a homeless black guy. I win. Isn't that how racism works? The white man or woman always wins. How's that for racism? So don't bring up racism to save you. You will lose."

I couldn't believe she could be so cynical. Was she serious or was she mocking me? She was wrong. Racism was not the last stand for black people. There was another reliable standby comeback. It was all I had left, and I uttered, "Bitch."

Lee didn't answer, but her look was one of disappointment. I was disappointed, as well. She looked at me, but I couldn't look her in the eye. Finally she broke the silence. "Why did you think I was black?"

I wanted to explain, but the words would not come out to her satisfaction. How could I tell her what I thought of her name and the size of her butt? Not to mention her hair texture and the size of her lips. She just wouldn't understand. What could I say? I was so glad when she stepped in and said, "Never mind."

The crisis was over. It was time to settle in for the evening. Tiger tapped me on the leg again to inform me it was time to go. Lee clipped the leash to his collar and we walked to the park. I noticed someone in an office window looking at us. They must have witnessed the entire argument, but they also saw the resolution. As we walked by, we must have looked like a typical family. Yes, looks are deceiving.

As I watched our reflection in the windows we passed, I thought back to Reverend Franklin's statement about companionship. He said it was the primary drive in humans. Maybe he was right. Maybe it was the most important thing in the whole world. What's love got to do with it? I don't know, maybe nothing. As long as we have somebody to be with, then I guess it fulfills the first and foremost ambition of us all. We need somebody.

Lee and I just argued, yet we made up. What was the motivation? Were we afraid to be apart? Is it love or desperation? I didn't know, but I finally understood the pastor. I looked at Tiger and he looked up at us, and I could see in his eyes he understood. Maybe God put the same imperative in everything. I needed to ask Reverend Franklin about that, when I saw him again.

During our stroll, we saw people assembling tents and tables. I knew what it was all about. The Stand Down happened every year. It was established by a homeless organization. It was mostly for veterans, but they never turned away anyone. It would be a good place for me to take Lee and connect her with people who could help her find someplace to live.

Living on the streets is like being in war. In my brief stint in the Navy, I never thought women should be fighting. It was a man's job. I needed to get her off the streets and the Stand Down was the best place to do so. I just had to convince her not to come looking for me, again. Women.

Chapter 21

Detective Innis walked into the audio-visual room to find Lois eating lunch. She greeted him with a bright smile.

"I haven't seen you in a while. Busy?"

"Very." He grabbed a chair, pulled it close to her and sat. "You were right."

"Aren't I, always?"

"No, but this time you are definitely right."

Offering him a piece of her sandwich, she replied, "What am I right about this time?"

He refused the sandwich. "About Renny's message. It is a message, but I can't figure it out. Well, I have a clue, but not all the pieces to the puzzle."

"You want help?"

"You're the only one I can trust."

Lois felt a bit uncomfortable and sat up, waiting for Greg to offer a reason for his comment.

"I can trust you, right?"

"Of course you can. What's going on? Do you want to talk here?"

Innis looked around and decided it was okay to continue the conversation in the room. "I'm serious, Lois. This has got to stay with us."

"Okay, okay," she reassured him. "You're kind of scaring me. What is his message about?"

Greg hesitated, but he began his thesis. "Okay, about a year ago, Renny and I busted a sex trade ring. We found the tunnel they were using."

Lois interrupted with, "I remember. It was a big story."

"Well, when we first found the tunnel, it led to an elevator shaft, and in the shaft was a place carved out just big enough to hide some money we found."

"Yes, it was about a million bucks."

"That's the key. It was about. It could have been more, it could have been less."

Lois was anticipating the story. "Oh, no. Did you take some?"

"No! I would never do that."

"But if you wouldn't, you know who would," Lois tried to calm him.

"I believe Renny took some of it. I don't know that. I never saw he him do it, but I believe he did."

"If you never saw him, then why do you believe he did it? Nobody knows how much money there was, exactly."

"You're right. Nobody knows, but I know he had serious money problems and he wasn't right afterward. It was our biggest case ever, and he didn't seem to enjoy being a part of solving it. He was different. And the crazy part, he never talked about money anymore. He was always complaining about money, then nothing. Like his problems were solved."

"I don't like bringing this up, but do you think the guilt made him commit suicide?" Lois asked.

It was hard for Greg to admit, but he said, "Yes."

"So if he was so guilty, why didn't he just give the money back?"

"Because he did the wrong thing for the right reason. He wanted to take care of his family."

She finally caught on to his train of thought. "Ooohhh. The money is out there. Who did he give it to? His wife?"

"I don't know. She overspends and lives beyond her means, but I don't see her spending like crazy, like she used to."

"Then who did he give it to? Or maybe he didn't give it to anyone. He put it somewhere, right?" she kept probing.

"He put it somewhere and answer is in the picture." Greg pulled out the photo and laid it on the desk for them to view again. After studying it for a moment, the detective tapped on the photograph and said, "Somewhere, in here, is the answer."

"Let's go for the obvious. He's standing in front of a building, with the address number visible and he seems to be pointing to the number. Does he want you to look there?"

"He wouldn't leave it there. That was the building where we found the money, but maybe the number means something."

After much examination, Lois thought she might have the answer. "Maybe it's not about the building he's pointing to, but the building reflected in the window. What do you think?"

"What building is that?

"I don't know, but we can find out."

"No it can't be that."

"Well, then I don't know. Nothing else is in the picture."

Without recognizing what he was doing, Greg took Lois' sandwich from her plate and sat back in his chair, looking again at the picture. He studied the note on the back. "'Yes, there is more. Keep hope alive.'"

"Does that make sense? Why keep hope alive and then kill yourself," he questioned.

"Everything is not logical, isn't that right?"

"Right."

"Maybe the number is to a safe deposit box."

"Now that makes sense," Greg said with excitement; then his enthusiasm waned. "No, that can't be it. How would anyone get to it?"

"His wife."

"She would have said something about that."

"That's why he sent you the picture, as well. Law enforcement can get into it."

"If we have proper cause. If I go to a judge, I'll have to tell him my partner stole the money, a year ago, and, by the way, I implicate myself in the theft. So that won't work, either."

"Okay, nothing means nothing. The picture means nothing, the number means nothing, so we're back to the very beginning."

Greg put the sandwich back on the plate and mumbled with frustration. "No, you're right. He sent me the picture, so there is something he wanted me to know. The message was for Carmen, but I was sent the clue. He wanted me to help. He knows I'll figure it out, and I will."

"Who said you were sent the clue?"

"Well, why did he send me the picture? I'm part of this."

"Yes, *part* of it. Maybe his wife is the other part."

"We got the same photo, so what do you mean?"

"I mean you got the photo, she got the clue. She got the original photo with the message. You got the photo, only."

Greg got excited again. "So he's telling me to figure out the riddle on the back. I thought it was about life. Makes sense, right?"

"Sounds logical, but you don't work with logic. You're the Hunchman of Notre Dame."

Detective Innis smiled at his nickname. "Yeah, that's what they call me."

"Well, start hunching, man," Lois demanded.

"My mother used to say she would pray on something and then go to sleep. The answer would be waiting for her in the morning."

"I've never heard you pray. Do you pray?"

He had to think a moment. "Yeah, I do. Not a lot, but I pray. Especially when I get stressed."

"My pastor says that's typical—to talk to God when you need something. He says you should pray all the time."

"Okay, okay," said Innis, irritated. "I don't need a sermon."

"Not a sermon, just a life lesson. I'm just saying you should pray all the time."

Still irritated, Greg responded, "Got it."

But Lois would not let it go. "God is with us all the time, so you can talk to Him all the time."

"Lois," the detective snapped. "I need help, right now. Can I get you to focus with me, right now? Here with me, right now. That's what I need, okay. I hope you understand."

"I hope *you* understand," she said. "I pray because I have hope in a God who is always there, at any time."

"I get it, babe, but can I get some of that hope right now? Let's hope I get the answer. I need the answer."

Her body language said she was backing off her stubborn stand. "Okay, I'll hope with you."

"How did we get from talking about this picture to God and hope? That's all I'm saying. Can we change the subject and get back to the picture and the words?"

"Sometimes God and hope is all you have, right? Maybe?"

Her response seemed to stun Greg. "What?"

"I'm not trying to beat a dead horse, but all I was trying—"

"No, you said it. I got it." He was so animated. Greg stood up. "I got it!"

"The answer? You have the answer?"

Detective Innis wouldn't answer her. He paced to and fro and then leaned over and kissed her, to her surprise and that of a police officer who just entered the room.

"My bad," the policeman said.

"No bad, no bad, at all. In fact it's all good."

Detective Innis leaned over and kissed Lois again and bounded out of the room, leaving the two to look at each other, bewildered. Greg poked his head back into the room. "I love you," he said and left again. Lois could only smile. The police officer sarcastically said, "Ain't love grand?"

"Yes. Yes, it is." She did not smile, but her tone said she was well pleased. "What can I do for you, officer?"

* * *

Detective Innis didn't bother to stop at his desk and inform his partner he was on another mission. It was a purposeful decision. As he rode the elevator to the garage level, he smiled to himself. At one point he said, in a low voice, "You son of a gun." The other elevator passengers looked to see if he was speaking to them, but quickly realized he was not when he apologized.

Greg's driving was marked by frequent horn blowing, but he finally reached his destination. He turned into the mission parking lot. There was no immediate parking space, but it didn't matter. He stopped and blocked several cars from exiting, if they needed to do so, while he was inside. He went directly to Reverend Franklin's office. Luckily the minister was there.

Franklin sat back in his chair and welcomed the detective. "What can I help you with, detective?"

"May I sit, Reverend?"

The pastor extended his hand, giving Innis permission to sit. The detective took his invitation and sat directly across from Franklin.

"Where's your partner?"

"I came alone, sir."

"Are you still looking for Mr. Barnes or have you found him?"

"Haven't found him, but we will, if we need to. Thanks for your willingness to help, but this is about something else." He hesitated a moment, then finished his thought. "This is something personal, so to speak."

"So to speak?" Franklin repeated.

"This is going to sound crazy, but I had to come. I'm working on a hunch of mine." When he saw the big grin on the minister's face, he was taken aback. "What? What did I say?"

"I apologize, detective. What can I help you with? Do you need some counseling?"

"Counseling? No. I don't know what to ask for, or how to ask."

"Would you like a drink?" Franklin asked, standing ready to accommodate his guest.

"No, no, no. Nothing for me, thanks."

His answer did not stop the reverend from going to a small refrigerator and taking out a bottle of pineapple soda. "I don't drink alcohol, detective, but I love pineapple soda. I'm hooked, I must say. I'm trying to cut back, but I always look for an opportunity to pull out a cold one." He produced a second bottle, offering it to Innis, and the detective accepted it.

"Thank you. There's only one thing better than drinking pineapple soda. It's sharing pineapple soda."

He opened the bottle and took a swig as if he were an alcoholic taking a drink after a year of sobriety. Innis smiled and took a drink, as well.

"I love pineapple soda, too," Innis said.

"There you go. We found common ground. We may be friends one day."

"Sure," Innis said with a chuckle, and another swallow. The reverend took his seat by the time the detective had put his bottle down on the desk.

"How do you feel, detective?"

"I'm fine, sir."

"Pineapple soda will do that to you. What's your name, if I may ask."

"Gregory Innis. Greg, for my friends."

"No nickname?"

Innis laughed out loud. "Funny you should ask. I have a few. Why would you ask that?"

"Sometimes when you know a person's nickname, it tells you

about the person without their telling you much about themselves. Names do mean something."

"I believe you. They call me 'School.' I like that one the best. Sometimes they call me the 'Hunchback' or 'Hunchman of Notre Dame.' I don't particularly care for that one."

"Probably doesn't fit your vision of yourself. Am I right?"

"I guess so. I like School because I'm a teacher, at least I believe so."

"I'm sure your colleagues believe it as well, or they would never have called you that."

Detective Innis felt very relaxed with Franklin. If he were not an interviewer, he would not have recognized the technique used to get him to talk. He was talking about subjects he never meant to speak about, yet this man made him talk. The reverend would have been best as the good cop.

"You're very good, Pastor," Innis said, admiringly.

"I like people. I guess it shows."

"It shows. I would imagine you have lots of people come to you."

"Of course. I run this place. There are a lot of homeless out there and I'm trying to do my part. God gave me the vision and I followed. It's that simple."

"I imagine it's not easy. I mean, there are a lot of mean people out there, bad people."

"A lot, sure, but I don't know who they are until they come to me. And more important, I don't know if they will stay that way. The Lord says come as you are, but He doesn't expect you to stay as you are. I want people to change once they are accepted to our program."

"How do you feel when they don't change?" Innis inquired.

"It used to hurt, but I've learned it's not me that's being rejected. I'm living out God's directive. If a person doesn't change, he has not rejected me, he has rejected God. I just wish they would listen, though."

"Yes, I know what you mean."

It took a moment for the detective to recognize he was talking again. He couldn't feel manipulated, since he willingly submitted to the gentle man before him. "Have you ever had important people come to you?"

"Surely you didn't mean that. Everyone is important."

"You're right. I felt wrong the moment I said the words. From the pictures you have, I see you are well connected," Innis said, referring to the many photos on the wall. "Do you ever have politicians, city leaders, police officers come by?"

Franklin gently pushed back from his desk and leaned back in his chair. "What do you want to know, Greg?"

Greg's response took longer than expected, but finally he asked, "Did my partner come to you?"

"Detective Turner came with you, and that was the first time I had met him."

"Not him. I mean my friend, Renny, Detective Jackson."

"I'm not sure if I should be divulging personal conversations with you. Especially since this is not about police business. What is this about?"

"It's about hope. My partner asked me to keep hope alive, and you are that hope, at least I think you are. You are the HOPE mission."

"It's our mission. We give it, we offer it."

Greg's frustration was starting to show. "Father, I mean, pastor or whatever you want to be called, did my partner, Renaldo Jackson, visit you?"

Franklin studied Detective Innis for a while before giving his answer. "Yes, he did."

Elated, Innis almost shouted, "I knew it!"

Reverend Franklin seemed relieved. "He said you would say that."

"What?" Innis was knocked from his train of thought. When he recovered he asked, "Who?"

"Your partner, Detective Jackson. He said you would say that."

The reverend rose from his chair and came around to the front of the desk to be closer to the detective. "Your partner seems to know you very well."

"We spent a lot of time together. I guess you could say he was my best friend."

Franklin continued. "He said my first clue would be that you would come alone. And that you would say you were acting on a hunch."

Greg listened intently. The pastor walked over to a large safe as he talked. "He also told me your nickname. He has a lot of respect for you."

"Had," Greg correct him.

"Sorry. Yes, he did." He opened the safe, but stopped and asked, "Do you have a number for me?"

"A number? I'm not understanding, Reverend. What number would I have for you, for what? What is this about that I would need a number."

"I wouldn't know. I was told to ask you for a number."

Detective Innis was puzzled. What number could unleash the rest of this mystery? Finally it did come to him. He partner was very clever. It was the number in the photograph. Greg recited the number, "Three, five, six, two."

Pastor Franklin reached into the safe and brought a metal box to Innis. "Here you go," he said with a smile.

Greg sat with the box and looked for a way to open it. The reverend offered him the key, but Greg was reluctant to open it, so he took it and stood to leave.

"Thank you, sir," Greg said.

"You're very welcome. He, your partner, said you would know what to do. He said you always do the right thing."

"I don't know about that, but I try."

"Well, obviously he trusted you. So do what you do."

The detective turned to leave, then thought to ask, "Did he tell you what was in here?"

"No."

The answer was only partially satisfying, so Greg had to ask, "Do you know what is in here?"

"No."

"Okay, thanks." On his way out, Greg turned and said, "Obviously he trusted you, too."

Reverend Franklin smiled and said, "Good luck, detective."

"Thank you, sir. One hunch down, one to go."

Chapter 22

I had been to only one other Stand Down, but I was pretty sure this one was the biggest. Lee and I were fortunate enough to get a bed. The beds were reserved for veterans only. Men and women were separated, of course. There were more sponsored tents than I remembered. I counted fifty, and each tent slept at least ten people. There was also another area for those who had their own personal tents, for veteran overflow and non-veterans.

The Stand Down had become one of the biggest events of the year. Ironically, it was festive. The gathering of the homeless from around the city had a carnival-like atmosphere. Reporters walked around looking for the best story they could find. Every story was engaging, especially when it came to veterans. I served only two years, and I never really felt like a veteran.

I never went to war or never really committed myself to the country. It was money for me—I just wanted a way to make some money. There is nothing heroic or honorable about that. It was obvious, and I had to realize my discharge was administered appropriately—other than honorable.

However, there were some who really took their service seriously. They had every intention to protect America. They believed in America and they deserved respect. I wondered if they hurt because they sacrificed to save the home of someone, only to find themselves homeless.

I looked around and watched men and women mingle and thought each of them came to the same place—homeless. We took different roads and made different decisions, but we arrived at the same place. There must have been something common to all of us, but I couldn't figure it out.

Maybe it was PTSD which brought us to this spot. So many military members suffered from the disorder. It was the diagnosis of the decade. It was so popular, every disadvantaged group was using it. It reminded me of groups using the black civil rights movement as an analogy to their struggle. Whatever works, I guess.

As I walked around, I felt as though I were at a homeless convention. I met people I hadn't seen for a long time. I heard of those who died and those who succeeded. There were few of each. Most of us remained homeless year to year. It was depressing if I thought too long about it.

Though the Stand Down had several agencies available to help us, we came for the camaraderie, the food, and the entertainment. We networked and mentored each other as to how to survive another day. Now I understood Graham's book. He was just trying to be a patriot.

I walked over to Lee's tent but she was not there. There was no need for me to panic this time. The security was obvious. Everywhere I looked, there were men and women with yellow jackets labeled *Security*. Lee was safe, but I searched for her, anyway. I came to get her some help and until I accomplished my mission, she was still in my charge.

A woman was approaching me with a smile which said she knew me. I hated that look. Maybe she was just being friendly, but her steps toward me were so deliberate, I knew it was me she was after.

"How are you?" the woman asked.

I was hesitant, but I answered with faked pleasure. "Fine. How are you?"

"You don't remember me, do you? That's okay. Last fall a woman and her daughter came to me for shelter. You helped them get out of some trouble."

"Lady, get to the point," is what I thought, but not what I said.

She continued, "Do you remember Sarah and Deborah?"

Still suspicious of her motives, I answered, "Yes."

"Sarah talked about you all the time. You made quite an impression on that little girl. Her mother, as well."

"Good," I replied. What else was I to say?

"My name is Beverly Nash. You won't recognize that, either, but I own Bernadette's House. Sarah and Deborah came to me after leaving the HOPE mission. They needed some anonymity after their ordeal. Anyway, I saw your picture in the paper and recognized you here. You're quite the hero."

I reluctantly accepted her compliment and was ready to move on, but she was a talker.

"How are you doing?"

"I'm doing fine, thanks."

"Where are you living now?"

Goodness! This lady is nosy. She was so polite, I tolerated her intrusion. "I'm living where I can, where I can get some rest."

"Weren't you at HOPE?"

Now she was truly getting on my nerves. "Yes, I was at HOPE."

"Well it's a shame you're on the street again. I only have women at my place, but I know many people out here. I'm sure I can help you find a place."

"I appreciate it, but I'm okay."

"Men." I didn't like her tone, though she said it with a smile.

"Yeah, men."

I guess she understood I was not in the mood to be helped, so she said her polite good-bye. It took me an instant to realize my need for her. I grabbed her arm and she looked a bit startled. Though we were in a public space, she looked frightened. I released my grip and apologized.

"I'm sorry. I just realized you might be able to help a friend of mine. She's here and could use a place to stay."

Ms. Nash just stared at me. It seemed our roles were reversed, but I kept speaking, anyway. "She really is a good person. She's a veteran." I was waiting to see if anything I said would break through her stone face. "Ms. Nash, she really could use you."

I guess I said the right thing. My father told me if you want to make friends, use their name. He was right again.

Her face softened. "Where is she?"

"Not sure, but she can't be far."

We walked the grounds looking for Lee. We approached a camera crew and I was prepared to let them know I was not interested in any interview. I had been asked earlier in the day. However, I noticed they were already engaged with a subject. I peered over the crew and seated in front of the camera was a reporter and Lee! The interview was not underway, as I heard the reporter giving some instructions about lighting. But it was Lee who took my breath. She was white! Her nappy hair was gone. I knew they had all kinds of services here, and one was a beauty makeover booth. She obviously took advantage of it. She had on different clothes. She looked like a woman. She even sat like a woman. My astonishment was interrupted by Ms. Nash.

"Is that her?"

I could hardly speak. "Yes, yes."

"Very pretty," Ms. Nash said.

I briefly glanced at her and then back at the pending interview. Apparently the setup was complete. The newscaster looked into the camera with ease and introduced Talitha. I looked at Lee to see if she was nervous and she appeared quite calm. The interviewer asked her what brought her to the Stand Down and Lee sat up in her seat and spoke directly to the reporter.

"I wish I could tell you how I got here. It has been a slow process. So slow, I feel as if I have cancer. Homelessness is like a cancer. The decisions you make, the food you eat, can give you cancer, but you don't know it's growing. Finally you find out you have cancer, and finally you find yourself homeless. "

The reporter seemed to be impressed with Lee's answer. "I've never heard homelessness compared to cancer. I think that analogy helps a lot of people understand."

"They tell you if you smoke, you will get cancer, but people don't listen. Then you get sick and you don't stop. You read labels and see commercials, and you don't stop. With homelessness, people make decisions that keep them from improving their lives and they, we, make the wrong choices. We don't save money. We spend money on the wrong things. Our priorities are all screwed up."

The reporter was intently listening and asked Lee another question. "Tell me about your military experience and how it affected you."

"Well, I joined the Army when I was twenty-two."

"Why would a woman want to do that?" asked the reporter.

"I guess for the same reason as a man. I love my country. I wanted a way out of the small town where I grew up. I wanted to be independent. It has always been important that I be independent.

So I joined. It wasn't that rough, really. I just did what they asked. I was good. I liked it."

"What did you do for the Army?"

"I was in Intelligence. I thought I wanted to be a medic, but my test scores said I should try Intelligence. They were right. I love it. I really enjoyed it when I went to Afghanistan."

"How many tours did you do there?"

She thought a moment and said, "Five," then corrected herself, "No, six."

The reporter was shocked. "You did six tours in Afghanistan?"

"Yes. I volunteered for two of them."

"Why?"

"Because I was making a difference. I felt I was saving the lives of my fellow soldiers and the people of Afghanistan."

"What do you think of our involvement there, now?"

"Well, I think we kind of lost focus, but I don't know enough to comment too much on that."

"Did you stop making a difference? Is that why you left?"

I could tell from Lee's hesitation she didn't want to say, but she was brave enough to tell her story.

"MST."

"Military sexual trauma," the reporter explained. "So, were you raped?"

"Yes." Lee didn't want to talk anymore, but the reporter did her job.

"Did you report it?"

Lee noticed I was there. "I always reported it. It never went anywhere. I told everyone I could. I was told it would be investigated, and I don't believe it ever was. I became a complainer, interfering with good order and discipline."

"Were you transferred?"

"I was. Three times, but it did no good. The Army is very small and before you get to your new assignment, they already know who you are and why you're there. I started to feel lonely. I got married, hoping it would solve things for me. We had two beautiful kids, but that didn't take away the pain."

"What do you need, to take away the pain?"

She waited, trying to think of the best answer she could. I could see her withdraw, and her eyes were looking into a painful past. Her interviewer was very patient. Lee finally responded, through her tears, "Justice. All I want is justice."

I wanted to yell out the interview was finished. Why would they expose her to the world in such a callous way? Was this all for ratings or manipulation? My intervention was not necessary. The reporter stopped the interview and consoled Lee. I was glad the reporter was a woman. She could relate to her. The reporter leaned over to Lee and said something which allowed Lee to stand and disconnect from some wires. I was surprised when she came directly to me.

"Are you okay?"I asked. Lee nodded yes, but kept walking. I wanted to walk with her, but Ms. Nash stopped me.

"Let me talk to her," she said, and walked after Lee until they were together. I watched them stroll, without talking. With any luck, this was the beginning of the end of my relationship with Lee. If I could find a home for Lee, surely I could do the same for Tiger. As much as I thought of leaving him at a pound, it didn't feel right. I would figure it out later. Besides, he was safe, for now, in the kennel provided at the site. It was time to eat.

This weekend would highlight one of two things for all involved. One, it inspired some to realize there was a future. Two, it was a reminder of all we lost. I was of the latter category. I watched people mingle with their backpacks or suitcases on rollers. Tomorrow we would return to the street, except for a select few who would find the help.

Unfortunately, this was a show for the organizers and not much aid to the homeless. Maybe because most of us didn't want to be helped, we just wanted some rest. All of us had a routine. We knew where to go for food. We knew the corners where we could panhandle. I could never bring myself to beg for money, though. I have accepted money, if offered. We could find anything, but here at the "fair," we didn't need to look for anything. Everything came to us.

We were celebrities, for a couple of days. People wanted to know our story. They wanted to give you a job, an education, beauty makeovers, and food. It was the food I was interested in, right now. I walked the buffet line and picked my favorite dish, spaghetti. Pasta was my weakness. It was so easy to fix and was the best comfort food, ever.

There was so much food, there was a sign to remind us to eat all we chose. We could always come back for more. The admonition sounded a lot like my mother. I sat quietly eating, at the end of a picnic table. A young Marine came by and asked if I wanted something to drink. I wanted some fruit punch, and he gladly and respectfully brought me a cup. This was nice.

Someone called out, "Hey, Featherman." I looked up to see Justino. He was a homeless guy I met a couple of years ago. He didn't have the same look as then. He looked so different it took me a moment to recognize him, but I could not forget his accent and his cleft lip.

It was good to see someone I knew, but I wasn't excited to see him, so I just politely returned his greeting with, "Don't call me that."

I continued to eat, and Justino joined me. He had roast beef and cabbage. I immediately decided I was going back to get seconds and get his choice. As good as my spaghetti tasted, I still felt a lack. I wanted more. I always wanted more.

Pastor Franklin once preached on a poverty mindset and never being satisfied. I always feared living in poverty, and poverty found me, anyway. All I did to hide from its ugly prowling face, it sniffed me out. It was a self-fulfilling prophecy. Someone told me once, the thing you fear the most is the thing you cause. I couldn't accept the philosophy, but it didn't take much thought to understand my gambling habit was my demise. However, hindsight is 20-20 and I never thought of gambling as a path to the poorhouse. It was my way out of all my woes. Money could solve all of them, or so I thought.

The reverend also said we should be content in whatever state we find ourselves. He cited some Bible verse, but I asked him if he had ever been homeless. He answered no, as I expected. Out of respect for him and his good heart toward the homeless, I never responded to his statement. I wanted to say, "Then what the hell do you know about living contentedly?"

He had money, he had friends. He didn't know about having nothing, constantly searching for something. He didn't know hunger. He didn't know the constant search for safety. Wherever he slept, I would bet he slept all night and it was on a mattress.

Pastor Franklin couldn't possibly understand my life, but I

give him credit for understanding he didn't want to be where I was. Neither did I.

My thought was broken by Justino trying to get my attention. I didn't know what he was saying to me, but I finally heard, "Are you okay?"

"Yeah, I'm okay."

"You were thinking too hard, man. Enjoy the day. You're somebody, today."

I recognized his sarcasm and smiled. I don't know why he took such an interest in me. We weren't friends. Our paths crossed a few times, but we had no meaningful conversations I could recall. Apparently he missed past opportunities to chat, and this was his time to make up for lost time.

"Why don't you like to be called Featherman? You are one of the classics, man."

"Do I look like a classic?" I responded, trying to shovel spaghetti into my mouth. He must have understood my point, since he had no immediate reply.

"You're, like, in the hall of fame, man," he tried again. What was he trying to do?

I finally stopped eating and tried to calm his enthusiasm for days gone by. "Did you ever wonder what happens to O-Gs?"

Justino's look told me he had never pondered the question before. For him, an O-G, an original gangster, was a title of respect. He was giving me "my props." To him I was a top dog, a gang trailblazer, a survivor. I made it past the age of thirty! His silence caused me to think he didn't know how to answer the question.

"Exactly," I said. "Nothing. Nothing good, at least. You play the game until you can't play it anymore, then you quit. If you're smart, you get out early, probably because you made a baby and don't want her to get caught up in that life." He seemed to be listening, so I ended my tutorial. "Then you die."

"Man, that's depressing. Is that what happened to you?"

"Which part?"

"Any of it."

"Yes. All of it."

Justino remained enamored of me. "You are still the man."

"Okay. I'm the man."

I didn't believe what I said. I wasn't the man or any man. I was a shell of a man. I was a father, but not a daddy. So many times I could hear Jenna call me "Daddy." It was such a common word, it rarely registered any emotion in me. But every once in a while, I could see her thought behind the expression. The title was not common to her. Every time she called me daddy, she was calling her protector, as well as her teacher. She used the term as if it were synonymous with, "I love you." I could see it in her face, though not often, because I wasn't paying attention. Every day I heard her voice and every day I saw her face beam with pride at the person she saw before her. Yes, I missed being a daddy.

"You have any children, Justino?"

"Oh, yeah. A son and two daughters," he beamed. "I finally got that boy. My daughter is sixteen and driving me crazy, man. She's trying to date. You kidding me? Her mother says it's okay. I say over my dead body, or more like, over his dead body. You know what I mean? Dating. I try and tell her what guys are like, but she's hardheaded. The strange thing is that when I describe the guys out there, I realize I'm really describing myself. That hurts, you know?"

I could only nod in agreement. It was a cruel reality discovered all too late for us men. The universe had a pathway for us all to follow. The dots were in place and they couldn't be moved. We chose the path and the path led only one way. We were looking for the yellow brick road, but too many of us chose another road—the wide road, the easier road, the crowded one.

Justino started to call me Featherman again, but he caught himself. "What's your name again?" he asked.

"Roman." It wasn't often I heard myself use my name. It was a pretty cool name. When I heard others say it, it didn't mean much, but from my lips it was an announcement.

"Cool. That's a cool name. That's a warrior's name."

I was sick of his groupie mentality toward me, so I tried to change the subject. "What happened to your eye?"

"Oh, my son. We were wrestling and he scratched my eye."

"Looks like it should hurt." I noticed that the white part of his left eye was almost filled with a brilliant red, as if it were paint.

"It's better now. Still red, though. The doctor said it will take time to clear up, though. My vision is still blurry, but the contact lens they put on my eye helps a little. The doc says it's more like a band-aid than to help me see. Imagine that. A band-aid for the eye."

Justino used the opportunity to change the subject back to me. "I see you got yourself in some trouble, too." He indicted the wound below my left eye.

"The hazards of living on the street," I volleyed back. "Why are you out here? Why aren't you with your family? Is your family here?"

"No, my wife and kids moved a couple of years ago. I talk to them, well, at least the kids. My wife and I argue."

I guess he didn't think I was paying attention. Didn't he just tell me his son scratched his eye? Why was he lying to me? I couldn't answer the question, but I knew I wanted to get away.

I excused myself with some excuse that I needed to meet a counselor. I walked toward the woman's tent area and noticed a security guard, at the ready. He was good at his job. No matter the argument I used to get in to see Lee, he rebuffed each and every one. At one point, he crudely remarked, "Ain't no booty calls happenin' here."

What an absurd thought, but his statement was enough to send me on my way. I was pretty sure Lee was okay. I had to repeat it to myself to reassure myself I had done I all I needed. I didn't want any bad outcomes cluttering my mind when it came to her. I had enough bad outcomes of my own. Her safety was the notch I needed to restore a small portion of my self-esteem. I don't know how many notches I need to erase my blunders, but this would help.

Once I asked my father how he managed to dress so well. He was always getting compliments. I wanted to know how he coordinated colors or how he chose the right suit. Dressing was a science, I learned from a guy in the Navy. Our uniforms had to be in just the right place. There were precise measurements to follow. He would tell me about where the buttons should be on a suit and how many buttons should be on the jacket sleeve. My father didn't seem to be concerned with such precise accuracy. He told me a good suit should make me feel good. "If it doesn't make you walk taller, then don't wear it," he told me. Lee was a good suit.

As I passed the chapel, I could hear someone praying. It was more than prayer. The women were speaking in tongues. When I was growing up, such prayer would frighten me, but now I tried to ignore it. At least I tried not to notice, but I heard the women say Talitha's name. I stopped and peeked inside to find a woman praying over Lee. Lee was on her knees with her arms stretched wide from her shoulders. She was bent over with her head just inches from the ground, and her torso moved up and down as the woman prayed over her.

Finally the woman touched her head and said, "*Talithacumi*." She repeated it several times, accompanied each time with more gibberish. With the prayer over, Lee stood up and tightly hugged the woman. Neither woman cared I was there. Once their embrace ended, Lee thanked the woman, and I heard her assure Lee she was healed. I wondered what she was healed from, but maybe she would fill me in later.

The woman left, and as she passed by, she smiled and I nodded. Lee looked exhausted, but she found the energy to smile at me and sat on a nearby chair. I just watched, until she extended her arm to me to invite me over. I sat in the row behind her. I didn't know what I should say to her, and she must have understood. She didn't say anything, either. Finally she turned and rested her hand on my shoulder and asked, "Are you okay?"

"Sure." I was impressed she was concerned for me. I returned the concern. "You?"

Lee smiled and gripped my shoulder. "I'll be fine." She released her grip and gently ran two fingers across my cheek and smiled. "Do you believe in God, Roman?" She called my name with the same affection I heard from my mother when she was pleased with me.

"Sometimes I do and sometimes I don't," I said.

She giggled. "What does that mean, sometimes you do?"

"I mean, sometimes I feel Him and sometimes I don't. Most of the time I don't think about Him."

"Maybe that's the problem. You don't think about Him, I mean."

"What's the problem? What has He done for me, lately?"

As the words came from my mouth, I was sure they would shock her, but she just looked at me, without much of a reaction at all. I did detect a very mild grin. Lee grabbed my hands and asked me the same question. Her words were so tender, it was as if she

259

were channeling God, Himself. "What has He done for you, lately, Roman? Do you believe in God?"

"What do you want from me? I told you. Sometimes I do."

"Sometimes you don't. When do you feel him?"

I didn't know what she was trying to understand. "What? Sometimes I feel Him. What's weird about that?"

"When do you feel Him?" She was looking directly into me when she asked.

What was she after? I felt like she was interrogating me. "I don't know. I just do, sometimes I do, that's all."

"When you don't feel Him, is He there?"

Shit! It was time for her to stop. "Listen, Lee, there's no point to this, is there? To be honest, I don't even know if there is a God. I try to, but what the hell, where is He? Can you answer that? Where is He?"

"Would you believe me, if I told you?"

Oh, now she wanted to be cryptic. I wasn't interested in her philosophy or religion. I tried my best not to be rude. After all, she just had a religious experience or something, so I guess she wanted me to experience the same. She was barking up the wrong tree. I was a hardheaded oak. That's what my mother told me. "Boy, your head is as hard as an oak."

I decided to change the subject. "I heard that woman call you *cumi*. Is that your middle name or something?" Lee found the question amusing. She laughed, but I persisted. "Is it?"

"No. *Talithacumi* means—" She stopped abruptly, and found a nearby Bible, flipped through the pages, then recited,

> While He was still speaking, some came from the ruler of the synagogue's house who said, 'Your daughter is dead. Why trouble the Teacher any further?' As soon as Jesus heard the word that was spoken, He said to the ruler of the synagogue, 'Do not be afraid; only believe.' And He permitted no one to follow Him except Peter, James, and John the brother of James. Then he came to the house of the ruler of the synagogue, and saw the tumult and those who wept and wailed loudly. When He came in, He said to them, 'Why make this commotion and weep? The child is not dead, but sleeping.' And they ridiculed Him. But when He had put them all outside, He took the father and

the mother of the child, and those who were with Him, and entered where the child was lying. Then He took the child by the hand, and said to her, 'Talithacumi,' which is translated, 'Little girl, I say to you, arise.'

I was wrong, again. Talitha was biblical, not ghetto. Of course, I would never tell her what I thought of her name, but I finally understood. It did have a meaning, a real meaning.

"So my mother named me Little Girl. When I was born, I wasn't breathing and the doctor performed CPR, while my mother and prayed. She overheard the doctor praying, too, and he recited the same phrase Jesus used to raise the girl from the dead."

"And the rest is history," I added.

"Amen," she responded. "Roman. What does your name mean?"

"I wouldn't know." I thought about it a moment, then answered, "Warrior? Maybe. I don't know."

"I like that," she said. She seemed so soft now. The earlier prayer must have transformed her. "You have to live your name. Your name was given to you for a reason. I am to rise, and do what I was born to do."

I didn't intend to be mean, but I had to ask, "And what might that be?"

"You know already. I need to get my children back."

"I wish you the best."

Though I meant her goodwill, my face must have portrayed my belief it would not happen. She was a good person, as far as I knew, but she had been on the street for years, had PTSD, and had some substance abuse issues. Who would return her children back to her?

"You don't believe, do you?"

I shrugged, "It doesn't matter what I believe."

"Of course it does. What do you want?"

"I don't want anything."

I was lying, of course, but I wasn't about to discuss anything more with her. She was on some spiritual thing I wasn't able to understand. Lee's look seemed to compel me to continue, though. "Sometimes I want things, but I don't get them. I want off the streets, but here I am back, running the street, scrounging for food, like some, uh—"

"Pigeon?" she filled in.

"Yes, like some damn filthy pigeon. But I'll be okay. The birds are okay, so I'll be okay. Sometimes I ask God for something and He gives me nothing."

"You have to be patient."

"I've been hearing that all my life. Be patient. Why? Why is God always making me wait for things? The devil doesn't make anyone wait. He gives you what you want when you want it. If God is supposed to be so smart, why doesn't He give me what I want when I want it? Maybe then He would have more believers. Give somebody something, sometime. Stop making people wait. Isn't life short? Then give us something. Give us what we want."

"Sometimes, what we want is not good for us."

"Yeah, that's brilliant. What is wrong with wanting a job, or money, or... I don't know. Everything a person wants is not bad. How long does a person need to suffer, anyway?"

"I wish I could answer your question, Roman, but I'm not that smart. I do believe. I see my life changing already. You came along and saved me, you brought me here and I met Ms. Nash and I'll be staying with her. She's even willing to take Tiger. I just got prayed for and prophesied over. I'm on my way."

"Good for you."

"Don't give up. God is real."

"If He's real, so is the devil. The devil knows what I want and he's willing to give it to me."

I felt so frustrated. The conversation was going nowhere and I stood up to leave, but I had to make one last remark to God, or whoever was listening. "Give me something," I yelled, looking up to the invisible God. I thought about my outburst and said in a calmer voice as I prepared to leave, "Never mind, I don't want anything."

Lee wouldn't let me leave. "I understand," she said.

"Maybe you do, but what difference does that make?"

"I don't know. I do know you saved me and I'm grateful. I feel safe now, and I have you to thank for that. I will miss you, man, and I know that, too. You are a man."

"Better than being a damn pigeon," I smiled.

"And you're that, too."

"That's not funny."

I watched her come closer to me as if she had no intention of stopping. She grasped my face in her hands and just looked at me. I stared back, looking for her intentions. In another life, it would have been obvious to me, but I lived in a different world. Her plan became obvious as she kissed me on the cheek, twice. Then she kissed me on the mouth and I returned her affection.

She pulled back and exposed her tongue. On the tip of her tongue was a mint, the tip resting in the center hole. She jiggled it as if asking me to grab it with my tongue. I stared, lost in confusion, so she pushed her tongue and candy into my mouth. This was a moment I never expected would come my way, and I took advantage of the time and the opportunity.

When she broke the kiss, she whispered, "I love you, pigeon." I didn't know how to respond to her, but it didn't matter. She didn't seem to expect a response from me. "Come. I want to give you Peter's book."

"Who?"

"Graham," she clarified. "His name was Peter. You should have it. You're the one who could do something good with it."

"What could I do with it? I don't have the patience to complete it."

"But you will do the right thing with it. I trust you."

"Don't do that," I insisted.

"Too late. I did it."

We walked over to the women's tents and I waited for her to go in and bring me Graham's book.

She left me with, "Do your thing, man. Oh, by the way, did you know pigeons are monogamous?" I knew I would never see her again.

Chapter 23

Alone again, naturally. I broke camp just before dawn. It was just me and my backpack. On this Sunday morning, the streets were empty and I claimed them. This was the best part of the day. Before people came to conquer the shops and restaurants, the city looked abandoned, save for the occasional cab and cat. There was no fear of police harassment or violence of any kind.

A black mutt exited from an alley about two hundred feet in front of me. I stood and watched her movements. It was obvious she was a recent mother from the large tits hanging from her belly. I wondered if she was hunting for her babies or just wandering. She didn't seem intent on anything, but moving. When the dog approached the street, she never looked for traffic. Geesh, was she suicidal? Finally she trotted down the street and around the corner.

The black sky was turning blue. It was such a peaceful transition. I thought of my Aunt Helen. She told me the sunrise was the best part of the day. She liked seeing the sunrise. She said it was like witnessing God taking His place on the throne. True or not, it was a pretty sight. The city had no color a moment ago, but slowly the sunlight painted every building, every street, and every store.

I had no particular destination. My mission was complete. I thought of visiting the Mayor again to tell him about Tiger, but I talked myself out of the idea. It was depressing to watch him and maybe he wouldn't like the news, anyway. I was thinking too much. I decided to walk, in any direction my feet took me, and enjoy the journey.

My walk took me past closed shops, a fast food restaurant. The smell of food wasn't as seductive as usual. I saw a homeless woman inside with a cup of coffee, her small suitcase resting close to her. I felt sorry for her, then I realized she had more than I did. I had my backpack, only. I knew they would throw her out soon and we would roam the streets together, but it was nice of the manager to give her some shelter for a little while. I think they were more inclined to do so when it was a woman. Homeless men were scary. So many of us had mental issues, not to mention we looked like deranged, rabid bears.

I came to a mall and walked around as if I were window shopping. I stopped at a shoe store, because the display caught my attention. In the center of the shoes was a foot standing on its toes, dressed in a ballet shoe. It reminded me of my times with Jenna. She loved dancing. Her mother put her in dance class, against my wishes. "She doesn't even show an interest in dancing," I told her. Sharon insisted we needed to expose her to many things. After one session, it was obvious she was hooked on dancing. Eventually, it became ballet classes and it was all she would talk about.

I thought about my many dreams. I originally tried to join the Air Force because I wanted to be a pilot, but I guess the test I took didn't show aptitude for that. Besides, I needed a college degree, too. I loved basketball, but I wasn't good enough to get a scholarship. My father said I didn't practice enough. I didn't practice anything, much.

My mother bought me a journal, when I was twelve. It took me about six months before I started writing in it. Eventually my daily entries morphed into poems. When I shared them with my mother, she was so surprised. Her reaction made me feel I was good at something. "It's not so much what you say, Roman. It's how you say it."

She was so impressed with the words I used to express myself. She asked me how I put words together, but I couldn't answer. I didn't know. She convinced me poetry was my talent, but all those poems went the way of my dreams. If I could resurrect my dreams, I would find my poems. They were probably in the same place—my head.

The city was starting to awaken. More cars and more people were on the street, especially the joggers. I was decided my best bet to maintain my peace was to make it to the river. There's something about water. Maybe it's the rhythm in its flow, like music. Or maybe it was the silence as it moved past. Watching water move is like watching a silent movie. You pay attention to every bit of motion, because there is no sound. It was mesmerizing and I was drawn to its soothing magic.

The longer I walked, the brighter the day became and the noise of the city became louder. At this moment, the scene before me looked chaotic, but I chose to stroll through the frenzy and breathe in the city air as if I were walking the beach, on a tropical island. My walk took about an hour and a half. I arrived at the river walk before the crowd. I had the choice of any location to rest, so I choose a bench. After the long walk, I lay down, using my back pack as a pillow. The sun was warm and comforting, the breeze soft enough to lullaby me to sleep.

I guessed I had been asleep for about thirty minutes, when the roar of skateboards rushed by. I was still groggy, so I just turned over and try to sleep again. It was not to be. I recognized an authoritarian voice call out to me. "Sir, sir. Are you all right?"

I twisted my head and saw the policeman I expected. I quietly sat up and assured him I was okay.

"Do you need any help?" he asked me.

Again, I told him I was fine. I knew what he wanted. He wanted me gone, so I told him I was on my way. As I walked away, he asked, "Have you been drinking?"

"No." I was insulted. Why didn't he just let me go? I bothered no one but him. His harassment continued.

"Where are you headed?"

"None of your damn business." Those were fighting words, and maybe a fight is what he wanted. He wanted a reason to push me around and exercise his machismo. I had some of my own.

"What was that, sir?" His demeanor was calm, but I knew he was raging inside. He could have chased down the skateboarders, but they were too fast. "Do you want to come with me?"

"No, I don't. Do you want me to come with you?" I felt good with my answers.

"What's in the back pack, sir?"

Now he was revealing what he was really after. He suspected I had drugs, and he was prodding me for a reason to search my bag. I recognized the game and to end it quickly, I opened my backpack and pointed into the opening for his inspection. He looked inside and poked around with his baton. It was another tactic designed to rile me.

"Would you take the contents out and lay them on the grass," he commanded.

I expected him to end the sentence with "sir," but his faux kindness was beginning to fade. I did as ordered. Again, he used his baton to move my socks, a couple of T-shirts, toiletries, a set of keys, and Graham's papers.

"Whose keys?"

Of course, I never said what was on my mind. I just replied, "Mine."

Maybe the keys were what he needed to legitimize my existence. If you have keys, you must own something. He didn't need to know they were my room and storage key, given to me at HOPE.

"Thank you, sir."

He returned to my title of respect. I guess I satisfied his curiosity, as well as fulfilled his need to express his authority. Some people passing by slowed their pace to witness his exhibition of manhood. Maybe it was a message to them, rather than to me. Either way, I was no match for a taser, a gun, and every other weapon he was wielding. He let me go, with a stern suggestion not to sleep on the benches. You win, pig.

So much for peace, but everything is but for a moment. As I walked away, I was sure he was still watching me, but I wasn't going to give him the satisfaction of looking back. He was onto another test. Who would blink first? This was one game I mastered long ago. You lose, pig.

My journey took me past a liquor store. My last drink was months ago, but today I felt I needed one. After all, who would I hurt? What could I lose I had not already lost?

The answer was quick and simple. A man can justify anything. I searched my pocket for my last remaining money, which came to twenty-three dollars. It was enough to buy me a bottle of vodka or a bottle of happiness, as my father would say. As many times I saw him unhappy, his philosophy was not enviable, but today he was a wise man. I heard his encouragement loud and clear.

I wasn't aiming for happiness, though. I was more interested in amnesia, the place where nothing matters. There is no right or wrong, no decisions to make. Ambition had no merit, and I could find contentment wherever I found myself. I wasn't there yet, but I was on the fast track to oblivion.

I gulped the vodka like it was soda. A buzz was on the way, and I was anxious to meet it halfway. I was certainly doing my part. As my head grew lighter, my legs became heavier. It was harder for me to move them with the control I had an hour ago. It was time to find a place to allow the alcohol to completely overwhelm my senses and it had to be soon.

My head was sweating and the street was spinning, so I sat against the wall of a local market. I could have stayed there for the remainder of the day, but the store owner made it clear I was not going to sit there scaring his customers. I understood what he wanted of me, but I had a very hard time executing his demands. My legs weren't following the commands of my head, but the store owner gave me the aid I needed, or he needed. He grabbed me by my arm and snatched me to my feet.

I was too weak to resist his aggressive behavior. I tried to pull my arm from his grasp, to no avail. I tried to kick him away from me, which made him angrier. He pushed and shoved me around as if he hated me. He didn't know me, yet he hated me. He jostled me around the corner as he hurled insults at me, in Spanish. Once off the main street, he kicked me to the ground and told me the next time he would, "kick your ass." The threat was meaningless. Could my life be more worthless than this moment?

I climbed to my feet, as the owner disappeared around the corner. I straightened my disheveled clothes, as if it mattered. I looked in my backpack for my bottle and it was intact. I had no other plan than to find a spot to down the rest of it. My goal was limited, but it was enough to move me.

I hadn't eaten all day, but it didn't matter. I shuffled through the streets looking for a place of refuge. At one point, I saw the HOPE mission in the distance. By instinct, I was coming home, but I had enough awareness to know I was no longer welcome there. My drunken journey took me to an alley, situated in a housing area. Trash cans were laid out for trash day.

As I walked through the alleyway, I spotted a sofa someone placed against the building. The back of it faced the alley, making for a nice place to sleep, undetected. A cushion was missing, the other was torn and stained. I pushed on the fabric and it was dry. This would be my home for the night. I looked around to see if anyone else was camping nearby. I noticed a shopping cart in the distance, but apparently the people with the cart were not interested in this territory. They had their territory and I had mine. There would be no border wars here.

I climbed over the back of the sofa and the broken frame squeaked. It made a noise every time I moved to get comfortable. It was time to finish off my bottle. Happiness was just a few gulps away and sleep was a close partner. Before I fully lost consciousness, I heard a couple arguing from one of the apartments. Another strong black woman was making it clear to her man, he was a piece of shit. She was probably right. He, on the other hand, made it clear she was nothing but a whore. Before long, I was unaware of anything. I was in paradise.

I don't know how long I was asleep, but the argument was still going on. On second thought, this was another argument, in Spanish, no less. The men stood in the alley within yards of my couch. It was best I stay still, but I had to turn because my hip was aching for relief. I turned as slowly as I could, but the couch squeaked, so I stayed still. Their conversation became cautious, then suspicious when my bottle hit the concrete. Shit!

Suddenly a light from a flashlight hit the wall and swept the area. I was so tuned to every sight and sound, I knew I was no longer drunk. I did have a slight headache, but I was totally awake, though I wished I weren't.

The ring of light grew brighter as they approached and my heart thumped so loud, I was sure they could hear it. The sweat on my brow was not alcohol-related this time. The sofa squeaked as a body leaned over and the man announced he found me. I didn't know what they were saying, but they were angry. The man pulled on me to get me up, while speaking his language. I sat up and climbed over the back of the sofa. I performed it with such ease, it was another sign I was as close to sober as expected.

It was so dark, I could not see any of the men or how many. I'm sure the flashlight, directly in my face, was to keep me blinded.

"Hey, I don't even speak Spanish. I don't know what you were saying, so you can let me be on my way." I pleaded.

They talked among themselves, as I tried to look around the beam of light. Finally one man came forward, but stayed in the darkness just enough to prevent my seeing his face. The one with the flashlight pushed me aside, and the other looked over the edge of the couch and found my backpack. As he dumped the contents on the ground, I noticed a third man, completely in the dark. He kept silent.

I was tired of being disrespected, so I walked up to the one with my backpack as he picked up some items. The one with the flashlight illuminated the items on the ground.

"There's no need for that. I have no valuables in there, no money, nothing."

He pushed me away and without thought, I kicked him. I knew what was coming, and I was ready. I was going down, but I was going down with someone's dick in my hand. The scuffle became a brawl. The flashlight became a weapon, and I looked for an advantage of my own. The trash bins were good enough and the brawl became a loud cockfight. The two men finally overpowered me and one pinned me to the ground. The other placed the tip of a blade to my chest and began to carve a mark around my heart. I barely felt the blade. It must be a sign I was ready to die.

A car turned into the alley flashing blue and red lights. My assailants fled more quickly than lightening. The police came ready for the chase, but they had to stop since I was blocking their advance, lying across the alleyway. One police officer quickly got out of the car, but I knew it was too late. The other officer came over me and helped me to my feet.

"What are you doing here?"

"Minding my damn business," I said, with my anger still intact. I tore away from his grip. Anger and resolve make all men descend to a level where they depend on instinct only. Add a bottle of vodka and fear becomes a hollow word. The cop grabbed me with both hands. I guess I was still a bit under the influence of alcohol, as well, because once he pulled me close to him, I head-butted him. It was lights out.

* * *

I awoke in a jail cell. When I sat up, I grabbed my head to

straighten the room. Liquor, rage, and the police are not a good mixture. I had been here before. Add a cup of testosterone and it's a recipe for death. I was fortunate my head was the only body part which hurt. I looked for a mirror or some reflective surface to see how I looked, but there was none to be had, so I touched my face to get a clue of any damage. I could feel a cut on my bottom lip; otherwise I was in one piece. I had to smile. Hours ago I wanted to be as close to death as possible, now I was pleased to be able to feel anything.

I leaned against the door and looked for other signs of intelligent life. It was quiet, so I sat on the bed and pondered my future in the court system. I started to itemize my charges—hit a cop, resisted arrest. I'm sure they could come up with a few more. Incarceration for a man who was just minding his business was not my idea of justice, but would a judge understand my situation? My guess was, he would not. Justice was for the wealthy, who could afford a lawyer. Jail was for those without a voice.

I fell down on the bed in despair, contemplating my options, which came to a total sum of nothing. Zero was a great complement to my life. These are the moments vodka, or any alcoholic beverage, are meant to erase. The next best thing is sleep, but I wasn't allowed to do that, either, as the door opened. A uniformed policeman beckoned me out. I slowly responded, but when I came through the door, Detective Innis was leaning against the opposite wall. He said nothing, he walked down the hall, and I was given permission to follow by a gesture from the police officer.

The detective said nothing as I followed him to the street. He walked to an unmarked police car. He was alone, which was suspicious. Before he got inside, he looked over and said, "Get in."

This had to be a trap, but there was no trap to be set for me. I had nothing to give, nothing to trade. Why did he want me to get in? After some thought, I opened the back door and he stopped me. "No. In the front."

What the hell was going on? It was midday and we were visible to the public, so it was obvious he wasn't out to harm me; I got in the car and remained silent. The detective reached in the back seat and brought up my backpack. I searched it.

I asked the detective how he knew I was in jail.

"I'm a cop. It's a very small club. Like being in a gang. We all know each other." He waited a while, then asked, "Did they take anything?"

"No."

"Liar." He said it so gently, I didn't know if he was joking or knew something. "Where's the book?"

"How did you know about it?"

"Your girlfriend told us."

"I don't have a girlfriend," I insisted.

"Whatever. Your social life doesn't interest me."

"What did she tell you?"

"You had the book, she knew you would use it."

"Use it for what?"

"Who knows, but she is worried about you."

"I'm okay."

He looked at me a moment, then commented, "Who else worries about you, Featherman? Take it when it comes. She cares."

"Don't call me that. I don't like it."

"What, Featherman? It's written all over your neck," he responded, indicating the tattoo of the bird on the left side of my neck. "What would you have me call you?"

I stared through the windshield and saw all the people walking by. They had identities. I answered, "I don't really know, anymore. Roman, I guess."

"Roman, it is. So, Roman, who were the Spanish guys in the alley?"

"They were Portuguese."

"How do you know that?"

I had recognized one of the guys. He stayed in the dark, didn't get involved, but I got a glimpse of him when the flashlight turned on him. "His name is Justino. He's a Brazilian Boy."

"Deuces, you mean?" The detective was surprised.

I recognized the other name, as well. Their original name became Deuces, which signified the two B's. "Yeah, that's them. I can't believe he did that. I talked to him the day before."

"Talked to him about what, where?"

"At the Stand Down. We didn't talk about much."

"Why do you think they wanted the book?"

I was still stuck on the previous question. "I can't believe he watched me get a beat-down. He praised me the day before, then he wants to see me killed. Son of a bitch."

"You know as well as I, they are one vicious gang. Did you think he cared about you?" Detective Innis made clear.

"Please. Who does?"

The conversation stopped. I'm sure he wanted to know what was on my mind, but was smart enough not to ask. The more I thought of Justino, the more agitated I became. "I'm gonna kick his ass."

I expected a response from the detective, but he just sat quietly, then said, "I have a better idea."

He opened the glove compartment and there sat a beautiful Glock! It looked new. As much as I wanted to touch it, I didn't move.

"Take it," Detective Innis prodded.

"Where's your partner?"

"This is between you and me. Do you want to hear my idea?" I indicated he should continue. "It's risky. It's dangerous."

"I got it. I could die. I got that."

"This is an unofficial thing."

I chuckled. "Is this a mission impossible sort of thing?" The detective answered with a shrug of his shoulders.

"Whatever," I said. "It may turn out to be my last good day."

I took the gun and played with it. The detective stopped me.

"What the hell am I supposed to do with this?" I asked.

"I told you it was dangerous. Play with it at home." He saw my expression and modified his statement. "Sorry. Look it over when you're alone. You'll know what to do."

I placed it in my bag and before I could leave, Innis grabbed my arm and offered me some cash. Whatever the amount, it wasn't enough, but I took it and went on my way. I had another mission and I knew who I could get to help me, but I needed some time to formulate a plan. I headed for the park, but soon realized I was hungry. Searching my pockets, I found the several twenty dollar bills the detective gave me. I could feast for days with the money. I headed toward the nearest fast food joint.

Once in the park, I slowly ate my burgers, fries and large drink. Though I was invisible to most people, I watched everyone. I listened to every conversation as people passed me. I judged their fashion and their hair. I was just like them.

I threw my remaining fries into the air and, as predicted, the pigeons came. First it was one, then the flock arrived. They cooed with satisfaction, and I watched to see if there were couples or a master bird. I watched their society play out, at my feet.

I waited for sunset and headed for HOPE. Carl, the security guard, greeted me at the door. He welcomed me back. Apparently he didn't know I was banned from the residence, especially since I flashed my keys at him.

I walked down the hall to a room and wondered if the reverend was still doing work. He was always doing work. Since I was a manager, I had a master key to this set of rooms and I slowly inserted the key, opened the door, and tiptoed my way to the resident's bedside.

"Tuba," I whispered, but he didn't budge. I spoke to him again, and this time shook his shoulder. It turned out to be a mistake, because the big man turned and wrapped his arm around my neck and squeezed the breath from me. My God! I couldn't breathe or shout out. I couldn't overpower him, in the least.

"Tuba, it's me. It's me." There was so much desperation in my voice.

He knew he had the advantage and he released his grip, a bit. It was enough to allow me to gasp for air. "It's Roman." He released me, and I fell to the floor and gasped for more air.

"What are you doing, man?"

It was hard for me to answer, but I said, "I need your help."

The big man sat up, while I stayed on the floor. I didn't have the energy to sit with him.

"What do you need?"

This is why I knew I wanted his help. Whatever I needed, I knew he would be there to help. I was the one who recruited him to HOPE and he was forever grateful. I also needed his anger. I was well aware he was attending anger management classes.

While he dressed, I was able to regain my equanimity and got up to sit on his bed. We walked to the front, but I made Tuba wait inside while I talked to Carl. I took him for a short walk up the block. It was the moment Tuba needed to walk out and disappear around the corner. I handed the keys to Carl. "I won't need these anymore. You take care of yourself." He returned the good wishes and I went to find Tuba. Together we went toward an abandoned building not far away.

"You ready?" I asked Tuba.

"Always." His answer was so immediate and confident, it gave me courage.

As we walked, we talked about old times. We laughed a few times as he recalled my fight with Seal. He made it clear he thought I was a fool for tackling the martial artist. He wanted to know what I was thinking, and I told him I wasn't thinking. It was instinct, like when he tried to choke me earlier, I explained. He understood because he understood his own anger.

We reached our destination in about twenty minutes. It was a nice walk but not a nice objective. We entered the abandoned building and were immediately stopped by two men. Before I could announcement my intentions, Tuba socked one so hard, it hurt all of us. The second man asked what we wanted. He was much more cooperative, now that his partner lay unconscious on the floor. I looked at the big man and, with every muscle behind me, I slugged the man and he, too, hit the floor and didn't move.

"That felt good," I confessed.

I didn't know how long they would stay incapacitated, so we had to find the mastermind, quickly. Tuba searched them, found a gun, and put it in his pocket. We hurried up the stairs to the second floor and peeked into the hallway. There was a light coming from one of the rooms, and we moved toward it. This was my moment. It was the beginning or the end, but it didn't matter. My only decision was whether to open the door slowly, or kick it open. My father told me the hardest thing to do is make a decision. Once made, the rest follows. "But be ready for the consequences," he admonished.

I kicked the door open, exposing the barren room with a bed, a card table with four chairs, and a lamp. Justino jumped to his feet from the bed. I didn't give him a chance to recover. I charged him, but was stopped by another man who grabbed me around my neck. We wrestled and he threw me to the ground, but Tuba grabbed his neck and began choking him. The man struggled until he could resist no more.

"Tuba...Tuba, stop." I wasn't sure he was listening. "Tuba, stop. Don't do it. Don't kill him. Please."

This situation had progressed much farther than I intended

already. Tuba's face was filled with such intense anger. As I tried to convince him to stop choking the man, I noticed Justino was creeping toward his bed. I had no doubt he was going toward a weapon. This was my dilemma. Do I stop Tuba from killing or stop Justino from killing us? I tried to do both. I kept shouting at Tuba. I reasoned he didn't want a murder to deal with.

"We didn't come here to kill, anyone!" I shouted.

Tuba looked at me and I knew I finally had his attention. It may have been too late. Justino reached beneath his pillow and pulled a gun. Tuba dropped his victim and pulled the gun he retrieved from the two men at the entrance. It was a face-off.

The prayer of a righteous man availeth much, my grand-mother would tell me. Every time I was in trouble, she would pray and then leave me with the verse.

"What do you want, Featherman?" Justino was nervous as he looked back and forth between me and Tuba.

"A lot of things," I said as I reached behind me and pulled the Glock, pointing it back at him.

"You waited too long. Now we're stuck."

We stared at each other for an uncomfortable amount of time.

"I'm betting that whistle don't blow. So let's begin with peace," I challenged him.

Before long, Justino threw his gun and on the bed and I followed suit. We looked at Tuba to see if he would relinquish his weapon. Finally, he threw his gun on the bed, as well.

"What else do you want?" Justino asked.

"Leave me alone," I said.

He thought about my proposal. It was simple enough, so he agreed. I looked at Tuba and told Justino, "I want you to leave my friends alone."

"No problem, Featherman."

Damn, I hated the title! Once I was proud of it, now I was ashamed of it. I could not properly represent the Feathermen. I couldn't represent manhood, let alone some irrelevant gang from my past. In this instance, the title helped me. Justino agreed, again, to leave me and my friends alone. My mission was over, or so I thought.

Justino felt compelled to apologize for what happened to my friend.

"Who?" I wanted to know.

"Graham." He was so nonchalant. Death meant nothing to him. We were brothers in that respect. I didn't care about my life, either. I guess it was the reason for the moment that had arrived. Two men at the end of life and seeing it clearly.

"What about Graham?" I encouraged him.

"He was a very stubborn man. Reminds me of the stories of the Korubo. Very resistant."

Was this guy high? I had no idea what he was trying to say. I looked at Tuba, and he was just as perplexed.

"What stories are you talking about?"

"I'm a descendant of the Korubo. All the Deuces are."

I could only respond with a blank stare. I was sure he really wanted to tell me something significant and I wished he would come to it. My grandmother used to babble just like this. I would just tune her out. "Pay attention, boy. Sooner or later, I'll say something important," she would say. I waited for Justino's important moment.

"The Korubo are one the ancients of Brazil."

If only I could respond with, "Who the fuck cares?" I was in his territory, trying my best to leave without bringing harm to Tuba. I couldn't let him die here. He was here for me, and I couldn't disappoint him. I had let down enough people.

I didn't mean to be rude, but I said, "Never heard of 'em."

"Neither did your friend. We're a very aggressive people, the clubbers. They used clubs to attack people. We never did like the Europeans and the destruction they brought to our country."

"What did Graham have to do with the destruction of your country?"

"Not a thing."

"So, I'm listening to this for what reason?" I was pretty sure I was being offensive, now. I saw it in his face.

"I guess, I was just sharing. We have exchanged the club for the knife." His voice was without affect. "How's your girlfriend?" Justino asked, in the same bland tone.

"She's not my girlfriend, and don't bother her, either," I demanded.

Though Justino nodded in agreement, I didn't believe him. I asked him what he wanted.

"The book," he said. "Do you know where the book is? Do you have the book?"

"What book?"

He muffled his snicker at my response. He didn't believe me either, but he was willing to let this particular episode end without any more violence. I watched him eyeing the guns on the bed. Justino wished me good luck—a bad sign. I looked at Tuba and apologized, with my eyes, but Tuba didn't seem to be fazed. His eyes told me he accepted our fate.

Yes, this was going to be my last good day.

Chapter 24

Talitha entered the kitchen of Bernadette's House and went over to the coffeemaker to make coffee for the other residents. The sun was just about to make its way over the landscape as she sat at the table to feel her surroundings, but she was interrupted by another resident, Nadine.

"Hey, girl, you're up early."

"Habit, ya know. I'm usually up at this time, breaking camp."

Nadine was sympathetic. "I know what you mean. I think it took me about six months before I realized I could sleep until eight," she chuckled.

"You're up early, too," Talitha reminded her.

"I'm always up early when Ms. Nash is coming. She's nice, but she likes things a certain way, so I'm up to make sure they are a certain way. You know what I mean?"

"I do, but isn't that what Stephanie should be doing?"

"She does, but it's just me. I'm like that. I get anxious."

Nadine looked at the coffeemaker and realized more time was needed before the first cup was ready, so she stared out the kitchen window. "Don't you just love this time of morning?"

"Yes, it's nice," Talitha agreed.

"It's even better when you wake up to such a morning, in a house, in a bed."

She took in a deep breath, as if she could smell fresh air through the closed window. She turned to Talitha and asked, "How you getting along with Stephanie?"

"All right, I guess," Talitha replied.

"She can be a piece of work. She's been here the longest.

Being the house manager goes to her head, sometimes. She thinks this is her house."

"Yeah, she can get bossy."

Nadine snorted a laugh. "Ain't you nice. She's a bitch."

"Well, I wouldn't say that."

"I would, and I did. I'll probably say it again, before the day is out."

Talitha was looking for a way out of the conversation, so she asked what brought Nadine to the house. Though she must have told the story many times, Nadine told it again, as if it were the first.

"Where to start? It is funny when you think about your past, how you remember the bad things that have happened, so clearly. The good things, you only remember bits and pieces. Funny thing is, it took thirty-four years for me to remember the details of the bad things, as good things."

Talitha had to ask, "The bad things were good things?"

Nadine explained. "Everything I have been through in my life has been a foundation God has made in order to build a strong structure of a skyscraper that reaches to the heavens. I didn't always see it this way. For a long time, I thought I was being punished for something I had done in a past life. I felt there was never going to be an end to the story of horror I was experiencing."

The thought of her life must have been exhausting. Nadine came to the table and sat down. "This is the one thing I regret, this is the one thing I wish I could change. I wish I could have seen, sooner, how much God loved me and was helping, guiding, and teaching me. All along, He was protecting me. I wish I had seen what an amazing female specimen he created, so long ago; He knew what he was doing the whole time and makes no mistakes."

Talitha waited for Nadine to tell more of her story and she obliged.

"The point in my life when I realized who my heavenly father truly was, was about four years ago. I like to say, that is when I saw the light at the end of the tunnel. When I was only thirty, I was diagnosed with stage three breast cancer, and this was all too big of a shock for me."

Talitha didn't think she could hear much more. The woman sitting here was not the same person she met when she arrived at the house three weeks before, yet she understood. When she thought of her children, she must have the same appearance.

Nadine continued her story. "I was afraid, sad, angry, and hopeless. That's the moment God brought me to my knees. See, I realize now that you will always end up, at the right time, in the right place where God wants you to be, no matter how you try to run, just like Jonah in the Bible. God will let you go through pain and turmoil, only to swallow you up and spit you out to the exact place He wants you to be. I had absolutely no choice but to humble myself before the Lord."

"I hear ya, girl. My momma used to tell me God will bring you so low all you can do is look up," Talitha added.

The aroma of coffee filled the room and Nadine poured two cups. The room was silent as they prepared their cups with cream or sugar and took the first sip. It brought another level of peace to the kitchen.

"So, tell me your story. This is the first time we've had to ourselves," Nadine said.

"I'm like you, where do I start?" Talitha began. "With all I've been through, I guess I have trust issues. As a child, I was violated multiple times by people I thought I could trust—friends of the family, my baby sitter."

"That's sick," Nadine chimed in. "I wish a man would put his hand on me."

"I had a best friend as a child, named Patsy. She had two sisters and a brother, named Josh. I was four, and he was eleven. I recall having play dates with Patsy, and her brother wanting to be involved. He would touch me, you know, in that way. In the way he wasn't supposed to."

Nadine nodded understanding and sipped more coffee. "Sometimes I hate men," she said. "I had a family friend do the same to me. A woman! Can you believe that shit? A woman. I was too young and naïve to understand it was wrong, though it didn't feel right. Well, God don't like ugly. Bitch was killed by her husband. You heard about the Calvary murder?"

Talitha admitted she did not hear the story.

"I'll tell you later," Nadine said. "What were you saying?"

"Well, after what I had been through, I felt as if no one could protect me, you know what I mean?"

"I know," Nadine answered sympathetically.

"I've been bitter a long time. Problem is, I had to trust someone on the street."

Nadine said, "I was on the street for about a year and a half and didn't let *no* man protect me. That's when the pimps show up."

"Tell me about it. I met up with a good guy, though." Talitha thought a moment. "Yeah, Graham was a good guy."

"You got lucky."

"Yes, I guess, I did," she said, but it was not with joy as she remembered his death.

"You okay?" Nadine inquired.

It took Talitha a moment, but she answered, "I'll be okay. I'm okay." Then she asked, "What do you fear the most?"

"Why?"

"I just wanna know. Someone told me that the thing you fear the most is the thing you cause."

"Who told you that?"

"Somebody."

"Probably your daddy, maybe your mother."

"My father was a smart man. I guess he will always be the only man I trust, really trust."

"Is he still alive?"

"Oh, yes, he's still living."

"Does he know about you? I mean does know you're homeless?"

"I never told him, but somehow I don't think he would be surprised. I've been living a pretty unstable life. He and my mother watch my kids, along with my husband, former husband."

"Would he still love you, if he knew?"

"Oh, yes, he would"

"You don't sound that sure."

Once Talitha thought more, she answered, "Yes, he would. There's something special about a father and daughter."

"Well, that's my fear. My biggest fear in life is that I will die not being able to love someone with my whole heart and have the feeling returned."

Talitha noticed she looked so distant and sad. She tried to comfort her. "Don't worry, hon. God got your back."

Nadine stood with her coffee cup in hand and started out of

the kitchen, but had a change of heart. "So what's *your* biggest fear, sister?"

"I will have to think about that."

"Uh-uh. No, you don't. How long were you living on the street?"

"About four years, off and on."

"Then you have thought about it, off and on. Besides you wouldn't have asked me if you didn't have the thought, first."

"Wow. You're like a therapist."

"I think I could be one. I like talking to people and figuring out how they think. So answer the question, woman." Her demand came with a smile.

"Loneliness. I don't want to be alone."

Nadine allowed the answer to sit a while, then said, "I hear ya. Funny, how we all are looking for the same thing—love. It's all about love, girl. It's always all about love."

Talitha had no response. The analysis seemed correct. She tried to find the fallacy in her housemate's theory, but she couldn't find one. She looked at Nadine, whose left shoulder started to move, up and down.

"You feel that?" Nadine asked.

Talitha was confused and Nadine asked again, as her right shoulder began to bounce. She had a rhythm. "Oh, what's that?" she said with a big smile. She twisted her foot to and fro on the ball of the foot. "You don't feel that?"

Talitha smiled with amusement. She watched, and before long Nadine was dancing and Talitha had to join. She stood up and mimicked her friend. Whatever the music in her head, it was enough to have them dancing in harmony. They stepped around the kitchen, until Stephanie stopped them.

"What in the world?" She was smiling, too.

"You don't feel that?" said Talitha.

They continued to dance and Stephanie's smile grew larger. They eventually danced their way to the kitchen entrance where the house manager stood. Their movements became more seductive and inviting. Stephanie tried to ignore their folly, but she recognized joy and she wasn't going to be the one to stop it. At one point, she started to join in, but stopped herself.

"Ms. Nash is coming, girls. I got work to do and so do you."

The celebration dissolved and they were off to do work.

Talitha began cleaning the kitchen sink and counter. She stopped when she heard Tiger barking. She tried to ignore it, but Stephanie came in. "What's up with that dog?"

Talitha excused herself and went to the yard. Tiger was running in the front yard along the fence, looking down the street. Talitha tried to calm him by calling to him, but the dog ignored her. Finally she picked him up and looked down the street, as well. Tiger stopped barking, but his tail continued to wag.

"Okay, okay, boy. Who's out there? You see somebody?" They scanned the distance together. "You smell somebody, Tiger? Who's out there?"

There was no one to be seen on the street. There was no movement to be detected. Talitha waited. The wait brought no satisfaction, but she understood. She spoke softly into the air. "We're okay, Roman." She rubbed Tiger. "Aren't we, boy? We're just fine."

She pressed her free hand to her lips and blew a kiss into the wind. Then she turned and put Tiger on the ground. The dog immediately returned to the fence, but did not bark. He looked back to Talitha for answers. "He's gone, boy."

She went back in the house and resumed her chores. Stephanie asked, "What was that all about?"

"Companionship. He just wants some company," Talitha answered.

Stephanie accepted the answer and went on her way. Talitha watched through the window as she scrubbed the sink.

Chapter 25

The end of summer used to mean the end of leisure. Labor Day was a reminder to return to work. It was a time to recall the summer vacations and review the photographs of a life which seemed so long ago. As a school child, I couldn't wait to tell my friends about my adventures during the school break.

My fondest memory to this day is my family trip to Disneyland. I was six years old. It was more than I imagined. It was bigger than the state of Texas, I thought. We stayed for five whole days which, of course, was one day too short. On the ride home, I stared out the car window and remembered every detail of every ride and every food I ate. Disneyland never left me. As I look back, I think my life was geared to recreating the ride home. It was one of the most satisfying and peaceful moments of my life.

Every once in a while my mother would turn around and look at me and ask how I was doing. Her loving smile told me she knew. "I'm okay," I answered, but she knew I was far beyond my brief description. It was hard for me to describe, so why bother.

I would glance in the rearview mirror and my father was intent on driving. Occasionally he glanced back at me, which told me he was thinking of me. He smiled and it made me smile in return. He was satisfied.

Though the memory of those days remained so clear, I wish I had the photographs to confirm it was not a dream. Some of my experiences seemed like dreams, today. As I stood in line for the opening of the winter shelter, I tried to reconstruct my journey. Sometimes I saw my mistakes. At other times, I blamed people. The one innocent person, in my life was my daughter, Jenna. She made life worthwhile, yet I was not able to make a life worth living for her. I failed her, of all people.

I sat against the building wall with at least two hundred other people, waiting to know if we would be accepted. There wasn't much to the process. I just had to be here early enough to get a bed. I thought of the long lines people would create to buy a new phone. This was no different, other than I *lived* and slept on the street. The television news made a big deal of the people who would bring tents to camp out, to be the first ones to buy a phone. No reporters were here this morning.

Though it was called the winter shelter, the city opened the facility early this year. The fall brought unseasonal, early cold. The mayor used her political skills to obtain the empty two-story building house for the homeless. It made her feel good to see her streets free of us sleeping on the sidewalk. It made the citizens feel safer.

They say it takes thirty days to form a habit, but it was not long at all for me to assimilate again in the homeless population. At HOPE, I was showering every day. The last time I showered was about two weeks earlier. I cleaned up from time to time at the public restrooms, but the days came few and far between. My black skin camouflaged some of the dirt. My fingernails couldn't. They were chipped with dirt, packed underneath. There was little reason to remove it.

My clothes carried a musty smell. Most of the time I was not aware of the odor. All of us stank. There was no one to impress. I watched the hundred or so men in front of me and was anxious I would not be able to get a bed. If I was denied here, I could always try the veterans' tent. It was a smaller facility and was probably already full, so I was trapped here, in this line.

A group of men walked along the line, handing out a packaged pastry and pouring a cup of coffee. Their smile was genuine, as they greeted each of us. They had popped out of a van, like clowns from a circus car. The side of the van read, *Let us not become weary in doing good, for at the proper time we will reap a harvest if we do not give up. Galatians 6:9.* Their enthusiasm at this early hour of the morning convinced me they believed in their mission.

It made me think of my good deeds. Did God notice the good I had done? From where I sat, I was doubtful, but these guys were true believers. I watched them pray with some of the men. Eventually, they came to me and handed me a pastry.

"Would you like some coffee?" the young man asked. I accepted and he prepared the cup and asked if I wanted sugar and cream. He treated me as if I were in a restaurant. He dumped two packets of sugar in the plastic cup and some cream. I watched him and I could feel he really wanted to serve me.

A young lady emerged from the group of missionaries and asked if she could pray for me. I declined and she didn't seem offended. They moved on to the guys behind me, and she prayed for the man there. She asked God to deliver him from his situation and give him peace. I looked at the man and his head was bowed, as he accepted her authority. I must admit, I always had an issue with those in authority. Maybe that's why I didn't accept her prayer. Maybe it's why I rejected God. My father told me I always had to ride my own horse.

I unwrapped and took a bite of my cherry and cheese Danish. A sip of coffee, and I was feeling good. This was just as good as any prayer. I hoped they had enough for everyone in line, and it appeared they did. With their mission completed, they drove by and shouted, "God bless you!"

One of the men in line occasionally coughed, and he brought to mind the Mayor. I was dirty. All of us were dirty, but some of us might be sick. Who would know? The nurse told me the Mayor might have gotten tuberculosis from one of the shelters.

He was not one to go to the shelters, but I do remember he gave in last year. He missed Tiger so he left, got his dog, and returned to the jungle. My last visit to the hospital, I learned he had died.

The coughing man made me think twice about my decision to come here, but I was tired of the sidewalk and the rain and the cold and the fights and the insecurity. My thoughts were interrupted by the man next to me.

"Good stuff, huh?" he said, hoisting his cup of coffee. "Nothing like a good cup of joe."

"You're right. What's better than satisfaction, right?"

He laughed and exposed his few remaining teeth. "I'm more than happy, girl, I satisfied."

"Amen," I replied. I smiled because I knew the Stevie Wonder song he was quoting. It was the only line I knew, but it made me feel good that he and I knew the same song.

"That was a pretty little girl, don't you think?" My facial expression told him I didn't know what girl he was speaking about. I hoped he was not a pervert and was about to share some obnoxious photos with me. He was giving me another reason why I didn't want to come here and be among freaks.

"The girl that prayed for us," he explained.

"Oh," I was relieved. "I guess she was."

At least he was talking about a grown woman. I couldn't fault him for recognizing beauty among us pigeons. His face was cracked and filthy. His beard was much longer than mine, but his blue eyes were as bright as a child's. Behind his dirt was a man, and his eyes announced his humanity. There is something about blue eyes which make people pay attention. Blue eyes reveal creativity, like burnt orange skin. My father talked about his burnt orange skin, mostly when he was drunk. "My orange skin is from the God within. Taste a li'l bit. It's just like chicken." I would laugh, but my mother's eyes would roll so far in her head, I thought she was about to faint.

Our conversation ended quickly. I watched the line of men, and soon a man came down the line offering his wares. He flashed a plastic bag of weed at me and I ignored him, and he moved on. I wondered if anyone would take his offer. As I watched, he stopped momentarily by a man who passed him some money, and the plastic bag was his.

I struggled to eat and stay clean and other daily activities, yet someone had the money to buy marijuana. But who was I to judge; if I had the money, I would be buying more liquor. At this point, it was my only friend. Another relationship dissolved for lack of finance. My father told me alcohol was like a woman. She will be there for you, when you have money. She will make you feel good, leave you feeling invincible, then leave you when you're poor. His logic wasn't sound. I watched my mother stay when he was down, broke and drunk. I don't even know why she stayed with him. I should have asked. I could have learned a valuable lesson from her, if I was interested enough to find out what loyalty involves.

I noticed the men at front entrance were standing. Everyone in succession stood. It was apparent the doors to the shelter were open and they started accepting residents. It would still take a while before I found out if I would be one of those accepted. It took time to register people, so we were reacting to the opening with anxiety, more than proximity.

Twenty minutes must have passed and I moved about five or six positions forward. Our excitement waned and everyone sat again. In time, another drug salesman passed by, and our curiosity perked up when a news van parked across the street. A camera man played with his equipment as a woman news reporter got herself ready. When her cue came, I couldn't hear her report, but she seemed prepared. There was no one to speak with her from the city, as far as I could tell, but they were likely to come.

The camera man lowered his equipment signaling the end of her lead-in. I watched as she and her crew came to the line of men. All I wanted, at this moment, was the ability to disappear. I hope they would get enough interviews before they came to me. I didn't even want to decline their invitation to speak. I didn't want any part of the press.

My anxiety was comforted when a city car arrived and parked by the news van. This must have been the interview she came to do. The mayor emerged and she looked smaller than she did on television. I wasn't used to seeing celebrities. The mayor looked like one, and she behaved like one. After some words with the reporter, she made her way down the line to shake hands with her fans. Only a few guys stood to greet her, but regardless of her reception, she shook hands and smiled. It was a quick greeting for all of us. No wonder she was the mayor. She knew public relations and the value of a photo opportunity. Even I liked her and I didn't know her, nor did I vote for her. Of course, I didn't vote, period.

She came along to me and extended her very clean hand. She was so pleasant, it would have been rude not to extend my hand. I looked to see if she would be reluctant to take my hand, but she wasn't. The mayor looked directly in my eyes and asked me my name. Why did she care, I thought.

"Roman," I answered.

My response caused her to pause. "That's a good name. I like that name. I'm Mayor Constantine," she said directly to my eyes.

I could only respond with, "Thank you."

"Is there anything I can do for you?"

Her question was presented with real sincerity, but I was still suspicious of her motives. The cameraman was following her every move. Who was she trying to impress, me or the camera?

"No, ma'am," I said. It was good enough for her and she moved to the next man, but she glanced at me one last time.

Once the mayor completed her rounds, she went inside the building, followed by the television news crew. I'm sure they would give her a polished tour of the facility. I wondered if she would ever hear about the drug deals or other crimes occurring among the homeless. If she cared, maybe close advisors did not.

The registration process must have improved, since it only took another hour and a half and I could see the building entrance. The mayor had long gone on her way to her other duties. My enthusiasm level was enough to have me stand. I noticed another homeless guy come toward me, and I was ready for another drug deal. He wasn't after me, though. He spoke with the man in front of me. Their conversation was friendly and nothing of importance. As we moved forward in line, he moved with us. Was he cutting in line?

"You realize the line is back there?" I said to him, indicating the end of the line. He didn't take my statement well. He just looked at me with the disdain I was used to seeing from those with means, those with a job or a home or the ability to change clothes by choice, at any time.

As he talked, he occasionally glanced at me for a response as we advanced to the door. I couldn't let the situation go on without any intervention. He could be the reason I was denied.

"Are you going to register?" I asked.

"Don't play with me, man," he warned me.

I didn't want to say the words, because I knew where this was headed, but they came out anyway. "I'm not playing, I just want to know if you plan to register."

"I plan to do what I want."

"Not here." I surprised myself with my quick and angry retort.

His response was just as quick. He grabbed my clothes and pushed me against the building wall. The one thing I learned as a Featherman was to stand my ground, scared or not.

"How far do you want to take this?" I asked.

"This is where it ends, brother. You want to die?"

It was an excellent question. Yes, I did want to die, on some days, but today was not that day. I would not have come to the shelter if I didn't have the hope of another day, which would be better than the day before. I wondered if he knew the significance of his question.

"Not today," I said. "Do you?"

He didn't have time to answer. The security personnel came and escorted him away. He went willingly. I was sure I would see him again. Maybe he would remember me. Maybe then, I would be ready to die.

My turn came to register and it went smoothly. I climbed the stairs to the second floor and stood at the entrance and watched other men mingling and settling in. The view was a bit overwhelming. The entire floor was filled with bunk beds. I remember my first time at Grand Central Station. People were moving everywhere. As chaotic as it looked, it was controlled.

I walked through the crowd and looked for bed number 238. For the most part, I ignored the men I passed. Occasionally I recognized someone and nodded, to recognize them. It was an unemotional gesture.

Bed 238 was the bottom bunk. Whoever occupied the top left their black plastic bag of belongings, in place. When he returned, I wondered if he would be amenable to switch. I wasn't claustrophobic, but being on the bottom seemed a tight fit, given the surrounding beds. Comfort was not the main mission of the shelter. I was one less bum on the street.

I shoved my backpack under the bed, pulled off my dirty sneakers. I placed my dirty jacket on the post. I was used to using it as a pillow, but I was surprised the shelter supplied one. There was nothing left to do but lie down and I did so as if pushed. This was heaven compared to the sidewalk or park grass.

I examined the exposed mattress above. I studied the design until my eyelids refused to stay open. I thought of the guy who threatened me, earlier. I wasn't ready to die, then, but at this moment, I was at peace. This would be a good time to die. I was ready. I was not aware when I lost consciousness, it was such a gentle transition. Even my crazy dream didn't give me a clue.

My surgeon was explaining to me the only way to relieve my personality disorder was to remove or destroy a part of my brain. I refused to get a lobotomy, and he explained it was not the procedure I thought it was. It was not electric shock. He explained he could locate the precise area of the brain and use a device to burn it. How could he find the right place, I wanted to know, and he said he would ask me certain questions and give me commands which would help him locate the correct area.

His theory was dubious and there were only twenty other procedures performed in the world. I didn't want to be number twenty-one, but I had no choice. My surgeon was already preparing me for the surgery, despite my objections. I didn't even sign a consent form. How could he do this without my signature?

He shaved my head, drilled a hole in my skull, and placed a wire in my brain. I watched on a screen as the probe snaked its way through my brain. It was incredible I didn't feel anything. Maybe I was so mesmerized by the moving wire in my brain, I stopped objecting and watched.

As promised, he gave me a command to lift my left arm. I did as he asked, but something was wrong. I couldn't breathe. I tried my best to draw a breath, but I couldn't. Finally he realized the surgery was not going as planned. "Are you okay?" he said. The anxiety in his voice created more stress and it became harder for me to breathe. He asked again, "Are you okay?"

I took control and sucked in all the air around me. I was okay, and I regained consciousness to see a man standing over me. "Are you okay?" he asked.

Now it was clear I had been asleep. My gasp for air was a symptom of my sleep apnea. I wasn't sure I had it, but I met a few guys with it, who described their symptoms. My episodes were becoming more frequent, making me fearful of sleep. I had enough reasons not to sleep while lying on a park bench, now I had another item to add to my list.

I assured the man I was okay, and he retreated to the bunk above. As he made himself comfortable, the bed squeaked until he settled into his relaxation zone. I sat up and blindly searched for my back pack. Once I found it, I brought it upon the bed and looked through the contents. There was the welcome packet from the city, containing a toothbrush, small bottle of lotion, a tube of toothpaste, a pair of white socks, and a coupon for a free sandwich from the local sandwich shop. Pretty good, I thought.

I pulled out a wool cap and a pair of black sweat pants. At the bottom was a T-shirt I never wore. It was the shirt Pastor Franklin gave me months ago. I kept it as a memory, but didn't use it because of its message. On the front, it read "In the end." I unfolded the shirt and turned it around to read the back. In bold red letters on the black shirt, it shouted, "I WIN!" In smaller letters was a reference verse, "Zephaniah 3:15."

I was interested in what the verse said, so I stood and asked the man above if he had a Bible. He didn't, but there was a library on the first floor. I wasn't interested enough to move away from my current place. It didn't apply to me, anyway.

I took the newspaper from my bag and looked over some of the headlines. It was an outdated paper, but it was helpful for the treatment of despair. One headline stated, *Drug Smuggling Uncovered.* Detective Innis was named, along with his partner. I smiled, knowing I did my part, though I was not identified. The police said they discovered a book which led to the arrests. They didn't give Graham any credit, either. However, I knew the truth.

The truth was, Detective Innis had approached me with a very dangerous idea and I was willing. Maybe I had a death wish when he presented it, but the idea was clever and risky. I took the Glock he offered and found Justino. Luckily there was minimal violence. He could have killed me at any time, but he didn't know that. My last moments with him convinced me I was about to die. I was sorry if Tuba had to die with me, but I had to do what I intended.

Justino wanted to kill me, but maybe in his unwarranted respect for my former life, he allowed us to leave. Tuba and I left. I was bold enough to turn my back on Justino and leave. I expected to hear the click of a gun hammer. It didn't happen. There was much he didn't know. My gun was not loaded, at least not with bullets. It was a shrewd way to hide a recorder and a video camera.

The gamble was that Justino would not examine the weapon until the police recorded enough information to find the masterminds of the ring. Before long, several names were revealed. The most surprising was a doctor at the HOPE mission. He was involved in drug trafficking through the mission. The homeless shuttled the drugs in and out of the building, in their small rolling suitcases. Dr. Maloney gave up other names, and a drug smuggling ring was discovered and dismantled, for a little while. Victories were applauded, but everyone knew it was a temporary win. The war on drugs had been waged since I was a kid. It was the longest war I knew.

I debated whether or not to toss the paper in the trash. I decided to keep it. It still felt good to read it, so I put it back into my bag and then sat on the edge of bed number 238, without a plan.

The man with the cough passed by and I covered my face. Whatever he had, I wanted no part of it. I was relieved when he walked several beds away, but maybe it was too late. Maybe this is how it started and ended for the Mayor. He was a good guy. He cared about us. It was a shame a man of his age had to end his life in homelessness. Who would miss him? The more I thought of the Mayor, I realized I was really asking questions about me. Who missed me?

My father asked me not to miss him. His death was so slow, and tiring. Each day he seemed to be disappointed he was still here. He used his last days to relay wisdom he was unable or not sure he had given me. Alcohol rotted his brain like a virus. One of his final admonishments was to live a good life. I thought it was too late. Though he was weak, he was aware enough to see my depression.

I peered through the row of beds and watched how each man accepted his fate. I watched one man reading a book. My guess is it took his mind from his situation. Another stared at the bed above him, maybe wondering how he got here. Maybe he was grateful. I couldn't tell.

I felt as if I were in an asylum and we were all crazy. We had our own sickness—drugs, pedophilia, alcoholism. Most of us were just guys who tried and failed. We tried to make a living, but chose the wrong job. We tried to care for our families, but made the wrong decision. Some of us had no plan and let life make a plan for us. Life didn't care who we were, it just placed us in a void left by another failure.

We were drifters, controlled by the wind, like tumbleweed. We moved from the street to a shelter, to a transition home, and back to the street. After a while we put up no resistance. Our roots were dead and soon we would follow, but we were men. My father would shout at my mother, he was a man. Sometimes I understood he was trying to convince her, but some of my most sad moments were the times I understood he was trying to convince me. I thought it was understood he was a man, but he was telling me something more. He was telling me, men do not give up.

I opened my wallet and found a note my father left for me. He really never gave it to me, though I'm sure he meant to, at an opportune time. I found it in one of his dresser drawers. It was the drawer where he kept all of his valuables—wallet, money, pieces of paper with reminders.

There was little need for a wallet nowadays. Mine held few treasures—a family photo of Jenna, Sharon, and me and six dollars. Once, I had a photo of my mother and me, taken on Mother's Day when I was about six. I was robbed a few years ago and someone took the wallet. They took the money, as expected, and tossed the contents. I found only my father's note. The only picture I had left of my mother was in my head. It never faded.

His note was as beaten and tattered as I was, but it had value. It was old but told a truth I was not ready to receive. I opened the worn paper and read, "There is no legacy I can leave you that you cannot change." He signed it, "Dad."

He repeated it on many occasions. I thought it was because he didn't remember he told me, but now I realize he wanted me to get the message. He knew he wasn't the best example of a father. He wanted more for me, but I became more like him than I wanted to be. His legacy was safe with me, unfortunately.

The man at bed number 240 fell on his bed and blocked my view. He introduced himself, kind enough to extend his hand. We shook hands and he asked, "How you doing?"

I tried to stifle the laugh. "I'm okay," I said.

"Really?"

He unclothed my lie and I smiled. "Well, as good as I can be."

We wouldn't be friends long, but at least we made a connection for now. His name was John and he was a talker. If we hadn't been interrupted by a staff member, I believe I would have been up all night listening to his stories.

The staffer's name tag announced who he was. Jeff Coleman came up to me and asked, "Are you Mr. Barnes?"

I was very suspicious. Why would he want to know? How could there be a problem after I had been here for just a few hours. I reluctantly confirmed, "I am."

"There is someone here to see you."

"Who?" I snapped.

"I don't know, sir. I was just asked to bring you the message."

He left, never caring if I followed. It took me a moment, but I did follow, with a little prompting from John.

"Could be money," he said.

I stood up and replied, "Could be trouble."

As I walked away, John said, "Could be that, too. Lord knows I've seen enough of that come along."

He increased my anxiety, but as I walked to the stairway entrance, I rationalized it could not be anything worse than I had already experienced. If it were the police, what could they do? Maybe it was Detective Innis. They were the only ones to know me by name.

I went down to the first floor. It was quiet, only a few people moving around. The area was large and was divided by function. There was the reception station and further back was a game area, and even farther in the distance was the library.

I stopped at reception and asked who might be looking for Mr. Barnes, and the young lady pointed to the far end of the floor. I was not halfway there when I noticed a women coming my way. Her brilliant coral dress swayed to and fro with her steps. Her smile grew larger with each step. I was speechless. This could not be. This was the mirage of those who have been in the desert too long without, food or drink.

The slender black women came to me with some caution, now, and asked me the most mundane question. "How are you?"

I could not think of a mundane answer. I felt like John. I wanted to tell my entire story and I didn't care how much time I had.

"How did you find me?"

"Persistence. Pure persistence."

I looked around behind this beautiful woman before me. She knew what I was after.

"She's over there. Come on."

Sharon grabbed my hand and, as we went forward, a young woman stood up from a large lounge chair and waited for us to approach. Her smile was not broad. I could see the anxiety in her face, and for the first time in a long while, I cared about how I smelled. I wished I had the time to shower. Suddenly I became aware of how my breath smelled. I needed time to change, but it was too late. The girl stood before me, and I fell to my knees before her as if I were approaching Jesus.

I don't know who started to tear-up first, but my emotions were in step with my rapid heartbeat. We stared at each other. Who would make the first move? She took control of the situation, pulled me to my feet, and hugged me with the embrace everyone wants. Her hug absorbed every hurt. My tears escalated to weeping and I was weak, but she kept me upright.

There was only one thing I needed and she must have known, because she squeezed tighter and said, "Are you okay, Daddy?"

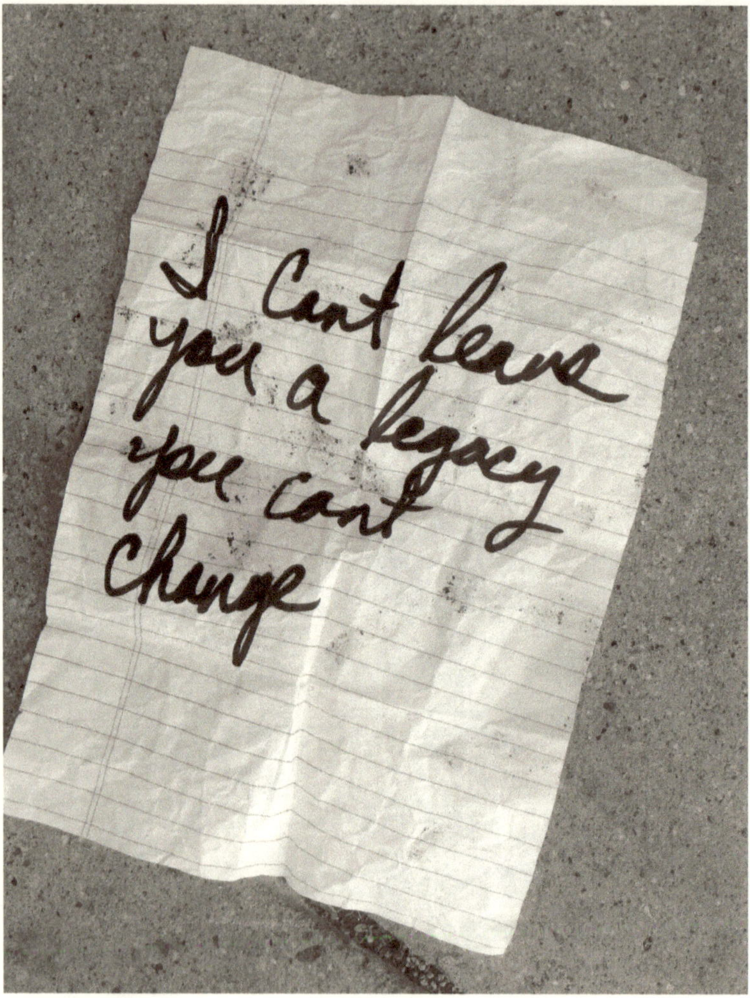
I cant leave
you a legacy
you cant
change

About the Author

Dr. Lawrence Wood is the author of numerous poems, screenplays, and short stories. His stage play, *No Marks Just Memories*, performed to sold-out audiences in Japan, and his first novel, *Among Pigeons*, is regarded as a triumphant voice for the homeless.

With his wife Vanessa, he founded Fan of the Feather, Inc., a nonprofit organization to benefit homeless veterans.

Dr. Wood is also a motivational speaker and lives with his wife and their youngest son in San Marcos, California.

To order additional copies of *Love and Death Among Pigeons* for your organization, book club, library, church or school, please contact:

Website: www.amongpigeons2.com
Mail: Productions2BE
310 So. Twin Oaks Valley Road
#107-314
San Marcos, CA 92078
Facebook: Lawrence A Wood MD
Twitter: @lawood

www.ingramcontent.com/pod-product-compliance
Lightning Source LLC
Chambersburg PA
CBHW060428030726
47495CB00003B/790